Maggie, A Girl of the Streets, and Other New York Writings

D0972790

STEPHEN CRANE

MAGGIE, A GIRL OF THE STREETS, AND OTHER NEW YORK WRITINGS

Introduction by Luc Sante

THE MODERN LIBRARY
NEW YORK

2001 Modern Library Paperback Edition

Biographical note copyright © 2001 by Random House, Inc.
Introduction copyright © 2001 by Luc Sante

All rights reserved under International and Pan-American Copyright Conventions. Published in the United States by Modern Library, an imprint of The Random House Publishing Group, a division of Random House, Inc., New York, and simultaneously in Canada by Random House of Canada Limited, Toronto.

Modern Library and the Torchbearer Design are registered trademarks of Random House, Inc.

Grateful acknowledgment is made to the University Press of Virginia for permission to reprint approximately 90 pages from "New York Journalism" in Volume VIII of *The Works of Stephen Crane*, edited by Fredson Bowers (Charlottesville, Virginia: University Press of Virginia, 1973). Copyright © 1973 by the Rectors and Visitors of the University of Virginia. Reprinted with permission of the University Press of Virginia.

Library of Congress Cataloging-in-Publication Data
Crane, Stephen.
Maggie, a girl of the streets, and other New York writings / Stephen Crane.
p. cm.
ISBN 0-375-75689-2
1. New York (N.Y.)—Social life and customs—Fiction. 2. City and town life—Fiction. 3. Slums—Fiction. 4. Poor—Fiction. I. Title.
PS1449.C85 A6 2001 813'.4—dc21 00-048726

Modern Library website address: www.modernlibrary.com

Printed in the United States of America

6 8 9 7

Stephen Crane

Stephen Townley Crane, the iconoclastic novelist, poet, short-story writer, journalist, and war correspondent who propelled American literature into the modernist age, was born in Newark, New Jersey, on November 1, 1871. The origins of his genius will perhaps always remain elusive: he was of the opinion that "writing was a business like any other" and believed that "one could train one's mind to observe and a man should be able to say something worthwhile about any event." Crane's tragically abbreviated career, which spanned less than ten years, dates from 1892, when the New York *Tribune* printed the novice reporter's so-called Sullivan County sketches, a series of rustic stories set in the New York countryside. His first novel, *Maggie, A Girl of the Streets,* was privately printed in 1893 and broke new ground with its realistic portrait of life in the slums of New York City. *The Black Riders,* a volume of poetry, came out in 1895.

Crane's next book, *The Red Badge of Courage,* brought him international fame when it was published in October 1895. "*The Red Badge of Courage* has long been considered the first great 'modern' novel of war by an American—the first novel of literary distinction to present war without heroics and this in a spirit of total irony and skepticism," wrote Alfred Kazin. "What makes [it] so remarkable, and a pioneer in the literature of war, is that it was written entirely from instinct by a young newspaperman in his early twenties who had never seen a war." "With *The Red Badge of Courage,* Crane burst upon the American public with the effect of a Civil War projectile lain dormant beneath a city square for thirty years," observed Ralph Ellison. "That *The Red Badge* was widely read during Crane's own time was a triumph of his art."

Afterward Crane led a vagabond existence as a journalist and war correspondent while continuing to write fiction. Capitalizing on the success of *The Red Badge of Courage,* he turned out *The Little Regiment* (1896), a collection of Civil War stories. In addition he completed two more novels: *George's Mother* (1896), a second Bowery tale often viewed as a companion volume to *Maggie,* and *The Third Violet* (1897), a portrait of bohemian life that is generally considered his least accomplished work. Crane's earlier travels in Mexico and the American Southwest inspired two of his most famous short stories, "The Bride Comes to Yellow Sky" (1897) and "The Blue Hotel" (1898). His harrowing misadventures at sea en route to Cuba resulted in "The Open Boat" (1897), a story many critics regard as his masterpiece. In 1899, the final year of his life, Crane published *War Is Kind,* a second book of verse; *Active Service,* an adventure-romance based on his experiences as a reporter in the Greco-Turkish War; and *The Monster and Other Stories,* whose disturbing title story provides a sharp study of community malice.

Stephen Crane suffered a series of tubercular hemorrhages while living in England during the spring of 1900 and died in a sanatorium in Badenweiler, Germany, on June 5, 1900. Several of Crane's last works were issued posthumously, including *Whilomville Stories* (1900), a volume of tales about small-town America; *Wounds in the Rain* (1900), a collection of short stories drawn from his exploits in the Spanish-American War; *Great Battles of the World* (1901), a work of nonfiction culled from a popular magazine series; *Last Words* (1902), a miscellany of articles, stories, and newspaper sketches; and *The O'Ruddy* (1903), a swashbuckling Irish romance left unfinished at the time of his death.

"Crane in his short life quickly showed himself the most original, most ruthlessly independent, most sardonic novelist of his talented generation," judged Alfred Kazin. "Nowhere in American writing was a godless world expressed with so much terseness and finality as in the work of Stephen Crane." The poet John Berryman, one of Crane's most celebrated biographers, concluded: "Crane was perhaps as original as an artist can be, and be valuable. . . . By a margin he is probably the greatest American story-writer, he stands as an artist not far below Hawthorne and James, he is one of our few poets, and one of the few manifest geniuses the country has produced."

Contents

Introduction

Luc Sante

Stephen Crane managed somehow or other to obtain for himself the special condensed edition of life. He was not long past his twentieth birthday when he wrote the first draft of *Maggie*—"in two days before Christmas," he claimed. He self-published it (under the pseudonym of Johnson Smith) not long after he turned twenty-one. *George's Mother* and two thirds of the stories in this book, as well as *The Red Badge of Courage,* were written the following year, before he had attained twenty-three. Thereafter, he wrote two more short novels (and began several others), wrote numerous short stories and pieces of reportage, traveled in the West and down to Mexico, covered the Spanish-American War and the Greco-Turkish War for Pulitzer and Hearst, moved to a baronial manor in England, and came down with tuberculosis, which killed him when he was twenty-eight. It may have been a short life, but it was a full one, conducted at three or four times the normal speed.

Prior to *Maggie,* he hardly had an apprenticeship: a handful of sketches at most. He had thrown over higher education after a semester apiece at two institutions. He was an orphan, his mother having just died and his father when he was eight. He lived variously: with brothers in New Jersey and in Sullivan County, New York, and in New York City in sundry ad hoc arrangements with artists his age, most often so poor they burned furniture for fuel and ate randomly. He zipped back and forth among domiciles, not seeming to spend more than two consecutive weeks in any one spot. The material for *Maggie* was undoubtedly drawn in part from his experiences of people from childhood onward, but the aspects specific to New York City he had absorbed in a matter of no more than three months before writing the first draft, since he arrived in the city in September and wrote the thing in December. He was a kid. His last years were studded with names; people like Joseph Conrad and Henry James were friends and neighbors. At the time of *Maggie,* however, he was a strange, impulsive, prodigious adolescent, half-silent and half-wild. The old men who published their memories of him in the 1930s or talked to his first biographer, Thomas Beer, in the previous decade remembered him in kid terms. One man, for example, recalled reading *Maggie* chapter by chapter "in a house over on the far East Side, where he lived with a crowd of irresponsibles." Translate this to the contemporary equivalent of your choice.

Being a kid gave him a number of advantages of stance. He could presume, for one thing, to understand the hearts of matters he had barely glimpsed—and this aspect looms largest in the clairvoyance of *The Red Badge of Courage,* which many war veterans were certain had to have been written by another war veteran. He could also overlook decorum, or, maybe, be innocent of it altogether. In the early 1890s, Realism was a sort of continental pornography; Zola was bought, more or less under the counter, by thrill-seeking schoolboys (not Crane, though, who didn't much like Zola). A homegrown Realism, employing the American slums as its focus and subject, simply didn't exist. The slums themselves were only just beginning to be discussed in a serious way, and then by reformers and crusaders—Jacob Riis's *How the Other Half Lives* had just come out, in 1890. Everything else lay in the future. The popular novelist Edward Townsend (*Chimmie Fadden* and *A Daughter of the Tenements,* both 1895), a friend of Crane's, virtually made a career of elaborating and sentimentalizing aspects of *Maggie.* Riis's fiction appears like so many banalizations of the "baby" tales herein, although there is no evidence he ever read Crane. Almost anything else of literary significance written about the Bowery and the Lower East Side, by Hutchins Hapgood, Rupert Hughes, James Huneker, Alfred Henry Lewis, even O. Henry, was published after 1900, after Crane's death.

It's not, of course, as if the New York slums lay beneath notice. *Harper's* and the other illustrated papers regularly sent reporters and sketch artists to do local-color items. The *Police Gazette,* which treated the Bowery as its private turf and made minor stars of its more notable loungers, was standard-issue reading in every barbershop in the country. The local accent and mannerisms were familiar nationwide from being relentlessly reproduced for laughs on the vaudeville stage. (Thomas Beer: "The Bowery language was humorous, as are a dozen dialects in which the fierce, defensive cynicism of the illiterate American takes on color and shape. There was a choppy rhythm in the speech from which the sound of *th* had been taken away. Many vowels were washed over so briskly that it took experience to tell whether they had been pronounced at all by some hasty group of lads hanging for a breath together while the policeman's back was turned.") All these avenues, however, fell below the level of art, which at the time was still supposed not only to be refined, but to concern itself exclusively with refined subjects. William Dean Howells, who was to champion Crane just as he championed nearly every worthwhile American writer of the era, had a character in *A Hazard of New Fortunes* (1890) wonder why it was that painters could see the beauty of a bustling slum thoroughfare if they happened upon it in Naples but overlook the same thing in New York, and Crane himself thought of genre painting ("Street Scene in Cairo") among the alleys of Coney Island. But such depictions would have to wait for the twentieth century and the Ashcan School.

The Lower East Side, then, before the great waves of immigration from Eastern Europe and Italy, was still largely Irish in ancestry and nurtured a lumpenproletarian style and customs in dissolution and vassalage that had been refined over a century. Most inhabitants weren't recent immigrants struggling to adjust, but treadmill-bound victims of compounded hopelessness and inertia. They might live in the same dumps and drink in the same deadfalls as their parents or grandparents before them. The Bowery, meanwhile, was the great clearinghouse that drew from all over the country thrill-seekers, lamsters, tramps, barflies, outcasts, predators, margin-players, small-time showbiz personalities, people with unconventional or unmarketable ambitions, people who knew nothing except how to hang out. The two spheres were distinct, although they blurred together in the popular mind. They were downtown, they were poor and vicious and uncultured and base, and that was all most people needed to know.

Soon after arriving, Crane thought the Bowery was "the only interesting place in New York," and a difference of opinion on the subject busted up one of his earliest serious romances. As the youngest son of a financially uncertain clerical family, he could not be said to be slumming, exactly, and he doesn't really seem like one of those writer types who go places merely to prospect for material. Rather, Crane throughout his life was interested in things that puzzled him, things that were off-kilter in human terms. He had to throw himself into the Bowery in order to dope it out, in the phrase of the time. After he had done so, he commented regarding "An Experiment in Misery" that "the root of Bowery life is a sort of cowardice. Perhaps I mean a lack of ambition or to willingly be knocked flat and accept the licking." This should not be interpreted as contempt, but it did settle the matter for him.

The Lower East Side posed a different sort of problem. *Maggie* is a study in tragic inevitability—Howells called it "Greek"—and that sort of thing was to go on fascinating him. It is also romantic, as John Berryman points out in his book on Crane. Maggie herself is fitted out for a kind of sainthood (even as her martyrdom seems to anticipate the judgment levied upon her opposite, Frank Wedekind's Lulu, who meets Jack the Ripper). Crane treated the Bowery sociologically, and *Maggie* may have begun as an inquiry along those lines, but Crane was pulled by tides of emotion toward the specific and the archetypal. In any case, it didn't go over with the wider public. Although copies got to Howells and Hamlin Garland and a few other writers who immediately understood, the original pseudonymous edition sold exactly two copies in the only bookstore that would handle it. After the triumph of *The Red Badge of Courage,* critics started to notice it, but they still didn't like it much. It was raw, uncouth, red (to employ Crane's favorite adjective). It was perceived as obscene, or close to it, and in 1896 Crane actually abetted a bowdlerized edition (which also incorporated his own revisions) that tamed the interjections and drew a discreet veil over the circumstances of Maggie's end. For half a century *Maggie* stood among the unknown American classics.

A few of the stories herein are stories, at least one of them ("A Dark Brown Dog") an anthology standard, and deservedly so. The rest are examples of what Crane thought of as reporting. Crane spent much of his brief writing life in the employ of newspapers and magazines, but such employments often ended unhappily. Thomas Beer again: "He could not report. Apparently he did not even try to report. Of what use to any newspaper was an impression of impatient horses kicking 'grey ice of the gutter into silvery angles that hurtled and clicked on frozen stone' when the boy had been sent to get the facts of a large and important fire?" Newspapers then had a lot more room for impressions, fancies, and word-pictures than they do today, but even so there were limits, which Crane habitually overstepped. You'd be hard pressed to find a single ephemeral fact or number in any of his pieces. He was hardly ignorant of what was required, but he couldn't help himself. For him, writing meant noticing certain kinds of marginal details that cut openings through to the emotional center of his subject, and language was a color wheel. It is always embarrassing to get mystical about literature, but there is little question that Crane was a votary, a practitioner of some witchcraft that defied calculation and often conventional better judgment. As he himself put it, memorably, "An artist, I think, is nothing but a powerful memory that can move itself at will through certain experiences sideways and every artist must be in some things powerless as a dead snake."

—

LUC SANTE is the author of *Low Life*, *Evidence*, and *The Factory of Facts*. He teaches at Bard College and lives in New York.

BIBLIOGRAPHY

Thomas Beer, *Stephen Crane*. New York: Alfred A. Knopf, 1923.

John Berryman, *Stephen Crane: A Critical Biography*. New York: William Sloane Associates, 1950; revised edition New York: Meridian Books, 1962.

J. C. Levenson, editor, *Stephen Crane: Prose and Poetry*. New York: The Library of America, 1984.

Maggie,
A Girl of the Streets

I

A very little boy stood upon a heap of gravel for the honor of Rum Alley. He was throwing stones at howling urchins from Devil's Row who were circling madly about the heap and pelting at him.

His infantile countenance was livid with fury. His small body was writhing in the delivery of great, crimson oaths.

"Run, Jimmie, run! Dey'll get yehs," screamed a retreating Rum Alley child.

"Naw," responded Jimmie with a valiant roar, "dese micks can't make me run."

Howls of renewed wrath went up from Devil's Row throats. Tattered gamins on the right made a furious assault on the gravel heap. On their small, convulsed faces there shone the grins of true assassins. As they charged, they threw stones and cursed in shrill chorus.

The little champion of Rum Alley stumbled precipitately down the other side. His coat had been torn to shreds in a scuffle, and his hat was gone. He had bruises on twenty parts of his body, and blood was dripping from a cut in his head. His wan features wore a look of a tiny, insane demon.

On the ground, children from Devil's Row closed in on their antagonist. He crooked his left arm defensively about his head and fought with cursing fury. The little boys ran to and fro, dodging, hurling stones and swearing in barbaric trebles.

From a window of an apartment house that upreared its form from amid squat, ignorant stables, there leaned a curious woman. Some laborers, unloading a scow at a dock at the river, paused for a moment and regarded the fight. The engineer of a passive tugboat hung lazily to a railing and watched. Over on the Island, a worm of yellow convicts came from the shadow of a grey ominous building and crawled slowly along the river's bank.

A stone had smashed into Jimmie's mouth. Blood was bubbling over his chin and down upon his ragged shirt. Tears made furrows on his dirt-stained cheeks. His thin legs had begun to tremble and turn weak, causing his small body to reel. His roaring curses of the first part of the fight had changed to a blasphemous chatter.

In the yells of the whirling mob of Devil's Row children there were notes of joy like songs of triumphant savagery. The little boys seemed to leer gloatingly at the blood upon the other child's face.

Down the avenue came boastfully sauntering a lad of sixteen years, although the chronic sneer of an ideal manhood already sat upon his lips. His hat was tipped with an air of challenge over his eye. Between his teeth, a cigar stump was tilted at the angle of defiance. He walked with a certain swing of the shoulders which appalled the timid. He glanced over into the vacant lot in which the little raving boys from Devil's Row seethed about the shrieking and tearful child from Rum Alley.

"Gee!" he murmured with interest, "A scrap. Gee!"

He strode over to the cursing circle, swinging his shoulders in a manner which denoted that he held victory in his fists. He approached at the back of one of the most deeply engaged of the Devil's Row children.

"Ah, what deh hell," he said, and smote the deeply-engaged one on the back of the head. The little boy fell to the ground and gave a hoarse, tremendous howl. He scrambled to his feet, and perceiving, evidently, the size of his assailant, ran quickly off, shouting alarms. The entire Devil's Row party followed him. They came to a stand a short distance away and yelled taunting oaths at the boy with the chronic sneer. The latter, momentarily, paid no attention to them.

"What deh hell, Jimmie?" he asked of the small champion.

Jimmie wiped his blood-wet features with his sleeve.

"Well, it was dis way, Pete, see! I was goin' teh lick dat Riley kid and dey all pitched on me."

Some Rum Alley children now came forward. The party stood for a moment exchanging vainglorious remarks with Devil's Row. A few stones were thrown at long distances, and words of challenge passed between small warriors. Then the Rum Alley contingent turned slowly in the direction of their home street. They began to give, each to each, distorted versions of the fight. Causes of retreat in particular cases were magnified. Blows dealt in the fight were enlarged to catapultian power, and stones thrown were alleged to have hurtled with infinite accuracy. Valor grew strong again, and the little boys began to swear with great spirit.

"Ah, we blokies kin lick deh hull damn Row," said a child, swaggering.

Little Jimmie was striving to stanch the flow of blood from his cut lips. Scowling, he turned upon the speaker.

"Ah, where deh hell was yeh when I was doin' all deh fightin'?" he demanded. "Youse kids makes me tired."

"Ah, go ahn," replied the other argumentatively.

Jimmie replied with heavy contempt. "Ah, youse can't fight, Blue Billie! I kin lick yeh wid one han'."

"Ah, go ahn," replied Billie again.

"Ah," said Jimmie threateningly.

"Ah," said the other in the same tone.

They struck at each other, clinched, and rolled over on the cobble stones.

"Smash 'im, Jimmie, kick deh damn guts out of 'im," yelled Pete, the lad with the chronic sneer, in tones of delight.

The small combatants pounded and kicked, scratched and tore. They began to weep and their curses struggled in their throats with sobs. The other little boys clasped their hands and wriggled their legs in excitement. They formed a bobbing circle about the pair.

A tiny spectator was suddenly agitated.

"Cheese it, Jimmie, cheese it! Here comes yer fader," he yelled.

The circle of little boys instantly parted. They drew away and waited in ecstatic awe for that which was about to happen. The two little boys fighting in the modes of four thousand years ago, did not hear the warning.

Up the avenue there plodded slowly a man with sullen eyes. He was carrying a dinner pail and smoking an apple-wood pipe.

As he neared the spot where the little boys strove, he regarded them listlessly. But suddenly he roared an oath and advanced upon the rolling fighters.

"Here, you Jim, git up, now, while I belt yer life out, you damned disorderly brat."

He began to kick into the chaotic mass on the ground. The boy Billie felt a heavy boot strike his head. He made a furious effort and disentangled himself from Jimmie. He tottered away, damning.

Jimmie arose painfully from the ground and confronting his father, began to curse him. His parent kicked him. "Come home, now," he cried, "an' stop yer jawin', er I'll lam the everlasting head off yehs."

They departed. The man paced placidly along with the applewood emblem of serenity between his teeth. The boy followed a dozen feet in the rear. He swore luridly, for he felt that it was degradation for one who aimed to be some vague soldier, or a man of blood with a sort of sublime license, to be taken home by a father.

II

Eventually they entered into a dark region where, from a careening building, a dozen gruesome doorways gave up loads of babies to the street and the gutter. A wind of early autumn raised yellow dust from cobbles and swirled it against an hundred windows. Long streamers of garments fluttered from fire-escapes. In all unhandy places there were buckets, brooms, rags and bottles. In the street infants played or fought with other infants or sat stupidly in the way of vehicles. Formidable women, with uncombed hair and disordered dress, gossiped while leaning on railings, or screamed in frantic quarrels. Withered persons, in curious postures of submission to something, sat smoking pipes in obscure corners. A thousand odors of cooking food came forth to the street. The building quivered and creaked from the weight of humanity stamping about in its bowels.

A small ragged girl dragged a red, bawling infant along the crowded ways. He was hanging back, baby-like, bracing his wrinkled, bare legs.

The little girl cried out: "Ah, Tommie, come ahn. Dere's Jimmie and fader. Don't be a-pullin' me back."

She jerked the baby's arm impatiently. He fell on his face, roaring. With a second jerk she pulled him to his feet, and they went on. With the obstinacy of his order, he protested against being dragged in a chosen direction. He made heroic endeavors to keep on his legs, denounce his sister and consume a bit of orange peeling which he chewed between the times of his infantile orations.

As the sullen-eyed man, followed by the blood-covered boy, drew near, the little girl burst into reproachful cries. "Ah, Jimmie, youse bin fightin' agin."

The urchin swelled disdainfully.

"Ah, what deh hell, Mag. See?"

The little girl upbraided him. "Youse allus fightin', Jimmie, an' yeh knows it puts mudder out when yehs come home half dead, an' it's like we'll all get a poundin'."

She began to weep. The babe threw back his head and roared at his prospects.

"Ah, what deh hell!" cried Jimmie. "Shut up er I'll smack yer mout'. See?"

As his sister continued her lamentations, he suddenly swore and struck her. The little girl reeled and, recovering herself, burst into tears and quaveringly cursed him. As she slowly retreated her brother advanced dealing her cuffs. The father heard and turned about.

"Stop that, Jim, d'yeh hear? Leave yer sister alone on the street. It's like I can never beat any sense into yer damned wooden head."

The urchin raised his voice in defiance to his parent and continued his attacks. The babe bawled tremendously, protesting with great violence. During his sister's hasty manœuvres, he was dragged by the arm.

Finally the procession plunged into one of the gruesome doorways. They crawled up dark stairways and along cold, gloomy halls. At last the father pushed open a door and they entered a lighted room in which a large woman was rampant.

She stopped in a career from a seething stove to a pan-covered table. As the father and children filed in she peered at them.

"Eh, what? Been fightin' agin, by Gawd!" She threw herself upon

Jimmie. The urchin tried to dart behind the others and in the scuffle the babe, Tommie, was knocked down. He protested with his usual vehemence, because they had bruised his tender shins against a table leg.

The mother's massive shoulders heaved with anger. Grasping the urchin by the neck and shoulder she shook him until he rattled. She dragged him to an unholy sink, and, soaking a rag in water, began to scrub his lacerated face with it. Jimmie screamed in pain and tried to twist his shoulders out of the clasp of the huge arms.

The babe sat on the floor watching the scene, his face in contortions like that of a woman at a tragedy. The father, with a newly-ladened pipe in his mouth, crouched on a backless chair near the stove. Jimmie's cries annoyed him. He turned about and bellowed at his wife:

"Let the damned kid alone for a minute, will yeh, Mary? Yer allus poundin' 'im. When I come nights I can't git no rest 'cause yer allus poundin' a kid. Let up, d'yeh hear? Don't be allus poundin' a kid."

The woman's operations on the urchin instantly increased in violence. At last she tossed him to a corner where he limply lay cursing and weeping.

The wife put her immense hands on her hips and with a chieftain-like stride approached her husband.

"Ho," she said, with a great grunt of contempt. "An' what in the devil are you stickin' your nose for?"

The babe crawled under the table and, turning, peered out cautiously. The ragged girl retreated and the urchin in the corner drew his legs carefully beneath him.

The man puffed his pipe calmly and put his great mudded boots on the back part of the stove.

"Go teh hell," he murmured, tranquilly.

The woman screamed and shook her fists before her husband's eyes. The rough yellow of her face and neck flared suddenly crimson. She began to howl.

He puffed imperturbably at his pipe for a time, but finally arose and began to look out at the window into the darkening chaos of back yards.

"You've been drinkin', Mary," he said. "You'd better let up on the bot', ol' woman, or you'll git done."

"You're a liar. I ain't had a drop," she roared in reply.

They had a lurid altercation, in which they damned each other's souls with frequence.

The babe was staring out from under the table, his small face working in his excitement.

The ragged girl went stealthily over to the corner where the urchin lay.

"Are yehs hurted much, Jimmie?" she whispered timidly.

"Not a damn bit! See?" growled the little boy.

"Will I wash deh blood?"

"Naw!"

"Will I"—

"When I catch dat Riley kid I'll break 'is face! Dat's right! See?"

He turned his face to the wall as if resolved to grimly bide his time.

In the quarrel between husband and wife, the woman was victor. The man grabbed his hat and rushed from the room, apparently determined upon a vengeful drunk. She followed to the door and thundered at him as he made his way down stairs.

She returned and stirred up the room until her children were bobbing about like bubbles.

"Git outa deh way," she persistently bawled, waving feet with their dishevelled shoes near the heads of her children. She shrouded herself, puffing and snorting, in a cloud of steam at the stove, and eventually extracted a frying-pan full of potatoes that hissed.

She flourished it. "Come teh yer suppers, now," she cried with sudden exasperation. "Hurry up, now, er I'll help yeh!"

The children scrambled hastily. With prodigious clatter they arranged themselves at table. The babe sat with his feet dangling high from a precarious infant chair and gorged his small stomach. Jimmie forced, with feverish rapidity, the grease-enveloped pieces between his wounded lips. Maggie, with side glances of fear of interruption, ate like a small pursued tigress.

The mother sat blinking at them. She delivered reproaches, swallowed potatoes and drank from a yellow-brown bottle. After a time her mood changed and she wept as she carried little Tommie into another room and laid him to sleep with his fists doubled in an old quilt of faded red and green grandeur. Then she came and moaned by the stove. She rocked to and fro upon a chair, shedding tears and crooning miserably to the two children about their "poor mother" and "yer fader, damn 'is soul."

The little girl plodded between the table and the chair with a dish-pan on it. She tottered on her small legs beneath burdens of dishes.

Jimmie sat nursing his various wounds. He cast furtive glances at his mother. His practised eye perceived her gradually emerge from a muddled mist of sentiment until her brain burned in drunken heat. He sat breathless.

Maggie broke a plate.

The mother started to her feet as if propelled.

"Good Gawd," she howled. Her eyes glittered on her child with sudden hatred. The fervent red of her face turned almost to purple. The little boy ran to the halls, shrieking like a monk in an earthquake.

He floundered about in darkness until he found the stairs. He stumbled, panic-stricken, to the next floor. An old woman opened a door. A light behind her threw a flare on the urchin's quivering face.

"Eh, Gawd, child, what is it dis time? Is yer fader beatin' yer mudder, or yer mudder beatin' yer fader?"

III

Jimmie and the old woman listened long in the hall. Above the muffled roar of conversation, the dismal wailings of babies at night, the thumping of feet in unseen corridors and rooms, mingled with the sound of varied hoarse shoutings in the street and the rattling of wheels over cobbles, they heard the screams of the child and the roars of the mother die away to a feeble moaning and a subdued bass muttering.

The old woman was a gnarled and leathery personage who could don, at will, an expression of great virtue. She possessed a small music-box capable of one tune, and a collection of "God bless yehs" pitched in assorted keys of fervency. Each day she took a position upon the stones of Fifth Avenue, where she crooked her legs under her and crouched immovable and hideous, like an idol. She received daily a small sum in pennies. It was contributed, for the most part, by persons who did not make their homes in that vicinity.

Once, when a lady had dropped her purse on the sidewalk, the gnarled woman had grabbed it and smuggled it with great dexterity beneath her cloak. When she was arrested she had cursed the lady into a partial swoon, and with her aged limbs, twisted from rheumatism, had almost kicked the stomach out of a huge policeman whose conduct upon that occasion she referred to when she said: "The police, damn 'em."

"Eh, Jimmie, it's cursed shame," she said. "Go, now, like a dear an' buy me a can, an' if yer mudder raises 'ell all night yehs can sleep here."

Jimmie took a tendered tin-pail and seven pennies and departed. He passed into the side door of a saloon and went to the bar. Straining up on his toes he raised the pail and pennies as high as his arms would let him. He saw two hands thrust down and take them. Directly the same hands let down the filled pail and he left.

In front of the gruesome doorway he met a lurching figure. It was his father, swaying about on uncertain legs.

"Give me deh can. See?" said the man, threateningly.

"Ah, come off! I got dis can fer dat ol' woman an' it 'ud be dirt teh swipe it. See?" cried Jimmie.

The father wrenched the pail from the urchin. He grasped it in both hands and lifted it to his mouth. He glued his lips to the under edge and tilted his head. His hairy throat swelled until it seemed to grow near his chin. There was a tremendous gulping movement and the beer was gone.

The man caught his breath and laughed. He hit his son on the head with the empty pail. As it rolled clanging into the street, Jimmie began to scream and kicked repeatedly at his father's shins.

"Look at deh dirt what yeh done me," he yelled. "Deh ol' woman 'ill be raisin' hell."

He retreated to the middle of the street, but the man did not pursue. He staggered toward the door.

"I'll club hell outa yeh when I ketch yeh," he shouted, and disappeared.

During the evening he had been standing against a bar drinking whiskies and declaring to all comers, confidentially: "My home reg'lar livin' hell! Damndes' place! Reg'lar hell! Why do I come an' drin' whisk' here thish way? 'Cause home reg'lar livin' hell!"

Jimmie waited a long time in the street and then crept warily up through the building. He passed with great caution the door of the gnarled woman, and finally stopped outside his home and listened.

He could hear his mother moving heavily about among the furniture of the room. She was chanting in a mournful voice, occasionally interjecting bursts of volcanic wrath at the father, who, Jimmie judged, had sunk down on the floor or in a corner.

"Why deh blazes don' chere try teh keep Jim from fightin'? I'll break yer jaw," she suddenly bellowed.

The man mumbled with drunken indifference. "Ah, wha' deh hell. W'a's odds? Wha' makes kick?"

"Because he tears 'is clothes, yeh damn fool," cried the woman in supreme wrath.

The husband seemed to become aroused. "Go teh hell," he thundered fiercely in reply. There was a crash against the door and something broke into clattering fragments. Jimmie partially suppressed a howl and darted down the stairway. Below he paused and listened. He heard howls and curses, groans and shrieks, confusingly in chorus as if a battle were raging. With all was the crash of splintering furniture. The eyes of the urchin glared in fear that one of them would discover him.

Curious faces appeared in doorways, and whispered comments passed to and fro. "Ol' Johnson's raisin' hell agin."

Jimmie stood until the noises ceased and the other inhabitants of the tenement had all yawned and shut their doors. Then he crawled upstairs with the caution of an invader of a panther den. Sounds of labored breathing came through the broken door-panels. He pushed the door open and entered, quaking.

A glow from the fire threw red hues over the bare floor, the cracked and soiled plastering, and the overturned and broken furniture.

In the middle of the floor lay his mother asleep. In one corner of the room his father's limp body hung across the seat of a chair.

The urchin stole forward. He began to shiver in dread of awakening his parents. His mother's great chest was heaving painfully. Jimmie paused and looked down at her. Her face was inflamed and swollen from drinking. Her yellow brows shaded eyelids that had grown blue. Her tangled hair tossed in waves over her forehead. Her mouth was set in the same lines of vindictive hatred that it had, perhaps, borne during the fight. Her bare, red arms were thrown out above her head in positions of exhaustion, something, mayhap, like those of a sated villain.

The urchin bended over his mother. He was fearful lest she should open her eyes, and the dread within him was so strong, that he could not forbear to stare, but hung as if fascinated over the woman's grim face.

Suddenly her eyes opened. The urchin found himself looking straight into that expression, which, it would seem, had the power to change his blood to salt. He howled piercingly and fell backward.

The woman floundered for a moment, tossed her arms about her head as if in combat, and again began to snore.

Jimmie crawled back in the shadows and waited. A noise in the next room had followed his cry at the discovery that his mother was awake. He grovelled in the gloom, the eyes from out his drawn face riveted upon the intervening door.

He heard it creak, and then the sound of a small voice came to him. "Jimmie! Jimmie! Are yehs dere?" it whispered. The urchin started. The thin, white face of his sister looked at him from the door-way of the other room. She crept to him across the floor.

The father had not moved, but lay in the same death-like sleep. The mother writhed in uneasy slumber, her chest wheezing as if she were in the agonies of strangulation. Out at the window a florid moon was peering over dark roofs, and in the distance the waters of a river glimmered pallidly.

The small frame of the ragged girl was quivering. Her features were haggard from weeping, and her eyes gleamed from fear. She grasped the urchin's arm in her little trembling hands and they huddled in a corner. The eyes of both were drawn, by some force, to stare at the woman's face, for they thought she need only to awake and all fiends would come from below.

They crouched until the ghost-mists of dawn appeared at the window, drawing close to the panes, and looking in at the prostrate, heaving body of the mother.

IV

The babe, Tommie, died. He went away in a white, insignificant coffin, his small waxen hand clutching a flower that the girl, Maggie, had stolen from an Italian.

She and Jimmie lived.

The inexperienced fibres of the boy's eyes were hardened at an early age. He became a young man of leather. He lived some red years without laboring. During that time his sneer became chronic. He studied human nature in the gutter, and found it no worse than he thought he had reason to believe it. He never conceived a respect for the world, because he had begun with no idols that it had smashed.

He clad his soul in armor by means of happening hilariously in at a mission church where a man composed his sermons of "yous." While they got warm at the stove, he told his hearers just where he calculated they stood with the Lord. Many of the sinners were impatient over the pictured depths of their degradation. They were waiting for soup-tickets.

A reader of words of wind-demons might have been able to see the portions of a dialogue pass to and fro between the exhorter and his hearers.

"You are damned," said the preacher. And the reader of sounds might have seen the reply go forth from the ragged people: "Where's our soup?"

Jimmie and a companion sat in a rear seat and commented upon the things that didn't concern them, with all the freedom of English gentlemen. When they grew thirsty and went out their minds confused the speaker with Christ.

Momentarily, Jimmie was sullen with thoughts of a hopeless altitude where grew fruit. His companion said that if he should ever meet God he would ask for a million dollars and a bottle of beer.

Jimmie's occupation for a long time was to stand on street-corners and watch the world go by, dreaming blood-red dreams at the passing of pretty women. He menaced mankind at the intersections of streets.

On the corners he was in life and of life. The world was going on and he was there to perceive it.

He maintained a belligerent attitude toward all well-dressed men. To him fine raiment was allied to weakness, and all good coats covered faint hearts. He and his order were kings, to a certain extent, over the men of untarnished clothes, because these latter dreaded, perhaps, to be either killed or laughed at.

Above all things he despised obvious Christians and ciphers with the chrysanthemums of aristocracy in their button-holes. He considered himself above both of these classes. He was afraid of neither the devil nor the leader of society.

When he had a dollar in his pocket his satisfaction with existence was the greatest thing in the world. So, eventually, he felt obliged to work. His father died and his mother's years were divided up into periods of thirty days.

He became a truck driver. He was given the charge of a painstaking pair of horses and a large rattling truck. He invaded the turmoil and tumble of the down-town streets and learned to breathe maledictory defiance at the police who occasionally used to climb up, drag him from his perch and beat him.

In the lower part of the city he daily involved himself in hideous tangles. If he and his team chanced to be in the rear he preserved a demeanor of serenity, crossing his legs and bursting forth into yells when foot passengers took dangerous dives beneath the noses of his champing horses. He smoked his pipe calmly for he knew that his pay was marching on.

If in the front and the key-truck of chaos, he entered terrifically into the quarrel that was raging to and fro among the drivers on their high seats, and sometimes roared oaths and violently got himself arrested.

After a time his sneer grew so that it turned its glare upon all things. He became so sharp that he believed in nothing. To him the police were always actuated by malignant impulses and the rest of the world was composed, for the most part, of despicable creatures who were all trying to take advantage of him and with whom, in defense, he was obliged to quarrel on all possible occasions. He himself occupied a downtrodden position that had a private but distinct element of grandeur in its isolation.

The most complete cases of aggravated idiocy were, to his mind, rampant upon the front platforms of all of the street cars. At first his tongue strove with these beings, but he eventually was superior. He became immured like an African cow. In him grew a majestic contempt for those strings of street cars that followed him like intent bugs.

He fell into the habit, when starting on a long journey, of fixing his eye on a high and distant object, commanding his horses to begin, and then going into a sort of a trance of observation. Multitudes of drivers might howl in his rear, and passengers might load him with opprobrium, he would not awaken until some blue policeman turned red and began to frenziedly tear bridles and beat the soft noses of the responsible horses.

When he paused to contemplate the attitude of the police toward himself and his fellows, he believed that they were the only men in the city who had no rights. When driving about, he felt that he was held liable by the police for anything that might occur in the streets, and was the common prey of all energetic officials. In revenge, he resolved never to move out of the way of anything, until formidable circumstances, or a much larger man than himself forced him to it.

Foot-passengers were mere pestering flies with an insane disregard for their legs and his convenience. He could not conceive their maniacal desires to cross the streets. Their madness smote him with eternal amazement. He was continually storming at them from his throne. He sat aloft and denounced their frantic leaps, plunges, dives and straddles.

When they would thrust at, or parry, the noses of his champing horses, making them swing their heads and move their feet, disturbing a solid dreamy repose, he swore at the men as fools, for he himself could perceive that Providence had caused it clearly to be written, that he and his team had the unalienable right to stand in the proper path of the sun chariot, and if they so minded, obstruct its mission or take a wheel off.

And, perhaps, if the god-driver had an ungovernable desire to step down, put up his flame-colored fists and manfully dispute the right of way, he would have probably been immediately opposed by a scowling mortal with two sets of very hard knuckles.

It is possible, perhaps, that this young man would have derided, in an axle-wide alley, the approach of a flying ferry boat. Yet he achieved a respect for a fire engine. As one charged toward his truck, he would drive fearfully upon a sidewalk, threatening untold people with annihilation. When an engine would strike a mass of blocked trucks, splitting it into fragments, as a blow annihilates a cake of ice, Jimmie's team could usually be observed high and safe, with whole wheels, on the sidewalk. The fearful coming of the engine could break up the most intricate muddle of heavy vehicles at which the police had been swearing for the half of an hour.

A fire-engine was enshrined in his heart as an appalling thing that he loved with a distant dog-like devotion. They had been known to overturn street-cars. Those leaping horses, striking sparks from the cobbles in their forward lunge, were creatures to be ineffably admired. The clang of the gong pierced his breast like a noise of remembered war.

When Jimmie was a little boy, he began to be arrested. Before he reached a great age, he had a fair record.

He developed too great a tendency to climb down from his truck and fight with other drivers. He had been in quite a number of miscellaneous fights, and in some general barroom rows that had become known to the police. Once he had been arrested for assaulting a Chinaman. Two women in different parts of the city, and entirely unknown to each other, caused him considerable annoyance by breaking forth, simultaneously, at fateful intervals, into wailings about marriage and support and infants.

Nevertheless, he had, on a certain star-lit evening, said wonderingly and quite reverently: "Deh moon looks like hell, don't it?"

V

The girl, Maggie, blossomed in a mud puddle. She grew to be a most rare and wonderful production of a tenement district, a pretty girl.

None of the dirt of Rum Alley seemed to be in her veins. The philosophers up-stairs, down-stairs and on the same floor, puzzled over it.

When a child, playing and fighting with gamins in the street, dirt disguised her. Attired in tatters and grime, she went unseen.

There came a time, however, when the young men of the vicinity, said: "Dat Johnson goil is a puty good looker." About this period her brother remarked to her: "Mag, I'll tell yeh dis! See? Yeh've edder got teh go teh hell or go teh work!" Whereupon she went to work, having the feminine aversion of going to hell.

By a chance, she got a position in an establishment where they made collars and cuffs. She received a stool and a machine in a room where sat twenty girls of various shades of yellow discontent. She perched on the stool and treadled at her machine all day, turning out collars, the name of whose brand could be noted for its irrelevancy to anything in connection with collars. At night she returned home to her mother.

Jimmie grew large enough to take the vague position of head of the family. As incumbent of that office, he stumbled up-stairs late at night, as his father had done before him. He reeled about the room, swearing at his relations, or went to sleep on the floor.

The mother had gradually arisen to that degree of fame that she could bandy words with her acquaintances among the police-justices. Court-officials called her by her first name. When she appeared they pursued a course which had been theirs for months. They invariably grinned and cried out: "Hello, Mary, you here again?" Her grey head wagged in many a court. She always besieged the bench with voluble excuses, explanations, apologies and prayers. Her flaming face and rolling eyes were a sort of familiar sight on the island. She measured time by means of sprees, and was eternally swollen and dishevelled.

One day the young man, Pete, who as a lad had smitten the Devil's Row urchin in the back of the head and put to flight the antagonists of his friend, Jimmie, strutted upon the scene. He met Jimmie one day on the street, promised to take him to a boxing match in Williamsburg, and called for him in the evening.

Maggie observed Pete.

He sat on a table in the Johnson home and dangled his checked legs with an enticing nonchalance. His hair was curled down over his forehead in an oiled bang. His rather pugged nose seemed to revolt from contact with a bristling moustache of short, wire-like hairs. His blue double-breasted coat, edged with black braid, buttoned close to a red puff tie, and his patent-leather shoes, looked like murder-fitted weapons.

His mannerisms stamped him as a man who had a correct sense of his personal superiority. There was valor and contempt for circumstances in the glance of his eye. He waved his hands like a man of the world, who dismisses religion and philosophy, and says

"Fudge." He had certainly seen everything and with each curl of his lip, he declared that it amounted to nothing. Maggie thought he must be a very elegant and graceful bartender.

He was telling tales to Jimmie.

Maggie watched him furtively, with half-closed eyes, lit with a vague interest.

"Hully gee! Dey makes me tired," he said. "Mos' e'ry day some farmer comes in an' tries teh run deh shop. See? But deh gits t'rowed right out! I jolt dem right out in deh street before dey knows where dey is! See?"

"Sure," said Jimmie.

"Dere was a mug come in deh place deh odder day wid an idear he wus goin' teh own deh place! Hully gee, he wus goin' teh own deh place! I see he had a still on an' I didn' wanna giv 'im no stuff, so I says: 'Git deh hell outa here an' don' make no trouble,' I says like dat! See? 'Git deh hell outa here an' don' make no trouble;' like dat. 'Git deh hell outa here,' I says. See?"

Jimmie nodded understandingly. Over his features played an eager desire to state the amount of his valor in a similar crisis, but the narrator proceeded.

"Well, deh blokie he says: 'T'hell wid it! I ain' lookin' for no scrap,' he says (See?) 'but' he says, 'I'm spectable cit'zen an' I wanna drink an' purtydamnsoon, too.' See? 'Deh hell,' I says. Like dat! 'Deh hell,' I says. See? 'Don't make no trouble,' I says. Like dat. 'Don' make no trouble.' See? Den deh mug he squared off an' said he was fine as silk wid his dukes (See?) an' he wanned a drink damnquick. Dat's what he said. See?"

"Sure," repeated Jimmie.

Pete continued. "Say, I jes' jumped deh bar an' deh way I plunked dat blokie was great. See? Dat's right! In deh jaw! See? Hully gee, he t'rowed a spittoon true deh front windee. Say, I taut I'd drop dead. But deh boss, he comes in after an' he says, 'Pete, yehs done jes' right! Yeh've gota keep order an' it's all right.' See? 'It's all right,' he says. Dat's what he said."

The two held a technical discussion.

"Dat bloke was a dandy," said Pete, in conclusion, "but he had'n' oughta made no trouble. Dat's what I says teh dem: 'Don' come in here an' make no trouble,' I says, like dat. 'Don' make no trouble.' See?"

As Jimmie and his friend exchanged tales descriptive of their prowess, Maggie leaned back in the shadow. Her eyes dwelt wonderingly and rather wistfully upon Pete's face. The broken furniture, grimey walls, and general disorder and dirt of her home of a sudden appeared before her and began to take a potential aspect. Pete's aristocratic person looked as if it might soil. She looked keenly at him, occasionally, wondering if he was feeling contempt. But Pete seemed to be enveloped in reminiscence.

"Hully gee," said he, "dose mugs can't phase me. Dey knows I kin wipe up deh street wid any tree of dem."

When he said, "Ah, what deh hell," his voice was burdened with disdain for the inevitable and contempt for anything that fate might compel him to endure.

Maggie perceived that here was the beau ideal of a man. Her dim thoughts were often searching for far away lands where, as God says, the little hills sing together in the morning. Under the trees of her dream-gardens there had always walked a lover.

VI

Pete took note of Maggie.

"Say, Mag, I'm stuck on yer shape. It's outa sight," he said, parenthetically, with an affable grin.

As he became aware that she was listening closely, he grew still more eloquent in his descriptions of various happenings in his career. It appeared that he was invincible in fights.

"Why," he said, referring to a man with whom he had had a misunderstanding, "dat mug scrapped like a damn dago. Dat's right. He was dead easy. See? He tau't he was a scrapper! But he foun' out diff'ent! Hully gee."

He walked to and fro in the small room, which seemed then to grow even smaller and unfit to hold his dignity, the attribute of a supreme warrior. That swing of the shoulders that had frozen the timid when he was but a lad had increased with his growth and education at the ratio of ten to one. It, combined with the sneer upon his mouth, told mankind that there was nothing in space which could appall him. Maggie marvelled at him and surrounded him with greatness. She vaguely tried to calculate the altitude of the pinnacle from which he must have looked down upon her.

"I met a chump deh odder day way up in deh city," he said. "I was goin' teh see a frien' of mine. When I was a-crossin' deh street deh chump runned plump inteh me, an' den he turns aroun' an' says, 'Yer insolen' ruffin,' he says, like dat. 'Oh, gee,' I says, 'oh, gee, go teh hell and git off deh eart',' I says, like dat. See? 'Go teh hell an' git off deh eart',' like dat. Den deh blokie he got wild. He says I was a contempt'ble scoun'el, er something like dat, an' he says I was doom' teh everlastin' pe'dition an' all like dat. 'Gee,' I says, 'gee! Deh hell I am,' I says. 'Deh hell I am,' like dat. An' den I slugged 'im. See?"

With Jimmie in his company, Pete departed in a sort of blaze of glory from the Johnson home. Maggie, leaning from the window, watched him as he walked down the street.

Here was a formidable man who disdained the strength of a world full of fists. Here was one who had contempt for brass-clothed power; one whose knuckles could defiantly ring against the granite of law. He was a knight.

The two men went from under the glimmering street-lamp and passed into shadows.

Turning, Maggie contemplated the dark, dust-stained walls, and the scant and crude furniture of her home. A clock, in a splintered and battered oblong box of varnished wood, she suddenly regarded as an abomination. She noted that it ticked raspingly. The almost vanished flowers in the carpet-pattern, she conceived to be newly hideous. Some faint attempts she had made with blue ribbon, to freshen the appearance of a dingy curtain, she now saw to be piteous.

She wondered what Pete dined on.

She reflected upon the collar and cuff factory. It began to appear to her mind as a dreary place of endless grinding. Pete's elegant occupation brought him, no doubt, into contact with people who had money and manners. It was probable that he had a large acquaintance of pretty girls. He must have great sums of money to spend.

To her the earth was composed of hardships and insults. She felt instant admiration for a man who openly defied it. She thought that if the grim angel of death should clutch his heart, Pete would shrug his shoulders and say: "Oh, ev'ryt'ing goes."

She anticipated that he would come again shortly. She spent some of her week's pay in the purchase of flowered cretonne for a lambrequin. She made it with infinite care and hung it to the slightly-careening mantel, over the stove, in the kitchen. She studied it with painful anxiety from different points in the room. She wanted it to look well on Sunday night when, perhaps, Jimmie's friend would come. On Sunday night, however, Pete did not appear.

Afterward the girl looked at it with a sense of humiliation. She was now convinced that Pete was superior to admiration for lambrequins.

A few evenings later Pete entered with fascinating innovations in his apparel. As she had seen him twice and he had different suits on each time, Maggie had a dim impression that his wardrobe was prodigiously extensive.

"Say, Mag," he said, "put on yer bes' duds Friday night an' I'll take yehs teh deh show. See?"

He spent a few moments in flourishing his clothes and then vanished, without having glanced at the lambrequin.

Over the eternal collars and cuffs in the factory Maggie spent the most of three days in making imaginary sketches of Pete and his daily environment. She imagined some half dozen women in love with him and thought he must lean dangerously toward an indefinite one, whom she pictured with great charms of person, but with an altogether contemptible disposition.

She thought he must live in a blare of pleasure. He had friends, and people who were afraid of him.

She saw the golden glitter of the place where Pete was to take her. An entertainment of many hues and many melodies where she was afraid she might appear small and mouse-colored.

Her mother drank whiskey all Friday morning. With lurid face and tossing hair she cursed and destroyed furniture all Friday afternoon. When Maggie came home at half-past six her mother lay asleep amidst the wreck of chairs and a table. Fragments of various household utensils were scattered about the floor. She had vented some phase of drunken fury upon the lambrequin. It lay in a bedraggled heap in the corner.

"Hah," she snorted, sitting up suddenly, "where deh hell yeh been? Why deh hell don' yeh come home earlier? Been loafin' 'round deh streets. Yer gettin' teh be a reg'lar devil."

When Pete arrived Maggie, in a worn black dress, was waiting for him in the midst of a floor strewn with wreckage. The curtain at the window had been pulled by a heavy hand and hung by one tack, dangling to and fro in the draft through the cracks at the sash. The knots of blue ribbons appeared like violated flowers. The fire in the stove had gone out. The displaced lids and open doors showed heaps of sullen grey ashes. The remnants of a meal, ghastly, like dead flesh, lay in a corner. Maggie's red mother, stretched on the floor, blasphemed and gave her daughter a bad name.

VII

An orchestra of yellow silk women and bald-headed men on an elevated stage near the centre of a great green-hued hall, played a popular waltz. The place was crowded with people grouped about little tables. A battalion of waiters slid among the throng, carrying trays of beer glasses and making change from the inexhaustible vaults of their trousers pockets. Little boys, in the costumes of French chefs, paraded up and down the irregular aisles vending fancy cakes. There was a low rumble of conversation and a subdued clinking of glasses. Clouds of tobacco smoke rolled and wavered high in air about the dull gilt of the chandeliers.

The vast crowd had an air throughout of having just quitted

labor. Men with calloused hands and attired in garments that showed the wear of an endless trudge for a living, smoked their pipes contentedly and spent five, ten, or perhaps fifteen cents for beer. There was a mere sprinkling of kid-gloved men who smoked cigars purchased elsewhere. The great body of the crowd was composed of people who showed that all day they strove with their hands. Quiet Germans, with maybe their wives and two or three children, sat listening to the music, with the expressions of happy cows. An occasional party of sailors from a war-ship, their faces pictures of sturdy health, spent the earlier hours of the evening at the small round tables. Very infrequent tipsy men, swollen with the value of their opinions, engaged their companions in earnest and confidential conversation. In the balcony, and here and there below, shone the impassive faces of women. The nationalities of the Bowery beamed upon the stage from all directions.

Pete aggressively walked up a side aisle and took seats with Maggie at a table beneath the balcony.

"Two beehs!"

Leaning back he regarded with eyes of superiority the scene before them. This attitude affected Maggie strongly. A man who could regard such a sight with indifference must be accustomed to very great things.

It was obvious that Pete had been to this place many times before, and was very familiar with it. A knowledge of this fact made Maggie feel little and new.

He was extremely gracious and attentive. He displayed the consideration of a cultured gentleman who knew what was due.

"Say, what deh hell? Bring deh lady a big glass! What deh hell use is dat pony?"

"Don't be fresh, now," said the waiter, with some warmth, as he departed.

"Ah, git off deh eart'," said Pete, after the other's retreating form.

Maggie perceived that Pete brought forth all his elegance and all his knowledge of high-class customs for her benefit. Her heart warmed as she reflected upon his condescension.

The orchestra of yellow silk women and bald-headed men gave vent to a few bars of anticipatory music and a girl, in a pink dress with short skirts, galloped upon the stage. She smiled upon the throng as if in acknowledgment of a warm welcome, and began to walk to and fro, making profuse gesticulations and singing, in brazen soprano tones, a song, the words of which were inaudible. When she broke into the swift rattling measures of a chorus some half tipsy men near the stage joined in the rollicking refrain and glasses were pounded rhythmically upon the tables. People leaned forward to watch her and to try to catch the words of the song. When she vanished there were long rollings of applause.

Obedient to more anticipatory bars, she reappeared amidst the half-suppressed cheering of the tipsy men. The orchestra plunged into dance music and the laces of the dancer fluttered and flew in the glare of gas jets. She divulged the fact that she was attired in some half dozen skirts. It was patent that any one of them would have proved adequate for the purpose for which skirts are intended. An occasional man bent forward, intent upon the pink stockings. Maggie wondered at the splendor of the costume and lost herself in calculations of the cost of the silks and laces.

The dancer's smile of stereotyped enthusiasm was turned for ten minutes upon the faces of her audience. In the finale she fell into some of those grotesque attitudes which were at the time popular among the dancers in the theatres up-town, giving to the Bowery public the phantasies of the aristocratic theatre-going public, at reduced rates.

"Say, Pete," said Maggie, leaning forward, "dis is great."

"Sure," said Pete, with proper complacence.

A ventriloquist followed the dancer. He held two fantastic dolls on his knees. He made them sing mournful ditties and say funny things about geography and Ireland.

"Do dose little men talk?" asked Maggie.

"Naw," said Pete, "it's some damn fake. See?"

Two girls, on the bills as sisters, came forth and sang a duet that is heard occasionally at concerts given under church auspices.

They supplemented it with a dance which of course can never be seen at concerts given under church auspices.

After the duettists had retired, a woman of debatable age sang a negro melody. The chorus necessitated some grotesque waddlings supposed to be an imitation of a plantation darkey, under the influence, probably, of music and the moon. The audience was just enthusiastic enough over it to have her return and sing a sorrowful lay, whose lines told of a mother's love and a sweetheart who waited and a young man who was lost at sea under the most harrowing circumstances. From the faces of a score or so in the crowd, the self-contained look faded. Many heads were bent forward with eagerness and sympathy. As the last distressing sentiment of the piece was brought forth, it was greeted by that kind of applause which rings as sincere.

As a final effort, the singer rendered some verses which described a vision of Britain being annihilated by America, and Ireland bursting her bonds. A carefully prepared crisis was reached in the last line of the last verse, where the singer threw out her arms and cried, "The star-spangled banner." Instantly a great cheer swelled from the throats of the assemblage of the masses. There was a heavy rumble of booted feet thumping the floor. Eyes gleamed with sudden fire, and calloused hands waved frantically in the air.

After a few moments' rest, the orchestra played crashingly, and a small fat man burst out upon the stage. He began to roar a song and stamp back and forth before the foot-lights, wildly waving a glossy silk hat and throwing leers, or smiles, broadcast. He made his face into fantastic grimaces until he looked like a pictured devil on a Japanese kite. The crowd laughed gleefully. His short, fat legs were never still a moment. He shouted and roared and bobbed his shock of red wig until the audience broke out in excited applause.

Pete did not pay much attention to the progress of events upon the stage. He was drinking beer and watching Maggie.

Her cheeks were blushing with excitement and her eyes were glistening. She drew deep breaths of pleasure. No thoughts of the atmosphere of the collar and cuff factory came to her.

When the orchestra crashed finally, they jostled their way to the sidewalk with the crowd. Pete took Maggie's arm and pushed a way for her, offering to fight with a man or two.

They reached Maggie's home at a late hour and stood for a moment in front of the gruesome doorway.

"Say, Mag," said Pete, "give us a kiss for takin' yeh teh deh show, will yer?"

Maggie laughed, as if startled, and drew away from him.

"Naw, Pete," she said, "dat wasn't in it."

"Ah, what deh hell?" urged Pete.

The girl retreated nervously.

"Ah, what deh hell?" repeated he.

Maggie darted into the hall, and up the stairs. She turned and smiled at him, then disappeared.

Pete walked slowly down the street. He had something of an astonished expression upon his features. He paused under a lamppost and breathed a low breath of surprise.

"Gawd," he said, "I wonner if I've been played fer a duffer."

VIII

As thoughts of Pete came to Maggie's mind, she began to have an intense dislike for all of her dresses.

"What deh hell ails yeh? What makes yeh be allus fixin' and fussin'? Good Gawd," her mother would frequently roar at her.

She began to note, with more interest, the well-dressed women she met on the avenues. She envied elegance and soft palms. She craved those adornments of person which she saw every day on the street, conceiving them to be allies of vast importance to women.

Studying faces, she thought many of the women and girls she chanced to meet, smiled with serenity as though forever cherished and watched over by those they loved.

The air in the collar and cuff establishment strangled her. She knew she was gradually and surely shrivelling in the hot, stuffy room. The begrimed windows rattled incessantly from the passing of elevated trains. The place was filled with a whirl of noises and odors.

She wondered as she regarded some of the grizzled women in the room, mere mechanical contrivances sewing seams and grinding out, with heads bended over their work, tales of imagined or real girlhood happiness, past drunks, the baby at home, and unpaid wages. She speculated how long her youth would endure. She began to see the bloom upon her cheeks as valuable.

She imagined herself, in an exasperating future, as a scrawny woman with an eternal grievance. Too, she thought Pete to be a very fastidious person concerning the appearance of women.

She felt she would love to see somebody entangle their fingers in the oily beard of the fat foreigner who owned the establishment. He was a detestable creature. He wore white socks with low shoes.

He sat all day delivering orations, in the depths of a cushioned chair. His pocketbook deprived them of the power of retort.

"What een hell do you sink I pie fife dolla a week for? Play? No, py damn!"

Maggie was anxious for a friend to whom she could talk about Pete. She would have liked to discuss his admirable mannerisms with a reliable mutual friend. At home, she found her mother often drunk and always raving.

It seems that the world had treated this woman very badly, and she took a deep revenge upon such portions of it as came within her reach. She broke furniture as if she were at last getting her rights. She swelled with virtuous indignation as she carried the lighter articles of household use, one by one under the shadows of the three gilt balls, where Hebrews chained them with chains of interest.

Jimmie came when he was obliged to by circumstances over which he had no control. His well-trained legs brought him staggering home and put him to bed some nights when he would rather have gone elsewhere.

Swaggering Pete loomed like a golden sun to Maggie. He took

her to a dime museum where rows of meek freaks astonished her. She contemplated their deformities with awe and thought them a sort of chosen tribe.

Pete, raking his brains for amusement, discovered the Central Park Menagerie and the Museum of Arts. Sunday afternoons would sometimes find them at these places. Pete did not appear to be particularly interested in what he saw. He stood around looking heavy, while Maggie giggled in glee.

Once at the Menagerie he went into a trance of admiration before the spectacle of a very small monkey threatening to thrash a cageful because one of them had pulled his tail and he had not wheeled about quickly enough to discover who did it. Ever after Pete knew that monkey by sight and winked at him, trying to induce him to fight with other and larger monkeys.

At the Museum, Maggie said, "Dis is outa sight."

"Oh hell," said Pete, "wait till next summer an' I'll take yehs to a picnic."

While the girl wandered in the vaulted rooms, Pete occupied himself in returning stony stare for stony stare, the appalling scrutiny of the watch-dogs of the treasures. Occasionally he would remark in loud tones: "Dat jay has got glass eyes," and sentences of the sort. When he tired of this amusement he would go to the mummies and moralize over them.

Usually he submitted with silent dignity to all which he had to go through, but, at times, he was goaded into comment.

"What deh hell," he demanded once. "Look at all dese little jugs! Hundred jugs in a row! Ten rows in a case an' 'bout a t'ousand cases! What deh blazes use is dem?"

Evenings during the week he took her to see plays in which the brain-clutching heroine was rescued from the palatial home of her guardian, who is cruelly after her bonds, by the hero with the beautiful sentiments. The latter spent most of his time out at soak in pale-green snow storms, busy with a nickel-plated revolver, rescuing aged strangers from villains.

Maggie lost herself in sympathy with the wanderers swooning in snow storms beneath happy-hued church windows. And a choir within singing "Joy to the World." To Maggie and the rest of the audience this was transcendental realism. Joy always within, and they, like the actor, inevitably without. Viewing it, they hugged themselves in ecstatic pity of their imagined or real condition.

The girl thought the arrogance and granite-heartedness of the magnate of the play was very accurately drawn. She echoed the maledictions that the occupants of the gallery showered on this individual when his lines compelled him to expose his extreme selfishness.

Shady persons in the audience revolted from the pictured villainy of the drama. With untiring zeal they hissed vice and applauded virtue. Unmistakably bad men evinced an apparently sincere admiration for virtue.

The loud gallery was overwhelmingly with the unfortunate and the oppressed. They encouraged the struggling hero with cries, and jeered the villain, hooting and calling attention to his whiskers. When anybody died in the pale-green snow storms, the gallery mourned. They sought out the painted misery and hugged it as akin.

In the hero's erratic march from poverty in the first act, to wealth and triumph in the final one, in which he forgives all the enemies that he has left, he was assisted by the gallery, which applauded his generous and noble sentiments and confounded the speeches of his opponents by making irrelevant but very sharp remarks. Those actors who were cursed with villainy parts were confronted at every turn by the gallery. If one of them rendered lines containing the most subtile distinctions between right and wrong, the gallery was immediately aware if the actor meant wickedness, and denounced him accordingly.

The last act was a triumph for the hero, poor and of the masses, the representative of the audience, over the villain and the rich man, his pockets stuffed with bonds, his heart packed with tyrannical purposes, imperturbable amid suffering.

Maggie always departed with raised spirits from the showing places of the melodrama. She rejoiced at the way in which the poor and virtuous eventually surmounted the wealthy and wicked. The theater made her think. She wondered if the culture and refinement she had seen imitated, perhaps grotesquely, by the heroine on the stage, could be acquired by a girl who lived in a tenement house and worked in a shirt factory.

IX

A group of urchins were intent upon the side door of a saloon. Expectancy gleamed from their eyes. They were twisting their fingers in excitement.

"Here she comes," yelled one of them suddenly.

The group of urchins burst instantly asunder and its individual fragments were spread in a wide, respectable half-circle about the point of interest. The saloon door opened with a crash, and the figure of a woman appeared upon the threshold. Her gray hair fell in knotted masses about her shoulders. Her face was crimsoned and wet with perspiration. Her eyes had a rolling glare.

"Not a damn cent more of me money will yehs ever get, not a damn cent. I spent me money here fer t'ree years an' now yehs tells me yeh'll sell me no more stuff! T'hell wid yeh, Johnnie Murckre! 'Disturbance'? Disturbance be damned! T'hell wid yeh, Johnnie—"

The door received a kick of exasperation from within and the woman lurched heavily out on the sidewalk.

The gamins in the half-circle became violently agitated. They began to dance about and hoot and yell and jeer. Wide dirty grins spread over each face.

The woman made a furious dash at a particularly outrageous cluster of little boys. They laughed delightedly and scampered off a short distance, calling out over their shoulders to her. She stood tottering on the curb-stone and thundered at them.

"Yeh devil's kids," she howled, shaking red fists. The little boys whooped in glee. As she started up the street they fell in behind and marched uproariously. Occasionally she wheeled about and made charges on them. They ran nimbly out of reach and taunted her.

In the frame of a gruesome doorway she stood for a moment cursing them. Her hair straggled, giving her crimson features a look of insanity. Her great fists quivered as she shook them madly in the air.

The urchins made terrific noises until she turned and disappeared. Then they filed quietly in the way they had come.

The woman floundered about in the lower hall of the tenement house and finally stumbled up the stairs. On an upper hall a door was opened and a collection of heads peered curiously out, watching her. With a wrathful snort the woman confronted the door, but it was slammed hastily in her face and the key was turned.

She stood for a few minutes, delivering a frenzied challenge at the panels.

"Come out in deh hall, Mary Murphy, damn yeh, if yehs want a row. Come ahn, yeh overgrown terrier, come ahn."

She began to kick the door with her great feet. She shrilly defied the universe to appear and do battle. Her cursing trebles brought heads from all doors save the one she threatened. Her eyes glared in every direction. The air was full of her tossing fists.

"Come ahn, deh hull damn gang of yehs, come ahn," she roared at the spectators. An oath or two, cat-calls, jeers and bits of facetious advice were given in reply. Missiles clattered about her feet.

"What deh hell's deh matter wid yeh?" said a voice in the gathered gloom, and Jimmie came forward. He carried a tin dinner-pail in his hand and under his arm a brown truckman's apron done in a bundle. "What deh hell's wrong?" he demanded.

"Come out, all of yehs, come out," his mother was howling. "Come ahn an' I'll stamp yer damn brains under me feet."

"Shet yer face, an' come home, yeh damned old fool," roared Jimmie at her. She strided up to him and twirled her fingers in his face. Her eyes were darting flames of unreasoning rage and her frame trembled with eagerness for a fight.

"T'hell wid yehs! An' who deh hell are yehs? I ain't givin' a snap of me fingers fer yehs," she bawled at him. She turned her huge back in tremendous disdain and climbed the stairs to the next floor.

Jimmie followed, cursing blackly. At the top of the flight he seized his mother's arm and started to drag her toward the door of their room.

"Come home, damn yeh," he gritted between his teeth.

"Take yer hands off me! Take yer hands off me," shrieked his mother.

She raised her arm and whirled her great fist at her son's face. Jimmie dodged his head and the blow struck him in the back of the neck. "Damn yeh," gritted he again. He threw out his left hand and writhed his fingers about her middle arm. The mother and the son began to sway and struggle like gladiators.

"Whoop!" said the Rum Alley tenement house. The hall filled with interested spectators.

"Hi, ol' lady, dat was a dandy!"

"T'ree to one on deh red!"

"Ah, stop yer damn scrappin'!"

The door of the Johnson home opened and Maggie looked out. Jimmie made a supreme cursing effort and hurled his mother into the room. He quickly followed and closed the door. The Rum Alley tenement swore disappointedly and retired.

The mother slowly gathered herself up from the floor. Her eyes glittered menacingly upon her children.

"Here, now," said Jimmie, "we've had enough of dis. Sit down, an' don' make no trouble."

He grasped her arm, and twisting it, forced her into a creaking chair.

"Keep yer hands off me," roared his mother again.

"Damn yer ol' hide," yelled Jimmie, madly. Maggie shrieked and ran into the other room. To her there came the sound of a storm of crashes and curses. There was a great final thump and Jimmie's voice cried: "Dere, damn yeh, stay still." Maggie opened the door now, and went warily out. "Oh, Jimmie."

He was leaning against the wall and swearing. Blood stood upon bruises on his knotty fore-arms where they had scraped against the floor or the walls in the scuffle. The mother lay screeching on the floor, the tears running down her furrowed face.

Maggie, standing in the middle of the room, gazed about her. The usual upheaval of the tables and chairs had taken place. Crockery was strewn broadcast in fragments. The stove had been disturbed on its legs, and now leaned idiotically to one side. A pail had been upset and water spread in all directions.

The door opened and Pete appeared. He shrugged his shoulders. "Oh, Gawd," he observed.

He walked over to Maggie and whispered in her ear. "Ah, what deh hell, Mag? Come ahn and we'll have a hell of a time."

The mother in the corner upreared her head and shook her tangled locks.

"Teh hell wid him and you," she said, glowering at her daughter in the gloom. Her eyes seemed to burn balefully. "Yeh've gone teh deh devil, Mag Johnson, yehs knows yehs have gone teh deh devil. Yer a disgrace teh yer people, damn yeh. An' now, git out an' go ahn wid dat doe-faced jude of yours. Go teh hell wid him, damn yeh, an' a good riddance. Go teh hell an' see how yeh likes it."

Maggie gazed long at her mother.

"Go teh hell now, an' see how yeh likes it. Git out. I won't have sech as yehs in me house! Get out, d'yeh hear! Damn yeh, git out!"

The girl began to tremble.

At this instant Pete came forward. "Oh, what deh hell, Mag, see," whispered he softly in her ear. "Dis all blows over. See? Deh ol' woman 'ill be all right in deh mornin'. Come ahn out wid me! We'll have a hell of a time."

The woman on the floor cursed. Jimmie was intent upon his bruised fore-arms. The girl cast a glance about the room filled with a chaotic mass of debris, and at the red, writhing body of her mother.

"Go teh hell an' good riddance."

She went.

X

Jimmie had an idea it wasn't common courtesy for a friend to come to one's home and ruin one's sister. But he was not sure how much Pete knew about the rules of politeness.

The following night he returned home from work at rather a late hour in the evening. In passing through the halls he came upon the gnarled and leathery old woman who possessed the music box. She was grinning in the dim light that drifted through dust-stained panes. She beckoned to him with a smudged forefinger.

"Ah, Jimmie, what do yehs tink I got onto las' night. It was deh funnies' ting I ever saw," she cried, coming close to him and leering. She was trembling with eagerness to tell her tale. "I was by me door las' night when yer sister and her jude feller came in late, oh, very late. An' she, the dear, she was a-cryin' as if her heart would break, she was. It was deh funnies' ting I ever saw. An' right out here by me door she asked him did he love her, did he. An' she was a-cryin' as if her heart would break, poor t'ing. An' him, I could see by deh way what he said it dat she had been askin' orften, he says: 'Oh, hell, yes,' he says, says he, 'Oh, hell, yes.' "

Storm-clouds swept over Jimmie's face, but he turned from the leathery old woman and plodded on up-stairs.

"Oh, hell, yes," called she after him. She laughed a laugh that was like a prophetic croak. " 'Oh, hell, yes,' he says, says he, 'Oh, hell, yes.' "

There was no one in at home. The rooms showed that attempts had been made at tidying them. Parts of the wreckage of the day before had been repaired by an unskilful hand. A chair or two and the table, stood uncertainly upon legs. The floor had been newly swept. Too, the blue ribbons had been restored to the curtains, and the lambrequin, with its immense sheaves of yellow wheat and red roses of equal size, had been returned, in a worn and sorry state, to its position at the mantel. Maggie's jacket and hat were gone from the nail behind the door.

Jimmie walked to the window and began to look through the blurred glass. It occurred to him to vaguely wonder, for an instant, if some of the women of his acquaintance had brothers.

Suddenly, however, he began to swear.

"But he was me frien'! I brought 'im here! Dat's deh hell of it!"

He fumed about the room, his anger gradually rising to the furious pitch.

"I'll kill deh jay! Dat's what I'll do! I'll kill deh jay!"

He clutched his hat and sprang toward the door. But it opened and his mother's great form blocked the passage.

"What deh hell's deh matter wid yeh?" exclaimed she, coming into the rooms.

Jimmie gave vent to a sardonic curse and then laughed heavily.

"Well, Maggie's gone teh deh devil! Dat's what! See?"

"Eh?" said his mother.

"Maggie's gone teh deh devil! Are yehs deaf?" roared Jimmie, impatiently.

"Deh hell she has," murmured the mother, astounded.

Jimmie grunted, and then began to stare out at the window. His mother sat down in a chair, but a moment later sprang erect and delivered a maddened whirl of oaths. Her son turned to look at her as she reeled and swayed in the middle of the room, her fierce face convulsed with passion, her blotched arms raised high in imprecation.

"May Gawd curse her forever," she shrieked. "May she eat nothin' but stones and deh dirt in deh street. May she sleep in deh gutter an' never see deh sun shine agin. Deh damn—"

"Here, now," said her son. "Take a drop on yourself."

The mother raised lamenting eyes to the ceiling.

"She's deh devil's own chil', Jimmie," she whispered. "Ah, who would tink such a bad girl could grow up in our fambly, Jimmie, me son. Many deh hour I've spent in talk wid dat girl an' tol' her if she ever went on deh streets I'd see her damned. An' after all her bringin' up an' what I tol' her and talked wid her, she goes teh deh bad, like a duck teh water."

The tears rolled down her furrowed face. Her hands trembled.

"An' den when dat Sadie MacMallister next door to us was sent teh deh devil by dat feller what worked in deh soap-factory, didn't I tell our Mag dat if she—"

"Ah, dat's anudder story," interrupted the brother. "Of course, dat Sadie was nice an' all dat—but—see—it ain't dessame as if—well, Maggie was diff'ent—see—she was diff'ent."

He was trying to formulate a theory that he had always unconsciously held, that all sisters, excepting his own, could advisedly be ruined.

He suddenly broke out again. "I'll go t'ump hell outa deh mug what did her deh harm. I'll kill 'im! He tinks he kin scrap, but when he gits me a-chasin' 'im he'll fin' out where he's wrong, deh damned duffer. I'll wipe up deh street wid 'im."

In a fury he plunged out of the doorway. As he vanished the mother raised her head and lifted both hands, entreating.

"May Gawd curse her forever," she cried.

In the darkness of the hallway Jimmie discerned a knot of women talking volubly. When he strode by they paid no attention to him.

"She allus was a bold thing," he heard one of them cry in an eager voice. "Dere wasn't a feller come teh deh house but she'd try teh mash 'im. My Annie says deh shameless t'ing tried teh ketch her feller, her own feller, what we useter know his fader."

"I could a' tol' yehs dis two years ago," said a woman, in a key of triumph. "Yesir, it was over two years ago dat I says teh my ol' man, I says, 'Dat Johnson girl ain't straight,' I says. 'Oh, hell,' he says. 'Oh, hell.' 'Dat's all right,' I says, 'but I know what I knows,' I says, 'an' it'ill come out later. You wait an' see,' I says, 'you see.' "

"Anybody what had eyes could see dat dere was somethin' wrong wid dat girl. I didn't like her actions."

On the street Jimmie met a friend. "What deh hell?" asked the latter.

Jimmie explained. "An' I'll tump 'im till he can't stand."

"Oh, what deh hell," said the friend. "What's deh use! Yeh'll git pulled in! Everybody 'ill be onto it! An' ten plunks! Gee!"

Jimmie was determined. "He t'inks he kin scrap, but he'll fin' out diff'ent."

"Gee," remonstrated the friend, "What deh hell?"

XI

On a corner a glass-fronted building shed a yellow glare upon the pavements. The open mouth of a saloon called seductively to passengers to enter and annihilate sorrow or create rage.

The interior of the place was papered in olive and bronze tints of imitation leather. A shining bar of counterfeit massiveness extended down the side of the room. Behind it a great mahogany-appearing sideboard reached the ceiling. Upon its shelves rested pyramids of shimmering glasses that were never disturbed. Mirrors set in the face of the sideboard multiplied them. Lemons, oranges and paper napkins, arranged with mathematical precision, sat among the glasses. Many-hued decanters of liquor perched at regular intervals on the lower shelves. A nickel-plated cash register occupied a position in the exact center of the general effect. The elementary senses of it all seemed to be opulence and geometrical accuracy.

Across from the bar a smaller counter held a collection of plates upon which swarmed frayed fragments of crackers, slices of boiled ham, dishevelled bits of cheese, and pickles swimming in vinegar. An odor of grasping, begrimed hands and munching mouths pervaded.

Pete, in a white jacket, was behind the bar bending expectantly toward a quiet stranger. "A beeh," said the man. Pete drew a foam-topped glassful and set it dripping upon the bar.

At this moment the light bamboo doors at the entrance swung open and crashed against the siding. Jimmie and a companion entered. They swaggered unsteadily but belligerently toward the bar and looked at Pete with bleared and blinking eyes.

"Gin," said Jimmie.

"Gin," said the companion.

Pete slid a bottle and two glasses along the bar. He bended his head sideways as he assiduously polished away with a napkin at the gleaming wood. He had a look of watchfulness upon his features.

Jimmie and his companion kept their eyes upon the bartender and conversed loudly in tones of contempt.

"He's a dindy masher, ain't he, by Gawd?" laughed Jimmie.

"Oh, hell, yes," said the companion, sneering widely. "He's great, he is. Git onto deh mug on deh blokie. Dat's enough to make a feller turn hand-springs in 'is sleep."

The quiet stranger moved himself and his glass a trifle further away and maintained an attitude of oblivion.

"Gee! ain't he hot stuff!"

"Git onto his shape! Great Gawd!"

"Hey," cried Jimmie, in tones of command. Pete came along slowly, with a sullen dropping of the under lip.

"Well," he growled, "what's eatin' yehs?"

"Gin," said Jimmie.

"Gin," said the companion.

As Pete confronted them with the bottle and the glasses, they laughed in his face. Jimmie's companion, evidently overcome with merriment, pointed a grimy forefinger in Pete's direction.

"Say, Jimmie," demanded he, "what deh hell is dat behind deh bar?"

"Damned if I knows," replied Jimmie. They laughed loudly. Pete put down a bottle with a bang and turned a formidable face toward them. He disclosed his teeth and his shoulders heaved restlessly.

"You fellers can't guy me," he said. "Drink yer stuff an' git out an' don' make no trouble."

Instantly the laughter faded from the faces of the two men and expressions of offended dignity immediately came.

"Who deh hell has said anyt'ing teh you," cried they in the same breath.

The quiet stranger looked at the door calculatingly.

"Ah, come off," said Pete to the two men. "Don't pick me up for no jay. Drink yer rum an' git out an' don' make no trouble."

"Oh, deh hell," airily cried Jimmie.

"Oh, deh hell," airily repeated his companion.

"We goes when we git ready! See!" continued Jimmie.

"Well," said Pete in a threatening voice, "don' make no trouble."

Jimmie suddenly leaned forward with his head on one side. He snarled like a wild animal.

"Well, what if we does? See?" said he.

Dark blood flushed into Pete's face, and he shot a lurid glance at Jimmie.

"Well, den we'll see whose deh bes' man, you or me," he said.

The quiet stranger moved modestly toward the door.

Jimmie began to swell with valor.

"Don' pick me up fer no tenderfoot. When yeh tackles me yeh tackles one of deh bes' men in deh city. See? I'm a scrapper, I am. Ain't dat right, Billie?"

"Sure, Mike," responded his companion in tones of conviction.

"Oh, hell," said Pete, easily. "Go fall on yerself."

The two men again began to laugh.

"What deh hell is dat talkin'?" cried the companion.

"Damned if I knows," replied Jimmie with exaggerated contempt.

Pete made a furious gesture. "Git outa here now, an' don' make no trouble. See? Youse fellers er lookin' fer a scrap an' it's damn likely yeh'll fin' one if yeh keeps on shootin' off yer mout's. I know yehs! See? I kin lick better men dan yehs ever saw in yer lifes. Dat's right! See? Don' pick me up fer no stuff er yeh might be jolted out in deh street before yeh knows where yeh is. When I comes from behind dis bar, I t'rows yehs boat inteh deh street. See?"

"Oh, hell," cried the two men in chorus.

The glare of a panther came into Pete's eyes. "Dat's what I said! Unnerstan'?"

He came through a passage at the end of the bar and swelled down upon the two men. They stepped promptly forward and crowded close to him.

They bristled like three roosters. They moved their heads pugnaciously and kept their shoulders braced. The nervous muscles about each mouth twitched with a forced smile of mockery.

"Well, what deh hell yer goin' teh do?" gritted Jimmie.

Pete stepped warily back, waving his hands before him to keep the men from coming too near.

"Well, what deh hell yer goin' teh do?" repeated Jimmie's ally. They kept close to him, taunting and leering. They strove to make him attempt the initial blow.

"Keep back, now! Don' crowd me," ominously said Pete.

Again they chorused in contempt. "Oh, hell!"

In a small, tossing group, the three men edged for positions like frigates contemplating battle.

"Well, why deh hell don' yeh try teh t'row us out?" cried Jimmie and his ally with copious sneers.

The bravery of bull-dogs sat upon the faces of the men. Their clenched fists moved like eager weapons.

The allied two jostled the bartender's elbows, glaring at him with feverish eyes and forcing him toward the wall.

Suddenly Pete swore redly. The flash of action gleamed from his eyes. He threw back his arm and aimed a tremendous, lightning-like blow at Jimmie's face. His foot swung a step forward and the weight of his body was behind his fist. Jimmie ducked his head, Bowery-like, with the quickness of a cat. The fierce, answering blows of him and his ally crushed on Pete's bowed head.

The quiet stranger vanished.

The arms of the combatants whirled in the air like flails. The faces of the men, at first flushed to flame-colored anger, now began to fade to the pallor of warriors in the blood and heat of a battle. Their lips curled back and stretched tightly over the gums in ghoul-like grins. Through their white, gripped teeth struggled hoarse whisperings of oaths. Their eyes glittered with murderous fire.

Each head was huddled between its owner's shoulders, and arms were swinging with marvelous rapidity. Feet scraped to and fro with a loud scratching sound upon the sanded floor. Blows left crimson blotches upon pale skin. The curses of the first quarter minute of the fight died away. The breaths of the fighters came wheezingly from their lips and the three chests were straining and heaving. Pete at intervals gave vent to low, labored hisses, that sounded like a desire to kill. Jimmie's ally gibbered at times like a wounded maniac. Jimmie was silent, fighting with the face of a sacrificial priest. The rage of fear shone in all their eyes and their blood-colored fists swirled.

At a tottering moment a blow from Pete's hand struck the ally and he crashed to the floor. He wriggled instantly to his feet and grasping the quiet stranger's beer glass from the bar, hurled it at Pete's head.

High on the wall it burst like a bomb, shivering fragments flying in all directions. Then missiles came to every man's hand. The place had heretofore appeared free of things to throw, but suddenly glass and bottles went singing through the air. They were thrown point blank at bobbing heads. The pyramid of shimmering glasses, that had never been disturbed, changed to cascades as heavy bottles were flung into them. Mirrors splintered to nothing.

The three frothing creatures on the floor buried themselves in a frenzy for blood. There followed in the wake of missiles and fists some unknown prayers, perhaps for death.

The quiet stranger had sprawled very pyrotechnically out on the sidewalk. A laugh ran up and down the avenue for the half of a block.

"Dey've trowed a bloke inteh deh street."

People heard the sound of breaking glass and shuffling feet within the saloon and came running. A small group, bending down to look under the bamboo doors, watching the fall of glass, and three pairs of violent legs, changed in a moment to a crowd.

A policeman came charging down the sidewalk and bounced through the doors into the saloon. The crowd bended and surged in absorbing anxiety to see.

Jimmie caught first sight of the on-coming interruption. On his feet he had the same regard for a policeman that, when on his truck, he had for a fire engine. He howled and ran for the side door.

The officer made a terrific advance, club in hand. One comprehensive sweep of the long night stick threw the ally to the floor and forced Pete to a corner. With his disengaged hand he made a furious effort at Jimmie's coat-tails. Then he regained his balance and paused.

"Well, well, you are a pair of pictures. What in hell yeh been up to?"

Jimmie, with his face drenched in blood, escaped up a side street, pursued a short distance by some of the more law-loving, or excited individuals of the crowd.

Later, from a corner safely dark, he saw the policeman, the ally and the bartender emerge from the saloon. Pete locked the doors and then followed up the avenue in the rear of the crowd-encompassed policeman and his charge.

On first thoughts Jimmie, with his heart throbbing at battle heat, started to go desperately to the rescue of his friend, but he halted.

"Ah, what deh hell?" he demanded of himself.

XII

In a hall of irregular shape sat Pete and Maggie drinking beer. A submissive orchestra dictated to by a spectacled man with frowsy hair and a dress suit, industriously followed the bobs of his head and the waves of his baton. A ballad singer, in a dress of flaming scarlet, sang in the inevitable voice of brass. When she vanished, men seated at the tables near the front applauded loudly, pounding the polished wood with their beer glasses. She returned attired in less gown, and sang again. She received another enthusiastic encore. She reappeared in still less gown and danced. The deafening rumble of glasses and clapping of hands that followed her exit indicated an overwhelming desire to have her come on for the fourth time, but the curiosity of the audience was not gratified.

Maggie was pale. From her eyes had been plucked all look of self-reliance. She leaned with a dependent air toward her companion. She was timid, as if fearing his anger or displeasure. She seemed to beseech tenderness of him.

Pete's air of distinguished valor had grown upon him until it threatened stupendous dimensions. He was infinitely gracious to the girl. It was apparent to her that his condescension was a marvel.

He could appear to strut even while sitting still and he showed that he was a lion of lordly characteristics by the air with which he spat.

With Maggie gazing at him wonderingly, he took pride in commanding the waiters who were, however, indifferent or deaf.

"Hi, you, git a russle on yehs! What deh hell yeh's lookin' at? Two more beehs, d'yeh hear?"

He leaned back and critically regarded the person of a girl with a straw-colored wig who upon the stage was flinging her heels in somewhat awkward imitation of a well-known danseuse.

At times Maggie told Pete long confidential tales of her former home life, dwelling upon the escapades of the other members of the family and the difficulties she had to combat in order to obtain a degree of comfort. He responded in tones of philanthropy. He pressed her arm with an air of reassuring proprietorship.

"Dey was damn jays," he said, denouncing the mother and brother.

The sound of the music which, by the efforts of the frowsy-headed leader, drifted to her ears through the smoke-filled atmosphere, made the girl dream. She thought of her former Rum Alley environment and turned to regard Pete's strong protecting fists. She thought of the collar and cuff manufactory and the eternal moan of the proprietor: "What een hell do you sink I pie fife dolla a week for? Play? No, py damn." She contemplated Pete's man-subduing eyes and noted that wealth and prosperity was indicated by his clothes. She imagined a future, rose-tinted, because of its distance from all that she previously had experienced.

As to the present she perceived only vague reasons to be miserable. Her life was Pete's and she considered him worthy of the charge. She would be disturbed by no particular apprehensions, so long as Pete adored her as he now said he did. She did not feel like a bad woman. To her knowledge she had never seen any better.

At times men at other tables regarded the girl furtively. Pete, aware of it, nodded at her and grinned. He felt proud.

"Mag, yer a bloomin' good-looker," he remarked, studying her face through the haze. The men made Maggie fear, but she blushed at Pete's words as it became apparent to her that she was the apple of his eye.

Grey-headed men, wonderfully pathetic in their dissipation, stared at her through clouds. Smooth-cheeked boys, some of them with faces of stone and mouths of sin, not nearly so pathetic as the grey heads, tried to find the girl's eyes in the smoke wreaths. Maggie considered she was not what they thought her. She confined her glances to Pete and the stage.

The orchestra played negro melodies and a versatile drummer pounded, whacked, clattered and scratched on a dozen machines to make noise.

Those glances of the men, shot at Maggie from under half-closed lids, made her tremble. She thought them all to be worse men than Pete.

"Come, let's go," she said.

As they went out Maggie perceived two women seated at a table with some men. They were painted and their cheeks had lost their roundness. As she passed them the girl, with a shrinking movement, drew back her skirts.

XIII

Jimmie did not return home for a number of days after the fight with Pete in the saloon. When he did, he approached with extreme caution.

He found his mother raving. Maggie had not returned home. The parent continually wondered how her daughter could come to such a pass. She had never considered Maggie as a pearl dropped unstained into Rum Alley from Heaven, but she could not conceive how it was possible for her daughter to fall so low as to bring disgrace upon her family. She was terrific in denunciation of the girl's wickedness.

The fact that the neighbors talked of it, maddened her. When women came in, and in the course of their conversation casually asked, "Where's Maggie dese days?" the mother shook her fuzzy head at them and appalled them with curses. Cunning hints inviting confidence she rebuffed with violence.

"An' wid all deh bringin' up she had, how could she?" moaningly she asked of her son. "Wid all deh talkin' wid her I did an' deh t'ings I tol' her to remember? When a girl is bringed up deh way I bringed up Maggie, how kin she go teh deh devil?"

Jimmie was transfixed by these questions. He could not conceive how under the circumstances his mother's daughter and his sister could have been so wicked.

His mother took a drink from a squdgy bottle that sat on the table. She continued her lament.

"She had a bad heart, dat girl did, Jimmie. She was wicked teh deh heart an' we never knowed it."

Jimmie nodded, admitting the fact.

"We lived in deh same house wid her an' I brought her up an' we never knowed how bad she was."

Jimmie nodded again.

"Wid a home like dis an' a mudder like me, she went teh deh bad," cried the mother, raising her eyes.

One day, Jimmie came home, sat down in a chair and began to wriggle about with a new and strange nervousness. At last he spoke shamefacedly.

"Well, look-a-here, dis t'ing queers us! See? We're queered! An' maybe it 'ud be better if I—well, I t'ink I kin look 'er up an'—maybe it 'ud be better if I fetched her home an—"

The mother started from her chair and broke forth into a storm of passionate anger.

"What! Let 'er come an' sleep under deh same roof wid her mudder agin! Oh, yes, I will, won't I? Sure? Shame on yehs, Jimmie Johnson, fer sayin' such a t'ing teh yer own mudder—teh yer own mudder! Little did I tink when yehs was a babby playin' about me feet dat ye'd grow up teh say sech a t'ing teh yer mudder—yer own mudder. I never taut—"

Sobs choked her and interrupted her reproaches.

"Dere ain't nottin teh raise sech hell about," said Jimmie. "I on'y says it 'ud be better if we keep dis t'ing dark, see? It queers us! See?"

His mother laughed a laugh that seemed to ring through the city and be echoed and re-echoed by countless other laughs. "Oh, yes, I will, won' I! Sure!"

"Well, yeh must take me fer a damn fool," said Jimmie, indignant at his mother for mocking him. "I didn't say we'd make 'er inteh a little tin angel, ner nottin, but deh way it is now she can queer us! Don' che see?"

"Aye, she'll git tired of deh life atter a while an' den she'll wanna be a-comin' home, won' she, deh beast! I'll let 'er in den, won' I?"

"Well, I didn' mean none of dis prod'gal bus'ness anyway," explained Jimmie.

"It wasn't no prod'gal dauter, yeh damn fool," said the mother. "It was prod'gal son, anyhow."

"I know dat," said Jimmie.

For a time they sat in silence. The mother's eyes gloated on a scene her imagination could call before her. Her lips were set in a vindictive smile.

"Aye, she'll cry, won' she, an' carry on, an' tell how Pete, or some odder feller, beats 'er an' she'll say she's sorry an' all dat an' she ain't happy, she ain't, an' she wants to come home agin, she does."

With grim humor, the mother imitated the possible wailing notes of the daughter's voice.

"Den I'll take 'er in, won't I, deh beast. She kin cry 'er two eyes out on deh stones of deh street before I'll dirty deh place wid her. She abused an' ill-treated her own mudder—her own mudder what loved her an' she'll never git anodder chance dis side of hell."

Jimmie thought he had a great idea of women's frailty, but he could not understand why any of his kin should be victims.

"Damn her," he fervidly said.

Again he wondered vaguely if some of the women of his acquaintance had brothers. Nevertheless, his mind did not for an instant confuse himself with those brothers nor his sister with theirs. After the mother had, with great difficulty, suppressed the neighbors, she went among them and proclaimed her grief. "May Gawd forgive dat girl," was her continual cry. To attentive ears she recited the whole length and breadth of her woes.

"I bringed 'er up deh way a dauter oughta be bringed up an' dis is how she served me! She went teh deh devil deh first chance she got! May Gawd forgive her."

When arrested for drunkenness she used the story of her daughter's downfall with telling effect upon the police justices. Finally one of them said to her, peering down over his spectacles: "Mary, the records of this and other courts show that you are the mother of forty-two daughters who have been ruined. The case is unparalleled in the annals of this court, and this court thinks—"

The mother went through life shedding large tears of sorrow. Her red face was a picture of agony.

Of course Jimmie publicly damned his sister that he might appear on a higher social plane. But, arguing with himself, stumbling about in ways that he knew not, he, once, almost came to a conclusion that his sister would have been more firmly good had she better known why. However, he felt that he could not hold such a view. He threw it hastily aside.

XIV

In a hilarious hall there were twenty-eight tables and twenty-eight women and a crowd of smoking men. Valiant noise was made on a stage at the end of the hall by an orchestra composed of men who looked as if they had just happened in. Soiled waiters ran to and fro, swooping down like hawks on the unwary in the throng; clattering along the aisles with trays covered with glasses; stumbling over women's skirts and charging two prices for everything but beer, all with a swiftness that blurred the view of the cocoanut palms and dusty monstrosities painted upon the walls of the room. A bouncer, with an immense load of business upon his hands, plunged about in the crowd, dragging bashful strangers to prominent chairs, ordering waiters here and there and quarreling furiously with men who wanted to sing with the orchestra.

The usual smoke cloud was present, but so dense that heads and arms seemed entangled in it. The rumble of conversation was replaced by a roar. Plenteous oaths heaved through the air. The room rang with the shrill voices of women bubbling o'er with drink-laughter. The chief element in the music of the orchestra was speed. The musicians played in intent fury. A woman was singing and smiling upon the stage, but no one took notice of her. The rate at which the piano, cornet and violins were going, seemed to impart wildness to the half-drunken crowd. Beer glasses were emptied at a gulp and conversation became a rapid chatter. The smoke eddied and swirled like a shadowy river hurrying toward some unseen falls.

Pete and Maggie entered the hall and took chairs at a table near the door. The woman who was seated there made an attempt to occupy Pete's attention and, failing, went away.

Three weeks had passed since the girl had left home. The air of spaniel-like dependence had been magnified and showed its direct effect in the peculiar off-handedness and ease of Pete's ways toward her.

She followed Pete's eyes with hers, anticipating with smiles gracious looks from him.

A woman of brilliance and audacity, accompanied by a mere boy, came into the place and took seats near them.

At once Pete sprang to his feet, his face beaming with glad surprise.

"By Gawd, there's Nellie," he cried.

He went over to the table and held out an eager hand to the woman.

"Why, hello, Pete, my boy, how are you," said she, giving him her fingers.

Maggie took instant note of the woman. She perceived that her black dress fitted her to perfection. Her linen collar and cuffs were spotless. Tan gloves were stretched over her well-shaped hands. A hat of a prevailing fashion perched jauntily upon her dark hair. She wore no jewelry and was painted with no apparent paint. She looked clear-eyed through the stares of the men.

"Sit down, and call your lady-friend over," she said cordially to Pete. At his beckoning Maggie came and sat between Pete and the mere boy.

"I thought yeh were gone away fer good," began Pete, at once. "When did yeh git back? How did dat Buff'lo bus'ness turn out?"

The woman shrugged her shoulders. "Well, he didn't have as many stamps as he tried to make out, so I shook him, that's all."

"Well, I'm glad teh see yehs back in deh city," said Pete, with awkward gallantry.

He and the woman entered into a long conversation, exchanging reminiscences of days together. Maggie sat still, unable to formulate an intelligent sentence upon the conversation and painfully aware of it.

She saw Pete's eyes sparkle as he gazed upon the handsome stranger. He listened smilingly to all she said. The woman was familiar with all his affairs, asked him about mutual friends, and knew the amount of his salary.

She paid no attention to Maggie, looking toward her once or twice and apparently seeing the wall beyond.

The mere boy was sulky. In the beginning he had welcomed with acclamations the additions.

"Let's all have a drink! What'll you take, Nell? And you, Miss what's-your-name. Have a drink, Mr. ——, you, I mean."

He had shown a sprightly desire to do the talking for the company and tell all about his family. In a loud voice he declaimed on various topics. He assumed a patronizing air toward Pete. As Maggie was silent, he paid no attention to her. He made a great show of lavishing wealth upon the woman of brilliance and audacity.

"Do keep still, Freddie! You gibber like an ape, dear," said the woman to him. She turned away and devoted her attention to Pete.

"We'll have many a good time together again, eh?"

"Sure, Mike," said Pete, enthusiastic at once.

"Say," whispered she, leaning forward, "let's go over to Billie's and have a heluva time."

"Well, it's dis way! See?" said Pete. "I got dis lady frien' here."

"Oh, t'hell with her," argued the woman.

Pete appeared disturbed.

"All right," said she, nodding her head at him. "All right for you! We'll see the next time you ask me to go anywheres with you."

Pete squirmed.

"Say," he said, beseechingly, "come wid me a minit an' I'll tell yer why."

The woman waved her hand.

"Oh, that's all right, you needn't explain, you know. You wouldn't come merely because you wouldn't come, that's all there is of it."

To Pete's visible distress she turned to the mere boy, bringing him speedily from a terrific rage. He had been debating whether it would be the part of a man to pick a quarrel with Pete, or would he be justified in striking him savagely with his beer glass without warning. But he recovered himself when the woman turned to renew her smilings. He beamed upon her with an expression that was somewhat tipsy and inexpressibly tender.

"Say, shake that Bowery jay," requested he, in a loud whisper.

"Freddie, you are so droll," she replied.

Pete reached forward and touched the woman on the arm.

"Come out a minit while I tells yeh why I can't go wid yer. Yer doin' me dirt, Nell! I never taut ye'd do me dirt, Nell. Come on, will yer?" He spoke in tones of injury.

"Why, I don't see why I should be interested in your explanations," said the woman, with a coldness that seemed to reduce Pete to a pulp.

His eyes pleaded with her. "Come out a minit while I tells yeh."

The woman nodded slightly at Maggie and the mere boy, "Scuse me."

The mere boy interrupted his loving smile and turned a shriveling glare upon Pete. His boyish countenance flushed and he spoke, in a whine, to the woman:

"Oh, I say, Nellie, this ain't a square deal, you know. You aren't goin' to leave me and go off with that duffer, are you? I should think—"

"Why, you dear boy, of course I'm not," cried the woman, affectionately. She bended over and whispered in his ear. He smiled again and settled in his chair as if resolved to wait patiently.

As the woman walked down between the rows of tables, Pete was at her shoulder talking earnestly, apparently in explanation. The woman waved her hands with studied airs of indifference. The doors swung behind them, leaving Maggie and the mere boy seated at the table.

Maggie was dazed. She could dimly perceive that something stupendous had happened. She wondered why Pete saw fit to remonstrate with the woman, pleading for forgiveness with his eyes. She thought she noted an air of submission about her leonine Pete. She was astounded.

The mere boy occupied himself with cock-tails and a cigar. He was tranquilly silent for half an hour. Then he bestirred himself and spoke.

"Well," he said, sighing, "I knew this was the way it would be." There was another stillness. The mere boy seemed to be musing.

"She was pulling m'leg. That's the whole amount of it," he said, suddenly. "It's a bloomin' shame the way that girl does. Why, I've spent over two dollars in drinks to-night. And she goes off with that plug-ugly who looks as if he had been hit in the face with a coin-dye. I call it rocky treatment for a fellah like me. Here, waiter, bring me a cock-tail and make it damned strong."

Maggie made no reply. She was watching the doors. "It's a mean piece of business," complained the mere boy. He explained to her how amazing it was that anybody should treat him in such a manner. "But I'll get square with her, you bet. She won't get far ahead of yours truly, you know," he added, winking. "I'll tell her plainly that it was bloomin' mean business. And she won't come it over me with any of her 'now-Freddie-dears.' She thinks my name is Freddie, you know, but of course it ain't. I always tell these people some name like that, because if they got onto your right name they might use it sometime. Understand? Oh, they don't fool me much."

Maggie was paying no attention, being intent upon the doors. The mere boy relapsed into a period of gloom, during which he exterminated a number of cock-tails with a determined air, as if replying defiantly to fate. He occasionally broke forth into sentences composed of invectives joined together in a long string.

The girl was still staring at the doors. After a time the mere boy began to see cobwebs just in front of his nose. He spurred himself into being agreeable and insisted upon her having a charlotte-russe and a glass of beer.

"They's gone," he remarked, "they's gone." He looked at her through the smoke wreaths. "Shay, lil' girl, we mightish well make bes' of it. You ain't such bad lookin' girl, y'know. Not half bad. Can't come up to Nell, though. No, can't do it! Well, I should shay not! Nell fine-lookin' girl! F—i—n—ine. You look damn bad longsider her, but by y'self ain't so bad. Have to do anyhow. Nell gone. O'ny you left. Not half bad, though."

Maggie stood up.

"I'm going home," she said.

The mere boy started.

"Eh? What? Home," he cried, struck with amazement. "I beg pardon, did hear say home?"

"I'm going home," she repeated.

"Great Gawd, what hava struck," demanded the mere boy of himself, stupefied.

In a semi-comatose state he conducted her on board an uptown car, ostentatiously paid her fare, leered kindly at her through the rear window and fell off the steps.

XV

A forlorn woman went along a lighted avenue. The street was filled with people desperately bound on missions. An endless crowd darted at the elevated station stairs and the horse cars were thronged with owners of bundles.

The pace of the forlorn woman was slow. She was apparently searching for some one. She loitered near the doors of saloons and watched men emerge from them. She scanned furtively the faces in the rushing stream of pedestrians. Hurrying men, bent on catching some boat or train, jostled her elbows, failing to notice her, their thoughts fixed on distant dinners.

The forlorn woman had a peculiar face. Her smile was no smile. But when in repose her features had a shadowy look that was like a sardonic grin, as if some one had sketched with cruel forefinger indelible lines about her mouth.

Jimmie came strolling up the avenue. The woman encountered him with an aggrieved air.

"Oh, Jimmie, I've been lookin' all over fer yehs—," she began.

Jimmie made an impatient gesture and quickened his pace.

"Ah, don't bodder me! Good Gawd!" he said, with the savageness of a man whose life is pestered.

The woman followed him along the sidewalk in somewhat the manner of a suppliant.

"But, Jimmie," she said, "yehs told me ye'd—"

Jimmie turned upon her fiercely as if resolved to make a last stand for comfort and peace.

"Say, fer Gawd's sake, Hattie, don' foller me from one end of deh city teh deh odder. Let up, will yehs! Give me a minute's res', can't yehs? Yehs makes me tired, allus taggin' me. See? Ain' yehs got no sense? Do yehs want people teh get onto me? Go chase yerself, fer Gawd's sake."

The woman stepped closer and laid her fingers on his arm. "But, look-a here—"

Jimmie snarled. "Oh, go teh hell."

He darted into the front door of a convenient saloon and a moment later came out into the shadows that surrounded the side door. On the brilliantly lighted avenue he perceived the forlorn woman dodging about like a scout. Jimmie laughed with an air of relief and went away.

When he arrived home he found his mother clamoring. Maggie had returned. She stood shivering beneath the torrent of her mother's wrath.

"Well, I'm damned," said Jimmie in greeting.

His mother, tottering about the room, pointed a quivering forefinger.

"Lookut her, Jimmie, lookut her. Dere's yer sister, boy. Dere's yer sister. Lookut her! Lookut her!"

She screamed in scoffing laughter.

The girl stood in the middle of the room. She edged about as if unable to find a place on the floor to put her feet.

"Ha, ha, ha," bellowed the mother. "Dere she stands! Ain' she purty? Lookut her! Ain' she sweet, deh beast? Lookut her! Ha, ha, lookut her!"

She lurched forward and put her red and seamed hands upon her daughter's face. She bent down and peered keenly up into the eyes of the girl.

"Oh, she's jes' dessame as she ever was, ain' she? She's her mudder's purty darlin' yit, ain' she? Lookut her, Jimmie! Come here, fer Gawd's sake, and lookut her."

The loud, tremendous sneering of the mother brought the denizens of the Rum Alley tenement to their doors. Women came in the hallways. Children scurried to and fro.

"What's up? Dat Johnson party on anudder tear?"

"Naw! Young Mag's come home!"

"Deh hell yeh say?"

Through the open doors curious eyes stared in at Maggie. Children ventured into the room and ogled her, as if they formed the front row at a theatre. Women, without, bended toward each other and whispered, nodding their heads with airs of profound philosophy. A baby, overcome with curiosity concerning this object at which all were looking, sidled forward and touched her dress, cautiously, as if investigating a red-hot stove. Its mother's voice rang out like a warning trumpet. She rushed forward and grabbed her child, casting a terrible look of indignation at the girl.

Maggie's mother paced to and fro, addressing the doorful of eyes, expounding like a glib showman at a museum. Her voice rang through the building.

"Dere she stands," she cried, wheeling suddenly and pointing with dramatic finger. "Dere she stands! Lookut her! Ain' she a dindy? An' she was so good as to come home teh her mudder, she was! Ain' she a beaut'? Ain' she a dindy? Fer Gawd's sake!"

The jeering cries ended in another burst of shrill laughter.

The girl seemed to awaken. "Jimmie—"

He drew hastily back from her.

"Well, now, yer a hell of a t'ing, ain' yeh?" he said, his lips curling in scorn. Radiant virtue sat upon his brow and his repelling hands expressed horror of contamination.

Maggie turned and went.

The crowd at the door fell back precipitately. A baby falling down in front of the door, wrenched a scream like a wounded animal from its mother. Another woman sprang forward and picked it up, with a chivalrous air, as if rescuing a human being from an oncoming express train.

As the girl passed down through the hall, she went before open doors framing more eyes strangely microscopic, and sending broad beams of inquisitive light into the darkness of her path. On the second floor she met the gnarled old woman who possessed the music box.

"So," she cried, " 'ere yehs are back again, are yehs? An' dey've kicked yehs out? Well, come in an' stay wid me teh-night. I ain' got no moral standin'."

From above came an unceasing babble of tongues, over all of which rang the mother's derisive laughter.

XVI

Pete did not consider that he had ruined Maggie. If he had thought that her soul could never smile again, he would have believed the mother and brother, who were pyrotechnic over the affair, to be responsible for it.

Besides, in his world, souls did not insist upon being able to smile. "What deh hell?"

He felt a trifle entangled. It distressed him. Revelations and scenes might bring upon him the wrath of the owner of the saloon, who insisted upon respectability of an advanced type.

"What deh hell do dey wanna' raise such a smoke about it fer?" demanded he of himself, disgusted with the attitude of the family. He saw no necessity for anyone's losing their equilibrium merely because their sister or their daughter had stayed away from home.

Searching about in his mind for possible reasons for their conduct, he came upon the conclusion that Maggie's motives were correct, but that the two others wished to snare him. He felt pursued.

The woman of brilliance and audacity whom he had met in the hilarious hall showed a disposition to ridicule him.

"A little pale thing with no spirit," she said. "Did you note the expression of her eyes? There was something in them about pumpkin pie and virtue. That is a peculiar way the left corner of her mouth has of twitching, isn't it? Dear, dear, my cloud-compelling Pete, what are you coming to?"

Pete asserted at once that he never was very much interested in the girl. The woman interrupted him, laughing.

"Oh, it's not of the slightest consequence to me, my dear young man. You needn't draw maps for my benefit. Why should I be concerned about it?"

But Pete continued with his explanations. If he was laughed at for his tastes in women, he felt obliged to say that they were only temporary or indifferent ones.

The morning after Maggie had departed from home, Pete stood behind the bar. He was immaculate in white jacket and apron and his hair was plastered over his brow with infinite correctness. No customers were in the place. Pete was twisting his napkined fist slowly in a beer glass, softly whistling to himself and occasionally holding the object of his attention between his eyes and a few weak beams of sunlight that had found their way over the thick screens and into the shaded room.

With lingering thoughts of the woman of brilliance and audacity, the bartender raised his head and stared through the varying cracks between the swaying bamboo doors. Suddenly the whistling pucker faded from his lips. He saw Maggie walking slowly past. He gave a great start, fearing for the previously-mentioned eminent respectability of the place.

He threw a swift, nervous glance about him, all at once feeling guilty. No one was in the room.

He went hastily over to the side door. Opening it and looking out, he perceived Maggie standing, as if undecided, on the corner. She was searching the place with her eyes.

As she turned her face toward him Pete beckoned to her hurriedly, intent upon returning with speed to a position behind the bar and to the atmosphere of respectability upon which the proprietor insisted.

Maggie came to him, the anxious look disappearing from her face and a smile wreathing her lips.

"Oh, Pete—," she began brightly.

The bartender made a violent gesture of impatience.

"Oh, my Gawd," cried he, vehemently. "What deh hell do yeh wanna hang aroun' here fer? Do yeh wanna git me inteh trouble?" he demanded with an air of injury.

Astonishment swept over the girl's features. "Why, Pete! yehs tol' me—"

Pete glanced profound irritation. His countenance reddened with the anger of a man whose respectability is being threatened.

"Say, yehs makes me tired. See? What deh hell deh yeh wanna tag aroun' atter me fer? Yeh'll git me inteh trouble wid deh ol' man an' dey'll be hell teh pay! If he sees a woman roun' here he'll go crazy an' I'll lose me job! See? Ain' yehs got no sense? Don' be allus bodderin' me. See? Yer brudder come in here an' raised hell an' deh ol' man hada put up fer it! An' now I'm done! See? I'm done."

The girl's eyes stared into his face. "Pete, don' yeh remem—"

"Oh, hell," interrupted Pete, anticipating.

The girl seemed to have a struggle with herself. She was apparently bewildered and could not find speech. Finally she asked in a low voice: "But where kin I go?"

The question exasperated Pete beyond the powers of endurance. It was a direct attempt to give him some responsibility in a matter that did not concern him. In his indignation he volunteered information.

"Oh, go teh hell," cried he. He slammed the door furiously and returned, with an air of relief, to his respectability.

Maggie went away.

She wandered aimlessly for several blocks. She stopped once and asked aloud a question of herself: "Who?"

A man who was passing near her shoulder, humorously took the questioning word as intended for him.

"Eh? What? Who? Nobody! I didn't say anything," he laughingly said, and continued his way.

Soon the girl discovered that if she walked with such apparent aimlessness, some men looked at her with calculating eyes. She quickened her step, frightened. As a protection, she adopted a demeanor of intentness as if going somewhere.

After a time she left rattling avenues and passed between rows of houses with sternness and stolidity stamped upon their features. She hung her head for she felt their eyes grimly upon her.

Suddenly she came upon a stout gentleman in a silk hat and a chaste black coat, whose decorous row of buttons reached from his chin to his knees. The girl had heard of the Grace of God and she decided to approach this man.

His beaming, chubby face was a picture of benevolence and kind-heartedness. His eyes shone good-will.

But as the girl timidly accosted him, he gave a convulsive movement and saved his respectability by a vigorous sidestep. He did not risk it to save a soul. For how was he to know that there was a soul before him that needed saving?

XVII

Upon a wet evening, several months after the last chapter, two interminable rows of cars, pulled by slipping horses, jangled along a prominent side-street. A dozen cabs, with coat-enshrouded drivers, clattered to and fro. Electric lights, whirring softly, shed a blurred radiance. A flower dealer, his feet tapping impatiently, his nose and his wares glistening with rain-drops, stood behind an array of roses and chrysanthemums. Two or three theatres emptied a crowd upon the storm-swept pavements. Men pulled their hats over their eyebrows and raised their collars to their ears. Women shrugged impatient shoulders in their warm cloaks and stopped to arrange their skirts for a walk through the storm. People having been comparatively silent for two hours burst into a roar of conversation, their hearts still kindling from the glowings of the stage.

The pavements became tossing seas of umbrellas. Men stepped forth to hail cabs or cars, raising their fingers in varied forms of polite request or imperative demand. An endless procession wended toward elevated stations. An atmosphere of pleasure and prosperity seemed to hang over the throng, born, perhaps, of good clothes and of having just emerged from a place of forgetfulness.

In the mingled light and gloom of an adjacent park, a handful of wet wanderers, in attitudes of chronic dejection, was scattered among the benches.

A girl of the painted cohorts of the city went along the street. She threw changing glances at men who passed her, giving smiling invitations to men of rural or untaught pattern and usually seemingly sedately unconscious of the men with a metropolitan seal upon their faces.

Crossing glittering avenues, she went into the throng emerging from the places of forgetfulness. She hurried forward through the crowd as if intent upon reaching a distant home, bending forward in her handsome cloak, daintily lifting her skirts and picking for her well-shod feet the dryer spots upon the pavements.

The restless doors of saloons, clashing to and fro, disclosed animated rows of men before bars and hurrying barkeepers.

A concert hall gave to the street faint sounds of swift, machine-like music, as if a group of phantom musicians were hastening.

A tall young man, smoking a cigarette with a sublime air, strolled near the girl. He had on evening dress, a moustache, a chrysanthemum, and a look of ennui, all of which he kept carefully under his eye. Seeing the girl walk on as if such a young man as he was not in existence, he looked back transfixed with interest. He stared glassily for a moment, but gave a slight convulsive start when he discerned that she was neither new, Parisian, nor theatrical. He wheeled about hastily and turned his stare into the air, like a sailor with a searchlight.

A stout gentleman, with pompous and philanthropic whiskers, went stolidly by, the broad of his back sneering at the girl.

A belated man in business clothes, and in haste to catch a car, bounced against her shoulder. "Hi, there, Mary, I beg your pardon! Brace up, old girl." He grasped her arm to steady her, and then was away running down the middle of the street.

The girl walked on out of the realm of restaurants and saloons. She passed more glittering avenues and went into darker blocks than those where the crowd travelled.

A young man in light overcoat and derby hat received a glance shot keenly from the eyes of the girl. He stopped and looked at her, thrusting his hands in his pockets and making a mocking smile curl his lips. "Come, now, old lady," he said, "you don't mean to tell me that you sized me up for a farmer?"

A laboring man marched along with bundles under his arms. To her remarks, he replied: "It's a fine evenin', ain't it?"

She smiled squarely into the face of a boy who was hurrying by with his hands buried in his overcoat, his blonde locks bobbing on his youthful temples, and a cheery smile of unconcern upon his lips. He turned his head and smiled back at her, waving his hands.

"Not this eve—some other eve!"

A drunken man, reeling in her pathway, began to roar at her. "I ain' ga no money, dammit," he shouted, in a dismal voice. He lurched on up the street, wailing to himself, "Dammit, I ain' ga no money. Damn ba' luck. Ain' ga no more money."

The girl went into gloomy districts near the river, where the tall black factories shut in the street and only occasional broad beams of light fell across the pavements from saloons. In front of one of these places, from whence came the sound of a violin vigorously scraped, the patter of feet on boards and the ring of loud laughter, there stood a man with blotched features.

"Ah, there," said the girl.

"I've got a date," said the man.

Further on in the darkness she met a ragged being with shifting, blood-shot eyes and grimey hands. "Ah, what deh hell? Tink I'm a millionaire?"

She went into the blackness of the final block. The shutters of the tall buildings were closed like grim lips. The structures seemed to have eyes that looked over her, beyond her, at other things. Afar off the lights of the avenues glittered as if from an impossible distance. Street car bells jingled with a sound of merriment.

When almost to the river the girl saw a great figure. On going forward she perceived it to be a huge fat man in torn and greasy garments. His grey hair straggled down over his forehead. His small, bleared eyes, sparkling from amidst great rolls of red fat, swept eagerly over the girl's upturned face. He laughed, his brown, disordered teeth gleaming under a grey, grizzled moustache from which beer-drops dripped. His whole body gently quivered and shook like that of a dead jelly fish. Chuckling and leering, he followed the girl of the crimson legions.

At their feet the river appeared a deathly black hue. Some hidden factory sent up a yellow glare, that lit for a moment the waters lapping oilily against timbers. The varied sounds of life, made joyous by distance and seeming unapproachableness, came faintly and died away to a silence.

XVIII

In a partitioned-off section of a saloon sat a man with a half dozen women, gleefully laughing, hovering about him. The man had arrived at that stage of drunkenness where affection is felt for the universe.

"I'm good f'ler, girls," he said, convincingly. "I'm damn good f'ler. An'body treats me right, I allus trea's zem right! See?"

The women nodded their heads approvingly. "To be sure," they cried in hearty chorus. "You're the kind of a man we like, Pete. You're outa sight! What yeh goin' to buy this time, dear?"

"An'thin' yehs wants, damn it," said the man in an abandonment of good will. His countenance shone with the true spirit of benevolence. He was in the proper mode of missionaries. He would have fraternized with obscure Hottentots. And above all, he was overwhelmed in tenderness for his friends, who were all illustrious.

"An'thing yehs wants, damn it," repeated he, waving his hands with beneficent recklessness. "I'm good f'ler, girls, an' if an'body treats me right I—here," called he through an open door to a waiter, "bring girls drinks, damn it. What 'ill yehs have, girls? An'thing yehs want, damn it!"

The waiter glanced in with the disgusted look of the man who serves intoxicants for the man who takes too much of them. He nodded his head shortly at the order from each individual, and went.

"Damn it," said the man, "we're havin' heluva time. I like you girls! Damn'd if I don't! Yer right sort! See?"

He spoke at length and with feeling, concerning the excellencies of his assembled friends.

"Don' try pull man's leg, but have a heluva time! Das right! Das way teh do! Now, if I sawght yehs tryin' work me fer drinks, wouldn' buy damn t'ing! But yer right sort, damn it! Yehs know how ter treat a f'ler, an' I stays by yehs 'til spen' las' cent! Das right! I'm good f'ler an' I knows when an'body treats me right!"

Between the times of the arrival and departure of the waiter, the man discoursed to the women on the tender regard he felt for all living things. He laid stress upon the purity of his motives in all dealings with men in the world and spoke of the fervor of his friendship for those who were amiable. Tears welled slowly from his eyes. His voice quavered when he spoke to them.

Once when the waiter was about to depart with an empty tray, the man drew a coin from his pocket and held it forth.

"Here," said he, quite magnificently, "here's quar'."

The waiter kept his hands on his tray.

"I don' want yer money," he said.

The other put forth the coin with tearful insistence.

"Here, damn it," cried he, "tak't! Yer damn goo' f'ler an' I wan' yehs tak't!"

"Come, come, now," said the waiter, with the sullen air of a man who is forced into giving advice. "Put yer mon in yer pocket! Yer loaded an' yehs on'y makes a damn fool of yerself."

As the latter passed out of the door the man turned pathetically to the women.

"He don' know I'm damn goo' f'ler," cried he, dismally.

"Never you mind, Pete, dear," said a woman of brilliance and audacity, laying her hand with great affection upon his arm. "Never you mind, old boy! We'll stay by you, dear!"

"Das ri'," cried the man, his face lighting up at the soothing tones of the woman's voice. "Das ri', I'm damn goo' f'ler an' w'en anyone trea's me ri', I treats zem ri'! Shee!"

"Sure!" cried the women. "And we're not goin' back on you, old man."

The man turned appealing eyes to the woman of brilliance and audacity. He felt that if he could be convicted of a contemptible action he would die.

"Shay, Nell, damn it, I allus trea's yehs shquare, didn' I? I allus been goo' f'ler wi' yehs, ain't I, Nell?"

"Sure you have, Pete," assented the woman. She delivered an oration to her companions. "Yessir, that's a fact. Pete's a square fellah, he is. He never goes back on a friend. He's the right kind an' we stay by him, don't we, girls?"

"Sure," they exclaimed. Looking lovingly at him they raised their glasses and drank his health.

"Girlsh," said the man, beseechingly, "I allus trea's yehs ri', didn' I? I'm goo' f'ler, ain' I, girlsh?"

"Sure," again they chorused.

"Well," said he finally, "le's have nozzer drink, zen."

"That's right," hailed a woman, "that's right. Yer no bloomin' jay! Yer spends yer money like a man. Dat's right."

The man pounded the table with his quivering fists.

"Yessir," he cried, with deep earnestness, as if someone disputed him. "I'm damn goo' f'ler, an' w'en anyone trea's me ri', I allus trea's—le's have nozzer drink."

He began to beat the wood with his glass.

"Shay," howled he, growing suddenly impatient. As the waiter did not then come, the man swelled with wrath.

"Shay," howled he again.

The waiter appeared at the door.

"Bringsh drinksh," said the man.

The waiter disappeared with the orders.

"Zat f'ler dam fool," cried the man. "He insul' me! I'm ge'man! Can' stan' be insul'! I'm goin' lickim when comes!"

"No, no," cried the women, crowding about and trying to subdue him. "He's all right! He didn't mean anything! Let it go! He's a good fellah!"

"Din' he insul' me?" asked the man earnestly.

"No," said they. "Of course he didn't! He's all right!"

"Sure he didn' insul' me?" demanded the man, with deep anxiety in his voice.

"No, no! We know him! He's a good fellah. He didn't mean anything."

"Well, zen," said the man, resolutely, "I'm go' 'pol'gize!"

When the waiter came, the man struggled to the middle of the floor.

"Girlsh shed you insul' me! I shay damn lie! I 'pol'gize!"

"All right," said the waiter.

The man sat down. He felt a sleepy but strong desire to straighten things out and have a perfect understanding with everybody.

"Nell, I allus trea's yeh shquare, din I? Yeh likes me, don' yehs, Nell? I'm goo' f'ler?"

"Sure," said the woman of brilliance and audacity.

"Yeh knows I'm stuck on yehs, don' yehs, Nell?"

"Sure," she repeated, carelessly.

Overwhelmed by a spasm of drunken adoration, he drew two or three bills from his pocket, and, with the trembling fingers of an offering priest, laid them on the table before the woman.

"Yehs knows, damn it, yehs kin have all got, 'cause I'm stuck on yehs, Nell, damn't, I—I'm stuck on yehs, Nell—buy drinksh—damn't—we're havin' heleva time—w'en anyone trea's me ri'—I—damn't, Nell—we're havin' heluva—time."

Shortly he went to sleep with his swollen face fallen forward on his chest.

The women drank and laughed, not heeding the slumbering man in the corner. Finally he lurched forward and fell groaning to the floor.

The women screamed in disgust and drew back their skirts.

"Come ahn," cried one, starting up angrily, "let's get out of here."

The woman of brilliance and audacity stayed behind, taking up the bills and stuffing them into a deep, irregularly-shaped pocket. A guttural snore from the recumbent man caused her to turn and look down at him.

She laughed. "What a damn fool," she said, and went.

The smoke from the lamps settled heavily down in the little compartment, obscuring the way out. The smell of oil, stifling in its intensity, pervaded the air. The wine from an overturned glass dripped softly down upon the blotches on the man's neck.

XIX

In a room a woman sat at a table eating like a fat monk in a picture.

A soiled, unshaven man pushed open the door and entered.

"Well," said he, "Mag's dead."

"What?" said the woman, her mouth filled with bread.

"Mag's dead," repeated the man.

"Deh hell she is," said the woman. She continued her meal. When she finished her coffee she began to weep.

"I kin remember when her two feet was no bigger dan yer tumb, and she weared worsted boots," moaned she.

"Well, whata dat?" said the man.

"I kin remember when she weared worsted boots," she cried.

The neighbors began to gather in the hall, staring in at the weeping woman as if watching the contortions of a dying dog. A dozen women entered and lamented with her. Under their busy hands the rooms took on that appalling appearance of neatness and order with which death is greeted.

Suddenly the door opened and a woman in a black gown rushed in with outstretched arms. "Ah, poor Mary," she cried, and tenderly embraced the moaning one.

"Ah, what ter'ble affliction is dis," continued she. Her vocabulary was derived from mission churches. "Me poor Mary, how I feel fer yehs! Ah, what a ter'ble affliction is a disobed'ent chile."

Her good, motherly face was wet with tears. She trembled in eagerness to express her sympathy. The mourner sat with bowed head, rocking her body heavily to and fro, and crying out in a high, strained voice that sounded like a dirge on some forlorn pipe.

"I kin remember when she weared worsted boots an' her two feets was no bigger dan yer tumb an' she weared worsted boots, Miss Smith," she cried, raising her streaming eyes.

"Ah, me poor Mary," sobbed the woman in black. With low, coddling cries, she sank on her knees by the mourner's chair, and put her arms about her. The other women began to groan in different keys.

"Yer poor misguided chil' is gone now, Mary, an' let us hope its fer deh bes'. Yeh'll fergive her now, Mary, won't yehs, dear, all her disobed'ence? All her tankless behavior to her mudder an' all her badness? She's gone where her ter'ble sins will be judged."

The woman in black raised her face and paused. The inevitable sunlight came streaming in at the windows and shed a ghastly cheerfulness upon the faded hues of the room. Two or three of the spectators were sniffling, and one was loudly weeping. The mourner arose and staggered into the other room. In a moment she emerged with a pair of faded baby shoes held in the hollow of her hand.

"I kin remember when she used to wear dem," cried she. The women burst anew into cries as if they had all been stabbed. The mourner turned to the soiled and unshaven man.

"Jimmie, boy, go git yer sister! Go git yer sister an' we'll put deh boots on her feets!"

"Dey won't fit her now, yeh damn fool," said the man.

"Go git yer sister, Jimmie," shrieked the woman, confronting him fiercely.

The man swore sullenly. He went over to a corner and slowly began to put on his coat. He took his hat and went out, with a dragging, reluctant step.

The woman in black came forward and again besought the mourner.

"Yeh'll fergive her, Mary! Yeh'll fergive yer bad, bad chil'! Her life was a curse an' her days were black an' yeh'll fergive yer bad girl? She's gone where her sins will be judged."

"She's gone where her sins will be judged," cried the other women, like a choir at a funeral.

"Deh Lord gives and deh Lord takes away," said the woman in black, raising her eyes to the sunbeams.

"Deh Lord gives and deh Lord takes away," responded the others.

"Yeh'll fergive her, Mary!" pleaded the woman in black. The mourner essayed to speak but her voice gave way. She shook her great shoulders frantically, in an agony of grief. Hot tears seemed to scald her quivering face. Finally her voice came and arose like a scream of pain.

"Oh, yes, I'll fergive her! I'll fergive her!"

George's Mother

I

In the swirling rain that came at dusk the broad avenue glistened with that deep bluish tint which is so widely condemned when it is put into pictures. There were long rows of shops, whose fronts shone with full, golden light. Here and there, from druggists' windows, or from the red street-lamps that indicated the positions of fire-alarm boxes, a flare of uncertain, wavering crimson was thrown upon the wet pavements.

The lights made shadows, in which the buildings loomed with a new and tremendous massiveness, like castles and fortresses. There were endless processions of people, mighty hosts, with umbrellas waving, banner-like, over them. Horse-cars, aglitter with new paint, rumbled in steady array between the pillars that supported the elevated railroad. The whole street resounded with the tinkle of bells, the roar of iron-shod wheels on the cobbles, the ceaseless trample of the hundreds of feet. Above all, too, could be heard the loud screams of the tiny newsboys, who scurried in all directions. Upon the corners, standing in from the dripping eaves, were many loungers, descended from the world that used to prostrate itself before pageantry.

A brown young man went along the avenue. He held a tin lunch-pail under his arm in a manner that was evidently uncomfortable. He was puffing at a corn-cob pipe. His shoulders had a self-reliant poise, and the hang of his arms and the raised veins of his hands showed him to be a man who worked with his muscles.

As he passed a street-corner a man in old clothes gave a shout of surprise, and rushing impetuously forward, grasped his hand.

"Hello, Kelcey, ol' boy," cried the man in old clothes. "How's th' boy, anyhow? Where in thunder yeh been fer th' last seventeen years? I'll be hanged if you ain't th' last man I ever expected t' see."

The brown youth put his pail to the ground and grinned. "Well, if it ain't ol' Charley Jones," he said, ecstatically shaking hands.

"How are yeh, anyhow? Where yeh been keepin' yerself? I ain't seen yeh fer a year!"

"Well, I should say so! Why, th' last time I saw you was up in Handyville!"

"Sure! On Sunday, we——"

"Sure! Out at Bill Sickles's place. Let's go get a drink!"

They made toward a little glass-fronted saloon that sat blinking jovially at the crowds. It engulfed them with a gleeful motion of its two widely smiling lips.

"What'll yeh take, Kelcey?"

"Oh, I guess I'll take a beer."

"Gimme little whiskey, John."

The two friends leaned against the bar and looked with enthusiasm upon each other.

"Well, well, I'm thunderin' glad t' see yeh," said Jones.

"Well, I guess," replied Kelcey. "Here's to yeh, ol' man."

"Let 'er go."

They lifted their glasses, glanced fervidly at each other, and drank.

"Yeh ain't changed much, on'y yeh've growed like th' devil," said Jones, reflectively, as he put down his glass. "I'd know yeh anywheres!"

"Certainly yeh would," said Kelcey. "An' I knew you, too, th' minute I saw yeh. Yer changed, though!"

"Yes," admitted Jones, with some complacency, "I s'pose I am." He regarded himself in the mirror that multiplied the bottles on the shelf back of the bar. He should have seen a grinning face with a rather pink nose. His derby was perched carelessly on the back part of his head. Two wisps of hair straggled down over his hollow temples. There was something very worldly and wise about him. Life did not seem to confuse him. Evidently he understood its complications. His hand thrust into his trousers' pocket, where he jingled keys, and his hat perched back on his head expressed a young man of vast knowledge. His extensive acquaintance with bartenders aided him materially in this habitual expression of wisdom.

Having finished he turned to the barkeeper. "John, has any of th' gang been in t'-night yet?"

"No—not yet," said the barkeeper. "Ol' Bleecker was aroun' this afternoon about four. He said if I seen any of th' boys t' tell 'em he'd be up t'-night if he could get away. I saw Connor an' that other fellah goin' down th' avenyeh about an hour ago. I guess they'll be back after awhile."

"This is th' hang-out fer a great gang," said Jones, turning to Kelcey. "They're a great crowd, I tell yeh. We own th' place when we get started. Come aroun' some night. Any night, almost. T'-night, b' jiminy. They'll almost all be here, an' I'd like t' interduce yeh. They're a great gang! Gre-e-at!"

"I'd like teh," said Kelcey.

"Well, come ahead, then," cried the other, cordially. "Yeh'd like t' know 'em. It's an outa sight crowd. Come aroun' t'-night!"

"I will if I can."

"Well, yeh ain't got anything t' do, have yeh?" demanded Jones. "Well, come along, then. Yeh might just as well spend yer time with a good crowd 'a fellahs. An' it's a great gang. Great! Gre-e-at!"

"Well, I must make fer home now, anyhow," said Kelcey. "It's late as blazes. What'll yeh take this time, ol' man?"

"Gimme little more whiskey, John!"

"Guess I'll take another beer!"

Jones emptied the whiskey into his large mouth and then put the glass upon the bar. "Been in th' city long?" he asked. "Um—well, three years is a good deal fer a slick man. Doin' well? Oh, well, nobody's doin' well these days." He looked down mournfully at his shabby clothes. "Father's dead, ain't 'ee? Yeh don't say so? Fell off a scaffoldin', didn't 'ee? I heard it somewheres. Mother's livin', of course? I thought she was. Fine ol' lady—fi-i-ne. Well, you're th' last of her boys. Was five of yeh onct, wasn't there? I knew four m'self. Yes, five! I thought so. An' all gone but you, hey? Well, you'll have t' brace up an' be a comfort t' th' ol' mother. Well, well, well, who would 'a thought that on'y you'd be left out 'a all that mob 'a tow-headed kids. Well, well, well, it's a queer world, ain't it?"

A contemplation of this thought made him sad. He sighed and moodily watched the other sip beer.

"Well, well, it's a queer world—a damn queer world."

"Yes," said Kelcey, "I'm th' on'y one left!" There was an accent of discomfort in his voice. He did not like this dwelling upon a sentiment that was connected with himself.

"How is th' ol' lady, anyhow?" continued Jones. "Th' last time I remember she was as spry as a little ol' cricket, an' was helpeltin' aroun' th' country lecturin' before W.C.T.U.'s an' one thing an' another."

"Oh, she's pretty well," said Kelcey.

"An' outa five boys you're th' on'y one she's got left? Well, well—have another drink before yeh go."

"Oh, I guess I've had enough."

A wounded expression came into Jones's eyes. "Oh, come on," he said.

"Well, I'll take another beer!"

"Gimme little more whiskey, John!"

When they had concluded this ceremony, Jones went with his friend to the door of the saloon. "Good-by, ol' man," he said, genially. His homely features shone with friendliness. "Come aroun', now, sure. T'-night! See? They're a great crowd. Gre-e-at!"

II

A man with a red, mottled face put forth his head from a window and cursed violently. He flung a bottle high across two backyards at a window of the opposite tenement. It broke against the bricks of the house and the fragments fell crackling upon the stones below. The man shook his fist.

A bare-armed woman, making an array of clothes on a line in one of the yards, glanced casually up at the man and listened to his words. Her eyes followed his to the other tenement. From a distant window, a youth with a pipe, yelled some comments upon the poor aim. Two children, being in the proper yard, picked up the bits of broken glass and began to fondle them as new toys.

From the window at which the man raged came the sound of an old voice, singing. It quavered and trembled out into the air as if a sound-spirit had a broken wing.

"Should I be car-reed tew th' skies
O-on flow'ry be-eds of ee-ease,
While others fought tew win th' prize
An' sailed through blood-ee seas."

The man in the opposite window was greatly enraged. He continued to swear.

A little old woman was the owner of the voice. In a fourth-story room of the red and black tenement she was trudging on a journey. In her arms she bore pots and pans, and sometimes a broom and dust-pan. She wielded them like weapons. Their weight seemed to have bended her back and crooked her arms until she walked with difficulty. Often she plunged her hands into water at a sink. She splashed about, the dwindled muscles working to and fro under the loose skin of her arms. She came from the sink, steaming and bedraggled as if she had crossed a flooded river.

There was the flurry of a battle in this room. Through the clouded dust or steam one could see the thin figure dealing mighty blows. Always her way seemed beset. Her broom was continually poised, lance-wise, at dust demons. There came clashings and clangings as she strove with her tireless foes.

It was a picture of indomitable courage. And as she went on her way her voice was often raised in a long cry, a strange war-chant, a shout of battle and defiance, that rose and fell in harsh screams, and exasperated the ears of the man with the red, mottled face.

"Should I be car-reed tew th' skies
O-on flow'ry be-eds of ee-ease——"

Finally she halted for a moment. Going to the window she sat down and mopped her face with her apron. It was a lull, a moment of respite. Still it could be seen that she even then was planning skirmishes, charges, campaigns. She gazed thoughtfully about the room and noted the strength and position of her enemies. She was very alert.

At last, she turned to the mantel. "Five o'clock," she murmured, scrutinizing a little, swaggering, nickel-plated clock.

She looked out at chimneys growing thickly on the roofs. A man at work on one seemed like a bee. In the intricate yards below, vine-like lines had strange leaves of cloth. To her ears there came the howl of the man with the red, mottled face. He was engaged in a furious altercation with the youth who had called attention to his poor aim. They were like animals in a jungle.

In the distance an enormous brewery towered over the other buildings. Great gilt letters advertised a brand of beer. Thick smoke came from funnels and spread near it like vast and powerful wings. The structure seemed a great bird, flying. The letters of the sign made a chain of gold hanging from its neck. The little old woman looked at the brewery. It vaguely interested her, for a moment, as a stupendous affair, a machine of mighty strength.

Presently she sprang from her rest and began to buffet with her shrivelled arms. In a moment the battle was again in full swing. Terrific blows were given and received. There arose the clattering uproar of a new fight. The little intent warrior never hesitated nor faltered. She fought with a strong and relentless will. Beads and lines of perspiration stood upon her forehead.

Three blue plates were leaning in a row on the shelf back of the stove. The little old woman had seen it done somewhere. In front of them swaggered the round nickel-plated clock. Her son had stuck many cigarette pictures in the rim of a looking-glass that hung near. Occasional chromos were tacked upon the yellowed walls of the room. There was one in a gilt frame. It was quite an affair, in reds and greens. They all seemed like trophies.

It began to grow dark. A mist came winding. Rain plashed softly upon the window-sill. A lamp had been lighted in the opposite tenement; the strong orange glare revealed the man with a red, mottled face. He was seated by a table, smoking and reflecting.

The little old woman looked at the clock again. "Quarter 'a six."

She had paused for a moment, but she now hurled herself fiercely at the stove that lurked in the gloom, red-eyed, like a dragon. It hissed, and there was renewed clangor of blows. The little old woman dashed to and fro.

III

As it grew toward seven o'clock the little old woman became nervous. She often would drop into a chair and sit staring at the little clock.

"I wonder why he don't come," she continually repeated. There was a small, curious note of despair in her voice. As she sat thinking and staring at the clock the expressions of her face changed swiftly. All manner of emotions flickered in her eyes and about her lips. She was evidently perceiving in her imagination the journey of a loved person. She dreamed for him mishaps and obstacles. Something tremendous and irritating was hindering him from coming to her.

She had lighted an oil-lamp. It flooded the room with vivid yellow glare. The table, in its oil-cloth covering, had previously appeared like a bit of bare, brown desert. It now was a white garden, growing the fruits of her labor.

"Seven o'clock," she murmured, finally. She was aghast.

Then suddenly she heard a step upon the stair. She sprang up and began to bustle about the room. The little fearful emotions passed at once from her face. She seemed now to be ready to scold.

Young Kelcey entered the room. He gave a sigh of relief, and dropped his pail in a corner. He was evidently greatly wearied by a hard day of toil.

The little old woman hobbled over to him and raised her wrinkled lips. She seemed on the verge of tears and an outburst of reproaches.

"Hello!" he cried, in a voice of cheer. "Been gettin' anxious?"

"Yes," she said, hovering about him. "Where yeh been, George?

What made yeh so late? I've been waitin' th' longest while. Don't throw your coat down there. Hang it up behind th' door."

The son put his coat on the proper hook, and then went to splatter water in a tin wash-basin at the sink.

"Well, yeh see, I met Jones—you remember Jones? Ol' Handyville fellah. An' we had t' stop an' talk over ol' times. Jones is quite a boy."

The little old woman's mouth set in a sudden straight line. "Oh, that Jones," she said. "I don't like him."

The youth interrupted a flurry of white towel to give a glance of irritation. "Well, now, what's th' use of talkin' that way?" he said to her. "What do yeh know 'bout 'im? Ever spoke to 'im in yer life?"

"Well, I don't know as I ever did since he grew up," replied the little old woman. "But I know he ain't th' kind 'a man I'd like t' have you go around with. He ain't a good man. I'm sure he ain't. He drinks."

Her son began to laugh. "Th' dickens he does?" He seemed amazed, but not shocked at this information.

She nodded her head with the air of one who discloses a dreadful thing. "I'm sure of it! Once I saw 'im comin' outa Simpson's Hotel, up in Handyville, an' he could hardly walk. He drinks! I'm sure he drinks!"

"Holy smoke!" said Kelcey.

They sat down at the table and began to wreck the little white garden. The youth leaned back in his chair, in the manner of a man who is paying for things. His mother bended alertly forward, apparently watching each mouthful. She perched on the edge of her chair, ready to spring to her feet and run to the closet or the stove for anything that he might need. She was as anxious as a young mother with a babe. In the careless and comfortable attitude of the son there was denoted a great deal of dignity.

"Yeh ain't eatin' much t'-night, George?"

"Well, I ain't very hungry, t' tell th' truth."

"Don't yeh like yer supper, dear? Yeh must eat somethin', chile. Yeh mustn't go without."

"Well, I'm eatin' somethin', ain't I?"

He wandered aimlessly through the meal. She sat over behind the little blackened coffee-pot and gazed affectionately upon him.

After a time she began to grow agitated. Her worn fingers were gripped. It could be seen that a great thought was within her. She was about to venture something. She had arrived at a supreme moment. "George," she said, suddenly, "come t' prayer-meetin' with me t'-night."

The young man dropped his fork. "Say, you must be crazy," he said, in amazement.

"Yes, dear," she continued, rapidly, in a small pleading voice, "I'd like t' have yeh go with me onct in a while. Yeh never go with me any more, dear, an' I'd like t' have yeh go. Yeh ain't been anywheres at all with me in th' longest while."

"Well," he said, "well, but what th' blazes——"

"Ah, come on," said the little old woman. She went to him and put her arms about his neck. She began to coax him with caresses.

The young man grinned. "Thunderation!" he said, "what would I do at a prayer-meetin'?"

The mother considered him to be consenting. She did a little antique caper.

"Well, yeh can come an' take care 'a yer mother," she cried, gleefully. "It's such a long walk every Thursday night alone, an' don't yeh s'pose that when I have such a big, fine, strappin' boy, I want 'im t' beau me aroun' some? Ah, I knew ye'd come."

He smiled for a moment, indulgent of her humor. But presently his face turned a shade of discomfort. "But—" he began, protesting.

"Ah, come on," she continually repeated.

He began to be vexed. He frowned into the air. A vision came to him of dreary blackness arranged in solemn rows. A mere dream of it was depressing.

"But—" he said again. He was obliged to make great search for an argument. Finally he concluded, "But what th' blazes would I do at prayer-meetin'?"

In his ears was the sound of a hymn, made by people who tilted their heads at a prescribed angle of devotion. It would be too apparent that they were all better than he. When he entered they would turn their heads and regard him with suspicion. This would be an enormous aggravation, since he was certain that he was as good as they.

"Well, now, y' see," he said, quite gently, "I don't wanta go, an' it wouldn't do me no good t' go if I didn't wanta go."

His mother's face swiftly changed. She breathed a huge sigh, the counterpart of ones he had heard upon like occasions. She put a tiny black bonnet on her head, and wrapped her figure in an old shawl. She cast a martyr-like glance upon her son and went mournfully away. She resembled a limited funeral procession.

The young man writhed under it to an extent. He kicked moodily at a table-leg. When the sound of her footfalls died away he felt distinctly relieved.

IV

That night, when Kelcey arrived at the little smiling saloon, he found his friend Jones standing before the bar engaged in a violent argument with a stout man.

"Oh, well," this latter person was saying, "you can make a lot of noise, Charlie, for a man that never says anything—let's have a drink!"

Jones was waving his arms and delivering splintering blows upon some distant theories. The stout man chuckled fatly and winked at the bartender.

The orator ceased for a moment to say, "Gimme little whiskey, John." At the same time he perceived young Kelcey. He sprang forward with a welcoming cry. "Hello, ol' man, didn't much think ye'd come." He led him to the stout man.

"Mr. Bleecker—my friend Mr. Kelcey!"

"How d'yeh do!"

"Mr. Kelcey, I'm happy to meet you, sir; have a drink."

They drew up in line and waited. The busy hands of the bartender made glasses clink. Mr. Bleecker, in a very polite way, broke the waiting silence.

"Never been here before, I believe, have you, Mr. Kelcey?"

The young man felt around for a high-bred reply. "Er—no—I've never had that—er—pleasure," he said.

After a time the strained and wary courtesy of their manners wore away. It became evident to Bleecker that his importance slightly dazzled the young man. He grew warmer. Obviously, the youth was one whose powers of perception were developed. Directly, then, he launched forth into a tale of by-gone days, when the world was better. He had known all the great men of that age. He reproduced his conversations with them. There were traces of pride and of mournfulness in his voice. He rejoiced at the glory of the world of dead spirits. He grieved at the youth and flippancy of the present one. He lived with his head in the clouds of the past, and he seemed obliged to talk of what he saw there.

Jones nudged Kelcey ecstatically in the ribs. "You've got th' ol' man started in great shape," he whispered.

Kelcey was proud that the prominent character of the place talked at him, glancing into his eyes for appreciation of fine points.

Presently they left the bar, and going into a little rear room, took seats about a table. A gas-jet with a colored globe shed a crimson radiance. The polished wood of walls and furniture gleamed with faint rose-colored reflections. Upon the floor sawdust was thickly sprinkled.

Two other men presently came. By the time Bleecker had told three tales of the grand past, Kelcey was slightly acquainted with everybody.

He admired Bleecker immensely. He developed a brotherly feeling for the others, who were all gentle-spoken. He began to feel that he was passing the happiest evening of his life. His companions were so jovial and good-natured; and everything they did was marked by such courtesy.

For a time the two men who had come in late did not presume to address him directly. They would say: "Jones, won't your friend have so and so, or so and so?" And Bleecker would begin his orations: "Now, Mr. Kelcey, don't you think——"

Presently he began to believe that he was a most remarkably fine fellow, who had at last found his place in a crowd of most remarkably fine fellows.

Jones occasionally breathed comments into his ear.

"I tell yeh, Bleecker's an ol'-timer. He was a husky guy in his day, yeh can bet. He was one 'a th' best known men in N' York onct. Yeh ought to hear him tell about——"

Kelcey listened intently. He was profoundly interested in these intimate tales of men who had gleamed in the rays of old suns.

"That O'Connor's a damn fine fellah," interjected Jones once, referring to one of the others. "He's one 'a th' best fellahs I ever knowed. He's always on th' dead level. An' he's always jest th' same as yeh see 'im now—good-natured an' grinnin'."

Kelcey nodded. He could well believe it.

When he offered to buy drinks there came a loud volley of protests. "No, no, Mr. Kelcey," cried Bleecker, "no, no. Tonight you are our guest. Some other time——"

"Here," said O'Connor, "it's my turn now."

He called and pounded for the bartender. He then sat with a coin in his hand warily eying the others. He was ready to frustrate them if they offered to pay.

After a time Jones began to develop qualities of great eloquence and wit. His companions laughed. "It's the whiskey talking now," said Bleecker.

He grew earnest and impassioned. He delivered speeches on various subjects. His lectures were to him very imposing. The force of his words thrilled him. Sometimes he was overcome.

The others agreed with him in all things. Bleecker grew almost tender, and considerately placed words here and there for his use. As Jones became fiercely energetic the others became more docile in agreeing. They soothed him with friendly interjections.

His mood changed directly. He began to sing popular airs with enthusiasm. He congratulated his companions upon being in his society. They were excited by his frenzy. They began to fraternize in jovial fashion. It was understood that they were true and tender spirits. They had come away from a grinding world filled with men who were harsh.

When one of them chose to divulge some place where the world had pierced him, there was a chorus of violent sympathy. They rejoiced at their temporary isolation and safety.

Once a man, completely drunk, stumbled along the floor of the saloon. He opened the door of the little room and made a show of entering. The men sprang instantly to their feet. They were ready to throttle any invader of their island. They elbowed each other in rivalry as to who should take upon himself the brunt of an encounter.

"Oh!" said the drunken individual, swaying on his legs and blinking at the party, "oh! thish private room?"

"That's what it is, Willie," said Jones. "An' you git outa here er we'll throw yeh out."

"That's what we will," said the others.

"Oh," said the drunken man. He blinked at them aggrievedly for an instant and then went away.

They sat down again. Kelcey felt, in a way, that he would have liked to display his fidelity to the others by whipping the intruder.

The bartender came often. "Gee, you fellahs er tanks," he said, in a jocular manner, as he gathered empty glasses and polished the table with his little towel.

Through the exertions of Jones the little room began to grow clamorous. The tobacco-smoke eddied about the forms of the men in ropes and wreaths. Near the ceiling there was a thick gray cloud.

Each man explained, in his way, that he was totally out of place in the before-mentioned world. They were possessed of various virtues which were unappreciated by those with whom they were commonly obliged to mingle; they were fitted for a tree-shaded land, where everything was peace. Now that five of them had congregated it gave them happiness to speak their inmost thoughts without fear of being misunderstood.

As he drank more beer Kelcey felt his breast expand with manly feeling. He knew that he was capable of sublime things. He wished that some day one of his present companions would come to him for relief. His mind pictured a little scene. In it he was magnificent in his friendship.

He looked upon the beaming faces and knew that if at that instant there should come a time for a great sacrifice he would blissfully make it. He would pass tranquilly into the unknown, or into bankruptcy, amid the ejaculations of his companions upon his many virtues.

They had no bickerings during the evening. If one chose to momentarily assert himself, the others instantly submitted.

They exchanged compliments. Once old Bleecker stared at Jones for a few moments. Suddenly he broke out: "Jones, you're one of the finest fellows I ever knew!" A flush of pleasure went over the other's face, and then he made a modest gesture, the protest of an humble man. "Don't flim-flam me, ol' boy," he said, with earnestness. But Bleecker roared that he was serious about it. The two men arose and shook hands emotionally. Jones bunted against the table and knocked off a glass.

Afterward a general hand-shaking was inaugurated. Brotherly sentiments flew about the room. There was an uproar of fraternal feeling.

Jones began to sing. He beat time with precision and dignity. He gazed into the eyes of his companions, trying to call music from their souls. O'Connor joined in heartily, but with another tune. Off in a corner old Bleecker was making a speech.

The bartender came to the door. "Gee, you fellahs er making a row. It's time fer me t' shut up th' front th' place, an' you mugs better sit on yerselves. It's one o'clock."

They began to argue with him. Kelcey, however, sprang to his feet. "One o'clock," he said. "Holy smoke, I mus' be flyin'!"

There came protesting howls from Jones. Bleecker ceased his oration. "My dear boy—" he began. Kelcey searched for his hat. "I've gota go t' work at seven," he said.

The others watched him with discomfort in their eyes. "Well," said O'Connor, "if one goes we might as well all go." They sadly took their hats and filed out.

The cold air of the street filled Kelcey with vague surprise. It made his head feel hot. As for his legs, they were like willow-twigs.

A few yellow lights blinked. In front of an all-night restaurant a huge red electric lamp hung and sputtered. Horse-car bells jingled far down the street. Overhead a train thundered on the elevated road.

On the sidewalk the men took fervid leave. They clutched hands with extraordinary force and proclaimed, for the last time, ardent and admiring friendships.

When he arrived at his home Kelcey proceeded with caution. His mother had left a light burning low. He stumbled once in his voyage across the floor. As he paused to listen he heard the sound of little snores coming from her room.

He lay awake for a few moments and thought of the evening. He had a pleasurable consciousness that he had made a good impression upon those fine fellows. He felt that he had spent the most delightful evening of his life.

V

Kelcey was cross in the morning. His mother had been obliged to shake him a great deal, and it had seemed to him a most unjust thing. Also, when he, blinking his eyes, had entered the kitchen, she had said: "Yeh left th' lamp burnin' all night last night, George. How many times must I tell yeh never t' leave th' lamp burnin'?"

He ate the greater part of his breakfast in silence, moodily stirring his coffee and glaring at a remote corner of the room with eyes that felt as if they had been baked. When he moved his eyelids there was a sensation that they were cracking. In his mouth there was a singular taste. It seemed to him that he had been sucking the end of a wooden spoon. Moreover, his temper was rampant within him. It sought something to devour.

Finally he said, savagely: "Damn these early hours!"

His mother jumped as if he had flung a missile at her. "Why, George—" she began.

Kelcey broke in again. "Oh, I know all that—but this gettin' up in th' mornin' so early makes me sick. Jest when a man is gettin' his mornin' nap he's gota get up. I——"

"George, dear," said his mother, "yeh know how I hate yeh t' swear, dear. Now please don't." She looked beseechingly at him.

He made a swift gesture. "Well, I ain't swearin', am I?" he demanded. "I was on'y sayin' that this gettin'-up business gives me a pain, wasn't I?"

"Well, yeh know how swearin' hurts me," protested the little old woman. She seemed about to sob. She gazed off retrospectively. She apparently was recalling persons who had never been profane.

"I don't see where yeh ever caught this way a' swearin' out at everything," she continued, presently. "Fred, ner John, ner Willie never swore a bit. Ner Tom neither, except when he was real mad."

The son made another gesture. It was directed into the air, as if he saw there a phantom injustice. "Oh, good thunder," he said, with an accent of despair. Thereupon, he relapsed into a mood of silence. He sombrely regarded his plate.

This demeanor speedily reduced his mother to meekness. When she spoke again it was in a conciliatory voice. "George, dear, won't yeh bring some sugar home t'-night?" It could be seen that she was asking for a crown of gold.

Kelcey aroused from his semi-slumber. "Yes, if I kin remember it," he said.

The little old woman arose to stow her son's lunch into the pail. When he had finished his breakfast he stalked for a time about the room in a dignified way. He put on his coat and hat, and taking his lunch-pail went to the door. There he halted, and without turning his head, stiffly said: "Well, good-by!"

The little old woman saw that she had offended her son. She did not seek an explanation. She was accustomed to these phenomena. She made haste to surrender.

"Ain't yeh goin' t' kiss me good-by," she asked in a little woful voice.

The youth made a pretence of going on, deaf-heartedly. He wore the dignity of an injured monarch.

Then the little old woman called again in forsaken accents: "George—George—ain't yeh goin' t' kiss me good-by?" When he moved he found that she was hanging to his coattails.

He turned eventually with a murmur of a sort of tenderness. "Why, 'a course I am," he said. He kissed her. Withal there was an undertone of superiority in his voice, as if he were granting an astonishing suit. She looked at him with reproach and gratitude and affection.

She stood at the head of the stairs and watched his hand sliding along the rail as he went down. Occasionally she could see his arm and part of his shoulder. When he reached the first floor she called to him: "Good-by!"

The little old woman went back to her work in the kitchen with a frown of perplexity upon her brow. "I wonder what was th' matter with George this mornin'," she mused. "He didn't seem a bit like himself!"

As she trudged to and fro at her labor she began to speculate. She was much worried. She surmised in a vague way that he was a sufferer from a great internal disease. It was something no doubt that devoured the kidneys or quietly fed upon the lungs. Later, she imagined a woman, wicked and fair, who had fascinated him and was turning his life into a bitter thing. Her mind created many wondrous influences that were swooping like green dragons at him. They were changing him to a morose man, who suffered silently. She longed to discover them, that she might go bravely to the rescue of her heroic son. She knew that he, generous in his pain, would keep it from her. She racked her mind for knowledge.

However, when he came home at night he was extraordinarily blithe. He seemed to be a lad of ten. He capered all about the room. When she was bringing the coffee-pot from the stove to the table, he made show of waltzing with her so that she spilled some of the coffee. She was obliged to scold him.

All through the meal he made jokes. She occasionally was compelled to laugh, despite the fact that she believed that she should not laugh at her own son's jokes. She uttered reproofs at times, but he did not regard them.

"Golly," he said once, "I feel fine as silk. I didn't think I'd get over feelin' bad so quick. It—" He stopped abruptly.

During the evening he sat content. He smoked his pipe and read from an evening paper. She bustled about at her work. She seemed utterly happy with him there, lazily puffing out little clouds of smoke and giving frequent brilliant dissertations upon the news of the day. It seemed to her that she must be a model mother to have such a son, one who came home to her at night and sat contented, in a languor of the muscles after a good day's toil. She pondered upon the science of her management.

The week thereafter, too, she was joyous, for he stayed at home each night of it, and was sunny-tempered. She became convinced that she was a perfect mother, rearing a perfect son. There came often a love-light into her eyes. The wrinkled, yellow face frequently warmed into a smile of the kind that a maiden bestows upon him who to her is first and perhaps last.

VI

The little old woman habitually discouraged all outbursts of youthful vanity upon the part of her son. She feared that he would get to think too much of himself, and she knew that nothing could do more harm. Great self-esteem was always passive, she thought, and if he grew to regard his qualities of mind as forming a dazzling constellation, he would tranquilly sit still and not do those wonders she expected of him. So she was constantly on the alert to suppress even a shadow of such a thing. As for him he ruminated with the savage, vengeful bitterness of a young man, and decided that she did not comprehend him.

But despite her precautions he often saw that she believed him to be the most marvellous young man on the earth. He had only to look at those two eyes that became lighted with a glow from her heart whenever he did some excessively brilliant thing. On these occasions he could see her glance triumphantly at a neighbor, or whoever happened to be present. He grew to plan for these glances. And then he took a vast satisfaction in detecting and appropriating them.

Nevertheless, he could not understand why, directly after a scene of this kind, his mother was liable to call to him to hang his coat on the hook under the mantel, her voice in a key of despair as if he were negligent and stupid in what was, after all, the only important thing in life.

"If yeh'll only get in the habit of doin' it, it'll be jest as easy as throwin' it down anywheres," she would say to him. "When yeh pitch it down anywheres, somebody's got t' pick it up, an' that'll most likely be your poor ol' mother. Yeh can hang it up yerself, if yeh'll on'y think." This was intolerable. He usually went then and hurled his coat savagely at the hook. The correctness of her position was maddening.

It seemed to him that anyone who had a son of his glowing attributes should overlook the fact that he seldom hung up his coat. It was impossible to explain this situation to his mother. She was unutterably narrow. He grew sullen.

There came a time, too, that, even in all his mother's tremendous admiration for him, he did not entirely agree with her. He was delighted that she liked his great wit. He spurred himself to new and flashing effort because of this appreciation. But for the greater part he could see that his mother took pride in him in quite a different way from that in which he took pride in himself. She rejoiced at qualities in him that indicated that he was going to become a white and looming king among men. From these she made pictures in which he appeared as a benign personage, blessed by the filled hands of the poor, one whose brain could hold massive thoughts and awe certain men about whom she had read. She was fêted as the mother of this enormous man. These dreams were her solace. She spoke of them to no one because she knew that, worded, they would be ridiculous. But she dwelt with them, and they shed a radiance of gold upon her long days, her sorry labor. Upon the dead altars of her life she had builded the little fires of hope for another.

He had a complete sympathy for as much as he understood of these thoughts of his mother. They were so wise that he admired her foresight. As for himself, however, most of his dreams were of a nearer time. He had many of the distant future when he would be a man with a cloak of coldness concealing his gentleness and his faults, and of whom the men and, more particularly, the women, would think with reverence. He agreed with his mother that at that time he would go through the obstacles to other men like a flung stone. And then he would have power and he would enjoy having his bounty and his wrath alike fall swiftly upon those below. They would be awed. And above all he would mystify them.

But then his nearer dreams were a multitude. He had begun to look at the great world revolving near to his nose. He had a vast curiosity concerning this city in whose complexities he was buried. It was an impenetrable mystery, this city. It was a blend of many enticing colors. He longed to comprehend it completely, that he might walk understandingly in its greatest marvels, its mightiest march of life, its sin. He dreamed of a comprehension whose pay was the admirable attitude of a man of knowledge. He remembered Jones. He could not help but admire a man who knew so many bartenders.

VII

An indefinite woman was in all of Kelcey's dreams. As a matter of fact it was not he whom he pictured as wedding her. It was a vision of himself greater, finer, more terrible. It was himself as he expected to be. In scenes which he took mainly from pictures, this vision conducted a courtship, strutting, posing, and lying through a drama which was magnificent from glow of purple. In it he was icy, self-possessed; but she, the dream-girl, was consumed by wild, torrential passion. He went to the length of having her display it before the people. He saw them wonder at his tranquillity. It amazed them infinitely to see him remain cold before the glory of this peerless woman's love. She was to him as beseeching for affection as a pet animal, but still he controlled appearances and none knew of his deep abiding love. Some day, at the critical romantic time, he was going to divulge it. In these long dreams there were accessories of castle-like houses, wide lands, servants, horses, clothes.

They began somewhere in his childhood. When he ceased to see himself as a stern general pointing a sword at the nervous and abashed horizon, he became this sublime king of a vague woman's heart. Later when he had read some books, it all achieved clearer expression. He was told in them that there was a goddess in the world whose business it was to wait until he should exchange a glance with her. It became a creed, subtly powerful. It saved discomfort for him and for several women who flitted by him. He used her as a standard.

Often he saw the pathos of her long wait, but his faith did not falter. The world was obliged to turn gold in time. His life was to be fine and heroic, else he would not have been born. He believed that the common-place lot was the sentence, the doom of certain people who did not know how to feel. His blood was a tender current of life. He thought that the usual should fall to others whose nerves were of lead. Occasionally he wondered how fate was going to begin in making an enormous figure of him; but he had no doubt of the result. A chariot of pink clouds was coming for him. His faith was his reason for existence. Meanwhile he could dream of the indefinite woman and the fragrance of roses that came from her hair.

One day he met Maggie Johnson on the stairs. She had a pail of beer in one hand and a brown-paper parcel under her arm. She glanced at him. He discovered that it would wither his heart to see another man signally successful in the smiles of her. And the glance that she gave him was so indifferent and so unresponsive to the sudden vivid admiration in his own eyes that he immediately concluded that she was magnificent in two ways.

As she came to the landing, the light from a window passed in a silver gleam over the girlish roundness of her cheek. It was a thing that he remembered.

He was silent for the most part at supper that night. He was particularly unkind when he did speak. His mother, observing him apprehensively, tried in vain to picture the new terrible catastrophe. She eventually concluded that he did not like the beef-stew. She put more salt in it.

He saw Maggie quite frequently after the meeting upon the stairs. He reconstructed his dreams and placed her in the full glory of that sun. The dream-woman, the goddess, pitched from her pedestal, lay prostrate, unheeded, save when he brought her forth to call her insipid and childish in the presence of his new religion.

He was relatively happy sometimes when Maggie's mother would get drunk and make terrific uproars. He used then to sit in the dark and make scenes in which he rescued the girl from her hideous environment.

He laid clever plans by which he encountered her in the halls, at the door, on the street. When he succeeded in meeting her he was always overcome by the thought that the whole thing was obvious to her. He could feel the shame of it burn his face and neck. To prove to her that she was mistaken he would turn away his head or regard her with a granite stare.

After a time he became impatient of the distance between them. He saw looming princes who would aim to seize her. Hours of his leisure and certain hours of his labor he spent in contriving. The shade of this girl was with him continually. With her he builded his grand dramas so that he trod in clouds, the matters of his daily life obscured and softened by a mist.

He saw that he need only break down the slight conventional barriers and she would soon discover his noble character. Sometimes he could see it all in his mind. It was very skilful. But then his courage flew away at the supreme moment. Perhaps the whole affair was humorous to her. Perhaps she was watching his mental contortions. She might laugh. He felt that he would then die or kill her. He could not approach the dread moment. He sank often from the threshold of knowledge. Directly after these occasions, it was his habit to avoid her to prove that she was a cipher to him.

He reflected that if he could only get a chance to rescue her from something, the whole tragedy would speedily unwind.

He met a young man in the halls one evening who said to him: "Say, me frien', where d' d' Johnson birds live in heh? I can't fin' me feet in dis bloomin' joint. I been battin' round heh fer a half-hour."

"Two flights up," said Kelcey stonily. He had felt a sudden quiver of his heart. The grandeur of the clothes, the fine worldly air, the experience, the self-reliance, the courage that shone in the countenance of this other young man made him suddenly sink to the depths of woe. He stood listening in the hall, flushing and ashamed of it, until he heard them coming down-stairs together. He slunk away then. It would have been a horror to him if she had discovered him there. She might have felt sorry for him.

They were going out to a show, perhaps. That pig of the world in his embroidered cloak was going to dazzle her with splendor. He mused upon how unrighteous it was for other men to dazzle women with splendor.

As he appreciated his handicap he swore with savage, vengeful bitterness. In his home his mother raised her voice in a high key of monotonous irritability. "Hang up yer coat, can't yeh, George?" she cried at him. "I can't go round after yeh all th' time. It's jest as easy t' hang it up as it is t' throw it down that way. Don't yeh ever git tired 'a hearin' me yell at yeh!"

"Yes," he exploded. In this word he put a profundity of sudden anger. He turned toward his mother a face, red, seamed, hard with hate and rage. They stared a moment in silence. Then she turned and staggered toward her room. Her hip struck violently against the corner of the table during this blind passage. A moment later the door closed.

Kelcey sank down in a chair with his legs thrust out straight and his hands deep in his trousers' pockets. His chin was forward upon his breast and his eyes stared before him. There swept over him all the self-pity that comes when the soul is turned back from a road.

VIII

During the next few days Kelcey suffered from his first gloomy conviction that the earth was not grateful to him for his presence upon it. When sharp words were said to him, he interpreted them with what seemed to be a lately acquired insight. He could now perceive that the universe hated him. He sank to the most sublime depths of despair.

One evening of this period he met Jones. The latter rushed upon him with enthusiasm. "Why, yer jest th' man I wanted t' see! I was comin' round t' your place t'-night. Lucky I met yeh! Ol' Bleecker's goin' t' give a blow-out t'-morrah night. Anything yeh want t' drink! All th' boys 'll be there an' everything. He tol' me expressly that he wanted yeh t' be there. Great time! Great! Can yeh come?"

Kelcey grasped the other's hand with fervor. He felt now that there was some solacing friendship in space. "You bet I will, ol' man," he said, huskily. "I'd like nothin' better in th' world!"

As he walked home he thought that he was a very grim figure. He was about to taste the delicious revenge of a partial self-destruction. The universe would regret its position when it saw him drunk.

He was a little late in getting to Bleecker's lodging. He was delayed while his mother read aloud a letter from an old uncle, who wrote in one place: "God bless the boy! Bring him up to be the man his father was." Bleecker lived in an old three-storied house on a side-street. A Jewish tailor lived and worked in the front parlor, and old Bleecker lived in the back parlor. A German, whose family took care of the house, occupied the basement. Another German, with a wife and eight children, rented the dining-room. The two upper floors were inhabited by tailors, dressmakers, a pedler, and mysterious people who were seldom seen. The door of the little hall-bedroom, at the foot of the second flight, was always open, and in there could be seen two bended men who worked at mending opera-glasses. The German woman in the dining-room was not friends with the little dressmaker in the rear room of the third floor, and frequently they yelled the vilest names up and down between the balusters. Each part of the woodwork was scratched and rubbed by the contact of innumerable persons. In one wall there was a long slit with chipped edges, celebrating the time when a man had thrown a hatchet at his wife. In the lower hall there was an eternal woman, with a rag and a pail of suds, who knelt over the worn oil-cloth. Old Bleecker felt that he had quite respectable and high-class apartments. He was glad to invite his friends.

Bleecker met Kelcey in the hall. He wore a collar that was cleaner and higher than his usual one. It changed his appearance greatly. He was now formidably aristocratic. "How are yeh, ol' man?" he shouted. He grasped Kelcey's arm, and, babbling jovially, conducted him down the hall and into the ex-parlor.

A group of standing men made vast shadows in the yellow glare of the lamp. They turned their heads as the two entered. "Why, hello, Kelcey, ol' man," Jones exclaimed, coming rapidly forward. "Good fer you! Glad yeh come! Yeh know O'Connor, 'a course! An' Schmidt! an' Woods! Then there's Zeusentell! Mr. Zeusentell—my friend Mr. Kelcey! Shake hands—both good fellows, damnitall! Then here is—oh, gentlemen, my friend Mr. Kelcey! A good fellow, he is, too! I've known 'im since I was a kid! Come, have a drink!" Everybody was excessively amiable. Kelcey felt that he had social standing. The strangers were cautious and respectful.

"By all means," said old Bleecker. "Mr. Kelcey, have a drink! An' by th' way, gentlemen, while we're about it, let's all have a drink!" There was much laughter. Bleecker was so droll at times.

With mild and polite gesturing they marched up to the table. There were upon it a keg of beer, a long row of whiskey bottles, a little heap of corn-cob pipes, some bags of tobacco, a box of cigars, and a mighty collection of glasses, cups, and mugs. Old Bleecker had arranged them so deftly that they resembled a primitive bar. There was considerable scuffling for possession of the cracked cups. Jones politely but vehemently insisted upon drinking from the worst of the assortment. He was quietly opposed by others. Everybody showed that they were awed by Bleecker's lavish hospitality. Their demeanors expressed their admiration at the cost of this entertainment.

Kelcey took his second mug of beer away to a corner and sat down with it. He wished to socially reconnoitre. Over in a corner a man was telling a story, in which at intervals he grunted like a pig. A half dozen men were listening. Two or three others sat alone in isolated places. They looked expectantly bright, ready to burst out cordially if anyone should address them. The row of bottles made quaint shadows upon the table, and upon a side-wall the keg of beer created a portentous black figure that reared toward the ceiling, hovering over the room and its inmates with spectral stature. Tobacco-smoke lay in lazy cloud-banks overhead.

Jones and O'Connor stayed near the table, occasionally being affable in all directions. Kelcey saw old Bleecker go to them and heard him whisper: "Come, we must git th' thing started. Git th' thing started." Kelcey saw that the host was fearing that all were not having a good time. Jones conferred with O'Connor and then O'Connor went to the man named Zeusentell. O'Connor evidently proposed something. Zeusentell refused at once. O'Connor beseeched. Zeusentell remained implacable. At last O'Connor broke off his argument, and going to the centre of the room, held up his hand. "Gentlemen," he shouted loudly, "we will now have a recitation by Mr. Zeusentell, entitled 'Patrick Clancy's Pig'!" He then glanced triumphantly at Zeusentell and said: "Come on!" Zeusentell had been twisting and making pantomimic appeals. He said, in a reproachful whisper: "You son of a gun."

The men turned their heads to glance at Zeusentell for a moment and then burst into a sustained clamor. "Hurray! Let 'er go! Come—give it t' us! Spring it! Spring it! Let it come!" As Zeusentell made no advances, they appealed personally. "Come, ol' man, let 'er go! Whatter yeh 'fraid of? Let 'er go! Go ahn! Hurry up!"

Zeusentell was protesting with almost frantic modesty. O'Connor took him by the lapel and tried to drag him; but he leaned back, pulling at his coat and shaking his head. "No, no, I don't know it, I tell yeh! I can't! I don't know it! I tell yeh I don't know it! I've forgotten it, I tell yeh! No—no—no—no. Ah, say, lookahere, le' go me, can't yeh? What's th' matter with yeh? I tell yeh I don't know it!" The men applauded violently. O'Connor did not relent. A little battle was waged until all of a sudden Zeusentell was seen to grow wondrously solemn. A hush fell upon the men. He was about to begin. He paused in the middle of the floor and nervously adjusted his collar and cravat. The audience became grave. " 'Patrick Clancy's Pig,' " announced Zeusentell in a shrill, dry, unnatural tone. And then he began in rapid sing-song:

"Patrick Clancy had a pig
  Th' pride uv all th' nation,
The half uv him was half as big
  As half uv all creation——"

When he concluded the others looked at each other to convey their appreciation. They then wildly clapped their hands or tinkled their glasses. As Zeusentell went toward his seat a man leaned over and asked: "Can yeh tell me where I kin git that." He had made a great success. After an enormous pressure he was induced to recite two more tales. Old Bleecker finally led him forward and pledged him in a large drink. He declared that they were the best things he had ever heard.

The efforts of Zeusentell imparted a gayety to the company. The men having laughed together were better acquainted, and there was now a universal topic. Some of the party, too, began to be quite drunk.

The invaluable O'Connor brought forth a man who could play the mouth-organ. The latter, after wiping his instrument upon his coat-sleeve, played all the popular airs. The men's heads swayed to and fro in the clouded smoke. They grinned and beat time with their feet. A valor, barbaric and wild, began to show in their poses and in their faces, red and glistening from perspiration. The conversation resounded in a hoarse roar. The beer would not run rapidly enough for Jones, so he remained behind to tilt the keg. This caused the black shadow on the wall to retreat and advance, sinking mystically to loom forward again with sudden menace, a huge dark figure controlled, as by some unknown emotion. The glasses, mugs, and cups travelled swift and regular, catching orange reflections from the lamp-light. Two or three men were grown so careless that they were continually spilling their drinks. Old Bleecker, cackling with pleasure, seized time to glance triumphantly at Jones. His party was going to be a success.

IX

Of a sudden Kelcey felt the buoyant thought that he was having a good time. He was all at once an enthusiast, as if he were at a festival of a religion. He felt that there was something fine and thrilling in this affair isolated from a stern world, and from which the laughter arose like incense. He knew that old sentiment of brotherly regard for those about him. He began to converse tenderly with them. He was not sure of his drift of thought, but he knew that he was immensely sympathetic. He rejoiced at their faces, shining red and wrinkled with smiles. He was capable of heroisms.

His pipe irritated him by going out frequently. He was too busy in amiable conversations to attend to it. When he arose to go for a match he discovered that his legs were a trifle uncertain under him. They bended and did not precisely obey his intent. At the table he lit a match and then, in laughing at a joke made near him, forgot to apply it to the bowl of his pipe. He succeeded with the next match after annoying trouble. He swayed so that the match would appear first on one side of the bowl and then on the other. At last he happily got it directly over the tobacco. He had burned his fingers. He inspected them, laughing vaguely.

Jones came and slapped him on the shoulder. "Well, ol' man, let's take a drink fer ol' Handyville's sake!"

Kelcey was deeply affected. He looked at Jones with moist eyes. "I'll go yeh," he said. With an air of profound melancholy, Jones poured out some whiskey. They drank reverently. They exchanged a glistening look of tender recollections and then went over to where Bleecker was telling a humorous story to a circle of giggling listeners. The old man sat like a fat, jolly god. "—and just at that moment th' old woman put her head out of th' window an' said: 'Mike, yez lezy divil, fer phwat do yez be slapin' in me new geranium bid?' An' Mike woke up an' said: 'Domn a wash-woman thot do niver wash her own bidclues. Here do I be slapin' in nothin' but dhirt an' wades.' " The men slapped their knees, roaring loudly. They begged him to tell another. A clamor of comment arose concerning the anecdote, so that when old Bleecker began a fresh one nobody was heeding.

It occurred to Jones to sing. Suddenly he burst forth with a ballad that had a rippling waltz movement, and seizing Kelcey, made a furious attempt to dance. They sprawled over a pair of outstretched legs and pitched headlong. Kelcey fell with a yellow crash.

Blinding lights flashed before his vision. But he arose immediately, laughing. He did not feel at all hurt. The pain in his head was rather pleasant.

Old Bleecker, O'Connor, and Jones, who now limped and drew breath through his teeth, were about to lead him with much care and tenderness to the table for another drink, but he laughingly pushed them away and went unassisted. Bleecker told him: "Great Gawd, your head struck hard enough t' break a trunk."

He laughed again, and with a show of steadiness and courage he poured out an extravagant portion of whiskey. With cold muscles he put it to his lips and drank it. It chanced that this addition dazed him like a powerful blow. A moment later it affected him with blinding and numbing power. Suddenly unbalanced, he felt the room sway. His blurred sight could only distinguish a tumbled mass of shadow through which the beams from the light ran like swords of flame. The sound of the many voices was to him like the roar of a distant river. Still, he felt that if he could only annul the force of these million winding fingers that gripped his senses, he was capable of most brilliant and entertaining things.

He was at first of the conviction that his feelings were only temporary. He waited for them to pass away, but the mental and physical pause only caused a new reeling and swinging of the room. Chasms with inclined approaches were before him; peaks leaned toward him. And withal he was blind and numb with surprise. He understood vaguely in his stupefaction that it would disgrace him to fall down a chasm.

At last he perceived a shadow, a form, which he knew to be Jones. The adorable Jones, the supremely wise Jones, was walking in this strange land without fear or care, erect and tranquil. Kelcey murmured in admiration and affection, and fell toward his friend. Jones's voice sounded as from the shores of the unknown. "Come, come, ol' man, this will never do. Brace up." It appeared after all that Jones was not wholly wise. "Oh, I'm—all ri' Jones! I'm all ri'! I wan' shing song! Tha's all! I wan' shing song!"

Jones was stupid. "Come now, sit down an' shut up."

It made Kelcey burn with fury. "Jones, le' me alone, I tell yeh! Le' me alone! I wan' shing song er te' story! G'l'm'n, I lovsh girl live down my shtreet. Thash reason 'm drunk, 'tis! She——"

Jones seized him and dragged him toward a chair. He heard him laugh. He could not endure these insults from his friend. He felt a blazing desire to strangle his companion. He threw out his hand violently, but Jones grappled him close and he was no more than a dried leaf. He was amazed to find that Jones possessed the strength of twenty horses. He was forced skilfully to the floor.

As he lay, he reflected in great astonishment upon Jones's muscle. It was singular that he had never before discovered it. The whole incident had impressed him immensely. An idea struck him that he might denounce Jones for it. It would be a sage thing. There would be a thrilling and dramatic moment in which he would dazzle all the others. But at this moment he was assailed by a mighty desire to sleep. Sombre and soothing clouds of slumber were heavily upon him. He closed his eyes with a sigh that was yet like that of a babe.

When he awoke, there was still the battleful clamor of the revel. He half arose with a plan of participating, when O'Connor came and pushed him down again, throwing out his chin in affectionate remonstrance and saying, "Now, now," as to a child.

The change that had come over these men mystified Kelcey in a great degree. He had never seen anything so vastly stupid as their idea of his state. He resolved to prove to them that they were dealing with one whose mind was very clear. He kicked and squirmed in O'Connor's arms, until, with a final wrench, he scrambled to his feet and stood tottering in the middle of the room. He would let them see that he had a strangely lucid grasp of events. "G'l'm'n, I lovsh girl! I ain' drunker'n yeh all are! She——"

He felt them hurl him to a corner of the room and pile chairs and tables upon him until he was buried beneath a stupendous mountain. Far above, as up a mine's shaft, there were voices, lights, and vague figures. He was not hurt physically, but his feelings were unutterably injured. He, the brilliant, the good, the sympathetic had been thrust fiendishly from the party. They had had the comprehension of red lobsters. It was an unspeakable barbarism. Tears welled piteously from his eyes. He planned long diabolical explanations!

X

At first the gray lights of dawn came timidly into the room, remaining near the windows, afraid to approach certain sinister corners. Finally, mellow streams of sunshine poured in, undraping the shadows to disclose the putrefaction, making pitiless revelation. Kelcey awoke with a groan of undirected misery. He tossed his stiffened arms about his head for a moment and then leaning heavily upon his elbow stared blinking at his environment. The grim truthfulness of the day showed disaster and death. After the tumults of the previous night the interior of this room resembled a decaying battle-field. The air hung heavy and stifling with the odors of tobacco, men's breaths, and beer half filling forgotten glasses. There was ruck of broken tumblers, pipes, bottles, spilled tobacco, cigar stumps. The chairs and tables were pitched this way and that way, as after some terrible struggle. In the midst of it all lay old Bleecker stretched upon a couch in deepest sleep, as abandoned in attitude, as motionless, as ghastly as if it were a corpse that had been flung there.

A knowledge of the thing came gradually into Kelcey's eyes. He looked about him with an expression of utter woe, regret, and loathing. He was compelled to lie down again. A pain above his eyebrows was like that from an iron-clamp.

As he lay pondering, his bodily condition created for him a bitter philosophy, and he perceived all the futility of a red existence. He saw his life problems confronting him like granite giants and he was no longer erect to meet them. He had made a calamitous retrogression in his war. Spectres were to him now as large as clouds.

Inspired by the pitiless ache in his head, he was prepared to reform and live a white life. His stomach informed him that a good man was the only being who was wise. But his perception of his future was hopeless. He was aghast at the prospect of the old routine. It was impossible. He trembled before its exactions.

Turning toward the other way, he saw that the gold portals of vice no longer enticed him. He could not hear the strains of alluring music. The beckoning sirens of drink had been killed by this pain in his head. The desires of his life suddenly lay dead like mullein stalks. Upon reflection, he saw, therefore, that he was perfectly willing to be virtuous if somebody would come and make it easy for him.

When he stared over at old Bleecker, he felt a sudden contempt and dislike for him. He considered him to be a tottering old beast. It was disgusting to perceive aged men so weak in sin. He dreaded to see him awaken lest he should be required to be somewhat civil to him.

Kelcey wished for a drink of water. For some time he had dreamed of the liquid, deliciously cool. It was an abstract, uncontained thing that poured upon him and tumbled him, taking away his pain like a kind of surgery. He arose and staggered slowly toward a little sink in a corner of the room. He understood that any rapid movement might cause his head to split.

The little sink was filled with a chaos of broken glass and spilled liquids. A sight of it filled him with horror, but he rinsed a glass with scrupulous care, and filling it, took an enormous drink. The water was an intolerable disappointment. It was insipid and weak to his scorched throat and not at all cool. He put down the glass with a gesture of despair. His face became fixed in the stony and sullen expression of a man who waits for the recuperative power of morrows.

Old Bleecker awakened. He rolled over and groaned loudly. For awhile he thrashed about in a fury of displeasure at his bodily stiffness and pain. Kelcey watched him as he would have watched a death agony. "Good Gawd," said the old man, "beer an' whiskey make th' devil of a mix. Did yeh see th' fight?"

"No," said Kelcey, stolidly.

"Why, Zeusentell an' O'Connor had a great old mill. They were scrappin' all over th' place. I thought we were all goin' t' get pulled. Thompson, that fellah over in th' corner, though, he sat down on th' whole business. He was a dandy! He had t' poke Zeusentell! He was a bird! Lord, I wish I had a Manhattan!"

Kelcey remained in bitter silence while old Bleecker dressed. "Come an' get a cocktail," said the latter briskly. This was part of his aristocracy. He was the only man of them who knew much about cocktails. He perpetually referred to them. "It'll brace yeh right up! Come along! Say, you get full too soon. You oughter wait until later, me boy! You're too speedy!" Kelcey wondered vaguely where his companion had lost his zeal for polished sentences, his iridescent mannerisms.

"Come along," said Bleecker.

Kelcey made a movement of disdain for cocktails, but he followed the other to the street. At the corner they separated. Kelcey attempted a friendly parting smile and then went on up the street. He had to reflect to know that he was erect and using his own muscles in walking. He felt like a man of paper, blown by the winds. Withal, the dust of the avenue was galling to his throat, eyes, and nostrils, and the roar of traffic cracked his head. He was glad, however, to be alone, to be rid of old Bleecker. The sight of him had been as the contemplation of a disease.

His mother was not at home. In his little room he mechanically undressed and bathed his head, arms, and shoulders. When he crawled between the two white sheets he felt a first lifting of his misery. His pillow was soothingly soft. There was an effect that was like the music of tender voices.

When he awoke again his mother was bending over him giving vent to alternate cries of grief and joy. Her hands trembled so that they were useless to her. "Oh, George, George, where have yeh been? What has happened t' yeh? Oh, George, I've been so worried! I didn't sleep a wink all night."

Kelcey was instantly wide awake. With a moan of suffering he turned his face to the wall before he spoke. "Never mind, mother, I'm all right. Don't fret now! I was knocked down by a truck last night in th' street, an' they took me t' th' hospital; but it's all right now. I got out jest a little while ago. They told me I'd better go home an' rest up."

His mother screamed in pity, horror, joy, and self-reproach for something unknown. She frenziedly demanded the details. He sighed with unutterable weariness. "Oh—wait—wait—wait," he said shutting his eyes as from the merciless monotony of a pain. "Wait—wait—please wait. I can't talk now. I want t' rest."

His mother condemned herself with a little cry. She adjusted his pillow, her hands shaking with love and tenderness. "There, there, don't mind, dearie! But yeh can't think how worried I was—an' crazy. I was near frantic. I went down t' th' shop, an' they said they hadn't seen anything 'a yeh there. The foreman was awful good t' me. He said he'd come up this afternoon t' see if yeh had come home yet. He tol' me not t' worry. Are yeh sure yer all right? Ain't there anythin' I kin git fer yeh? What did th' docter say?"

Kelcey's patience was worn. He gestured, and then spoke querulously. "Now—now—mother, it's all right, I tell yeh! All I need is a little rest an' I'll be as well as ever. But it makes it all th' worse if yeh stand there an' ask me questions an' make me think. Jest leave me alone fer a little while, an' I'll be as well as ever. Can't yeh do that?"

The little old woman puckered her lips funnily. "My, what an old bear th' boy is!" She kissed him blithely. Presently she went out, upon her face a bright and glad smile that must have been a reminiscence of some charming girlhood.

XI

At one time Kelcey had a friend who was struck in the head by the pole of a truck and knocked senseless. He was taken to the hospital, from which he emerged in the morning an astonished man, with rather a dim recollection of the accident. He used to hold an old brier-wood pipe in his teeth in a manner peculiar to himself, and, with a brown derby hat tilted back on his head, recount his strange sensations. Kelcey had always remembered it as a bit of curious history. When his mother cross-examined him in regard to the accident, he told this story with barely a variation. Its truthfulness was incontestable.

At the shop he was welcomed on the following day with considerable enthusiasm. The foreman had told the story and there were already jokes created concerning it. Mike O'Donnell, whose wit was famous, had planned a humorous campaign, in which he made charges against Kelcey, which were, as a matter of fact, almost the exact truth. Upon hearing it, Kelcey looked at him suddenly from the corners of his eyes, but otherwise remained imperturbable. O'Donnell eventually despaired. "Yez can't goiy that kid! He tekes ut all loike mate an' dhrink." Kelcey often told the story, his pipe held in his teeth peculiarly, and his derby tilted back on his head.

He remained at home for several evenings, content to read the papers and talk with his mother. She began to look around for the tremendous reason for it. She suspected that his nearness to death in the recent accident had sobered his senses and made him think of high things. She mused upon it continually. When he sat moodily pondering she watched him. She said to herself that she saw the light breaking in upon his spirit. She felt that it was a very critical period of his existence. She resolved to use all her power and skill to turn his eyes toward the lights in the sky. Accordingly she addressed him one evening. "Come, go t' prayer-meetin' t'-night with me, will yeh, George?" It sounded more blunt than she intended.

He glanced at her in sudden surprise. "Huh?"

As she repeated her request, her voice quavered. She felt that it was a supreme moment. "Come, go t' prayer-meetin' t'-night, won't yeh?"

He seemed amazed. "Oh, I don't know," he began. He was fumbling in his mind for a reason for refusing. "I don't wanta go. I'm tired as th' dickens!" His obedient shoulders sank down languidly. His head mildly drooped.

The little old woman, with a quick perception of her helplessness, felt a motherly rage at her son. It was intolerable that she could not impart motion to him in a chosen direction. The waves of her desires were puny against the rocks of his indolence. She had a great wish to beat him. "I don't know what I'm ever goin' t' do with yeh," she told him, in a choking voice. "Yeh won't do anything I ask yeh to. Yeh never pay th' least bit 'a attention t' what I say. Yeh don't mind me any more than yeh would a fly. Whatever am I goin' t' do with yeh?" She faced him in a battleful way, her eyes blazing with a sombre light of despairing rage.

He looked up at her ironically. "I don't know," he said, with calmness. "What are yeh?" He had traced her emotions and seen her fear of his rebellion. He thrust out his legs in the easy scorn of a rapier-bravo. "What are yeh?"

The little old woman began to weep. They were tears without a shame of grief. She allowed them to run unheeded down her cheeks. As she stared into space her son saw her regarding there the powers and influences that she had held in her younger life. She was in some way acknowledging to fate that she was now but withered grass, with no power but the power to feel the winds. He was smitten with a sudden shame. Besides, in the last few days he had gained quite a character for amiability. He saw something grand in relenting at this point. "Well," he said, trying to remove a sulky quality from his voice, "well, if yer bound t' have me go, I s'pose I'll have t' go."

His mother, with strange, immobile face, went to him and kissed him on the brow. "All right, George!" There was in her wet eyes an emotion which he could not fathom.

She put on her bonnet and shawl, and they went out together. She was unusually silent, and made him wonder why she did not appear gleeful at his coming. He was resentful because she did not display more appreciation of his sacrifice. Several times he thought of halting and refusing to go farther, to see if that would not wring from her some acknowledgment.

In a dark street the little chapel sat humbly between two towering apartment-houses. A red street-lamp stood in front. It threw a marvellous reflection upon the wet pavements. It was like the death-stain of a spirit. Farther up the brilliant lights of an avenue made a span of gold across the black street. A roar of wheels and a clangor of bells came from this point, interwoven into a sound emblematic of the life of the city. It seemed somehow to affront this solemn and austere little edifice. It suggested an approaching barbaric invasion. The little church, pierced, would die with a fine, illimitable scorn for its slayers.

When Kelcey entered with his mother he felt a sudden quaking. His knees shook. It was an awesome place to him. There was a menace in the red padded carpet and the leather doors, studded with little brass tacks that penetrated his soul with their pitiless glances. As for his mother, she had acquired such a new air that he would have been afraid to address her. He felt completely alone and isolated at this formidable time.

There was a man in the vestibule who looked at them blandly. From within came the sound of singing. To Kelcey there was a million voices. He dreaded the terrible moment when the doors should swing back. He wished to recoil, but at that instant the bland man pushed the doors aside and he followed his mother up the centre aisle of the little chapel. To him there was a riot of lights that made him transparent. The multitudinous pairs of eyes that turned toward him were implacable in their cool valuations.

They had just ceased singing. He who conducted the meeting motioned that the services should wait until the new-comers found seats. The little old woman went slowly on toward the first rows. Occasionally she paused to scrutinize vacant places, but they did not seem to meet her requirements. Kelcey was in agony. He thought the moment of her decision would never come. In his unspeakable haste he walked a little faster than his mother. Once she paused to glance in her calculating way at some seats and he forged ahead. He halted abruptly and returned, but by that time she had resumed her thoughtful march up the aisle. He could have assassinated her. He felt that everybody must have seen his torture, during which his hands were to him like monstrous swollen hides. He was wild with a rage in which his lips turned slightly livid. He was capable of doing some furious, unholy thing.

When the little old woman at last took a seat, her son sat down beside her slowly and stiffly. He was opposing his strong desire to drop.

When from the mists of his shame and humiliation the scene came before his vision, he was surprised to find that all eyes were not fastened upon his face. The leader of the meeting seemed to be the only one who saw him. He stared gravely, solemnly, regretfully. He was a pale-faced, but plump young man in a black coat that buttoned to his chin. It was evident to Kelcey that his mother had spoken of him to the young clergyman, and that the latter was now impressing upon him the sorrow caused by the contemplation of his sin. Kelcey hated the man.

A man seated alone over in a corner began to sing. He closed his eyes and threw back his head. Others, scattered sparsely throughout the innumerable light-wood chairs, joined him as they caught the air. Kelcey heard his mother's frail, squeaking soprano. The chandelier in the centre was the only one lighted, and far at the end of the room one could discern the pulpit swathed in gloom, solemn and mystic as a bier. It was surrounded by vague shapes of darkness on which at times was the glint of brass, or of glass that shone like steel, until one could feel there the presence of the army of the unknown, possessors of the great eternal truths, and silent listeners at this ceremony. High up, the stained-glass windows loomed in leaden array like dull-hued banners, merely catching occasional splashes of dark wine-color from the lights. Kelcey fell to brooding concerning this indefinable presence which he felt in a church.

One by one people arose and told little tales of their religious faith. Some were tearful and others calm, emotionless, and convincing. Kelcey listened closely for a time. These people filled him with a great curiosity. He was not familiar with their types.

At last the young clergyman spoke at some length. Kelcey was amazed, because, from the young man's appearance, he would not have suspected him of being so glib; but the speech had no effect on Kelcey, excepting to prove to him again that he was damned.

XII

Kelcey sometimes wondered whether he liked beer. He had been obliged to cultivate a talent for imbibing it. He was born with an abhorrence which he had steadily battled until it had come to pass that he could drink from ten to twenty glasses of beer without the act of swallowing causing him to shiver. He understood that drink was an essential to joy, to the coveted position of a man of the world and of the streets. The saloons contained the mystery of a street for him. When he knew its saloons he comprehended the street. Drink and its surroundings were the eyes of a superb green dragon to him. He followed a fascinating glitter, and the glitter required no explanation.

Directly after old Bleecker's party he almost reformed. He was tired and worn from the tumult of it, and he saw it as one might see a skeleton emerged from a crimson cloak. He wished then to turn his face away. Gradually, however, he recovered his mental balance. Then he admitted again by his point of view that the thing was not so terrible. His headache had caused him to exaggerate. A drunk was not the blight which he had once remorsefully named it. On the contrary, it was a mere unpleasant incident. He resolved, however, to be more cautious.

When prayer-meeting night came again his mother approached him hopefully. She smiled like one whose request is already granted. "Well, will yeh go t' prayer-meetin' with me t'-night again?"

He turned toward her with eloquent suddenness, and then riveted his eyes upon a corner of the floor. "Well, I guess not," he said.

His mother tearfully tried to comprehend his state of mind. "What has come over yeh?" she said, tremblingly. "Yeh never used t' be this way, George. Yeh never used t' be so cross an' mean t' me——"

"Oh, I ain't cross an' mean t' yeh," he interpolated, exasperated and violent.

"Yes, yeh are, too! I ain't hardly had a decent word from yeh in ever so long. Yer as cross an' as mean as yeh can be. I don't know what t' make of it. It can't be—" There came a look in her eyes that told that she was going to shock and alarm him with her heaviest sentence—"it can't be that yeh've got t' drinkin'."

Kelcey grunted with disgust at the ridiculous thing. "Why, what an old goose yer gettin' t' be."

She was compelled to laugh a little, as a child laughs between tears at a hurt. She had not been serious. She was only trying to display to him how she regarded his horrifying mental state. "Oh, of course, I didn't mean that, but I think yeh act jest as bad as if yeh did drink. I wish yeh would do better, George!"

She had grown so much less frigid and stern in her censure that Kelcey seized the opportunity to try to make a joke of it. He laughed at her, but she shook her head and continued: "I do wish yeh would do better. I don't know what's t' become 'a yeh, George. Yeh don't mind what I say no more'n if I was th' wind in th' chimbly. Yeh don't care about nothin' 'cept goin' out nights. I can't ever get yeh t' prayer-meetin' ner church; yeh never go out with me anywheres unless yeh can't get out of it; yeh swear an' take on sometimes like everything, yeh never——"

He gestured wrathfully in interruption. "Say, lookahere, can't yeh think 'a something I do?"

She ended her oration then in the old way. "An' I don't know what's goin' t' become 'a yeh."

She put on her bonnet and shawl and then came and stood near him, expectantly. She imparted to her attitude a subtle threat of unchangeableness. He pretended to be engrossed in his newspaper. The little swaggering clock on the mantel became suddenly evident, ticking with loud monotony. Presently she said, firmly: "Well, are yeh comin'?"

He was reading.

"Well, are yeh comin'?"

He threw his paper down, angrily. "Oh, why don't yeh go on an' leave me alone?" he demanded in supreme impatience. "What do yeh wanta pester me fer? Yeh'd think there was robbers. Why can't yeh go alone er else stay home? You wanta go an' I don't wanta go, an' yeh keep all time tryin' t' drag me. Yeh know I don't wanta go." He concluded in a last defiant wounding of her. "What do I care 'bout those ol' bags-'a-wind anyhow? They gimme a pain!"

His mother turned her face and went from him. He sat staring with a mechanical frown. Presently he went and picked up his newspaper.

Jones told him that night that everybody had had such a good time at old Bleecker's party that they were going to form a club. They waited at the little smiling saloon, and then amid much enthusiasm all signed a membership-roll. Old Bleecker, late that night, was violently elected president. He made speeches of thanks and gratification during the remainder of the meeting. Kelcey went home rejoicing. He felt that at any rate he would have true friends. The dues were a dollar for each week.

He was deeply interested. For a number of evenings he fairly gobbled his supper in order that he might be off to the little smiling saloon to discuss the new organization. All the men were wildly enthusiastic. One night the saloon-keeper announced that he would donate half the rent of quite a large room over his saloon. It was an occasion for great cheering. Kelcey's legs were like whalebone when he tried to go upstairs upon his return home, and the edge of each step was moved curiously forward.

His mother's questions made him snarl. "Oh, nowheres!" At other times he would tell her: "Oh, t' see some friends 'a mine! Where d' yeh s'pose?"

Finally, some of the women of the tenement concluded that the little old mother had a wild son. They came to condole with her. They sat in the kitchen for hours. She told them of his wit, his cleverness, his kind heart.

XIII

At a certain time Kelcey discovered that some young men who stood in the cinders between a brick wall and the pavement, and near the side-door of a corner saloon, knew more about life than other people. They used to lean there smoking and chewing, and comment upon events and persons. They knew the neighborhood extremely well. They debated upon small typical things that transpired before them until they had extracted all the information that existence contained. They sometimes inaugurated little fights with foreigners or well-dressed men. It was here that Sapristi Glielmi, the pedler, stabbed Pete Brady to death, for which he got a life-sentence. Each patron of the saloon was closely scrutinized as he entered the place. Sometimes they used to throng upon the heels of a man and in at the bar assert that he had asked them in to drink. When he objected, they would claim with one voice that it was too deep an insult and gather about to thrash him. When they had caught chance customers and absolute strangers, the barkeeper had remained in stolid neutrality, ready to serve one or seven, but two or three times they had encountered the wrong men. Finally, the proprietor had come out one morning and told them, in the fearless way of his class, that their pastime must cease. "It quits right here! See? Right here! Th' nex' time yeh try t' work it, I come with th' bung-starter, an' th' mugs I miss with it git pulled. See? It quits!" Infrequently, however, men did ask them in to drink.

The policeman of that beat grew dignified and shrewd whenever he approached this corner. Sometimes he stood with his hands behind his back and cautiously conversed with them. It was understood on both sides that it was a good thing to be civil.

In winter this band, a trifle diminished in numbers, huddled in their old coats and stamped little flat places in the snow, their faces turned always toward the changing life in the streets. In the summer they became more lively. Sometimes, then, they walked out to the curb to look up and down the street. Over in a trampled vacant lot, surrounded by high tenement-houses, there was a sort of a den among some bowlders. An old truck was made to form a shelter. The small hoodlums of that vicinity all avoided the spot. So many of them had been thrashed upon being caught near it. It was the summer-time lounging-place of the band from the corner.

They were all too clever to work. Some of them had worked, but these used their experiences as stores from which to draw tales. They were like veterans with their wars. One lad in particular used to recount how he whipped his employer, the proprietor of a large grain and feed establishment. He described his victim's features and form and clothes with minute exactness. He bragged of his wealth and social position. It had been a proud moment of the lad's life. He was like a savage who had killed a great chief.

Their feeling for contemporaneous life was one of contempt. Their philosophy taught that in a large part the whole thing was idle and a great bore. With fine scorn they sneered at the futility of it. Work was done by men who had not the courage to stand still and let the skies clap together if they willed.

The vast machinery of the popular law indicated to them that there were people in the world who wished to remain quiet. They awaited the moment when they could prove to them that a riotous upheaval, a cloud-burst of destruction would be a delicious thing. They thought of their fingers buried in the lives of these people. They longed dimly for a time when they could run through decorous streets with crash and roar of war, an army of revenge for pleasures long possessed by others, a wild sweeping compensation for their years without crystal and gilt, women and wine. This thought slumbered in them, as the image of Rome might have lain small in the hearts of the barbarians.

Kelcey respected these youths so much that he ordinarily used the other side of the street. He could not go near to them, because if a passer-by minded his own business he was a disdainful prig and had insulted them; if he showed that he was aware of them they were likely to resent his not minding his own business and prod him into a fight if the opportunity were good. Kelcey longed for their acquaintance and friendship, for with it came social safety and ease; they were respected so universally.

Once in another street Fidsey Corcoran was whipped by a short, heavy man. Fidsey picked himself up, and in the fury of defeat hurled pieces of brick at his opponent. The short man dodged with skill and then pursued Fidsey for over a block. Sometimes he got near enough to punch him. Fidsey raved in maniacal fury. The moment the short man would attempt to resume his own affairs, Fidsey would turn upon him again, tears and blood upon his face, with the lashed rage of a vanquished animal. The short man used to turn about, swear madly, and make little dashes. Fidsey always ran and then returned as pursuit ceased. The short man apparently wondered if this maniac was ever going to allow him to finish whipping him. He looked helplessly up and down the street. People were there who knew Fidsey, and they remonstrated with him; but he continued to confront the short man, gibbering like a wounded ape, using all the eloquence of the street in his wild oaths.

Finally the short man was exasperated to black fury. He decided to end the fight. With low snarls, ominous as death, he plunged at Fidsey.

Kelcey happened there then. He grasped the short man's shoulder. He cried out in the peculiar whine of the man who interferes. "Oh, hol' on! Yeh don't wanta hit 'im any more! Yeh've done enough to 'im now! Leave 'im be!"

The short man wrenched and tugged. He turned his face until his teeth were almost at Kelcey's cheek: "Le' go me! Le' go me, you——" The rest of his sentence was screamed curses.

Kelcey's face grew livid from fear, but he somehow managed to keep his grip. Fidsey, with but an instant's pause, plunged into the new fray.

They beat the short man. They forced him against a high board-fence where for a few seconds their blows sounded upon his head in swift thuds. A moment later Fidsey descried a running policeman. He made off, fleet as a shadow. Kelcey noted his going. He ran after him.

Three or four blocks away they halted. Fidsey said: "I'd 'a licked dat big stuff in 'bout a minute more," and wiped the blood from his eyes.

At the gang's corner, they asked: "Who soaked yeh, Fidsey?" His description was burning. Everybody laughed. "Where is 'e now?" Later they began to question Kelcey. He recited a tale in which he allowed himself to appear prominent and redoubtable. They looked at him then as if they thought he might be quite a man.

Once when the little old woman was going out to buy something for her son's supper, she discovered him standing at the side-door of the saloon engaged intimately with Fidsey and the others. She slunk away, for she understood that it would be a terrible thing to confront him and his pride there with youths who were superior to mothers.

When he arrived home he threw down his hat with a weary sigh, as if he had worked long hours, but she attacked him before he had time to complete the falsehood. He listened to her harangue with a curled lip. In defence he merely made a gesture of supreme exasperation. She never understood the advanced things in life. He felt the hopelessness of ever making her comprehend. His mother was not modern.

XIV

The little old woman arose early and bustled in the preparation of breakfast. At times she looked anxiously at the clock. An hour before her son should leave for work she went to his room and called him in the usual tone of sharpness, "George! George!"

A sleepy growl came to her.

"Come, come it's time t' git up," she continued. "Come now, git right up!"

Later she went again to the door. "George, are yeh gittin' up?"

"Huh?"

"Are yeh gittin' up?"

"Yes, I'll git right up!" He had introduced a valor into his voice which she detected to be false. She went to his bedside and took him by the shoulder. "George—George—git up!"

From the mist-lands of sleep he began to protest incoherently. "Oh, le' me be, won' yeh? 'M sleepy!"

She continued to shake him. "Well, it's time t' git up. Come—come—come on, now."

Her voice, shrill with annoyance, pierced his ears in a slender, piping thread of sound. He turned over on the pillow to bury his head in his arms. When he expostulated, his tones came half-smothered. "Oh le' me be, can't yeh? There's plenty 'a time! Jest fer ten minutes! 'M sleepy!"

She was implacable. "No, yeh must git up now! Yeh ain't got more'n time enough t' eat yer breakfast an' git t' work."

Eventually he arose, sullen and grumbling. Later he came to his breakfast, blinking his dry eyelids, his stiffened features set in a mechanical scowl.

Each morning his mother went to his room, and fought a battle to arouse him. She was like a soldier. Despite his pleadings, his threats, she remained at her post, imperturbable and unyielding.

These affairs assumed large proportions in his life. Sometimes he grew beside himself with a bland, unformulated wrath. The whole thing was a consummate imposition. He felt that he was being cheated of his sleep. It was an injustice to compel him to arise morning after morning with bitter regularity, before the sleep-gods had at all loosened their grasp. He hated that unknown force which directed his life.

One morning he swore a tangled mass of oaths, aimed into the air, as if the injustice poised there. His mother flinched at first; then her mouth set in the little straight line. She saw that the momentous occasion had come. It was the time of the critical battle. She turned upon him valorously. "Stop your swearin', George Kelcey. I won't have yeh talk so before me! I won't have it! Stop this minute! Not another word! Do yeh think I'll allow yeh t' swear b'fore me like that? Not another word! I won't have it! I declare I won't have it another minute!"

At first her projected words had slid from his mind as if striking against ice, but at last he heeded her. His face grew sour with passion and misery. He spoke in tones dark with dislike. "Th' 'ell yeh won't? Whatter yeh goin' t' do 'bout it?" Then, as if he considered that he had not been sufficiently impressive, he arose and slowly walked over to her. Having arrived at point-blank range he spoke again. "Whatter yeh goin' t' do 'bout it?" He regarded her then with an unaltering scowl, albeit his mien was as dark and cowering as that of a condemned criminal.

She threw out her hands in the gesture of an impotent one. He was acknowledged victor. He took his hat and slowly left her.

For three days they lived in silence. He brooded upon his mother's agony and felt a singular joy in it. As opportunity offered, he did little despicable things. He was going to make her abject. He was now uncontrolled, ungoverned; he wished to be an emperor. Her suffering was all a sort of compensation for his own dire pains.

She went about with a gray, impassive face. It was as if she had survived a massacre in which all that she loved had been torn from her by the brutality of savages.

One evening at six he entered and stood looking at his mother as she peeled potatoes. She had hearkened to his coming listlessly, without emotion, and at his entrance she did not raise her eyes.

"Well, I'm fired," he said, suddenly.

It seemed to be the final blow. Her body gave a convulsive movement in the chair. When she finally lifted her eyes, horror possessed her face. Her under jaw had fallen. "Fired? Outa work? Why—George?" He went over to the window and stood with his back to her. He could feel her gray stare upon him.

"Yep! Fired!"

At last she said, "Well—whatter yeh goin' t' do?"

He tapped the pane with his finger-nail. He answered in a tone made hoarse and unnatural by an assumption of gay carelessness, "Oh, nothin'!"

She began, then, her first weeping. "Oh—George—George—George——"

He looked at her scowling. "Ah, whatter yeh givin' us? Is this all I git when I come home f'm being fired? Anybody 'ud think it was my fault. I couldn't help it."

She continued to sob in a dull, shaking way. In the pose of her head there was an expression of her conviction that comprehension of her pain was impossible to the universe. He paused for a moment, and then, with his usual tactics, went out, slamming the door. A pale flood of sunlight, imperturbable at its vocation, streamed upon the little old woman, bowed with pain, forlorn in her chair.

XV

Kelcey was standing on the corner next day when three little boys came running. Two halted some distance away, and the other came forward. He halted before Kelcey, and spoke importantly.

"Hey, your ol' woman's sick."

"What?"

"Your ol' woman's sick."

"Git out!"

"She is, too!"

"Who tol' yeh?"

"Mis' Callahan. She said fer me t' run an' tell yeh. Dey want yeh."

A swift dread struck Kelcey. Like flashes of light little scenes from the past shot through his brain. He had thoughts of a vengeance from the clouds. As he glanced about him the familiar view assumed a meaning that was ominous and dark. There was prophecy of disaster in the street, the buildings, the sky, the people. Something tragic and terrible in the air was known to his nervous, quivering nostrils. He spoke to the little boy in a tone that quavered. "All right!"

Behind him he felt the sudden contemplative pause of his companions of the gang. They were watching him. As he went rapidly up the street he knew that they had come out to the middle of the walk and were staring after him. He was glad that they could not see his face, his trembling lips, his eyes wavering in fear. He stopped at the door of his home and stared at the panel as if he saw written thereon a word. A moment later he entered. His eye comprehended the room in a frightened glance.

His mother sat gazing out at the opposite walls and windows. She was leaning her head upon the back of the chair. Her face was overspread with a singular pallor, but the glance of her eyes was strong and the set of her lips was tranquil.

He felt an unspeakable thrill of thanksgiving at seeing her seated there calmly. "Why, mother, they said yeh was sick," he cried, going toward her impetuously. "What's th' matter?"

She smiled at him. "Oh, it ain't nothin'! I on'y got kinda dizzy, that's all." Her voice was sober and had the ring of vitality in it.

He noted her common-place air. There was no alarm or pain in her tones, but the misgivings of the street, the prophetic twinges of his nerves made him still hesitate. "Well—are you sure it ain't? They scared me 'bout t' death."

"No, it ain't anything, on'y some sorta dizzy feelin'. I fell down b'hind th' stove. Missis Callahan, she came an' picked me up. I must 'a laid there fer quite a while. Th' docter said he guessed I'd be all right in a couple 'a hours. I don't feel nothin'!"

Kelcey heaved a great sigh of relief. "Lord, I was scared." He began to beam joyously, since he was escaped from his fright. "Why, I couldn't think what had happened," he told her.

"Well, it ain't nothin'," she said.

He stood about awkwardly, keeping his eyes fastened upon her in a sort of surprise, as if he had expected to discover that she had vanished. The reaction from his panic was a thrill of delicious contentment. He took a chair and sat down near her, but presently he jumped up to ask: "There ain't nothin' I can git fer yeh, is ther?" He looked at her eagerly. In his eyes shone love and joy. If it were not for the shame of it he would have called her endearing names.

"No, ther ain't nothin'," she answered. Presently she continued, in a conversational way, "Yeh ain't found no work yit, have yeh?"

The shadow of his past fell upon him then and he became suddenly morose. At last he spoke in a sentence that was a vow, a declaration of change. "No, I ain't, but I'm goin' t' hunt fer it hard, you bet."

She understood from his tone that he was making peace with her. She smiled at him gladly. "Yer a good boy, George!" A radiance from the stars lit her face.

Presently she asked, "D' yeh think yer old boss would take yeh on ag'in if I went t' see him?"

"No," said Kelcey, at once. "It wouldn't do no good! They got all th' men they want. There ain't no room there. It wouldn't do no good." He ceased to beam for a moment as he thought of certain disclosures. "I'm goin' t' try to git work everywheres. I'm goin' t' make a wild break t' git a job, an' if there's one anywheres I'll git it."

She smiled at him again. "That's right, George!"

When it came supper-time he dragged her in her chair over to the table and then scurried to and fro to prepare a meal for her. She laughed gleefully at him. He was awkward and densely ignorant. He exaggerated his helplessness sometimes until she was obliged to lean back in her chair to laugh. Afterward they sat by the window. Her hand rested upon his hair.

XVI

When Kelcey went to borrow money from old Bleecker, Jones and the others, he discovered that he was below them in social position.

Old Bleecker said gloomily that he did not see how he could loan money at that time. When Jones asked him to have a drink, his tone was careless. O'Connor recited at length some bewildering financial troubles of his own. In them all he saw that something had been reversed. They remained silent upon many occasions, when they might have grunted in sympathy for him.

As he passed along the street near his home he perceived Fidsey Corcoran and another of the gang. They made eloquent signs. "Are yeh wid us?"

He stopped and looked at them. "What's wrong with yeh?"

"Are yeh wid us er not," demanded Fidsey. "New barkeep'! Big can! We got it over in d' lot. Big can, I tell yeh." He drew a picture in the air, so to speak, with his enthusiastic fingers.

Kelcey turned dejectedly homeward. "Oh, I guess not, this roun'."

"What's d' matter wi'che?" said Fidsey. "Yer gittin' t' be a reg'lar willie! Come ahn, I tell yeh! Youse gits one smoke at d' can b'cause yeh b'longs t' d' gang, an' yeh don't wanta give it up widout er scrap! See? Some udder john'll git yer smoke. Come ahn!"

When they arrived at the place among the bowlders in the vacant lot, one of the band had a huge and battered tin-pail tilted afar up. His throat worked convulsively. He was watched keenly and anxiously by five or six others. Their eyes followed carefully each fraction of distance that the pail was lifted. They were very silent.

Fidsey burst out violently as he perceived what was in progress. "Heh, Tim, yeh big sojer, le' go d' can! What 'a yeh tink! Wese er in dis! Le' go dat!"

He who was drinking made several angry protesting contortions of his throat. Then he put down the pail and swore. "Who's a big sojer? I ain't gittin' more'n me own smoke! Yer too bloomin' swift! Yeh'd tink yeh was d' on'y mug what owned dis can! Close yer face while I gits me smoke!"

He took breath for a moment and then returned the pail to its tilted position. Fidsey went to him and worried and clamored. He interfered so seriously with the action of drinking that the other was obliged to release the pail again for fear of choking.

Fidsey grabbed it and glanced swiftly at the contents. "Dere! Dat's what I was hollerin' at! Lookut d' beer! Not 'nough t' wet yer t'roat! Yehs can't have not'in' on d' level wid youse damn' tanks! Youse was a reg'lar resevoiy, Tim Connigan! Look what yeh lef' us! Ah, say, youse was a dandy! What 'a yeh tink we ah? Willies? Don' we want no smoke? Say, lookut dat can! It's drier'n hell! What 'a yeh tink?"

Tim glanced in at the beer. Then he said: "Well, d' mug what come b'fore me, he on'y lef' me dat much. Blue Billee, he done d' swallerin'! I on'y had a tas'e!"

Blue Billie, from his seat near, called out in wrathful protest: "Yeh lie, Tim. I never had more'n a mouf-ful!" An inspiration evidently came to him then, for his countenance suddenly brightened, and, arising, he went toward the pail. "I ain't had me reg'lar smoke yit! Guess I come in aheader Fidsey, don' I?"

Fidsey, with a sardonic smile, swung the pail behind him. "I guess nit! Not dis minnet! Youse hadger smoke. If yeh ain't, yeh don't git none. See?"

Blue Billie confronted Fidsey determinedly. "D' 'ell I don't!"

"Nit," said Fidsey.

Billie sat down again.

Fidsey drank his portion. Then he manœuvred skilfully before the crowd until Kelcey and the other youth took their shares. "Youse er a mob 'a tanks," he told the gang. "Nobody 'ud git not'in' if dey wasn't on t' yehs!"

Blue Billie's soul had been smouldering in hate against Fidsey. "Ah, shut up! Youse ain't gota take care 'a dose two mugs, dough. Youse hadger smoke, ain't yeh? Den yer tr'u. G' home!"

"Well, I hate t' see er bloke use 'imself fer a tank," said Fidsey. "But youse don't wanta go jollyin' 'round 'bout d' can, Blue, er youse'll git done."

"Who'll do me?" demanded Blue Billie, casting his eye about him.

"Kel' will," said Fidsey, bravely.

"D' 'ell he will?"

"Dat's what he will!"

Blue Billie made the gesture of a warrior. "He never saw d' day 'a his life dat he could do me little finger. If 'e says much t' me, I'll push 'is face all over d' lot."

Fidsey called to Kelcey. "Say, Kel, hear what dis mug is chewin'?"

Kelcey was apparently deep in other matters. His back was half-turned.

Blue Billie spoke to Fidsey in a battleful voice. "Did 'e ever say 'e could do me?"

Fidsey said: "Soitenly 'e did. Youse is dead easy, 'e says. He says he kin punch holes in you, Blue!"

"When did 'e say it?"

"Oh—any time. Youse is a cinch, Kel' says."

Blue Billie walked over to Kelcey. The others of the band followed him exchanging joyful glances.

"Did youse say yeh could do me?"

Kelcey slowly turned, but he kept his eyes upon the ground. He heard Fidsey darting among the others telling of his prowess, preparing them for the downfall of Blue Billie. He stood heavily on one foot and moved his hands nervously. Finally he said, in a low growl, "Well, what if I did?"

The sentence sent a happy thrill through the band. It was the formidable question. Blue Billie braced himself. Upon him came the responsibility of the next step. The gang fell back a little upon all sides. They looked expectantly at Blue Billie.

He walked forward with a deliberate step until his face was close to Kelcey.

"Well, if you did," he said, with a snarl between his teeth, "I'm goin' t' t'ump d' life outa yeh right heh!"

A little boy, wild of eye and puffing, came down the slope as from an explosion. He burst out in a rapid treble, "Is dat Kelcey feller here? Say, yeh ol' woman's sick again. Dey want yeh! Yehs better run! She's awful sick!"

The gang turned with loud growls. "Ah, git outa here!" Fidsey threw a stone at the little boy and chased him a short distance, but he continued to clamor, "Youse better come, Kelcey feller! She's awful sick! She was hollerin'! Dey been lookin' fer yeh over'n hour!" In his eagerness he returned part way, regardless of Fidsey!

Kelcey had moved away from Blue Billie. He said: "I guess I'd better go!" They howled at him. "Well," he continued, "I can't—I don't wanta—I don't wanta leave me mother be—she—"

His words were drowned in the chorus of their derision. "Well, lookahere"—he would begin and at each time their cries and screams ascended. They dragged at Blue Billie. "Go fer 'im, Blue! Slug 'im! Go ahn!"

Kelcey went slowly away while they were urging Blue Billie to do a decisive thing. Billie stood fuming and blustering and explaining himself. When Kelcey had achieved a considerable distance from him, he stepped forward a few paces and hurled a terrible oath. Kelcey looked back darkly.

XVII

When he entered the chamber of death, he was brooding over the recent encounter and devising extravagant revenges upon Blue Billie and the others.

The little old woman was stretched upon her bed. Her face and hands were of the hue of the blankets. Her hair, seemingly of a new and wondrous grayness, hung over her temples in whips and tangles. She was sickeningly motionless, save for her eyes, which rolled and swayed in maniacal glances.

A young doctor had just been administering medicine. "There," he said, with a great satisfaction, "I guess that'll do her good!" As he went briskly toward the door he met Kelcey. "Oh," he said. "Son?"

Kelcey had that in his throat which was like fur. When he forced his voice, the words came first low and then high as if they had broken through something. "Will she—will she——"

The doctor glanced back at the bed. She was watching them as she would have watched ghouls, and muttering. "Can't tell," he said. "She's wonderful woman! Got more vitality than you and I together! Can't tell! May—may not! Good-day! Back in two hours."

In the kitchen Mrs. Callahan was feverishly dusting the furniture, polishing this and that. She arranged everything in decorous rows. She was preparing for the coming of death. She looked at the floor as if she longed to scrub it.

The doctor paused to speak in an undertone to her, glancing at the bed. When he departed she labored with a renewed speed.

Kelcey approached his mother. From a little distance he called to her. "Mother—mother——" He proceeded with caution lest this mystic being upon the bed should clutch at him.

"Mother—mother—don't yeh know me?" He put forth apprehensive, shaking fingers and touched her hand.

There were two brilliant steel-colored points upon her eyeballs. She was staring off at something sinister.

Suddenly she turned to her son in a wild babbling appeal. "Help me! Help me! Oh, help me! I see them coming."

Kelcey called to her as to a distant place. "Mother! Mother!" She looked at him, and then there began within her a struggle to reach him with her mind. She fought with some implacable power whose fingers were in her brain. She called to Kelcey in stammering, incoherent cries for help.

Then she again looked away. "Ah, there they come! There they come! Ah, look—look—loo—" She arose to a sitting posture without the use of her arms.

Kelcey felt himself being choked. When her voice pealed forth in a scream he saw crimson curtains moving before his eyes. "Mother—oh, mother—there's nothin'—there's nothin'——"

She was at a kitchen-door with a dish-cloth in her hand. Within there had just been a clatter of crockery. Down through the trees of the orchard she could see a man in a field ploughing. "Bill—o-o-oh, Bill—have yeh seen Georgie? Is he out there with you? Georgie! Georgie! Come right here this minnet! Right—this—minnet!"

She began to talk to some people in the room. "I want t' know what yeh want here! I want yeh t' git out! I don't want yeh here! I don't feel good t'-day, an' I don't want yeh here! I don't feel good t'-day! I want yeh t' git out!" Her voice became peevish. "Go away! Go away! Go away!"

Kelcey lay in a chair. His nerveless arms allowed his fingers to sweep the floor. He became so that he could not hear the chatter from the bed, but he was always conscious of the ticking of the little clock out on the kitchen shelf.

When he aroused, the pale-faced but plump young clergyman was before him.

"My poor lad——" began this latter.

The little old woman lay still with her eyes closed. On the table at the head of the bed was a glass containing a water-like medicine. The reflected lights made a silver star on its side. The two men sat side by side, waiting. Out in the kitchen Mrs. Callahan had taken a chair by the stove and was waiting.

Kelcey began to stare at the wall-paper. The pattern was clusters of brown roses. He felt them like hideous crabs crawling upon his brain.

Through the door-way he saw the oil-cloth covering of the table catching a glimmer from the warm afternoon sun. The window disclosed a fair, soft sky, like blue enamel, and a fringe of chimneys and roofs, resplendent here and there. An endless roar, the eternal trample of the marching city, came mingled with vague cries. At intervals the woman out by the stove moved restlessly and coughed.

Over the transom from the hall-way came two voices.

"Johnnie!"

"Wot!"

"You come right here t' me! I want yehs t' go t' d' store fer me!"

"Ah, ma, send Sally!"

"No, I will not! You come right here!"

"All right, in a minnet!"

"Johnnie!"

"In a minnet, I tell yeh!"

"Johnnie——" There was the sound of a heavy tread, and later a boy squealed. Suddenly the clergyman started to his feet. He rushed forward and peered. The little old woman was dead.

NEW YORK TALES AND SKETCHES

A Great Mistake

An Italian kept a fruit-stand on a corner where he had good aim at the people who came down from the elevated station, and at those who went along two thronged streets. He sat most of the day in a backless chair that was placed strategically.

There was a babe living hard by, up five flights of stairs, who regarded this Italian as a tremendous being. The babe had investigated this fruit-stand. It had thrilled him as few things he had met with in his travels had thrilled him. The sweets of the world had laid there in dazzling rows, tumbled in luxurious heaps. When he gazed at this Italian seated amid such splendid treasures, his lower lip hung low and his eyes, raised to the vendor's face, were filled with deep respect, worship, as if he saw omnipotence.

The babe came often to this corner. He hovered about the stand and watched each detail of the business. He was fascinated by the tranquillity of the vendor, the majesty of power and possession. At times he was so engrossed in his contemplation that people, hurrying, had to use care to avoid bumping him down.

He had never ventured very near to the stand. It was his habit to hang warily about the curb. Even there he resembled a babe who looks unbidden at a feast of gods.

One day, however, as the baby was thus staring, the vendor arose, and going along the front of the stand, began to polish oranges with a red pocket handkerchief. The breathless spectator moved across the sidewalk until his small face almost touched the vendor's sleeve. His fingers were gripped in a fold of his dress.

At last, the Italian finished with the oranges and returned to his chair. He drew a newspaper printed in his language from behind a bunch of bananas. He settled himself in a comfortable position, and began to glare savagely at the print. The babe was left face to face with the massed joys of the world. For a time he was a simple worshipper at this golden shrine. Then tumultuous desires began to shake him. His dreams were of conquest. His lips moved. Presently into his head there came a little plan. He sidled nearer, throwing swift and cunning glances at the Italian. He strove to maintain his conventional manner, but the whole plot was written upon his countenance.

At last he had come near enough to touch the fruit. From the tattered skirt came slowly his small dirty hand. His eyes were still fixed upon the vendor. His features were set, save for the under lip, which had a faint fluttering movement. The hand went forward.

Elevated trains thundered to the station and the stairway poured people upon the sidewalks. There was a deep sea roar from feet and wheels going ceaselessly. None seemed to perceive the babe engaged in a great venture.

The Italian turned his paper. Sudden panic smote the babe. His hand dropped, and he gave vent to a cry of dismay. He remained for a moment staring at the vendor. There was evidently a great debate in his mind. His infant intellect had defined this Italian. The latter was undoubtedly a man who would eat babes that provoked him. And the alarm in the babe when this monarch had turned his newspaper brought vividly before him the consequences if he were detected. But at this moment the vendor gave a blissful grunt, and tilting his chair against a wall, closed his eyes. His paper dropped unheeded.

The babe ceased his scrutiny and again raised his hand. It was moved with supreme caution toward the fruit. The fingers were bent, claw-like, in the manner of great heart-shaking greed. Once he stopped and chattered convulsively, because the vendor moved in his sleep. The babe, with his eyes still upon the Italian, again put forth his hand, and the rapacious fingers closed over a round bulb.

And it was written that the Italian should at this moment open his eyes. He glared at the babe a fierce question. Thereupon the babe thrust the round bulb behind him, and with a face expressive of the deepest guilt, began a wild but elaborate series of gestures declaring his innocence. The Italian howled. He sprang to his feet, and with three steps overtook the babe. He whirled him fiercely, and took from the little fingers a lemon.

An Ominous Baby

A baby was wandering in a strange country. He was a tattered child with a frowsled wealth of yellow hair. His dress, of a checked stuff, was soiled and showed the marks of many conflicts like the chain-shirt of a warrior. His sun-tanned knees shone above wrinkled stockings which he pulled up occasionally with an impatient movement when they entangled his feet. From a gaping shoe there appeared an array of tiny toes.

He was toddling along an avenue between rows of stolid, brown houses. He went slowly, with a look of absorbed interest on his small, flushed face. His blue eyes stared curiously. Carriages went with a musical rumble over the smooth asphalt. A man with a chrysanthemum was going up steps. Two nursery-maids chatted as they walked slowly, while their charges hobnobbed amiably between perambulators. A truck wagon roared thunderously in the distance.

The child from the poor district made way along the brown street filled with dull gray shadows. High up, near the roofs, glancing sunrays changed cornices to blazing gold and silvered the fronts of windows. The wandering baby stopped and stared at the two children laughing and playing in their carriages among the heaps of rugs and cushions. He braced his legs apart in an attitude of earnest attention. His lower jaw fell and disclosed his small, even teeth. As they moved on, he followed the carriages with awe in his face as if contemplating a pageant. Once one of the babies, with twittering laughter, shook a gorgeous rattle at him. He smiled jovially in return.

Finally a nursery-maid ceased conversation and, turning, made a gesture of annoyance.

"Go 'way, little boy," she said to him. "Go 'way. You're all dirty."

He gazed at her with infant tranquillity for a moment and then went slowly off, dragging behind him a bit of rope he had acquired in another street. He continued to investigate the new scenes. The people and houses struck him with interest as would flowers and trees. Passengers had to avoid the small, absorbed figure in the middle of the sidewalk. They glanced at the intent baby face covered with scratches and dust as with scars and powder smoke.

After a time, the wanderer discovered upon the pavement, a pretty child in fine clothes playing with a toy. It was a tiny fire engine painted brilliantly in crimson and gold. The wheels rattled as its small owner dragged it uproariously about by means of a string. The babe with his bit of rope trailing behind him paused and regarded the child and the toy. For a long while he remained motionless, save for his eyes, which followed all movements of the glittering thing.

The owner paid no attention to the spectator but continued his joyous imitations of phases of the career of a fire engine. His gleeful baby laugh rang against the calm fronts of the houses. After a little, the wandering baby began quietly to sidle nearer. His bit of rope, now forgotten, dropped at his feet. He removed his eyes from the toy and glanced expectantly at the other child.

"Say," he breathed, softly.

The owner of the toy was running down the walk at top speed. His tongue was clanging like a bell and his legs were galloping. An iron post on the corner was all ablaze. He did not look around at the coaxing call from the small, tattered figure on the curb.

The wandering baby approached still nearer and, presently, spoke again. "Say," he murmured, "le' me play wif it?"

The other child interrupted some shrill tootings. He bended his head and spoke disdainfully over his shoulder.

"No," he said.

The wanderer retreated to the curb. He failed to notice the bit of rope, once treasured. His eyes followed as before the winding course of the engine, and his tender mouth twitched.

"Say," he ventured at last, "is dat yours?"

"Yes," said the other, tilting his round chin. He drew his property suddenly behind him as if it were menaced. "Yes," he repeated, "it's mine."

"Well, le' me play wif it?" said the wandering baby, with a trembling note of desire in his voice.

"No," cried the pretty child with determined lips. "It's mine! My ma-ma buyed it."

"Well, tan't I play wif it?" His voice was a sob. He stretched forth little, covetous hands.

"No," the pretty child continued to repeat. "No, it's mine."

"Well, I want to play wif it," wailed the other. A sudden, fierce frown mantled his baby face. He clenched his thin hands and advanced with a formidable gesture. He looked some wee battler in a war.

"It's mine! It's mine," cried the pretty child, his voice in the treble of outraged rights.

"I want it," roared the wanderer.

"It's mine! It's mine!"

"I want it!"

"It's mine!"

The pretty child retreated to the fence, and there paused at bay. He protected his property with outstretched arms. The small vandal made a charge. There was a short scuffle at the fence. Each grasped the string to the toy and tugged. Their faces were wrinkled with baby rage, the verge of tears.

Finally, the child in tatters gave a supreme tug and wrenched the string from the other's hands. He set off rapidly down the street, bearing the toy in his arms. He was weeping with the air of a wronged one who has at last succeeded in achieving his rights. The other baby was squalling lustily. He seemed quite helpless. He wrung his chubby hands and railed.

After the small barbarian had got some distance away, he paused and regarded his booty. His little form curved with pride. A soft, gleeful smile loomed through the storm of tears. With great care, he prepared the toy for travelling. He stopped a moment on a corner and gazed at the pretty child whose small figure was quivering with sobs. As the latter began to show signs of beginning pursuit, the little vandal turned and vanished down a dark side street as into a swallowing cavern.

A Dark-Brown Dog

A child was standing on a street-corner. He leaned with one shoulder against a high board-fence and swayed the other to and fro, the while kicking carelessly at the gravel.

Sunshine beat upon the cobbles, and a lazy summer wind raised yellow dust which trailed in clouds down the avenue. Clattering trucks moved with indistinctness through it. The child stood dreamily gazing.

After a time, a little dark-brown dog came trotting with an intent air down the sidewalk. A short rope was dragging from his neck. Occasionally he trod upon the end of it and stumbled.

He stopped opposite the child, and the two regarded each other. The dog hesitated for a moment, but presently he made some little advances with his tail. The child put out his hand and called him. In an apologetic manner the dog came close, and the two had an interchange of friendly pattings and waggles. The dog became more enthusiastic with each moment of the interview, until with his gleeful caperings he threatened to overturn the child. Whereupon the child lifted his hand and struck the dog a blow upon the head.

This thing seemed to overpower and astonish the little dark-brown dog, and wounded him to the heart. He sank down in despair at the child's feet. When the blow was repeated, together with an admonition in childish sentences, he turned over upon his back, and held his paws in a peculiar manner. At the same time with his ears and his eyes he offered a small prayer to the child.

He looked so comical on his back, and holding his paws peculiarly, that the child was greatly amused and gave him little taps repeatedly, to keep him so. But the little dark-brown dog took this chastisement in the most serious way, and no doubt considered that he had committed some grave crime, for he wriggled contritely and showed his repentance in every way that was in his power. He pleaded with the child and petitioned him, and offered more prayers.

At last the child grew weary of this amusement and turned toward home. The dog was praying at the time. He lay on his back and turned his eyes upon the retreating form.

Presently he struggled to his feet and started after the child. The latter wandered in a perfunctory way toward his home, stopping at times to investigate various matters. During one of these pauses he discovered the little dark-brown dog who was following him with the air of a footpad.

The child beat his pursuer with a small stick he had found. The dog lay down and prayed until the child had finished, and resumed his journey. Then he scrambled erect and took up the pursuit again.

On the way to his home the child turned many times and beat the dog, proclaiming with childish gestures that he held him in contempt as an unimportant dog, with no value save for a moment. For being this quality of animal the dog apologized and eloquently expressed regret, but he continued stealthily to follow the child. His manner grew so very guilty that he slunk like an assassin.

When the child reached his door-step, the dog was industriously ambling a few yards in the rear. He became so agitated with shame when he again confronted the child that he forgot the dragging rope. He tripped upon it and fell forward.

The child sat down on the step and the two had another interview. During it the dog greatly exerted himself to please the child. He performed a few gambols with such abandon that the child suddenly saw him to be a valuable thing. He made a swift, avaricious charge and seized the rope.

He dragged his captive into a hall and up many long stairways in a dark tenement. The dog made willing efforts, but he could not hobble very skillfully up the stairs because he was very small and soft, and at last the pace of the engrossed child grew so energetic that the dog became panic-stricken. In his mind he was being dragged toward a grim unknown. His eyes grew wild with the terror of it. He began to wiggle his head frantically and to brace his legs.

The child redoubled his exertions. They had a battle on the stairs. The child was victorious because he was completely absorbed in his purpose, and because the dog was very small. He dragged his acquirement to the door of his home, and finally with triumph across the threshold.

No one was in. The child sat down on the floor and made overtures to the dog. These the dog instantly accepted. He beamed with affection upon his new friend. In a short time they were firm and abiding comrades.

When the child's family appeared, they made a great row. The dog was examined and commented upon and called names. Scorn was leveled at him from all eyes, so that he became much embarrassed and dropped like a scorched plant. But the child went sturdily to the center of the floor, and, at the top of his voice, championed the dog. It happened that he was roaring protestations, with his arms clasped about the dog's neck, when the father of the family came in from work.

The parent demanded to know what the blazes they were making the kid howl for. It was explained in many words that the infernal kid wanted to introduce a disreputable dog into the family.

A family council was held. On this depended the dog's fate, but he in no way heeded, being busily engaged in chewing the end of the child's dress.

The affair was quickly ended. The father of the family, it appears, was in a particularly savage temper that evening, and when he perceived that it would amaze and anger everybody if such a dog were allowed to remain, he decided that it should be so. The child, crying softly, took his friend off to a retired part of the room to hobnob with him, while the father quelled a fierce rebellion of his wife. So it came to pass that the dog was a member of the household.

He and the child were associated together at all times save when the child slept. The child became a guardian and a friend. If the large folk kicked the dog and threw things at him, the child made loud and violent objections. Once when the child had run, protesting loudly, with tears raining down his face and his arms outstretched, to protect his friend, he had been struck in the head with a very large saucepan from the hand of his father, enraged at some seeming lack of courtesy in the dog. Ever after, the family were careful how they threw things at the dog. Moreover, the latter grew very skilful in avoiding missiles and feet. In a small room containing a stove, a table, a bureau and some chairs, he would display strategic ability of a high order, dodging, feinting and scuttling about among the furniture. He could force three or four people armed with brooms, sticks and handfuls of coal, to use all their ingenuity to get in a blow. And even when they did, it was seldom that they could do him a serious injury or leave any imprint.

But when the child was present, these scenes did not occur. It came to be recognized that if the dog was molested, the child would burst into sobs, and as the child, when started, was very riotous and practically unquenchable, the dog had therein a safeguard.

However, the child could not always be near. At night, when he was asleep, his dark-brown friend would raise from some black corner a wild, wailful cry, a song of infinite lowliness and despair, that would go shuddering and sobbing among the buildings of the block and cause people to swear. At these times the singer would often be chased all over the kitchen and hit with a great variety of articles.

Sometimes, too, the child himself used to beat the dog, although it is not known that he ever had what could be truly called a just cause. The dog always accepted these thrashings with an air of admitted guilt. He was too much of a dog to try to look to be a martyr or to plot revenge. He received the blows with deep humility, and furthermore he forgave his friend the moment the child had finished, and was ready to caress the child's hand with his little red tongue.

When misfortune came upon the child, and his troubles overwhelmed him, he would often crawl under the table and lay his small distressed head on the dog's back. The dog was ever sympathetic. It is not to be supposed that at such times he took occasion to refer to the unjust beatings his friend, when provoked, had administered to him.

He did not achieve any notable degree of intimacy with the other members of the family. He had no confidence in them, and the fear that he would express at their casual approach often exasperated them exceedingly. They used to gain a certain satisfaction in underfeeding him, but finally his friend the child grew to watch the matter with some care, and when he forgot it, the dog was often successful in secret for himself.

So the dog prospered. He developed a large bark, which came wondrously from such a small rug of a dog. He ceased to howl persistently at night. Sometimes, indeed, in his sleep, he would utter little yells, as from pain, but that occurred, no doubt, when in his dreams he encountered huge flaming dogs who threatened him direfully.

His devotion to the child grew until it was a sublime thing. He wagged at his approach; he sank down in despair at his departure. He could detect the sound of the child's step among all the noises of the neighborhood. It was like a calling voice to him.

The scene of their companionship was a kingdom governed by this terrible potentate, the child; but neither criticism nor rebellion ever lived for an instant in the heart of the one subject. Down in the mystic, hidden fields of his little dog-soul bloomed flowers of love and fidelity and perfect faith.

The child was in the habit of going on many expeditions to observe strange things in the vicinity. On these occasions his friend usually jogged aimfully along behind. Perhaps, though, he went ahead. This necessitated his turning around every quarter-minute to make sure the child was coming. He was filled with a large idea of the importance of these journeys. He would carry himself with such an air! He was proud to be the retainer of so great a monarch.

One day, however, the father of the family got quite exceptionally drunk. He came home and held carnival with the cooking utensils, the furniture and his wife. He was in the midst of this recreation when the child, followed by the dark-brown dog, entered the room. They were returning from their voyages.

The child's practised eye instantly noted his father's state. He dived under the table, where experience had taught him was a rather safe place. The dog, lacking skill in such matters, was, of course, unaware of the true condition of affairs. He looked with interested eyes at his friend's sudden dive. He interpreted it to mean: Joyous gambol. He started to patter across the floor to join him. He was the picture of a little dark-brown dog en route to a friend.

The head of the family saw him at this moment. He gave a huge howl of joy, and knocked the dog down with a heavy coffee-pot. The dog, yelling in supreme astonishment and fear, writhed to his feet and ran for cover. The man kicked out with a ponderous foot. It caused the dog to swerve as if caught in a tide. A second blow of the coffee-pot laid him upon the floor.

Here the child, uttering loud cries, came valiantly forth like a knight. The father of the family paid no attention to these calls of the child, but advanced with glee upon the dog. Upon being knocked down twice in swift succession, the latter apparently gave up all hope of escape. He rolled over on his back and held his paws in a peculiar manner. At the same time with his eyes and his ears he offered up a small prayer.

But the father was in a mood for having fun, and it occurred to him that it would be a fine thing to throw the dog out of the window. So he reached down and grabbing the animal by a leg, lifted him, squirming, up. He swung him two or three times hilariously about his head, and then flung him with great accuracy through the window.

The soaring dog created a surprise in the block. A woman watering plants in an opposite window gave an involuntary shout and dropped a flower-pot. A man in another window leaned perilously out to watch the flight of the dog. A woman, who had been hanging out clothes in a yard, began to caper wildly. Her mouth was filled with clothes-pins, but her arms gave vent to a sort of exclamation. In appearance she was like a gagged prisoner. Children ran whooping.

The dark-brown body crashed in a heap on the roof of a shed five stories below. From thence it rolled to the pavement of an alleyway.

The child in the room far above burst into a long, dirgelike cry, and toddled hastily out of the room. It took him a long time to reach the alley, because his size compelled him to go downstairs backward, one step at a time, and holding with both hands to the step above.

When they came for him later, they found him seated by the body of his dark-brown friend.

The Broken-Down Van

The gas lamps had just been lit and the two great red furniture vans with impossible landscapes on their sides rolled and plunged slowly along the street. Each was drawn by four horses, and each almost touched the roaring elevated road above. They were on the uptown track of the surface road—indeed the street was so narrow that they must be on one track or the other.

They tossed and pitched and proceeded slowly, and a horse car with a red light came up behind. The car was red, and the bullseye light was red, and the driver's hair was red. He blew his whistle shrilly and slapped the horse's lines impatiently. Then he whistled again. Then he pounded on the red dash board with his car-hook till the red light trembled. Then a car with a green light crept up behind the car with the red light; and the green driver blew his whistle and pounded on his dash board; and the conductor of the red car seized his strap from his position on the rear platform and rung such a rattling tattoo on the gong over the red driver's head that the red driver became frantic and stood up on his toes and puffed out his cheeks as if he were playing the trombone in a German streetband and blew his whistle till an imaginative person could see slivers flying from it, and pounded his red dash board till the metal was dented in and the car-hook was bent. And just as the driver of a newly-come car with a blue light began to blow his whistle and pound his dash board and the green conductor began to ring his bell like a demon which drove the green driver mad and made him rise up and blow and pound as no man ever blew or pounded before, which made the red conductor lose the last vestige of control of himself and caused him to bounce up and down on his bell strap as he grasped it with both hands in a wild, maniacal dance, which of course served to drive uncertain Reason from her tottering throne in the red driver, who dropped his whistle and his hook and began to yell, and ki-yi, and whoop harder than the worst personal devil encountered by the sternest of Scotch Presbyterians ever yelled and ki-yied and whooped on the darkest night after the good man had drunk the most hot Scotch whiskey; just then the left-hand forward wheel on the rear van fell off and the axle went down. The van gave a mighty lurch and then swayed and rolled and rocked and stopped; the red driver applied his brake with a jerk and his horses turned out to keep from being crushed between car and van; the other drivers applied their brakes with a jerk and their horses turned out; the two cliff-dwelling men on the shelf half-way up the front of the stranded van began to shout loudly to their brother cliff-dwellers on the forward van; a girl, six years old, with a pail of beer crossed under the red car horses' necks; a boy, eight years old, mounted the red car with the sporting extras of the evening papers; a girl, ten years old, went in front of the van horses with two pails of beer; an unclassified boy poked his finger in the black grease in the hub of the right-hand hind van wheel and began to print his name on the red landscape on the van's side; a boy with a little head and big ears examined the white rings on the martingales of the van leaders with a view of stealing them in the confusion; a sixteen-year-old girl without any hat and with a roll of half-finished vests under her arm crossed the front platform of the green car. As she stepped up on to the sidewalk a barber from a ten-cent shop said "Ah! there!" and she answered "smarty!" with withering scorn and went down a side street. A few drops of warm summer rain began to fall.

Well, the van was wrecked and something had got to be done. It was on the busiest car track on Manhattan Island. The cliff-dwellers got down in some mysterious way—probably on a rope ladder. Their brethren drove their van down a side street and came back to see what was the matter.

"The nut is off," said the captain of the wrecked van.

"Yes," said the first mate, "the nut is off."

"Hah," said the captain of the other van, "the nut is off."

"Yer right," said his first mate, "the nut is off."

The driver of the red car came up, hot and irritated. But he had regained his reason. "The nut is off," he said.

The drivers of the green and of the blue car came along. "The nut," they said in chorus, "is off."

The red, green and blue conductors came forward. They examined the situation carefully as became men occupying a higher position. Then they made this report through the chairman, the red conductor:

"The nut is gone."

"Yes," said the driver of the crippled van, who had spoken first, "yes, the damned nut is lost."

Then the driver of the other van swore, and the two assistants swore, and the three car drivers swore and the three car conductors used some polite but profane expressions. Then a strange man, an unknown man and an outsider, with his trousers held up by a trunk-strap, who stood at hand, swore harder than any of the rest. The others turned and looked at him inquiringly and savagely. The man wriggled nervously.

"You wanter tie it up," he said at last.

"Wot yo' goin' to tie it to, you cussed fool?" asked the assistant of the head van scornfully, "a berloon?"

"Ha, ha!" laughed the others.

"Some folks make me tired," said the second van driver.

"Go and lose yourself with the nut," said the red conductor, severely.

"That's it," said the others. "Git out, 'fore we t'row you out."

The officiously profane stranger slunk away.

The crisis always produces the man.

In this crisis the man was the first van driver.

"Bill," said the first van driver, "git some candles." Bill vanished.

A car with a white light, a car with a white and red light, a car with a white light and a green bar across it, a car with a blue light and a white circle around it, another car with a red bullseye light and one with a red flat light had come up and stopped. More were coming to extend the long line. The elevated trains thundered overhead, and made the street tremble. A dozen horse cars went down on the other track, and the drivers made derisive noises, rather than speaking derisive words at their brother van-bound drivers. Each delayed car was full of passengers, and they craned their necks and peppery old gentlemen inquired what the trouble was, and a happy individual who had been to Coney Island began to sing.

Trucks, mail-wagons and evening paper carts crowded past. A jam was imminent. A Chatham Square cab fought its way along with a man inside wearing a diamond like an arc-light. A hundred people stopped on either sidewalk; ten per cent of them whistled "Boom-de-ay." A half dozen small boys managed to just miss being killed by passing teams. Four Jews looked out of four different pawnshops. Pullers-in for three clothing stores were alert. The ten-cent barber eyed a Division-st. girl who was a millinery puller-in and who was chewing gum with an earnest, almost fierce, motion of the jaw. The ever-forward flowing tide of the growlers flowed on. The men searched under the slanting rays of the electric light for the lost nut, back past a dozen cars; scattering drops of rain continued to fall and a hand-organ came up and began an overture.

Just then Bill rose up from somewhere with four candles. The leader lit them and each van man took one and they continued the search for the nut. The humorous driver on a blue car asked them why they didn't get a fire-fly; the equally playful driver of a white car advised them of the fact that the moon would be up in the course of two or three hours. Then a gust of wind came and blew out the candles. The hand-organ man played on. A dozen newsboys arrived with evening paper extras about the Presidential nomination. The passengers bought the extras and found that they contained nothing new. A man with a stock of suspenders on his arm began to look into the trade situation. He might have made a sale to the profane man with the trunk-strap but he had disappeared. The leader again asserted himself.

"Bill," he shouted, "you git a lager beer-keg." Bill was gone in an instant.

"Jim," continued the leader, in a loud voice, as if Jim were up at the sharp end of the mainmast and the leader was on the deck, "Jim, unhitch them hosses and take out the pole."

Jim started to obey orders. A policeman came and walked around the van, looked at the prostrated wheel, started to say something, concluded not to, made the hand-organ man move on, and then went to the edge of the sidewalk and began talking to the Division-st. girl with the gum, to the infinite disgust of the cheap barber. The trunk-strap man came out of a restaurant with a sign of "Breakfast, 13 cents; Dinner, 15 cents," where he had been hidden and slunk into the liquor store next door with a sign of "Hot spiced rum, 6 cents; Sherry with a Big Egg in it, 5 cents." At the door he almost stepped on a small boy with a pitcher of beer so big that he had to set it down and rest every half block.

Bill was now back with the keg. "Set it right there," said the leader. "Now you, Jim, sock that pole under the axle and we'll h'ist 'er up and put the keg under."

One of the horses began kicking the front of the van. "Here, there!" shouted the leader and the horse subsided. "Six or seven o' you fellers git under that pole," commanded the leader, and he was obeyed. "Now all together!" The axle slowly rose and Bill slipped under the chime of the keg. But it was not high enough to allow the wheel to go on. "Git a paving block," commanded the leader to Bill. Just then a truck loaded with great, noisy straps of iron tried to pass. The wheels followed the car track too long, the truck struck the rear of the van and the axle went down with a crash while the keg rolled away into the gutter. Even great leaders lose their self-control sometimes; Washington swore at the Battle of Long Island; so this van leader now swore. His language was plain and scandalous. The truckman offered to lick the van man till he couldn't walk. He stopped his horses to get down to do it. But the policeman left the girl and came and made the truckman give over his warlike movement, much to the disgust of the crowd. Then he punched the suspender man in the back with the end of his club and went back to the girl. But the second delay was too much for the driver of the green car, and he turned out his horses and threw his car from the track. It pitched like a skiff in the swell of a steamer. It staggered and rocked and as it went past the van plunged into the gutter and made the crowd stand back, but the horses strained themselves and finally brought it up and at last it blundered on to its track and rolled away at a furious rate with the faces of the passengers wreathed in smiles and the conductor looking proudly back. Two other cars followed the example of the green and went lumbering past on the stones.

"Tell them fellers we'll be out of their way now in a minute," said the leader to the red conductor. Bill had arrived with the paving block. "Up with 'er, now," called the leader. The axle went up again and the keg with the stone on top of it went under. The leader seized the wheel himself and slipped it on "Hitch on them hosses!" he commanded, and it was done. "Now pull slow there, Bill," and Bill pulled slow. The great red car with the impossible landscape gave a preliminary rock and roll, the wheel which had made the trouble dropped down an inch or two from the keg and the van moved slowly forward. There was nothing to hold the wheel on and the leader walked close to it and watched it anxiously. But it stayed on to the corner, and around the corner, and into the side street. The red driver gave a triumphant ki-yi and his horses plunged forward in their collars eagerly. The other drivers gave glad ki-yis and the other horses plunged ahead. Twenty cars rolled past at a fast gait. "Now, youse fellys, move on!" said the policeman, and the crowd broke up. The cheap barber was talking to a girl with one black eye, but he retreated to his shop with the sign which promised "bay rum and a clean towel to every customer." Inside the liquor store the trunk-strap man was telling a man with his sleeves rolled up how two good men could have put their shoulders under the van and h'isted it up while a ten-year-old boy put on the wheel.

An Experiment in Misery

It was late at night, and a fine rain was swirling softly down, causing the pavements to glisten with hue of steel and blue and yellow in the rays of the innumerable lights. A youth was trudging slowly, without enthusiasm, with his hands buried deep in his trousers' pockets, toward the downtown places where beds can be hired for coppers. He was clothed in an aged and tattered suit, and his derby was a marvel of dust-covered crown and torn rim. He was going forth to eat as the wanderer may eat, and sleep as the homeless sleep. By the time he had reached City Hall Park he was so completely plastered with yells of "bum" and "hobo," and with various unholy epithets that small boys had applied to him at intervals, that he was in a state of the most profound dejection. The sifting rain saturated the old velvet collar of his overcoat, and as the wet cloth pressed against his neck, he felt that there no longer could be pleasure in life. He looked about him searching for an outcast of highest degree that the two might share miseries. But the lights threw a quivering glare over rows and circles of deserted benches that glistened damply, showing patches of wet sod behind them. It seemed that their usual freights had fled on this night to better things. There were only squads of well-dressed Brooklyn people who swarmed toward the Bridge.

The young man loitered about for a time and then went shuffling off down Park Row. In the sudden descent in style of the dress of the crowd he felt relief, and as if he were at last in his own country. He began to see tatters that matched his tatters. In Chatham Square there were aimless men strewn in front of saloons and lodging houses, standing sadly, patiently, reminding one vaguely of the attitudes of chickens in a storm. He aligned himself with these men, and turned slowly to occupy himself with the flowing life of the great street.

Through the mists of the cold and storming night, the cable cars went in silent procession, great affairs shining with red and brass, moving with formidable power, calm and irresistible, dangerful and gloomy, breaking silence only by the loud fierce cry of the gong. Two rivers of people swarmed along the sidewalks, spattered with black mud, which made each shoe leave a scar-like impression. Overhead elevated trains with a shrill grinding of the wheels stopped at the station, which upon its leg-like pillars seemed to resemble some monstrous kind of crab squatting over the street. The quick fat puffings of the engines could be heard. Down an alley there were sombre curtains of purple and black, on which street lamps dully glittered like embroidered flowers.

A saloon stood with a voracious air on a corner. A sign leaning against the front of the doorpost announced: "Free hot soup to-night." The swing doors snapping to and fro like ravenous lips, made gratified smacks as the saloon gorged itself with plump men, eating with astounding and endless appetite, smiling in some indescribable manner as the men came from all directions like sacrifices to a heathenish superstition.

Caught by the delectable sign, the young man allowed himself to be swallowed. A bartender placed a schooner of dark and portentous beer on the bar. Its monumental form upreared until the froth a-top was above the crown of the young man's brown derby.

"Soup over there, gents," said the bartender, affably. A little yellow man in rags and the youth grasped their schooners and went with speed toward a lunch counter, where a man with oily but imposing whiskers ladled genially from a kettle until he had furnished his two mendicants with a soup that was steaming hot and in which there were little floating suggestions of chicken. The young man, sipping his broth, felt the cordiality expressed by the warmth of the mixture, and he beamed at the man with oily but imposing whiskers, who was presiding like a priest behind an altar. "Have some more, gents?" he inquired of the two sorry figures before him. The little yellow man accepted with a swift gesture, but the youth shook his head and went out, following a man whose wondrous seediness promised that he would have a knowledge of cheap lodging-houses.

On the side-walk he accosted the seedy man. "Say, do you know a cheap place t' sleep?"

The other hesitated for a time, gazing sideways. Finally he nodded in the direction of up the street. "I sleep up there," he said, "when I've got th' price."

"How much?"

"Ten cents."

The young man shook his head dolefully. "That's too rich for me."

At that moment there approached the two a reeling man in strange garments. His head was a fuddle of bushy hair and whiskers from which his eyes peered with a guilty slant. In a close scrutiny it was possible to distinguish the cruel lines of a mouth, which looked as if its lips had just closed with satisfaction over some tender and piteous morsel. He appeared like an assassin steeped in crimes performed awkwardly.

But at this time his voice was tuned to the coaxing key of an affectionate puppy. He looked at the men with wheedling eyes and began to sing a little melody for charity.

"Say, gents, can't yeh give a poor feller a couple of cents t' git a bed. I got five an I gits anudder two I gits me a bed. Now, on th' square, gents, can't yeh jest gimme two cents t' git a bed. Now, yeh know how a respecter'ble gentlem'n feels when he's down on his luck an' I——"

The seedy man, staring with imperturbable countenance at a train which clattered overhead, interrupted in an expressionless voice: "Ah, go t' h——!"

But the youth spoke to the prayerful assassin in tones of astonishment and inquiry. "Say, you must be crazy! Why don't yeh strike somebody that looks as if they had money?"

The assassin, tottering about on his uncertain legs, and at intervals brushing imaginary obstacles from before his nose, entered into a long explanation of the psychology of the situation. It was so profound that it was unintelligible.

When he had exhausted the subject the young man said to him: "Let's see th' five cents."

The assassin wore an expression of drunken woe at this sentence, filled with suspicion of him. With a deeply pained air he began to fumble in his clothing, his red hands trembling. Presently he announced in a voice of bitter grief, as if he had been betrayed: "There's on'y four."

"Four," said the young man thoughtfully. "Well, look-a-here, I'm a stranger here, an' if ye'll steer me to your cheap joint I'll find the other three."

The assassin's countenance became instantly radiant with joy. His whiskers quivered with the wealth of his alleged emotions. He seized the young man's hand in a transport of delight and friendliness.

"B'gawd," he cried, "if ye'll do that, b'gawd, I'd say yeh was a damned good feller, I would, an' I'd remember yeh all m' life, I would, b'gawd, an' if I ever got a chance I'd return th' compliment"—he spoke with drunken dignity—"b'gawd, I'd treat yeh white, I would, an' I'd allus remember yeh——"

The young man drew back, looking at the assassin coldly. "Oh, that's all right," he said. "You show me th' joint—that's all you've got t' do."

The assassin, gesticulating gratitude, led the young man along a dark street. Finally he stopped before a little dusty door. He raised his hand impressively. "Look-a-here," he said, and there was a thrill of deep and ancient wisdom upon his face, "I've brought yeh here, an' that's my part, ain't it? If th' place don't suit yeh yeh needn't git mad at me, need yeh? There won't be no bad feelin', will there?"

"No," said the young man.

The assassin waved his arm tragically and led the march up the steep stairway. On the way the young man furnished the assassin with three pennies. At the top a man with benevolent spectacles looked at them through a hole in the board. He collected their money, wrote some names on a register, and speedily was leading the two men along a gloom-shrouded corridor.

Shortly after the beginning of this journey the young man felt his liver turn white, for from the dark and secret places of the building there suddenly came to his nostrils strange and unspeakable odors that assailed him like malignant diseases with wings. They seemed to be from human bodies closely packed in dens; the exhalations from a hundred pairs of reeking lips; the fumes from a thousand bygone debauches; the expression of a thousand present miseries.

A man, naked save for a little snuff colored undershirt, was parading sleepily along the corridor. He rubbed his eyes, and, giving vent to a prodigious yawn, demanded to be told the time.

"Half past one."

The man yawned again. He opened a door, and for a moment his form was outlined against a black, opaque interior. To this door came the three men, and as it was again opened the unholy odors rushed out like released fiends, so that the young man was obliged to struggle as against an overpowering wind.

It was some time before the youth's eyes were good in the intense gloom within, but the man with benevolent spectacles led him skilfully, pausing but a moment to deposit the limp assassin upon a cot. He took the youth to a cot that lay tranquilly by the window, and, showing him a tall locker for clothes that stood near the head with the ominous air of a tombstone, left him.

The youth sat on his cot and peered about him. There was a gas-jet in a distant part of the room that burned a small flickering orange-hued flame. It caused vast masses of tumbled shadows in all parts of the place, save where, immediately about it, there was a little gray haze. As the young man's eyes became used to the darkness he could see upon the cots that thickly littered the floor the forms of men sprawled out, lying in death-like silence or heaving and snoring with tremendous effort, like stabbed fish.

The youth locked his derby and his shoes in the mummy-case near him and then lay down with his old and familiar coat around his shoulders. A blanket he handled gingerly, drawing it over part of the coat. The cot was leather covered and cold as melting snow. The youth was obliged to shiver for some time on this affair, which was like a slab. Presently, however, his chill gave him peace, and during this period of leisure from it he turned his head to stare at his friend, the assassin, whom he could dimly discern where he lay sprawled on a cot in the abandon of a man filled with drink. He was snoring with incredible vigor. His wet hair and beard dimly glistened and his inflamed nose shone with subdued luster like a red light in a fog.

Within reach of the youth's hand was one who lay with yellow breast and shoulders bare to the cold drafts. One arm hung over the side of the cot and the fingers lay full length upon the wet cement floor of the room. Beneath the inky brows could be seen the eyes of the man exposed by the partly opened lids. To the youth it seemed that he and this corpse-like being were exchanging a prolonged stare and that the other threatened with his eyes. He drew back, watching his neighbor from the shadows of his blanket-edge. The man did not move once through the night, but lay in this stillness as of death, like a body stretched out, expectant of the surgeon's knife.

And all through the room could be seen the tawny hues of naked flesh, limbs thrust into the darkness, projecting beyond the cots; upreared knees; arms hanging, long and thin, over the cot-edges. For the most part they were statuesque, carven, dead. With the curious lockers standing all about like tombstones there was a strange effect of a graveyard, where bodies were merely flung.

Yet occasionally could be seen limbs wildly tossing in fantastic, nightmare gestures, accompanied by guttural cries, grunts, oaths. And there was one fellow off in a gloomy corner, who in his dreams was oppressed by some frightful calamity, for of a sudden he began to utter long wails that went almost like yells from a hound, echoing wailfully and weird through this chill place of tombstones, where men lay like the dead.

The sound, in its high piercing beginnings that dwindled to final melancholy moans, expressed a red and grim tragedy of the unfathomable possibilities of the man's dreams. But to the youth these were not merely the shrieks of a vision-pierced man. They were an utterance of the meaning of the room and its occupants. It was to him the protest of the wretch who feels the touch of the imperturbable granite wheels and who then cries with an impersonal eloquence, with a strength not from him, giving voice to the wail of a whole section, a class, a people. This, weaving into the young man's brain and mingling with his views of these vast and somber shadows that like mighty black fingers curled around the naked bodies, made the young man so that he did not sleep, but lay carving biographies for these men from his meager experience. At times the fellow in the corner howled in a writhing agony of his imaginations.

Finally a long lance-point of gray light shot through the dusty panes of the window. Without, the young man could see roofs drearily white in the dawning. The point of light yellowed and grew brighter, until the golden rays of the morning sun came in bravely and strong. They touched with radiant color the form of a small, fat man, who snored in stuttering fashion. His round and shiny bald head glowed suddenly with the valor of a decoration. He sat up, blinked at the sun, swore fretfully and pulled his blanket over the ornamental splendors of his head.

The youth contentedly watched this rout of the shadows before the bright spears of the sun and presently he slumbered. When he awoke he heard the voice of the assassin raised in valiant curses. Putting up his head he perceived his comrade seated on the side of the cot engaged in scratching his neck with long finger nails that rasped like files.

"Hully Jee dis is a new breed. They've got can-openers on their feet," he continued in a violent tirade.

The young man hastily unlocked his closet and took out his shoes and hat. As he sat on the side of the cot, lacing his shoes, he glanced about and saw that daylight had made the room comparatively commonplace and uninteresting. The men, whose faces seemed stolid, serene or absent, were engaged in dressing, while a great crackle of bantering conversation arose.

A few were parading in unconcerned nakedness. Here and there were men of brawn, whose skins shone clear and ruddy. They took splendid poses, standing massively, like chiefs. When they had dressed in their ungainly garments there was an extraordinary change. They then showed bumps and deficiencies of all kinds.

There were others who exhibited many deformities. Shoulders were slanting, humped, pulled this way and pulled that way. And notable among these latter men was the little fat man who had refused to allow his head to be glorified. His pudgy form, builded like a pear, bustled to and fro, while he swore in fishwife fashion. It appeared that some article of his apparel had vanished.

The young man, attired speedily, went to his friend, the assassin. At first the latter looked dazed at the sight of the youth. This face seemed to be appealing to him through the cloud-wastes of his memory. He scratched his neck and reflected. At last he grinned, a broad smile gradually spreading until his countenance was a round illumination. "Hello, Willie," he cried, cheerily.

"Hello," said the young man. "Are yeh ready t' fly?"

"Sure." The assassin tied his shoe carefully with some twine and came ambling.

When he reached the street the young man experienced no sudden relief from unholy atmospheres. He had forgotten all about them, and had been breathing naturally and with no sensation of discomfort or distress.

He was thinking of these things as he walked along the street, when he was suddenly startled by feeling the assassin's hand, trembling with excitement, clutching his arm, and when the assassin spoke, his voice went into quavers from a supreme agitation.

"I'll be hully, bloomin' blowed, if there wasn't a feller with a nightshirt on up there in that joint!"

The youth was bewildered for a moment, but presently he turned to smile indulgently at the assassin's humor.

"Oh, you're a d——liar," he merely said.

Whereupon the assassin began to gesture extravagantly and take oath by strange gods. He frantically placed himself at the mercy of remarkable fates if his tale were not true. "Yes, he did! I cross m' heart thousan' times!" he protested, and at the time his eyes were large with amazement, his mouth wrinkled in unnatural glee. "Yessir! A nightshirt! A hully white nightshirt!"

"You lie!"

"Nosir! I hope ter die b'fore I kin git anudder ball if there wasn't a jay wid a hully, bloomin' white nightshirt!"

His face was filled with the infinite wonder of it. "A hully white nightshirt," he continually repeated.

The young man saw the dark entrance to a basement restaurant. There was a sign which read, "No mystery about our hash," and there were other age-stained and world-battered legends which told him that the place was within his means. He stopped before it and spoke to the assassin. "I guess I'll git somethin' t' eat."

At this the assassin, for some reason, appeared to be quite embarrassed. He gazed at the seductive front of the eating place for a moment. Then he started slowly up the street. "Well, good-by, Willie," he said, bravely.

For an instant the youth studied the departing figure. Then he called out, "Hol' on a minnet." As they came together he spoke in a certain fierce way, as if he feared that the other would think him to be weak. "Look-a-here, if yeh wanta git some breakfas' I'll lend yeh three cents t' do it with. But say, look-a-here, you've gota git out an' hustle. I ain't goin' t' support yeh, or I'll go broke b'fore night. I ain't no millionaire."

"I take me oath, Willie," said the assassin, earnestly, "th' on'y thing I really needs is a ball. Me t'roat feels like a fryin' pan. But as I can't git a ball, why, th' next bes' thing is breakfast, an' if yeh do that fer me, b'gawd, I'd say yeh was th' whitest lad I ever see."

They spent a few moments in dexterous exchanges of phrases, in which they each protested that the other was, as the assassin had originally said, a "respecter'ble gentlem'n." And they concluded with mutual assurances that they were the souls of intelligence and virtue. Then they went into the restaurant.

There was a long counter, dimly lighted from hidden sources. Two or three men in soiled white aprons rushed here and there.

The youth bought a bowl of coffee for two cents and a roll for one cent. The assassin purchased the same. The bowls were webbed with brown seams, and the tin spoons wore an air of having emerged from the first pyramid. Upon them were black, moss-like encrustations of age, and they were bent and scarred from the attacks of long-forgotten teeth. But over their repast the wanderers waxed warm and mellow. The assassin grew affable as the hot mixture went soothingly down his parched throat, and the young man felt courage flow in his veins.

Memories began to throng in on the assassin, and he brought forth long tales, intricate, incoherent, delivered with a chattering swiftness as from an old woman. "——great job out'n Orange. Boss keep yeh hustlin', though, all time. I was there three days, and then I went an' ask'im t' lend me a dollar. "G-g-go ter the devil,' he ses, an' I lose me job.

——"South no good. Damn niggers work for twenty-five an' thirty cents a day. Run white man out. Good grub, though. Easy livin'.

——"Yas; useter work little in Toledo, raftin' logs. Make two or three dollars er day in the spring. Lived high. Cold as ice, though, in the winter——

"I was raised in northern N'York. O-o-o-oh, yeh jest ough to live there. No beer ner whisky, though, way off in the woods. But all th' good hot grub yeh can eat. B'gawd, I hung around there long as I could till th' ol' man fired me. 'Git t'hell outa here, yeh wuthless skunk, git t'hell outa here an' go die,' he ses. 'You're a hell of a father,' I ses, 'you are,' an' I quit 'im."

As they were passing from the dim eating-place they encountered an old man who was trying to steal forth with a tiny package of food, but a tall man with an indomitable mustache stood dragon-fashion, barring the way of escape. They heard the old man raise a plaintive protest. "Ah, you always want to know what I take out, and you never see that I usually bring a package in here from my place of business."

As the wanderers trudged slowly along Park Row, the assassin began to expand and grow blithe. "B'gawd, we've been livin' like kings," he said, smacking appreciative lips.

"Look out or we'll have t' pay fer it t'-night," said the youth, with gloomy warning.

But the assassin refused to turn his gaze toward the future. He went with a limping step, into which he injected a suggestion of lamb-like gambols. His mouth was wreathed in a red grin.

In the City Hall Park the two wanderers sat down in the little circle of benches sanctified by traditions of their class. They huddled in their old garments, slumbrously conscious of the march of the hours which for them had no meaning.

The people of the street hurrying hither and thither made a blend of black figures, changing, yet frieze-like. They walked in their good clothes as upon important missions, giving no gaze to the two wanderers seated upon the benches. They expressed to the young man his infinite distance from all that he valued. Social position, comfort, the pleasures of living, were unconquerable kingdoms. He felt a sudden awe.

And in the background a multitude of buildings, of pitiless hues and sternly high, were to him emblematic of a nation forcing its regal head into the clouds, throwing no downward glances; in the sublimity of its aspirations ignoring the wretches who may flounder at its feet. The roar of the city in his ear was to him the confusion of strange tongues, babbling heedlessly; it was the clink of coin, the voice of the city's hopes which were to him no hopes.

He confessed himself an outcast, and his eyes from under the lowered rim of his hat began to glance guiltily, wearing the criminal expression that comes with certain convictions.

NOTE ON THE TEXT

Original publication of this article in the *New York Press* contained the following introductory passage and conclusion. This material was omitted by Crane when he prepared the piece for book publication.

Introductory Material:

Two men stood regarding a tramp.

"I wonder how he feels," said one, reflectively. "I suppose he is homeless, friendless, and has, at the most, only a few cents in his pocket. And if this is so, I wonder how he feels."

The other being the elder, spoke with an air of authoritative wisdom. "You can tell nothing of it unless you are in that condition yourself. It is idle to speculate about it from this distance."

"I suppose so," said the younger man, and then he added as from an inspiration: "I think I'll try it. Rags and tatters, you know, a couple of dimes, and hungry, too, if possible. Perhaps I could discover his point of view or something near it."

"Well, you might," said the other, and from those words begins this veracious narrative of an experiment in misery.

The youth went to the studio of an artist friend, who, from his store, rigged him out in an aged suit and a brown derby hat that had been made long years before. And then the youth went forth to try to eat as the tramp may eat, and sleep as the wanderers sleep. It was late at night, and a fine rain was swirling softly down, covering the pavements with a bluish luster. He began a weary trudge toward the downtown places, where beds can be hired for coppers. By the time he had reached City Hall Park he was so completely plastered with yells of "bum" and "hobo," and with various unholy epithets that small boys had applied to him at intervals that he was in a state of profound dejection, and looking searchingly for an outcast of high degree that the two might share miseries. But the lights threw a quivering glare over rows and circles of deserted benches that glistened damply, showing patches of wet sod behind them. It seemed that their usual freights of sorry humanity had fled on this night to better things. There were only squads of well dressed Brooklyn people, who swarmed toward the Bridge.

The young man loitered about for a time, and then went shuffling off down Park row. In the sudden descent in style of the dress of the crowd he felt relief. He began to see others whose tatters matched his tatters. In Chatham square there were aimless men strewn in front of saloons and lodging houses. He aligned himself with these men, and turned slowly to occupy himself with the pageantry of the street.

The mists of the cold and damp night made an intensely blue haze, through which the gaslights in the windows of stores and saloons shone with a golden radiance. The street cars rumbled softly, as if going upon carpet stretched in the aisle made by the pillars of the elevated road. Two interminable processions of people went along the wet pavements, spattered with black mud that made each shoe leave a scar-like impression. The high buildings lurked a-back, shrouded in shadows. Down a side street there were mystic curtains of purple and black, on which lamps dully glittered like embroidered flowers.

Following the last word, the newspaper version concluded:

"Well," said the friend, "did you discover his point of view?"

"I don't know that I did," replied the young man; "but at any rate I think mine own has undergone a considerable alteration."

At a time about halfway between the original and the revision, Crane commented: "In a story of mine called 'An Experiment in Misery' I tried to make plain that the root of Bowery life is a sort of cowardice. Perhaps I mean a lack of ambition or to willingly be knocked flat and accept the licking."

An Experiment in Luxury

"If you accept this invitation you will have an opportunity to make another social study," said the old friend.

The youth laughed. "If they caught me making a study of them they'd attempt a murder. I would be pursued down Fifth avenue by the entire family."

"Well," persisted the old friend who could only see one thing at a time, "it would be very interesting. I have been told all my life that millionaires have no fun, and I know that the poor are always assured that the millionaire is a very unhappy person. They are informed that miseries swarm around all wealth, that all crowned heads are heavy with care, and——"

"But still——" began the youth.

"And, in the irritating, brutalizing, enslaving environment of their poverty, they are expected to solace themselves with these assurances," continued the old friend. He extended his gloved palm and began to tap it impressively with a finger of his other hand. His legs were spread apart in a fashion peculiar to his oratory. "I believe that it is mostly false. It is true that wealth does not release a man from many things from which he would gladly purchase release. Consequences cannot be bribed. I suppose that every man believes steadfastly that he has a private tragedy which makes him yearn for other existences. But it is impossible for me to believe that these things equalize themselves; that there are burrs under all rich cloaks and benefits in all ragged jackets, and the preaching of it seems wicked to me. There are those who have opportunities; there are those who are robbed of——"

"But look here," said the young man; "what has this got to do with my paying Jack a visit?"

"It has got a lot to do with it," said the old friend sharply. "As I said, there are those who have opportunities; there are those who are robbed——"

"Well, I won't have you say Jack ever robbed anybody of anything, because he's as honest a fellow as ever lived," interrupted the youth, with warmth. "I have known him for years, and he is a perfectly square fellow. He doesn't know about these infernal things. He isn't criminal because you say he is benefited by a condition which other men created."

"I didn't say he was," retorted the old friend. "Nobody is responsible for anything. I wish to Heaven somebody was, and then we could all jump on him. Look here, my boy, our modern civilization is——"

"Oh, the deuce!" said the young man.

The old friend then stood very erect and stern. "I can see by your frequent interruptions that you have not yet achieved sufficient pain in life. I hope one day to see you materially changed. You are yet——"

"There he is now," said the youth, suddenly. He indicated a young man who was passing. He went hurriedly toward him, pausing once to gesture adieu to his old friend.

—

The house was broad and brown and stolid like the face of a peasant. It had an inanity of expression, an absolute lack of artistic strength that was in itself powerful because it symbolized something. It stood, a homely pile of stone, rugged, grimly self reliant, asserting its quality as a fine thing when in reality the beholder usually wondered why so much money had been spent to obtain a complete negation. Then from another point of view it was important and mighty because it stood as a fetich, formidable because of traditions of worship.

When the great door was opened the youth imagined that the footman who held a hand on the knob looked at him with a quick, strange stare. There was nothing definite in it; it was all vague and elusive, but a suspicion was certainly denoted in some way. The youth felt that he, one of the outer barbarians, had been detected to be a barbarian by the guardian of the portal, he of the refined nose, he of the exquisite sense, he who must be more atrociously aristocratic than any that he serves. And the youth, detesting himself for it, found that he would rejoice to take a frightful revenge upon this lackey who, with a glance of his eyes, had called him a name. He would have liked to have been for a time a dreadful social perfection whose hand, waved lazily, would cause hordes of the idolatrous imperfect to be smitten in the eyes. And in the tumult of his imagination he did not think it strange that he should plan in his vision to come around to this house and with the power of his new social majesty, reduce this footman to ashes.

He had entered with an easy feeling of independence, but after this incident the splendor of the interior filled him with awe. He was a wanderer in a fairy land, and who felt that his presence marred certain effects. He was an invader with a shamed face, a man who had come to steal certain colors, forms, impressions that were not his. He had a dim thought that some one might come to tell him to begone.

His friend, unconscious of this swift drama of thought, was already upon the broad staircase. "Come on," he called. When the youth's foot struck from a thick rug and changed upon the tiled floor he was almost frightened.

There was cool abundance of gloom. High up stained glass caught the sunlight, and made it into marvelous hues that in places touched the dark walls. A broad bar of yellow gilded the leaves of lurking plants. A softened crimson glowed upon the head and shoulders of a bronze swordsman, who perpetually strained in a terrific lunge, his blade thrust at random into the shadow, piercing there an unknown something.

An immense fire place was at one end, and its furnishings gleamed until it resembled a curious door of a palace, and on the threshold, where one would have to pass a fire burned redly. From some remote place came the sound of a bird twittering busily. And from behind heavy portieres came a subdued noise of the chatter of three, twenty or a hundred women.

He could not relieve himself of this feeling of awe until he had reached his friend's room. There they lounged carelessly and smoked pipes. It was an amazingly comfortable room. It expressed to the visitor that he could do supremely as he chose, for it said plainly that in it the owner did supremely as he chose. The youth wondered if there had not been some domestic skirmishing to achieve so much beautiful disorder. There were various articles left about defiantly, as if the owner openly flaunted the feminine ideas of precision. The disarray of a table that stood prominently defined the entire room. A set of foils, a set of boxing gloves, a lot of illustrated papers, an inkstand and a hat lay entangled upon it. Here was surely a young man, who, when his menacing mother, sisters or servants knocked, would open a slit in the door like a Chinaman in an opium joint, and tell them to leave him to his beloved devices. And yet, withal, the effect was good, because the disorder was not necessary, and because there are some things that when flung down, look to have been flung by an artist. A baby can create an effect with a guitar. It would require genius to deal with the piled up dishes in a Cherry street sink.

The youth's friend lay back upon the broad seat that followed the curve of the window and smoked in blissful laziness. Without one could see the windowless wall of a house overgrown with a green, luxuriant vine. There was a glimpse of a side street. Below were the stables. At intervals a little fox terrier ran into the court and barked tremendously.

The youth, also blissfully indolent, kept up his part of the conversation on the recent college days, but continually he was beset by a stream of sub-conscious reflection. He was beginning to see a vast wonder in it that they two lay sleepily chatting with no more apparent responsibility than rabbits, when certainly there were men, equally fine perhaps, who were being blackened and mashed in the churning life of the lower places. And all this had merely happened; the great secret hand had guided them here and had guided others there. The eternal mystery of social condition exasperated him at this time. He wondered if incomprehensible justice were the sister of open wrong.

And, above all, why was he impressed, awed, overcome by a mass of materials, a collection of the trophies of wealth, when he knew that to him their dominant meaning was that they represented a lavish expenditure? For what reason did his nature so deeply respect all this? Perhaps his ancestors had been peasants bowing heads to the heel of appalling pomp of princes or rows of little men who stood to watch a king kill a flower with his cane. There was one side of him that said there were finer things in life, but the other side did homage.

Presently he began to feel that he was a better man than many—entitled to a great pride. He stretched his legs like a man in a garden, and he thought that he belonged to the garden. Hues and forms had smothered certain of his comprehensions. There had been times in his life when little voices called to him continually from the darkness; he heard them now as an idle, half-smothered babble on the horizon edge. It was necessary that it should be so, too. There was the horizon, he said, and, of course, there should be a babble of pain on it. Thus it was written; it was a law, he thought. And, anyway, perhaps it was not so bad as those who babbled tried to tell.

In this way and with this suddenness he arrived at a stage. He was become a philosopher, a type of the wise man who can eat but three meals a day, conduct a large business and understand the purposes of infinite power. He felt valuable. He was sage and important.

There were influences, knowledges that made him aware that he was idle and foolish in his new state, but he inwardly reveled like a barbarian in his environment. It was delicious to feel so high and mighty, to feel that the unattainable could be purchased like a penny bun. For a time, at any rate, there was no impossible. He indulged in monarchical reflections.

As they were dressing for dinner his friend spoke to him in this wise: "Be sure not to get off anything that resembles an original thought before my mother. I want her to like you, and I know that when any one says a thing cleverly before her he ruins himself with her forever. Confine your talk to orthodox expressions. Be dreary and unspeakably commonplace in the true sense of the word. Be damnable."

"It will be easy for me to do as you say," remarked the youth.

"As far as the old man goes," continued the other, "he's a blooming good fellow. He may appear like a sort of a crank if he happens to be in that mood, but he's all right when you come to know him. And besides he doesn't dare do that sort of thing with me, because I've got nerve enough to bully him. Oh, the old man is all right."

On their way down the youth lost the delightful mood that he had enjoyed in his friend's rooms. He dropped it like a hat on the stairs. The splendor of color and form swarmed upon him again. He bowed before the strength of this interior; it said a word to him which he believed he should despise, but instead he crouched. In the distance shone his enemy, the footman.

"There will be no people here to-night, so you may see the usual evening row between my sister Mary and me, but don't be alarmed or uncomfortable, because it is quite an ordinary matter," said his friend, as they were about to enter a little drawing room that was well apart from the grander rooms.

The head of the family, the famous millionaire, sat on a low stool before the fire. He was deeply absorbed in the gambols of a kitten who was plainly trying to stand on her head that she might use all four paws in grappling with an evening paper with which her playmate was poking her ribs. The old man chuckled in complete glee. There was never such a case of abstraction, of want of care. The man of millions was in a far land where mechanics and bricklayers go, a mystic land of little, universal emotions, and he had been guided to it by the quaint gestures of a kitten's furry paws.

His wife, who stood near, was apparently not at all a dweller in thought lands. She was existing very much in the present. Evidently she had been wishing to consult with her husband on some tremendous domestic question, and she was in a state of rampant irritation, because he refused to acknowledge at this moment that she or any such thing as a tremendous domestic question was in existence. At intervals she made savage attempts to gain his attention.

As the youth saw her she was in a pose of absolute despair. And her eyes expressed that she appreciated all the tragedy of it. Ah, they said, hers was a life of terrible burden, of appalling responsibility; her pathway was beset with unsolved problems, her horizon was lined with tangled difficulties, while her husband—the man of millions—continued to play with the kitten. Her expression was an admission of heroism.

The youth saw that here at any rate was one denial of his oratorical old friend's statement. In the face of this woman there was no sign that life was sometimes a joy. It was impossible that there could be any pleasure in living for her. Her features were as lined and creased with care and worriment as those of an apple woman. It was as if the passing of each social obligation, of each binding form of her life had left its footprints, scarring her face.

Somewhere in her expression there was terrible pride, that kind of pride which, mistaking the form for the real thing, worships itself because of its devotion to the form.

In the lines of the mouth and the set of the chin could be seen the might of a grim old fighter. They denoted all the power of machination of a general, veteran of a hundred battles. The little scars at the corners of her eyes made a wondrously fierce effect, baleful, determined, without regard somehow to ruck of pain. Here was a savage, a barbarian, a spear woman of the Philistines, who fought battles to excel in what are thought to be the refined and worthy things in life; here was a type of Zulu chieftainess who scuffled and scrambled for place before the white altars of social excellence. And woe to the socially weaker who should try to barricade themselves against that dragon.

It was certain that she never rested in the shade of the trees. One could imagine the endless churning of that mind. And plans and other plans coming forth continuously, defeating a rival here, reducing a family there, bludgeoning a man here, a maid there. Woe and wild eyes followed like obedient sheep upon her trail.

Too, the youth thought he could see that here was the true abode of conservatism—in the mothers, in those whose ears displayed their diamonds instead of their diamonds displaying their ears, in the ancient and honorable controllers who sat in remote corners and pulled wires and respected themselves with a magnitude of respect that heaven seldom allows on earth. There lived tradition and superstition. They were perhaps ignorant of that which they worshiped, and, not comprehending it at all, it naturally followed that the fervor of their devotion could set the sky ablaze.

As he watched, he saw that the mesmeric power of a kitten's waving paws was good. He rejoiced in the spectacle of the little fuzzy cat trying to stand on its head, and by this simple antic defeating some intention of a great domestic Napoleon.

The three girls of the family were having a musical altercation over by the window. Then and later the youth thought them adorable. They were wonderful to him in their charming gowns. They had time and opportunity to create effects, to be beautiful. And it would have been a wonder to him if he had not found them charming, since making themselves so could but be their principal occupation.

Beauty requires certain justices, certain fair conditions. When in a field no man can say: "Here should spring up a flower; here one should not." With incomprehensible machinery and system, nature sends them forth in places both strange and proper, so that, somehow, as we see them each one is a surprise to us. But at times, at places, one can say: "Here no flower can flourish." The youth wondered then why he had been sometimes surprised at seeing women fade, shrivel, their bosoms flatten, their shoulders crook forward, in the heavy swelter and wrench of their toil. It must be difficult, he thought, for a woman to remain serene and uncomplaining when she contemplated the wonder and the strangeness of it.

The lights shed marvelous hues of softened rose upon the table.

In the encircling shadows the butler moved with a mournful, deeply solemn air. Upon the table there was color of pleasure, of festivity, but this servant in the background went to and fro like a slow religious procession.

The youth felt considerable alarm when he found himself involved in conversation with his hostess. In the course of this talk he discovered the great truth that when one submits himself to a thoroughly conventional conversation he runs risks of being most amazingly stupid. He was glad that no one cared to overhear it.

The millionaire, deprived of his kitten, sat back in his chair and laughed at the replies of his son to the attacks of one of the girls. In the rather good wit of his offspring he took an intense delight, but he laughed more particularly at the words of the son.

Indicated in this light chatter about the dinner table there was an existence that was not at all what the youth had been taught to see. Theologians had for a long time told the poor man that riches did not bring happiness, and they had solemnly repeated this phrase until it had come to mean that misery was commensurate with dollars, that each wealthy man was inwardly a miserable wretch. And when a wail of despair or rage had come from the night of the slums they had stuffed this epigram down the throat of he who cried out and told him that he was a lucky fellow. They did this because they feared.

The youth, studying this family group, could not see that they had great license to be pale and haggard. They were no doubt fairly good, being not strongly induced toward the by-paths. Various worlds turned open doors toward them. Wealth in a certain sense is liberty. If they were fairly virtuous he could not see why they should be so persistently pitied.

And no doubt they would dispense their dollars like little seeds upon the soil of the world if it were not for the fact that since the days of the ancient great political economist, the more exalted forms of virtue have grown to be utterly impracticable.

Mr. Binks' Day Off

When Binks was coming up town in a Broadway cable car one afternoon he caught some superficial glimpses of Madison square as he ducked his head to peek through between a young woman's bonnet and a young man's newspaper. The green of the little park vaguely astonished Binks. He had grown accustomed to a white and brown park; now, all at once, it was radiant green. The grass, the leaves, had come swiftly, silently, as if a great green light from the sky had shone suddenly upon the little desolate hued place.

The vision cheered the mind of Binks. It cried to him that nature was still supreme; he had begun to think the banking business to be the pivot on which the universe turned. Produced by this wealth of young green, faint faraway voices called to him. Certain subtle memories swept over him. The million leaves looked into his soul and said something sweet and pure in an unforgotten song, the melody of his past. Binks began to dream.

When he arrived at the little Harlem flat he sat down to dinner with an air of profound dejection, which Mrs. Binks promptly construed into an insult to her cooking, and to the time and thought she had expended in preparing the meal. She promptly resented it.

"Well, what's the matter now?" she demanded. Apparently she had asked this question ten thousand times.

"Nothin'," said Binks, shortly, filled with gloom. He meant by this remark that his ailment was so subtle that her feminine mind would not be enlightened by any explanation.

The head of the family was in an ugly mood. The little Binkses suddenly paused in their uproar and became very wary children. They knew that it would be dangerous to do anything irrelevant to their father's bad temper. They studied his face with their large eyes, filled with childish seriousness and speculation. Meanwhile they ate with the most extraordinary caution. They handled their little forks with such care that there was barely a sound. At each slight movement of their father they looked apprehensively at him, expecting the explosion.

The meal continued amid a somber silence. At last, however, Binks spoke, clearing his throat of the indefinite rage that was in it and looking over at his wife. The little Binkses seemed to inwardly dodge, but he merely said: "I wish I could get away into the country for awhile!"

His wife bristled with that brave anger which agitates a woman when she sees fit to assume that her husband is weak spirited. "If I worked as hard as you do, if I slaved over those old books the way you do, I'd have a vacation once in awhile or I'd tear their old office down." Upon her face was a Roman determination. She was a personification of all manner of courages and rebellions and powers.

Binks felt the falsity of her emotion in a vague way, but at that time he only made a sullen gesture. Later, however, he cried out in a voice of sudden violence: "Look at Tommie's dress! Why the dickens don't you put a bib on that child?"

His wife glared over Tommie's head at her husband, as she leaned around in her chair to tie on the demanded bib. The two looked as hostile as warring redskins. In the wife's eyes there was an intense opposition and defiance, an assertion that she now considered the man she had married to be beneath her in intellect, industry, valor. There was in this glance a jeer at the failures of his life.

And Binks, filled with an inexpressible rebellion at what was to him a lack of womanly perception and sympathy in her, replied with a look that called his wife a drag, an uncomprehending thing of vain ambitions, the weight of his existence.

The baby meanwhile began to weep because his mother, in her exasperation, had yanked him and hurt his neck. Her anger, groping for an outlet, had expressed itself in the nervous strength of her fingers. "Keep still, Tommie," she said to him. "I didn't hurt you. You needn't cry the minute anybody touches you!" He made a great struggle and repressed his loud sobs, but the tears continued to fall down his cheeks and his under lip quivered from a baby sense of injury, the anger of an impotent child who seems as he weeps to be planning revenges.

"I don't see why you don't keep that child from eternally crying," said Binks, as a final remark. He then arose and went away to smoke, leaving Mrs. Binks with the children and the dishevelled table.

Later that night, when the children were in bed, Binks said to his wife: "We ought to get away from the city for awhile at least this spring. I can stand it in the summer, but in the spring——" He made a motion with his hand that represented the new things that are born in the heart when spring comes into the eyes.

"It will cost something, Phil," said Mrs. Binks.

"That's true," said Binks. They both began to reflect, contemplating the shackles of their poverty. "And besides, I don't believe I could get off," said Binks after a time.

Nothing more was said of it that night. In fact, it was two or three days afterward that Binks came home and said: "Margaret, you get the children ready on Saturday noon and we'll all go out and spend Sunday with your Aunt Sarah!"

When he came home on Saturday his hat was far back on the back of his head from the speed he was in. Mrs. Binks was putting on her bonnet before the glass, turning about occasionally to admonish the little Binkses, who, in their new clothes, were wandering around, stiffly, and getting into all sorts of small difficulties. They had been ready since 11 o'clock. Mrs. Binks had been obliged to scold them continually, one after the other, and sometimes three at once.

"Hurry up," said Binks, immediately, "ain't got much time. Say, you ain't going to let Jim wear that hat, are you? Where's his best one? Good heavens, look at Margaret's dress! It's soiled already! Tommie, stop that, do you hear? Well, are you ready?"

Indeed, it was not until the Binkses had left the city far behind and were careering into New Jersey that they recovered their balances. Then something of the fresh quality of the country stole over them and cooled their nerves. Horse cars and ferryboats were maddening to Binks when he was obliged to convoy a wife and three children. He appreciated the vast expanses of green, through which ran golden hued roads. The scene accented his leisure and his lack of responsibility.

Near the track a little river jostled over the stones. At times the cool thunder of its roar came faintly to the ear. The Ramapo Hills were in the background, faintly purple, and surmounted with little peaks that shone with the luster of the sun. Binks began to joke heavily with the children. The little Binkses, for their part, asked the most superhuman questions about details of the scenery. Mrs. Binks leaned contentedly back in her seat and seemed to be at rest, which was a most extraordinary thing.

When they got off the train at the little rural station they created considerable interest. Two or three loungers began to view them in a sort of concentrated excitement. They were apparently fascinated by the Binkses and seemed to be indulging in all manner of wild and intense speculation. The agent, as he walked into his station, kept his head turned. Across the dusty street, wide at this place, a group of men upon the porch of a battered grocery store shaded their eyes with their hands. The Binkses felt dimly like a circus and were a trifle bewildered by it. Binks gazed up and down, this way and that; he tried to be unaware of the stare of the citizens. Finally, he approached the loungers, who straightened their forms suddenly and looked very expectant.

"Can you tell me where Miss Pattison lives?"

The loungers arose as one man. "It's th' third house up that road there."

"It's a white house with green shutters!"

"There, that's it—yeh can see it through th' trees!" Binks discerned that his wife's aunt was a well known personage, and also that the coming of the Binkses was an event of vast importance. When he marched off at the head of his flock, he felt like a drum-major. His course was followed by the unwavering, intent eyes of the loungers.

The street was lined with two rows of austere and solemn trees. In one way it was like parading between the plumes on an immense hearse. These trees, lowly sighing in a breath-like wind, oppressed one with a sense of melancholy and dreariness. Back from the road, behind flower beds, controlled by box-wood borders, the houses were asleep in the drowsy air. Between them one could get views of the fields lying in a splendor of gold and green. A monotonous humming song of insects came from the regions of sunshine, and from some hidden barnyard a hen suddenly burst forth in a sustained cackle of alarm. The tranquillity of the scene contained a meaning of peace and virtue that was incredibly monotonous to the warriors from the metropolis. The sense of a city is battle. The Binkses were vaguely irritated and astonished at the placidity of this little town. This life spoke to them of no absorbing nor even interesting thing. There was something unbearable about it. "I should go crazy if I had to live here," said Mrs. Binks. A warrior in the flood-tide of his blood, going from the hot business of war to a place of utter quiet, might have felt that there was an insipidity in peace. And thus felt the Binkses from New York. They had always named the clash of the swords of commerce as sin, crime, but now they began to imagine something admirable in it. It was high wisdom. They put aside their favorite expressions: "The curse of gold," "A mad passion to get rich," "The rush for the spoils." In the light of their contempt for this stillness, the conflicts of the city were exalted. They were at any rate wondrously clever.

But what they did feel was the fragrance of the air, the radiance of the sunshine, the glory of the fields and the hills. With their ears still clogged by the tempest and fury of city uproars, they heard the song of the universal religion, the mighty and mystic hymn of nature, whose melody is in each landscape. It appealed to their elemental selves. It was as if the earth had called recreant and heedless children and the mother word, of vast might and significance, brought them to sudden meekness. It was the universal thing whose power no one escapes. When a man hears it he usually remains silent. He understands then the sacrilege of speech.

When they came to the third house, the white one, with the green blinds, they perceived a woman, in a plaid sun bonnet, walking slowly down a path. Around her was a riot of shrubbery and flowers. From the long and tangled grass of the lawn grew a number of cherry trees. Their dark green foliage was thickly sprinkled with bright red fruit. Some sparrows were scuffling among the branches. The little Binkses began to whoop at sight of the woman in the plaid sun bonnet.

"Hay-oh, Aunt Sarah, hay-oh!" they shouted.

The woman shaded her eyes with her hand. "Well, good gracious, if it ain't Marg'ret Binks! An' Phil, too! Well, I am surprised!"

She came jovially to meet them. "Why, how are yeh all? I'm awful glad t' see yeh!"

The children, filled with great excitement, babbled questions and ejaculations while she greeted the others.

"Say, Aunt Sarah, gimme some cherries!"

"Look at th' man over there!"

"Look at th' flowers!"

"Gimme some flowers, Aunt Sarah!"

And little Tommie, red faced from the value of his information, bawled out: "Aunt Sah-wee, dey have horse tars where I live!" Later he shouted: "We come on a twain of steam tars!"

Aunt Sarah fairly bristled with the most enthusiastic hospitality. She beamed upon them like a sun. She made desperate attempts to gain possession of everybody's bundles that she might carry them to the house. There was a sort of a little fight over the baggage. The children clamored questions at her; she tried heroically to answer them. Tommie, at times, deluged her with news.

The curtains of the dining room were pulled down to keep out the flies. This made a deep, cool gloom in which corners of the old furniture caught wandering rays of light and shone with a mild luster. Everything was arranged with an unspeakable neatness that was the opposite of comfort. A branch of an apple tree moved by the gentle wind, brushed softly against the closed blinds.

"Take off yer things," said Aunt Sarah.

Binks and his wife remained talking to Aunt Sarah, but the children speedily swarmed out over the farm, raiding in countless directions. It was only a matter of seconds before Jimmie discovered the brook behind the barn. Little Margaret roamed among the flowers, bursting into little cries at sight of new blossoms, new glories. Tommie gazed at the cherry trees for a few moments in profound silence. Then he went and procured a pole. It was very heavy, relatively. He could hardly stagger under it, but with infinite toil he dragged it to the proper place and somehow managed to push it erect. Then with a deep earnestness of demeanor he began a little onslaught upon the trees. Very often his blow missed the entire tree and the pole thumped on the ground. This necessitated the most extraordinary labor. But then at other times he would get two or three cherries at one wild swing of his weapon.

Binks and his wife spent the larger part of the afternoon out under the apple trees at the side of the house. Binks lay down on his back, with his head in the long lush grass. Mrs. Binks moved lazily to and fro in a rocking chair that had been brought from the house. Aunt Sarah, sometimes appearing, was strenuous in an account of relatives, and the Binkses had only to listen. They were glad of it, for this warm, sleepy air, pulsating with the sounds of insects, had enchained them in a great indolence.

It was to this place that Jimmie ran after he had fallen into the brook and scrambled out again. Holding his arms out carefully from his dripping person, he was roaring tremendously. His new sailor suit was a sight. Little Margaret came often to describe the wonders of her journeys, and Tommie, after a frightful struggle with the cherry trees, toddled over and went to sleep in the midst of a long explanation of his operations. The breeze stirred the locks on his baby forehead. His breath came in long sighs of content. Presently he turned his head to cuddle deeper into the grass. One arm was thrown in childish abandon over his head. Mrs. Binks stopped rocking to gaze at him. Presently she bended and noiselessly brushed away a spear of grass that was troubling the baby's temple. When she straightened up she saw that Binks, too, was absorbed in a contemplation of Tommie. They looked at each other presently, exchanging a vague smile. Through the silence came the voice of a plowing farmer berating his horses in a distant field.

The peace of the hills and the fields came upon the Binkses. They allowed Jimmie to sit up in bed and eat cake while his clothes were drying. Uncle Daniel returned from a wagon journey and recited them a ponderous tale of a pig that he had sold to a man with a red beard. They had no difficulty in feeling much interest in the story.

Binks began to expand with enormous appreciations. He would not go into the house until they compelled him. And as soon as the evening meal was finished he dragged his wife forth on a trip to the top of the hill behind the house. There was a great view from there, Uncle Daniel said.

The path, gray with little stones in the dusk, extended above them like a pillar. The pines were beginning to croon in a mournful key, inspired by the evening winds. Mrs. Binks had great difficulty in climbing this upright road. Binks was obliged to assist her, which he did with a considerable care and tenderness. In it there was a sort of a reminiscence of their courtship. It was a repetition of old days. Both enjoyed it because of this fact, although they subtly gave each other to understand that they disdained this emotion as an altogether un-American thing, for she, as a woman, was proud, and he had great esteem for himself as a man.

At the summit they seated themselves upon a fallen tree, near the edge of a cliff. The evening silence was upon the earth below them. Far in the west the sun lay behind masses of corn colored clouds, tumbled and heaved into crags, peaks and canyons. On either hand stood the purple hills in motionless array. The valley lay wreathed in somber shadows. Slowly there went on the mystic process of the closing of the day. The corn colored clouds faded to yellow and finally to a faint luminous green, inexpressibly vague. The rim of the hills was then an edge of crimson. The mountains became a profound blue. From the night, approaching in the east, came a wind. The trees of the mountain raised plaintive voices, bending toward the faded splendors of the day.

This song of the trees arose in low, sighing melody into the still air. It was filled with an infinite sorrow—a sorrow for birth, slavery, death. It was a wail telling the griefs, the pains of all ages. It was the symbol of agonies. It celebrated all suffering. Each man finds in this sound the expression of his own grief. It is the universal voice raised in lamentations.

As the trees huddled and bended as if to hide from their eyes a certain sight the green tints became blue. A faint suggestion of yellow replaced the crimson. The sun was dead.

The Binkses had been silent. These songs of the trees awe. They had remained motionless during this ceremony, their eyes fixed upon the mighty and indefinable changes which spoke to them of the final thing—the inevitable end. Their eyes had an impersonal expression. They were purified, chastened by this sermon, this voice calling to them from the sky. The hills had spoken and the trees had crooned their song. Binks finally stretched forth his arm in a wondering gesture.

"I wonder why," he said; "I wonder why the dickens it—why it—why——"

Tangled in his tongue was the unformulated question of the centuries, but Mrs. Binks had stolen forth her arm and linked it with his. Her head leaned softly against his shoulder.

Stories Told by an Artist

A Tale About How "Great Grief" Got His Holiday Dinner

Wrinkles had been peering into the little drygoods box that acted as a cupboard. "There is only two eggs and a half of a loaf of bread left," he announced brutally.

"Heavens!" said Warwickson from where he lay smoking on the bed. He spoke in his usual dismal voice. By it he had earned his popular name of Great Grief.

Wrinkles was a thrifty soul. A sight of an almost bare cupboard maddened him. Even when he was not hungry, the ghosts of his careful ancestors caused him to rebel against it. He sat down with a virtuous air. "Well, what are we going to do?" he demanded of the others. It is good to be the thrifty man in a crowd of unsuccessful artists, for then you can keep the others from starving peacefully. "What are we going to do?"

"Oh, shut up, Wrinkles," said Grief from the bed. "You make me think."

Little Pennoyer, with head bended afar down, had been busily scratching away at a pen and ink drawing. He looked up from his board to utter his plaintive optimism.

"The *Monthly Amazement* may pay me to-morrow. They ought to.

I've waited over three months now. I'm going down there tomorrow, and perhaps I'll get it."

His friends listened to him tolerantly, but at last Wrinkles could not omit a scornful giggle. He was such an old man, almost twenty-eight, and he had seen so many little boys be brave. "Oh, no doubt, Penny, old man." Over on the bed, Grief croaked deep down in his throat. Nothing was said for a long time thereafter.

The crash of the New York streets came faintly. Occasionally one could hear the tramp of feet in the intricate corridors of this begrimed building that squatted, slumbering and aged between two exalted commercial structures that would have had to bend afar down to perceive it. The light snow beat pattering into the window corners and made vague and grey the vista of chimneys and roofs. Often, the wind scurried swiftly and raised a long cry.

Great Grief leaned upon his elbow. "See to the fire, will you, Wrinkles?"

Wrinkles pulled the coal box out from under the bed and threw open the stove door preparatory to shoveling some fuel. A red glare plunged at the first faint shadows of dusk. Little Pennoyer threw down his pen and tossed his drawing over on the wonderful heap of stuff that hid the table. "It's too dark to work." He lit his pipe and walked about, stretching his shoulders like a man whose labor was valuable.

When the dusk came it saddened these youths. The solemnity of darkness always caused them to ponder. "Light the gas, Wrinkles," said Grief.

The flood of orange light showed clearly the dull walls lined with sketches, the tousled bed in one corner, the mass of boxes and trunks in another, the little fierce stove and the wonderful table. Moreover, there were some wine colored draperies flung in some places, and on a shelf, high up, there was a plaster cast dark with dust in the creases. A long stovepipe wandered off in the wrong direction and then twined impulsively toward a hole in the wall. There were some extensive cobwebs on the ceiling.

"Well, let's eat," said Grief.

Later there came a sad knock at the door. Wrinkles, arranging a tin pail on the stove, little Pennoyer busy at slicing the bread, and Great Grief, affixing the rubber tube to the gas stove, yelled: "Come in!"

The door opened and Corinson entered dejectedly. His overcoat was very new. Wrinkles flashed an envious glance at it, but almost immediately he cried: "Hello, Corrie, old boy!"

Corinson sat down and felt around among the pipes until he found a good one. Great Grief had fixed the coffee to boil on the gas stove, but he had to watch it closely, for the rubber tube was short, and a chair was balanced on a trunk and then the gas stove was balanced on the chair. Coffee making was a feat.

"Well," said Grief, with his back turned, "how goes it, Corrie? How's Art, hey?" He fastened a terrible emphasis upon the word.

"Crayon portraits," said Corinson.

"What?" They turned toward him with one movement, as if from a lever connection. Little Pennoyer dropped his knife.

"Crayon portraits," repeated Corinson. He smoked away in profound cynicism. "Fifteen dollars a week, or more, this time of year, you know." He smiled at them calmly like a man of courage.

Little Pennoyer picked up his knife again. "Well, I'll be blowed," said Wrinkles. Feeling it incumbent upon him to think, he dropped into a chair and began to play serenades on his guitar and watch to see when the water for the eggs would boil. It was a habitual pose.

Great Grief, however, seemed to observe something bitter in the affair. "When did you discover that you couldn't draw?" he said, stiffly.

"I haven't discovered it yet," replied Corinson, with a serene air. "I merely discovered that I would rather eat."

"Oh!" said Grief.

"Hand me the eggs, Grief," said Wrinkles. "The water's boiling."

Little Pennoyer burst into the conversation. "We'd ask you to dinner, Corrie, but there's only three of us and there's two eggs. I dropped a piece of bread on the floor, too. I'm shy one."

"That's all right, Penny," said the other, "don't trouble yourself.

You artists should never be hospitable. I'm going, anyway. I've got to make a call. Well, good night, boys. I've got to make a call. Drop in and see me."

When the door closed upon him, Grief said: "The coffee's done. I hate that fellow. That overcoat cost thirty dollars, if it cost a red. His egotism is so tranquil. It isn't like yours, Wrinkles. He——"

The door opened again and Corinson thrust in his head. "Say, you fellows, you know it's Thanksgiving to-morrow."

"Well, what of it?" demanded Grief.

Little Pennoyer said: "Yes, I know it is, Corrie, I thought of it this morning."

"Well, come out and have a table d'hote with me to-morrow night. I'll blow you off in good style."

While Wrinkles played an exuberant air on his guitar, little Pennoyer did part of a ballet. They cried ecstatically: "Will we? Well, I guess yes!"

When they were alone again Grief said: "I'm not going, anyhow. I hate that fellow."

"Oh, fiddle," said Wrinkles. "You're an infernal crank. And, besides, where's your dinner coming from to-morrow night if you don't go? Tell me that."

Little Pennoyer said: "Yes, that's so, Grief. Where's your dinner coming from if you don't go?"

Grief said: "Well, I hate him, anyhow."

AS TO PAYMENT OF THE RENT

Little Pennoyer's four dollars could not last forever. When he received it he and Wrinkles and Great Grief went to a table d'hote. Afterward little Pennoyer discovered that only two dollars and a half remained. A small magazine away down town had accepted one out of the six drawings that he had taken them, and later had given him four dollars for it. Penny was so disheartened when he saw that his money was not going to last forever that, even with two dollars and a half in his pockets, he felt much worse then he had when he was penniless, for at that time he anticipated twenty-four. Wrinkles lectured upon "Finance."

Great Grief said nothing, for it was established that when he received six dollar checks from comic weeklies he dreamed of renting studios at seventy-five dollars per month, and was likely to go out and buy five dollars' worth of second hand curtains and plaster casts.

When he had money Penny always hated the cluttered den in the old building. He desired then to go out and breathe boastfully like a man. But he obeyed Wrinkles, the elder and the wise, and if you had visited that room about ten o'clock of a morning or about seven of an evening you would have thought that rye bread, frankfurters and potato salad from Second avenue were the only foods in the world.

Purple Sanderson lived there, too, but then he really ate. He had learned parts of the gasfitter's trade before he came to be such a great artist, and when his opinions disagreed with that of every art manager in New York he went to see a plumber, a friend of his, for whose opinion he had a great deal of respect. In consequence he frequented a very neat restaurant on Twenty-third street and sometimes on Saturday nights he openly scorned his companions.

Purple was a good fellow, Grief said, but one of his singularly bad traits was that he always remembered everything. One night, not long after little Pennoyer's great discovery, Purple came in and as he was neatly hanging up his coat, said: "Well, the rent will be due in four days."

"Will it?" demanded Penny, astounded. Penny was always astounded when the rent came due. It seemed to him the most extraordinary occurrence.

"Certainly it will," said Purple with the irritated air of a superior financial man.

"My soul!" said Wrinkles.

Great Grief lay on the bed smoking a pipe and waiting for fame. "Oh, go home, Purple. You resent something. It wasn't me—it was the calendar."

"Try and be serious a moment, Grief."

"You're a fool, Purple."

Penny spoke from where he was at work. "Well, if those *Amazement* people pay me when they said they would I'll have money then."

"So you will, dear," said Grief, satirically. "You'll have money to burn. Did the *Amazement* people ever pay you when they said they would? You're wonderfully important all of a sudden, it seems to me. You talk like an artist."

Wrinkles, too, smiled at little Pennoyer. "The *Established Magazine* people wanted Penny to hire models and make a try for them, too. It will only cost him a big blue chip. By the time he has invested all the money he hasn't got and the rent is two weeks overdue he will be able to tell the landlord to wait seven months until the Monday morning after the day of publication. Go ahead, Penny."

It was the habit to make game of little Pennoyer. He was always having gorgeous opportunities, with no opportunity to take advantage of his opportunities.

Penny smiled at them, his tiny, tiny smile of courage.

"You're a confident little cuss," observed Grief, irrelevantly.

"Well, the world has no objection to your being confident, also, Grief," said Purple.

"Hasn't it?" said Grief. "Well, I want to know!"

Wrinkles could not be light spirited long. He was obliged to despair when occasion offered. At last he sank down in a chair and seized his guitar. "Well, what's to be done?" he said. He began to play mournfully.

"Throw Purple out," mumbled Grief from the bed.

"Are you fairly certain that you will have money then, Penny?" asked Purple.

Little Pennoyer looked apprehensive. "Well, I don't know," he said.

And then began that memorable discussion, great in four minds. The tobacco was of the "Long John" brand. It smelled like burning mummies.

HOW PENNOYER DISPOSED OF HIS SUNDAY DINNER

Once Purple Sanderson went to his home in St. Lawrence county to enjoy some country air, and, incidentally, to explain his life failure to his people. Previously, Great Grief had given him odds that he would return sooner than he then planned, and everybody said that Grief had a good bet. It is not a glorious pastime, this explaining of life failures.

Later, Great Grief and Wrinkles went to Haverstraw to visit Grief's cousin and sketch. Little Pennoyer was disheartened, for it is bad to be imprisoned in brick and dust and cobbles when your ear can hear in the distance the harmony of the summer sunlight upon leaf and blade of green. Besides, he did not hear Wrinkles and Grief discoursing and quarreling in the den and Purple coming in at six o'clock with contempt.

On Friday afternoon he discovered that he only had fifty cents to last until Saturday morning, when he was to get his check from the *Gamin.* He was an artful little man by this time, however, and it is as true as the sky that when he walked toward the *Gamin* office on Saturday he had twenty cents remaining.

The cashier nodded his regrets. "Very sorry, Mr.—er—Pennoyer, but our pay day, you know, is on Monday. Come around any time after ten."

"Oh, it don't matter," said Penny. As he walked along on his return he reflected deeply how he could invest his twenty cents in food to last until Monday morning any time after ten. He bought two coffee cakes in a Third avenue bakery. They were very beautiful. Each had a hole in the center and a handsome scallop all around the edges.

Penny took great care of those cakes. At odd times he would rise from his work and go to see that no escape had been made. On Sunday he got up at noon and compressed breakfast and noon into one meal. Afterward he had almost three-quarters of a cake still left to him. He congratulated himself that with strategy he could make it endure until Monday morning, any time after ten.

At three in the afternoon there came a faint-hearted knock. "Come in," said Penny. The door opened and old Tim Connegan, who was trying to be a model, looked in apprehensively. "I beg pardon, sir," he said, at once.

"Come in, Tim, you old thief," said Penny. Tim entered, slowly and bashfully. "Sit down," said Penny. Tim sat down and began to rub his knees, for rheumatism had a mighty hold upon him.

Penny lit his pipe and crossed his legs. "Well, how goes it?"

Tim moved his square jaw upward and flashed Penny a little glance.

"Bad?" said Penny.

The old man raised his hand impressively. "I've been to every studio in the hull city and I never see such absences in my life. What with the seashore and the mountains, and this and that resort, I think all the models will be starved by fall. I found one man in up on Fifty-seventh street. He ses to me: 'Come around Tuesday—I may want yez and I may not.' That was last week. You know, I live down on the Bowery, Mr. Pennoyer, and when I got up there on Tuesday, he ses: 'Confound you, are you here again?' ses he. I went and sat down in the park, for I was too tired for the walk back. And there you are, Mr. Pennoyer. What with tramping around to look for men that are a thousand miles away, I'm near dead."

"It's hard," said Penny.

"It is, sir. I hope they'll come back soon. The summer is the death of us all, sir, it is. Sure, I never know where my next meal is coming until I get it. That's true."

"Had anything to-day?"

"Yes, sir—a little."

"How much?"

"Well, sir, a lady give me a cup of coffee this morning. It was good, too, I'm telling you."

Penny went to his cupboard. When he returned, he said: "Here's some cake."

Tim thrust forward his hands, palms erect. "Oh, now, Mr. Pennoyer, I couldn't. You——"

"Go ahead. What's the odds?"

"Oh, now——"

"Go ahead, you old bat."

Penny smoked.

When Tim was going out, he turned to grow eloquent again. "Well, I can't tell you how much I'm obliged to you, Mr. Pennoyer. You——"

"Don't mention it, old man."

Penny smoked.

The Men in the Storm

At about three o'clock of the February afternoon, the blizzard began to swirl great clouds of snow along the streets, sweeping it down from the roofs and up from the pavements until the faces of pedestrians tingled and burned as from a thousand needle-prickings. Those on the walks huddled their necks closely in the collars of their coats and went along stooping like a race of aged people. The drivers of vehicles hurried their horses furiously on their way. They were made more cruel by the exposure of their positions, aloft on high seats. The street cars, bound up-town, went slowly, the horses slipping and straining in the spongy brown mass that lay between the rails. The drivers, muffled to the eyes, stood erect and facing the wind, models of grim philosophy. Overhead the trains rumbled and roared, and the dark structure of the elevated railroad, stretching over the avenue, dripped little streams and drops of water upon the mud and snow beneath it.

All the clatter of the street was softened by the masses that lay upon the cobbles until, even to one who looked from a window, it became important music, a melody of life made necessary to the ear by the dreariness of the pitiless beat and sweep of the storm.

Occasionally one could see black figures of men busily shovelling the white drifts from the walks. The sounds from their labor created new recollections of rural experiences which every man manages to have in a measure. Later, the immense windows of the shops became aglow with light, throwing great beams of orange and yellow upon the pavement. They were infinitely cheerful, yet in a way they accented the force and discomfort of the storm, and gave a meaning to the pace of the people and the vehicles, scores of pedestrians and drivers, wretched with cold faces, necks and feet, speeding for scores of unknown doors and entrances, scattering to an infinite variety of shelters, to places which the imagination made warm with the familiar colors of home.

There was an absolute expression of hot dinners in the pace of the people. If one dared to speculate upon the destination of those who came trooping, he lost himself in a maze of social calculations; he might fling a handful of sand and attempt to follow the flight of each particular grain. But as to the suggestion of hot dinners, he was in firm lines of thought, for it was upon every hurrying face. It is a matter of tradition; it is from the tales of childhood. It comes forth with every storm.

However, in a certain part of a dark West-side street, there was a collection of men to whom these things were as if they were not. In this street was located a charitable house where for five cents the homeless of the city could get a bed at night and, in the morning, coffee and bread.

During the afternoon of the storm, the whirling snows acted as drivers, as men with whips, and at half-past three, the walk before the closed doors of the house was covered with wanderers of the street, waiting. For some distance on either side of the place they could be seen lurking in doorways and behind projecting parts of buildings, gathering in close bunches in an effort to get warm. A covered wagon drawn up near the curb sheltered a dozen of them. Under the stairs that led to the elevated railway station, there were six or eight, their hands stuffed deep in their pockets, their shoulders stooped, jiggling their feet. Others always could be seen coming, a strange procession, some slouching along with the characteristic hopeless gait of professional strays, some coming with hesitating steps wearing the air of men to whom this sort of thing was new.

It was an afternoon of incredible length. The snow, blowing in twisting clouds, sought out the men in their meagre hiding-places and skilfully beat in among them, drenching their persons with showers of fine, stinging flakes. They crowded together, muttering, and fumbling in their pockets to get their red, inflamed wrists covered by the cloth.

Newcomers usually halted at one of the groups and addressed a question, perhaps much as a matter of form, "Is it open yet?"

Those who had been waiting inclined to take the questioner seriously and become contemptuous. "No; do yeh think we'd be standin' here?"

The gathering swelled in numbers steadily and persistently. One could always see them coming, trudging slowly through the storm.

Finally, the little snow plains in the street began to assume a leaden hue from the shadows of evening. The buildings upreared gloomily save where various windows became brilliant figures of light that made shimmers and splashes of yellow on the snow. A street lamp on the curb struggled to illuminate, but it was reduced to impotent blindness by the swift gusts of sleet crusting its panes.

In this half-darkness, the men began to come from their shelter places and mass in front of the doors of charity. They were of all types, but the nationalities were mostly American, German and Irish. Many were strong, healthy, clear-skinned fellows with that stamp of countenance which is not frequently seen upon seekers after charity. There were men of undoubted patience, industry and temperance, who in time of ill-fortune, do not habitually turn to rail at the state of society, snarling at the arrogance of the rich and bemoaning the cowardice of the poor, but who at these times are apt to wear a sudden and singular meekness, as if they saw the world's progress marching from them and were trying to perceive where they had failed, what they had lacked, to be thus vanquished in the race. Then there were others of the shifting, Bowery lodging-house element who were used to paying ten cents for a place to sleep, but who now came here because it was cheaper.

But they were all mixed in one mass so thoroughly that one could not have discerned the different elements but for the fact that the laboring men, for the most part, remained silent and impassive in the blizzard, their eyes fixed on the windows of the house, statues of patience.

The sidewalk soon became completely blocked by the bodies of the men. They pressed close to one another like sheep in a winter's gale, keeping one another warm by the heat of their bodies. The snow came down upon this compressed group of men until, directly from above, it might have appeared like a heap of snow-covered merchandise, if it were not for the fact that the crowd swayed gently with a unanimous, rhythmical motion. It was wonderful to see how the snow lay upon the heads and shoulders of these men, in little ridges an inch thick perhaps in places, the flakes steadily adding drop and drop, precisely as they fall upon the unresisting grass of the fields. The feet of the men were all wet and cold and the wish to warm them accounted for the slow, gentle, rhythmical motion. Occasionally some man whose ears or nose tingled acutely from the cold winds would wriggle down until his head was protected by the shoulders of his companions.

There was a continuous murmuring discussion as to the probability of the doors being speedily opened. They persistently lifted their eyes toward the windows. One could hear little combats of opinion.

"There's a light in th' winder!"

"Naw; it's a reflection f'm across th' way."

"Well, didn't I see 'em lite it?"

"You did?"

"I did!"

"Well, then, that settles it!"

As the time approached when they expected to be allowed to enter, the men crowded to the doors in an unspeakable crush, jamming and wedging in a way that it seemed would crack bones. They surged heavily against the building in a powerful wave of pushing shoulders. Once a rumor flitted among all the tossing heads.

"They can't open th' doors! Th' fellers er smack up ag'in 'em."

Then a dull roar of rage came from the men on the outskirts; but all the time they strained and pushed until it appeared to be impossible for those that they cried out against to do anything but be crushed to pulp.

"Ah, git away f'm th' door!"

"Git outa that!"

"Throw 'em out!"

"Kill 'em!"

"Say, fellers, now, what th' 'ell? Give 'em a chanct t' open th' door!"

"Yeh damned pigs, give 'em a chanct t' open th' door!"

Men in the outskirts of the crowd occasionally yelled when a boot-heel of one of frantic trampling feet crushed on their freezing extremities.

"Git off me feet, yeh clumsy tarrier!"

"Say, don't stand on me feet! Walk on th' ground!"

A man near the doors suddenly shouted: "O-o-oh! Le' me out—le' me out!" And another, a man of infinite valor, once twisted his head so as to half face those who were pushing behind him. "Quit yer shovin', yeh——" and he delivered a volley of the most powerful and singular invective straight into the faces of the men behind him. It was as if he was hammering the noses of them with curses of triple brass. His face, red with rage, could be seen; upon it, an expression of sublime disregard of consequences. But nobody cared to reply to his imprecations; it was too cold. Many of them snickered and all continued to push.

In occasional pauses of the crowd's movement the men had opportunity to make jokes; usually grim things, and no doubt very uncouth. Nevertheless, they are notable—one does not expect to find the quality of humor in a heap of old clothes under a snowdrift.

The winds seemed to grow fiercer as time wore on. Some of the gusts of snow that came down on the close collection of heads cut like knives and needles, and the men huddled, and swore, not like dark assassins, but in a sort of an American fashion, grimly and desperately, it is true, but yet with a wondrous under-effect, indefinable and mystic, as if there was some kind of humor in this catastrophe, in this situation in a night of snow-laden winds.

Once, the window of the huge dry-goods shop across the street furnished material for a few moments of forgetfulness. In the brilliantly-lighted space appeared the figure of a man. He was rather stout and very well clothed. His whiskers were fashioned charmingly after those of the Prince of Wales. He stood in an attitude of magnificent reflection. He slowly stroked his moustache with a certain grandeur of manner, and looked down at the snow-encrusted mob. From below, there was denoted a supreme complacence in him. It seemed that the sight operated inversely, and enabled him to more clearly regard his own environment, delightful relatively.

One of the mob chanced to turn his head and perceive the figure in the window. "Hello, lookit 'is whiskers," he said genially.

Many of the men turned then, and a shout went up. They called to him in all strange keys. They addressed him in every manner, from familiar and cordial greetings to carefully-worded advice concerning changes in his personal appearance. The man presently fled, and the mob chuckled ferociously like ogres who had just devoured something.

They turned then to serious business. Often they addressed the stolid front of the house.

"Oh, let us in fer Gawd's sake!"

"Let us in or we'll all drop dead!"

"Say, what's th' use o' keepin' all us poor Indians out in th' cold?"

And always some one was saying, "Keep off me feet."

The crushing of the crowd grew terrific toward the last. The men, in keen pain from the blasts, began almost to fight. With the pitiless whirl of snow upon them, the battle for shelter was going to the strong. It became known that the basement door at the foot of a little steep flight of stairs was the one to be opened, and they jostled and heaved in this direction like laboring fiends. One could hear them panting and groaning in their fierce exertion.

Usually some one in the front ranks was protesting to those in the rear: "O—o—ow! Oh, say, now, fellers, let up, will yeh? Do yeh wanta kill somebody?"

A policeman arrived and went into the midst of them, scolding and berating, occasionally threatening, but using no force but that of his hands and shoulders against these men who were only struggling to get in out of the storm. His decisive tones rang out sharply: "Stop that pushin' back there! Come, boys, don't push! Stop that! Here, you, quit yer shovin'! Cheese that!"

When the door below was opened, a thick stream of men forced a way down the stairs, which were of an extraordinary narrowness and seemed only wide enough for one at a time. Yet they somehow went down almost three abreast. It was a difficult and painful operation. The crowd was like a turbulent water forcing itself through one tiny outlet. The men in the rear, excited by the success of the others, made frantic exertions, for it seemed that this large band would more than fill the quarters and that many would be left upon the pavements. It would be disastrous to be of the last, and accordingly men with the snow biting their faces, writhed and twisted with their might. One expected that from the tremendous pressure, the narrow passage to the basement door would be so choked and clogged with human limbs and bodies that movement would be impossible. Once indeed the crowd was forced to stop, and a cry went along that a man had been injured at the foot of the stairs. But presently the slow movement began again, and the policeman fought at the top of the flight to ease the pressure on those who were going down.

A reddish light from a window fell upon the faces of the men when they, in turn, arrived at the last three steps and were about to enter. One could then note a change of expression that had come over their features. As they thus stood upon the threshold of their hopes, they looked suddenly content and complacent. The fire had passed from their eyes and the snarl had vanished from their lips. The very force of the crowd in the rear, which had previously vexed them, was regarded from another point of view, for it now made it inevitable that they should go through the little doors into the place that was cheery and warm with light.

The tossing crowd on the sidewalk grew smaller and smaller. The snow beat with merciless persistence upon the bowed heads of those who waited. The wind drove it up from the pavements in frantic forms of winding white, and it seethed in circles about the huddled forms, passing in, one by one, three by three, out of the storm.

Coney Island's Failing Days

"Down here at your Coney Island, toward the end of the season, I am made to feel very sad," said the stranger to me. "The great mournfulness that settles upon a summer resort at this time always depresses me exceedingly. The mammoth empty buildings, planned by extraordinarily optimistic architects, remind me in an unpleasant manner of my youthful dreams. In those days of visions I erected huge castles for the reception of my friends and admirers, and discovered later that I could have entertained them more comfortably in a small two story frame structure. There is a mighty pathos in these gaunt and hollow buildings, impassively and stolidly suffering from an enormous hunger for the public. And the unchangeable, ever imperturbable sea pursues its quaint devices blithely at the feet of these mournful wooden animals, gabbling and frolicking, with no thought for absent man nor maid!"

As the stranger spoke, he gazed with considerable scorn at the emotions of the sea; and the breeze from the far Navesink hills gently stirred the tangled, philosophic hair upon his forehead. Presently he went on: "The buildings are in effect more sad than the men, but I assure you that some of the men look very sad. I watched a talented and persuasive individual who was operating in front of a tintype gallery, and he had only the most marvelously infrequent opportunities to display his oratory and finesse. The occasional stragglers always managed to free themselves before he could drag them into the gallery and take their pictures. In the long intervals he gazed about him with a bewildered air, as if he felt his world dropping from under his feet. Once I saw him spy a promising youth afar off. He lurked with muscles at a tension, and then at the proper moment he swooped. 'Look-a-here,' he said, with tears of enthusiasm in his eyes, 'the best picture in the world! An' on'y four fer a quarter. On'y jest try it, an' you'll go away perfectly satisfied!'

" 'I'll go away perfectly satisfied without trying it,' replied the promising youth, and he did. The tintype man wanted to dash his samples to the ground and whip the promising youth. He controlled himself, however, and went to watch the approach of two women and a little boy who were nothing more than three dots, away down the board walk.

"At one place I heard the voice of a popcorn man raised in a dreadful note, as if he were chanting a death hymn. It made me shiver as I felt all the tragedy of the collapsed popcorn market. I began to see that it was an insult to the pain and suffering of these men to go near to them without buying anything. I took new and devious routes sometimes.

"As for the railroad guards and station men, they were so tolerant of the presence of passengers that I felt it to be an indication of their sense of relief from the summer's battle. They did not seem so greatly irritated by patrons of the railroad as I have seen them at other times. And in all the beer gardens the waiters had opportunity to indulge that delight in each other's society and conversation which forms so important a part in a waiter's idea of happiness. Sometimes the people in a sparsely occupied place will fare more strange than those in a crowded one. At one time I waited twenty minutes for a bottle of the worst beer in Christendom while my waiter told a charmingly naive story to a group of his compatriots. I protested sotto voce at the time that such beer might at least have the merit of being brought quickly.

"The restaurants, however, I think to be quite delicious, being in a large part thoroughly disreputable and always provided with huge piles of red boiled crabs. These huge piles of provision around on the floor and on the oyster counters always give me the opinion that I am dining on the freshest food in the world, and I appreciate the sensation. If need be, it also allows a man to revel in dreams of unlimited quantity.

"I found countless restaurants where I could get things almost to my taste, and, as I ate, watch the grand, eternal motion of the sea and have the waiter come up and put the pepper castor on the menu card to keep the salt breeze from interfering with my order for dinner.

"And yet I have an occasional objection to the sea when dining in sight of it; for a man with a really artistic dining sense always feels important as a duke when he is indulging in his favorite pastime, and, as the sea always makes me feel that I am a trivial object, I cannot dine with absolute comfort in its presence. The conflict of the two perceptions disturbs me. This is why I have grown to prefer the restaurants down among the narrow board streets. I tell you this because I think an explanation is due to you."

As we walked away from the beach and around one of those huge buildings whose pathos had so aroused the stranger's interest, we came into view of two acres of merry-go-rounds, circular swings, roller coasters, observation wheels and the like. The stranger paused and regarded them.

"Do you know," he said, "I am deeply fascinated by all these toys. For, of course, you perceive that they are really enlarged toys. They reinforce me in my old opinion that humanity only needs to be provided for ten minutes with a few whirligigs and things of the sort, and it can forget at least four centuries of misery. I rejoice in these whirligigs," continued the stranger, eloquently, "and as I watch here and there a person going around and around or up and down, or over and over, I say to myself that whirligigs must be made in heaven.

"It is a mystery to me why some man does not provide a large number of wooden rocking horses and let the people sit and dreamfully rock themselves into temporary forgetfulness. There could be intense quiet enforced by special policemen, who, however, should allow subdued conversation on the part of the patrons of the establishment. Deaf mutes should patrol to and fro selling slumberous drinks. These things are none of them insane. They are particularly rational. A man needs a little nerve quiver, and he gets it by being flopped around in the air like a tailless kite. He needs the introduction of a reposeful element, and he procures it upon a swing that makes him feel like thirty-five emotional actresses all trying to swoon upon one rug. There are some people who stand apart and deride these machines. If you could procure a dark night for them and the total absence of their friends they would smile, many of them. I assure you that I myself would indulge in these forms of intoxication if I were not a very great philosopher."

We strolled to the music hall district, where the sky lines of the rows of buildings are wondrously near to each other, and the crowded little thoroughfares resemble the eternal "Street Scene in Cairo." There was an endless strumming and tooting and shrill piping in clamor and chaos, while at all times there were interspersed the sharp cracking sounds from the shooting galleries and the coaxing calls of innumerable fakirs. At the stand where one can throw at wooden cats and negro heads and be in danger of winning cigars, a self reliant youth bought a whole armful of base balls, and missed with each one. Everybody grinned. A heavily built man openly jeered. "You couldn't hit a church!" "Couldn't I?" retorted the young man, bitterly. Near them three bad men were engaged in an intense conversation. The fragment of a sentence suddenly dominated the noises. "He's got money to burn." The sun, meanwhile, was muffled in the clouds back of Staten Island and the Narrows. Softened tones of sapphire and carmine touched slantingly the sides of the buildings. A view of the sea, to be caught between two of the houses, showed it to be of a pale, shimmering green. The lamps began to be lighted, and shed a strong orange radiance. In one restaurant the only occupants were a little music hall singer and a youth. She was laughing and chatting in a light hearted way not peculiar to music hall girls. The youth looked as if he desired to be at some other place. He was singularly wretched and uncomfortable. The stranger said he judged from appearances that the little music hall girl must think a great deal of that one youth. His sympathies seemed to be for the music hall girl. Finally there was a sea of salt meadow, with a black train shooting across it.

"I have made a discovery in one of these concert halls," said the stranger, as we retraced our way. "It is an old gray haired woman, who occupies proudly the position of chief pianiste. I like to go and sit and wonder by what mighty process of fighting and drinking she achieved her position. To see her, you would think she was leading an orchestra of seventy pieces, although she alone composes it. It is great reflection to watch that gray head. At those moments I am willing to concede that I must be relatively happy, and that is a great admission from a philosopher of my attainments.

"How seriously all these men out in front of the dens take their vocations. They regard people with a voracious air, as if they contemplated any moment making a rush and a grab and mercilessly compelling a great expenditure. This scant and feeble crowd must madden them. When I first came to this part of the town I was astonished and delighted, for it was the nearest approach to a den of wolves that I had encountered since leaving the West. Oh, no, of course the Coney Island of to-day is not the Coney Island of the ancient days. I believe you were about to impale me upon that sentence, were you not?"

We walked along for some time in silence until the stranger went to buy a frankfurter. As he returned, he said: "When a man is respectable he is fettered to certain wheels, and when the chariot of fashion moves, he is dragged along at the rear. For his agony, he can console himself with the law that if a certain thing has not yet been respectable, he need only wait a sufficient time and it will eventually be so. The only disadvantage is that he is obliged to wait until other people wish to do it, and he is likely to lose his own craving. Now I have a great passion for eating frankfurters on the street, and if I were respectable I would be obliged to wait until the year 3365, when men will be able to hold their positions in society only by consuming immense quantities of frankfurters on the street. And by that time I would have undoubtedly developed some new pastime. But I am not respectable. I am a philosopher. I eat frankfurters on the street with the same equanimity that you might employ toward a cigarette.

"See those three young men enjoying themselves. With what rakish, daredevil airs they smoke those cigars. Do you know, the spectacle of three modern young men enjoying themselves is something that I find vastly interesting and instructive. I see revealed more clearly the purposes of the inexorable universe which plans to amuse us occasionally to keep us from the rebellion of suicide. And I see how simply and drolly it accomplishes its end. The insertion of a mild quantity of the egotism of sin into the minds of these young men causes them to wildly enjoy themselves. It is necessary to encourage them, you see, at this early day. After all, it is only great philosophers who have the wisdom to be utterly miserable."

As we walked toward the station the stranger stopped often to observe types which interested him. He did it with an unconscious calm insolence as if the people were bugs. Once a bug threatened to beat him. "What 'cher lookin' at?" he asked of him. "My friend," said the stranger, "if any one displays real interest in you in this world, you should take it as an occasion for serious study and reflection. You should be supremely amazed to find that a man can be interested in anybody but himself!" The belligerent seemed quite abashed. He explained to a friend: "He ain't right! What? I dunno. Something 'bout 'study' er something! He's got wheels in his head!"

On the train the cold night wind blew transversely across the reeling cars, and in the dim light of the lamps one could see the close rows of heads swaying and jolting with the motion. From directly in front of us peanut shells fell to the floor amid a regular and interminable crackling. A stout man, who slept with his head forward upon his breast, crunched them often beneath his uneasy feet. From some unknown place a drunken voice was raised in song.

"This return of the people to their battles always has a stupendous effect upon me," said the stranger. "The gayety which arises upon these Sunday night occasions is different from all other gayeties. There is an unspeakable air of recklessness and bravado and grief about it. This train load is going toward that inevitable, overhanging, devastating Monday. That singer there to-morrow will be a truckman, perhaps, and swearing ingeniously at his horses and other truckmen. He feels the approach of this implacable Monday. Two hours ago he was engulfed in whirligigs and beer and had forgotten that there were Mondays. Now he is confronting it, and as he can't battle it, he scorns it. You can hear the undercurrent of it in that song, which is really as grievous as the cry of a child. If he had no vanity—well, it is fortunate for the world that we are not all great thinkers."

We sat on the lower deck of the Bay Ridge boat and watched the marvelous lights of New York looming through the purple mist. The little Italian band situated up one stairway, through two doors and around three corners from us, sounded in beautiful, faint and slumberous rhythm. The breeze fluttered again in the stranger's locks. We could hear the splash of the waves against the bow. The sleepy lights looked at us with hue of red and green and orange. Overhead some dust colored clouds scudded across the deep indigo sky. "Thunderation," said the stranger, "if I did not know of so many yesterdays and have such full knowledge of to-morrows, I should be perfectly happy at this moment, and that would create a sensation among philosophers all over the world."

The Fire

We were walking on one of the shadowy side streets, west of Sixth avenue. The midnight silence and darkness was upon it save where at the point of intersection with the great avenue, there was a broad span of yellow light. From there came the steady monotonous jingle of streetcar bells and the weary clatter of hoofs on the cobbles. While the houses in this street turned black and mystically silent with the night, the avenue continued its eternal movement and life, a great vein that never slept nor paused. The gorgeous orange-hued lamps of a saloon flared plainly, and the figures of some loungers could be seen as they stood on the corner. Passing to and fro, the tiny black figures of people made an ornamental border on this fabric of yellow light.

The stranger was imparting to me some grim midnight reflections upon existence, and in the heavy shadows and in the great stillness pierced only by the dull thunder of the avenue, they were very impressive.

Suddenly the muffled cry of a woman came from one of those dark, impassive houses near us. There was the sound of the splinter and crash of broken glass, falling to the pavement. "What's that," gasped the stranger. The scream contained that ominous quality, that weird timbre which denotes fear of imminent death.

A policeman, huge and panting, ran past us with glitter of buttons and shield in the darkness. He flung himself upon the fire-alarm box at the corner where the lamp shed a flicker of carmine tints upon the pavement. "Come on," shouted the stranger. He dragged me excitedly down the street. We came upon an old four story structure, with a long sign of a bakery over the basement windows, and the region about the quaint front door plastered with other signs. It was one of those ancient dwellings which the churning process of the city had changed into a hive of little industries.

At this time some dull grey smoke, faintly luminous in the night, writhed out from the tops of the second story windows, and from the basement there glared a deep and terrible hue of red, the color of satanic wrath, the color of murder. "Look! Look!" shouted the stranger.

It was extraordinary how the street awakened. It seemed but an instant before the pavements were studded with people. They swarmed from all directions, and from the dark mass arose countless exclamations, eager and swift.

"Where is it? Where is it?"

"No. 135."

"It's that old bakery."

"Is everybody out?"

"Look—gee—say, lookut 'er burn, would yeh?"

The windows of almost every house became crowded with people, clothed and partially clothed, many having rushed from their beds. Here were many women, and as their eyes fastened upon that terrible growing mass of red light one could hear their little cries, quavering with fear and dread. The smoke oozed in greater clouds from the spaces between the sashes of the windows, and urged by the fervor of the heat within, ascended in more rapid streaks and curves.

Upon the sidewalk there had been a woman who was fumbling mechanically with the buttons at the neck of her dress. Her features were lined in anguish; she seemed to be frantically searching her memory—her memory, that poor feeble contrivance that had deserted her at the first of the crisis, at the momentous time. She really struggled and tore hideously at some frightful mental wall that upreared between her and her senses, her very instincts. The policeman, running back from the fire-alarm box, grabbed her, intending to haul her away from danger of falling things. Then something came to her like a bolt from the sky. The creature turned all grey, like an ape. A loud shriek rang out that made the spectators bend their bodies, twisting as if they were receiving sword thrusts.

"My baby! My baby! My baby!"

The policeman simply turned and plunged into the house. As the woman tossed her arms in maniacal gestures about her head, it could then be seen that she waved in one hand a little bamboo easel, of the kind which people sometimes place in corners of their parlors. It appeared that she had with great difficulty saved it from the flames. Its cost should have been about 30 cents.

A long groaning sigh came from the crowd in the street, and from all the thronged windows. It was full of distress and pity, and a sort of cynical scorn for their impotency. Occasionally the woman screamed again. Another policeman was fending her off from the house, which she wished to enter in the frenzy of her motherhood, regardless of the flames. These people of the neighborhood, aroused from their beds, looked at the spectacle in a half-dazed fashion at times, as if they were contemplating the ravings of a red beast in a cage. The flames grew as if fanned by tempests, a sweeping, inexorable appetite of a thing, shining, with fierce, pitiless brilliancy, gleaming in the eyes of the crowd that were upturned to it in an ecstasy of awe, fear and, too, half barbaric admiration. They felt the human helplessness that comes when nature breaks forth in passion, overturning the obstacles, emerging at a leap from the position of a slave to that of a master, a giant. There became audible a humming noise, the buzzing of curious machinery. It was the voices of the demons of the flame. The house, in manifest heroic indifference to the fury that raged in its entrails, maintained a stolid and imperturbable exterior, looming black and immovable against the turmoil of crimson.

Eager questions were flying to and fro in the street.

"Say, did a copper go in there?"

"Yeh! He come out again, though."

"He did not! He's in there yet!"

"Well, didn't I see 'im?"

"How long ago was the alarm sent in?"

" 'Bout a minute."

A woman leaned perilously from a window of a nearby apartment house and spoke querulously into the shadowy, jostling crowd beneath her, "Jack!"

And the voice of an unknown man in an unknown place answered her gruffly and short in the tones of a certain kind of downtrodden husband who rebels upon occasion, "What?"

"Will you come up here," cried the woman, shrilly irritable. "Supposin' this house should get afire——" It came to pass that during the progress of the conflagration these two held a terse and bitter domestic combat, infinitely commonplace in language and mental maneuvers.

The blaze had increased with a frightful vehemence and swiftness. Unconsciously, at times, the crowd dully moaned, their eyes fascinated by this exhibition of the strength of nature, their master after all, that ate them and their devices at will whenever it chose to fling down their little restrictions. The flames changed in color from crimson to lurid orange as glass was shattered by the heat, and fell crackling to the pavement. The baker, whose shop had been in the basement, was running about, weeping. A policeman had fought interminably to keep the crowd away from the front of the structure.

"Thunderation!" yelled the stranger, clutching my arm in a frenzy of excitement, "did you ever see anything burn so? Why, it's like an explosion. It's only been a matter of seconds since it started."

In the street, men had already begun to turn toward each other in that indefinite regret and sorrow, as if they were not quite sure of the reason of their mourning.

"Well, she's a goner!"

"Sure—went up like a box of matches!"

"Great Scott, lookut 'er burn!"

Some individual among them furnished the inevitable grumble. "Well, these——" It was a half-coherent growling at conditions, men, fate, law.

Then, from the direction of the avenue there suddenly came a tempestuous roar, a clattering, rolling rush and thunder, as from the headlong sweep of a battery of artillery. Wild and shrill, like a clangorous noise of war, arose the voice of a gong.

One could see a sort of a delirium of excitement, of ardorous affection, go in a wave of emotion over this New York crowd, usually so stoical. Men looked at each other. "Quick work, eh?" They crushed back upon the pavements, leaving the street almost clear. All eyes were turned toward the corner where the lights of the avenue glowed.

The roar grew and grew until it was as the sound of an army, charging. That policeman's hurried fingers sending the alarm from the box at the corner had aroused a tornado, a storm of horses, machinery, men. And now they were coming in clamor and riot of hoofs and wheels, while over all rang the piercing cry of the gong, tocsin-like, a noise of barbaric fights.

It thrilled the blood, this thunder. The stranger jerked his shoulders nervously and kept up a swift muttering. "Hear 'em come!" he said, breathlessly.

Then in an instant a fire patrol wagon, as if apparitional flashed into view at the corner. The lights of the avenue gleamed for an instant upon the red and brass of the wagon, the helmets of the crew and the glossy sides of the galloping horses. Then it swung into the dark street and thundered down upon its journey, with but a half-view of a driver making his reins to be steel ribbons over the backs of his horses, mad from the fervor of their business.

The stranger's hand tightened convulsively upon my arm. His enthusiasm was like the ardor of one who looks upon the pageantry of battles. "Ah, look at 'em! Look at 'em! Ain't that great? Why it hasn't been any time at all since the alarm was sent in, and now look!" As this clanging, rolling thing, drawn swiftly by the beautiful might of the horses, clamored through the street, one could feel the cheers, wild and valorous, at the very lips of these people habitually so calm, cynical, impassive. The crew tumbled from their wagon and ran toward the house. A hoarse shout arose high above the medley of noises.

Other roars, other clangings, were to be heard from all directions. It was extraordinary, the loud rumblings of wheels and the pealings of gongs aroused by a movement of the policeman's fingers.

Of a sudden, three white horses dashed down the street with their engine, a magnificent thing of silver-like glitter, that sent a storm of red sparks high into the air and smote the heart with the wail of its whistle.

A hosecart swept around the corner and into the narrow lane, whose close walls made the reverberations like the crash of infantry volleys. There was shine of lanterns, of helmets, of rubber coats, of the bright, strong trappings of the horses. The driver had been confronted by a dreadful little problem in street cars and elevated railway pillars just as he was about to turn into the street, but there had been no pause, no hesitation. A clever dodge, a shrill grinding of the wheels in the street-car tracks, a miss of this and an escape of that by a beautifully narrow margin, and the hosecart went on its headlong way. When the gleam-white and gold of the cart stopped in the shadowy street, it was but a moment before a stream of water, of a cold steel color, was plunging through a window into the yellow glare, into this house which was now a den of fire wolves, lashing, carousing, leaping, straining. A wet snake-like hose trailed underfoot to where the steamer was making the air pulsate with its swift vibrations.

From another direction had come another thunder that developed into a crash of sounds, as a hook-and-ladder truck, with long and graceful curves, spun around the other corner, with the horses running with steady leaps toward the place of the battle. It was always obvious that these men who drove were drivers in blood and fibre, charioteers incarnate.

When the ladders were placed against the side of the house, firemen went slowly up them, dragging their hose. They became outlined like black beetles against the red and yellow expanses of flames. A vast cloud of smoke, sprinkled thickly with sparks, went coiling heavily toward the black sky. Touched by the shine of the blaze, the smoke sometimes glowed dull red, the color of bricks. A crowd that, it seemed, had sprung from the cobbles, born at the sound of the wheels rushing through the night, thickly thronged the walks, pushed here and there by the policemen who scolded them roundly, evidently in an eternal state of injured surprise at their persistent desire to get a view of things.

As we walked to the corner we looked back and watched the red glimmer from the fire shine on the dark surging crowd over which towered at times the helmets of police. A billow of smoke swept away from the structure. Occasionally, burned out sparks, like fragments of dark tissue, fluttered in the air. At the corner a steamer was throbbing, churning, shaking in its power as if overcome with rage. A fireman was walking tranquilly about it scrutinizing the mechanism. He wore a blasé air. They all, in fact, seemed to look at fires with the calm, unexcited vision of veterans. It was only the populace with their new nerves, it seemed, who could feel the thrill and dash of these attacks, these furious charges made in the dead of night, at high noon, at any time, upon the common enemy, the loosened flame.

When Man Falls, a Crowd Gathers

A man and a boy were trudging slowly along an East-Side street. It was nearly six o'clock in the evening and this street, which led to one of the East River ferries, was crowded with laborers, shop men and shop women, hurrying to their dinners. The store windows were a-glare.

The man and the boy conversed in Italian, mumbling the soft syllables and making little quick egotistical gestures. They walked with the lumbering peasant's gait, slowly, and blinking their black eyes at the passing show of the street.

Suddenly the man wavered on his limbs and glared bewildered and helpless as if some blinding light had flashed before his vision; then he swayed like a drunken man and fell. The boy grasped his companion's arm frantically and made an attempt to support him so that the limp form slid to the sidewalk with an easy motion as a body sinks in the sea. The boy screamed.

Instantly, from all directions people turned their gaze upon the prone figure. In a moment there was a dodging, pushing, peering group about the man. A volley of questions, replies, speculations flew to and fro above all the bobbing heads.

"What's th' matter? What's th' matter?"

"Oh, a jag, I guess!"

"Nit; he's got a fit!"

"What's th' matter? What's th' matter?"

Two streams of people coming from different directions met at this point to form a crowd. Others came from across the street.

Down under their feet, almost lost under this throng, lay the man, hidden in the shadows caused by their forms which in fact barely allowed a particle of light to pass between them. Those in the foremost rank bended down, shouldering each other, eager, anxious to see everything. Others behind them crowded savagely for a place like starving men fighting for bread. Always, the question could be heard flying in the air. "What's the matter?" Some, near to the body and perhaps feeling the danger of being forced over upon it, twisted their heads and protested violently to those unheeding ones who were scuffling in the rear. "Say, quit yer shovin', can't yeh? What d' yeh want, anyhow? Quit!"

A man back in the crowd suddenly said: "Say, young feller, you're a peach wid dose feet o' yours. Keep off me!"

Another voice said: "Well, dat's all right——"

The boy who had been walking with the man who fell was standing helplessly, a terrified look in his eyes. He held the man's hand. Sometimes he gave it a little jerk that was at once an appeal, a reproach, a caution. And, withal, it was a timid calling to the limp and passive figure as if he half expected to arouse it from its coma with a pleading touch of his fingers. Occasionally, he looked about him with swift glances of indefinite hope, as if assistance might come from the clouds. The men near him questioned him, but he did not seem to understand. He answered them "Yes" or "No," blindly, with no apparent comprehension of their language. They frequently jostled him until he was obliged to put his hand upon the breast of the body to maintain his balance.

Those that were nearest to the man upon the side-walk at first saw his body go through a singular contortion. It was as if an invisible hand had reached up from the earth and had seized him by the hair. He seemed dragged slowly, relentlessly backward, while his body stiffened convulsively, his hands clenched, and his arms swung rigidly upward. A slight froth was upon his chin. Through his pallid half-closed lids could be seen the steel-colored gleam of his eyes that were turned toward all the bending, swaying faces and in the inanimate thing upon the pave yet burned threateningly, dangerously, shining with a mystic light, as a corpse might glare at those live ones who seemed about to trample it under foot.

As for the men near, they hung back, appearing as if they expected it to spring erect and clutch at them. Their eyes however were held in a spell of fascination. They seemed scarcely to breathe. They were contemplating a depth into which a human being had sunk and the marvel of this mystery of life or death held them chained. Occasionally from the rear, a man came thrusting his way impetuously, satisfied that there was a horror to be seen and apparently insane to get a view of it. Less curious persons swore at these men when they trod upon their toes.

The loaded street-cars jingled past this scene in endless parade. Occasionally, from where the elevated railroad crossed the street there came a rhythmical roar, suddenly begun and suddenly ended. Over the heads of the crowd hung an immovable canvas sign. "Regular dinner twenty cents."

After the first spasm of curiosity had passed away, there were those in the crowd who began to consider ways to help. A voice called: "Rub his wrists." The boy and some one on the other side of the man began to rub his wrists and slap his palms, but still the body lay inert, rigid. When a hand was dropped the arm fell like a stick. A tall German suddenly appeared and resolutely began to push the crowd back. "Get back there—get back," he continually repeated as he pushed them. He had psychological authority over this throng; they obeyed him. He and another knelt by the man in the darkness and loosened his shirt at the throat. Once they struck a match and held it close to the man's face. This livid visage suddenly appearing under their feet in the light of the match's yellow glare, made the throng shudder. Half articulate exclamations could be heard. There were men who nearly created a battle in the madness of their desire to see the thing.

Meanwhile others with magnificent passions for abstract statistical information were questioning the boy. "What's his name?" "Where does he live?"

Then a policeman appeared. The first part of the little play had gone on without his assistance but now he came swiftly, his helmet towering above the multitude of black derbys and shading that confident, self-reliant police face. He charged the crowd as if he were a squadron of Irish lancers. The people fairly withered before this onslaught. He shouted: "Come, make way there! Make way!" He was evidently a man whose life was half-pestered out of him by the inhabitants of the city who were sufficiently unreasonable and stupid as to insist on being in the streets. His was the rage of a placid cow, who wishes to lead a life of tranquillity, but who is eternally besieged by flies that hover in clouds.

When he arrived at the centre of the crowd he first demanded threateningly: "Well, what's th' matter here?" And then when he saw that human bit of wreckage at the bottom of the sea of men he said to it: "Come, git up outa that! Git outa here!"

Whereupon hands were raised in the crowd and a volley of decorated information was blazed at the officer.

"Ah, he's got a fit! Can't yeh see!"

"He's got a fit!"

"He's sick!"

"What th' ell yeh doin'? Leave 'm be!"

The policeman menaced with a glance the crowd from whose safe interior the defiant voices had emerged.

A doctor had come. He and the policeman bended down at the man's side. Occasionally the officer upreared to create room. The crowd fell away before his threats, his admonitions, his sarcastic questions and before the sweep of those two huge buckskin gloves.

At last, the peering ones saw the man on the side-walk begin to breathe heavily, with the strain of overtaxed machinery, as if he had just come to the surface from some deep water. He uttered a low cry in his foreign tongue. It was a babyish squeal or like the sad wail of a little storm-tossed kitten. As this cry went forth to all those eager ears the jostling and crowding recommenced until the doctor was obliged to yell warningly a dozen times. The policeman had gone to send an ambulance call.

When a man struck another match and in its meagre light the doctor felt the skull of the prostrate one to discover if any wound or fracture had been caused by his fall to the stone side-walk, the crowd pressed and crushed again. It was as if they fully anticipated a sight of blood in the gleam of the match and they scrambled and dodged for positions. The policeman returned and fought with them. The doctor looked up frequently to scold at them and to sharply demand more space.

At last out of the golden haze made by the lamps far up the street, there came the sound of a gong beaten rapidly, impatiently. A monstrous truck loaded to the sky with barrels scurried to one side with marvelous agility. And then the black ambulance with its red light, its galloping horse, its dull gleam of lettering and bright shine of gong clattered into view. A young man, as imperturbable always as if he were going to a picnic, sat thoughtfully upon the rear seat.

When they picked up the limp body, from which came little moans and howls, the crowd almost turned into a mob, a silent mob, each member of which struggled for one thing. Afterward some resumed their ways with an air of relief, as if they themselves had been in pain and were at last recovered. Others still continued to stare at the ambulance on its banging, clanging return journey until it vanished into the golden haze. It was as if they had been cheated. Their eyes expressed discontent at this curtain which had been rung down in the midst of the drama. And this impenetrable fabric suddenly intervening between a suffering creature and their curiosity, seemed to appear to them as an injustice.

New York's Bicycle Speedway

The Bowery has had its day as a famous New York street. It is now a mere tradition. Broadway will long hold its place as the chief vein of the city's life. No process of expansion can ever leave it abandoned to the cheap clothing dealers and dime museum robbers. It is too strategic in position. But lately the Western Boulevard which slants from the Columbus monument at the southwest corner of Central Park to the river has vaulted to a startling prominence and is now one of the sights of New York. This is caused by the bicycle. Once the Boulevard was a quiet avenue whose particular distinctions were its shade trees and its third foot-walk which extended in Parisian fashion down the middle of the street. Also it was noted for its billboards and its huge and slumberous apartment hotels. Now, however, it is the great thoroughfare for bicycles. On these gorgeous spring days they appear in thousands. All mankind is a-wheel apparently and a person on nothing but legs feels like a strange animal. A mighty army of wheels streams from the brick wilderness below Central Park and speeds over the asphalt. In the cool of the evening it returns with swaying and flashing of myriad lamps.

The bicycle crowd has completely subjugated the street. The glittering wheels dominate it from end to end. The cafes and dining rooms of the apartment hotels are occupied mainly by people in bicycle clothes. Even the billboards have surrendered. They advertise wheels and lamps and tires and patent saddles with all the flaming vehemence of circus art. Even when they do condescend to still advertise a patent medicine, you are sure to confront a lithograph of a young person in bloomers who is saying in large type: "Yes, George, I find that Willowrum always refreshes me after these long rides."

Down at the Circle where stands the patient Columbus, the stores are crowded with bicycle goods. There are innumerable repair shops. Everything is bicycle. In the afternoon the parade begins. The great discoverer, erect on his tall grey shaft, must feel his stone head whirl when the battalions come swinging and shining around the curve.

It is interesting to note the way in which the blasphemous and terrible truck-drivers of the lower part of the city will hunt a bicyclist. A truck-driver, of course, believes that a wheelman is a pest. The average man could not feel more annoyance if nature had suddenly invented some new kind of mosquito. And so the truck-driver resolves in his dreadful way to make life as troublous and thrilling for the wheelman as he possibly can. The wheelman suffers under a great handicap. He is struggling over the most uneven cobbles which bless a metropolis. Twenty horses threaten him and forty wheels miss his shoulder by an inch. In his ears there is a hideous din. It surrounds him, envelopes him.

Add to this trouble, then, a truckman with a fiend's desire to see dead wheelmen. The situation affords deep excitement for everyone concerned.

But when a truck-driver comes to the Boulevard the beautiful balance of the universe is apparent. The teamster sits mute, motionless, casting sidelong glances at the wheels which spin by him. He still contrives to exhibit a sort of a sombre defiance, but he has no oath nor gesture nor wily scheme to drive a three-ton wagon over the prostrate body of some unhappy cyclist. On the Boulevard this roaring lion from down town is so subdued, so isolated that he brings tears to the sympathetic eye.

There is a new game on the Boulevard. It is the game of Bicycle Cop and Scorcher. When the scorcher scorches beyond the patience of the law, the bicycle policeman, if in sight, takes after him. Usually the scorcher has a blissful confidence in his ability to scorch and thinks it much easier to just ride away from the policeman than to go to court and pay a fine. So they go flying up the Boulevard with the whole mob of wheelmen and wheelwomen, eager to see the race, sweeping after them. But the bicycle police are mighty hard riders and it takes a flier to escape them. The affair usually ends in calamity for the scorcher, but in the meantime fifty or sixty cyclists have had a period of delirious joy.

Bicycle Cop and Scorcher is a good game, but after all it is not as good as the game that was played in the old days when the suggestion of a corps of bicycle police in neat knickerbockers would have scandalized Mulberry street. This was the game of Fat Policeman on Foot Trying to Stop a Spurt. A huge, unwieldy officer rushing out into the street and wildly trying to head off and grab some rider who was spinning along in just one silver flash was a sight that caused the populace to turn out in a body. If some madman started at a fierce gait from the Columbus monument, he could have the consciousness that at frequent and exciting intervals, red-faced policemen would gallop out at him and frenziedly clutch at his coattails. And owing to a curious dispensation, the majority of the policemen along the Boulevard were very stout and could swear most graphically in from two to five languages.

But they changed all that. The un-police-like bicycle police are wonderfully clever and the vivid excitement of other days is gone. Even the scorcher seems to feel depressed and narrowly looks over the nearest officer before he starts on his frantic career.

The girl in bloomers is, of course, upon her native heath when she steers her steel steed into the Boulevard. One becomes conscious of a bewildering variety in bloomers. There are some that fit and some that do not fit. There are some that were not made to fit and there are some that couldn't fit anyhow. As a matter of fact the bloomer costume is now in one of the primary stages of its evolution. Let us hope so at any rate. Of course every decent citizen concedes that women shall wear what they please and it is supposed that he covenants with himself not to grin and nudge his neighbor when anything particularly amazing passes him on the street but resolves to simply and industriously mind his own affairs. Still the situation no doubt harrows him greatly. No man was ever found to defend bloomers. His farthest statement, as an individual, is to advocate them for all women he does not know and cares nothing about. Most women become radical enough to say: "Why shouldn't I wear 'em, if I choose." Still, a second look at the Boulevard convinces one that the world is slowly, solemnly, inevitably coming to bloomers. We are about to enter an age of bloomers and the bicycle, that machine which has gained an economic position of the most tremendous importance, is going to be responsible for more than the bruises on the departed fat policemen of the Boulevard.

An Eloquence of Grief

The windows were high and saintly, of the shape that is found in churches. From time to time a policeman at the door spoke sharply to some incoming person. "Take your hat off!" He displayed in his voice the horror of a priest when the sanctity of a chapel is defied or forgotten. The court-room was crowded with people who sloped back comfortably in their chairs, regarding with undeviating glances the procession and its attendant and guardian policemen that moved slowly inside the spear-topped railing. All persons connected with a case went close to the magistrate's desk before a word was spoken in the matter, and then their voices were toned to the ordinary talking strength. The crowd in the court-room could not hear a sentence; they could merely see shifting figures, men that gestured quietly, women that sometimes raised an eager eloquent arm. They could not always see the judge, although they were able to estimate his location by the tall stands surmounted by white globes that were at either hand of him. And so those who had come for curiosity's sweet sake wore an air of being in wait for a cry of anguish, some loud painful protestation that would bring the proper thrill to their jaded, world-weary nerves—wires that refused to vibrate for ordinary affairs.

Inside the railing the court officers shuffled the various groups with speed and skill; and behind the desk the magistrate patiently toiled his way through mazes of wonderful testimony.

In a corner of this space, devoted to those who had business before the judge, an officer in plain clothes stood with a girl that wept constantly. None seemed to notice the girl and there was no reason why she should be noticed if the curious in the body of the courtroom were not interested in the devastation which tears bring upon some complexions. Her tears seemed to burn like acid and they left fierce pink marks on her face. Occasionally the girl looked across the room where two well-dressed young women and a man stood waiting with the serenity of people who are not concerned as to the interior fittings of a jail.

The business of the court progressed and presently the girl, the officer and the well-dressed contingent stood before the judge. Thereupon two lawyers engaged in some preliminary fire-wheels which were endured, generally, in silence. The girl, it appeared, was accused of stealing fifty dollars' worth of silk clothing from the room of one of the well-dressed women. She had been a servant in the house.

In a clear way and with none of the ferocity that an accuser often exhibits in a police-court, calmly and moderately, the two young women gave their testimony. Behind them stood their escort, always mute. His part, evidently, was to furnish the dignity, and he furnished it heavily, almost massively.

When they had finished, the girl told her part. She had full, almost Afric, lips, and they had turned quite white. The lawyer for the others asked some questions, which he did—be it said, in passing—with the air of a man throwing flower-pots at a stone house.

It was a short case and soon finished. At the end of it the judge said that, considering the evidence, he would have to commit the girl for trial. Instantly the quick-eyed court officer began to clear the way for the next case. The well-dressed women and their escort turned one way and the girl turned another, toward a door with an austere arch leading into a stone-paved passage. Then it was that a great cry rang through the court-room, the cry of this girl who believed that she was lost.

The loungers, many of them, underwent a spasmodic movement as if they had been knived. The court officers rallied quickly. The girl fell back opportunely for the arms of one of them, and her wild heels clicked twice on the floor. "I am innocent! Oh, I am innocent!"

People pity those who need none, and the guilty sob alone; but innocent or guilty, this girl's scream described such a profound depth of woe—it was so graphic of grief, that it slit with a dagger's sweep the curtain of common-place, and disclosed the gloom-shrouded spectre that sat in the young girl's heart so plainly, in so universal a tone of the mind, that a man heard expressed some far-off midnight terror of his own thought.

The cries died away down the stone-paved passage. A patrolman leaned one arm composedly on the railing, and down below him stood an aged, almost toothless wanderer, tottering and grinning.

"Plase, yer honer," said the old man as the time arrived for him to speak, "if ye'll lave me go this time, I've niver been dhrunk befoor, sir."

A court officer lifted his hand to hide a smile.

In the Tenderloin: A Duel Between an Alarm Clock and a Suicidal Purpose

Everybody knows all about the Tenderloin district of New York. There is no man that has the slightest claim to citizenship that does not know all there is to know concerning the Tenderloin. It is wonderful—this amount of truth which the world's clergy and police forces have collected concerning the Tenderloin. My friends from the stars obtain all this information, if possible, and then go into this wilderness and apply it. Upon observing you, certain spirits of the jungle will term you a wise guy, but there is no gentle humor in the Tenderloin, so you need not fear that this remark is anything but a tribute to your knowledge.

Once upon a time there was fought in the Tenderloin a duel between an Alarm Clock and a Suicidal Purpose. That such a duel was fought is a matter of no consequence, but it may be worth a telling, because it may be the single Tenderloin incident about which every man in the world has not exhaustive information.

It seems that Swift Doyer and his girl quarreled. Swift was jealous in the strange and devious way of his kind, and at midnight, his voice burdened with admonition, grief and deadly menace, roared through the little flat and conveyed news of the strife up the air-shaft and down the air-shaft.

"Lied to me, didn't you?" he cried. "Told me a lie and thought I wouldn't get onto you. Lied to me! Lied to me! There's where I get crazy. If you hadn't lied to me in one thing, and I hadn't collared you flat in it, I might believe all the rest, but now—how do I know you ever tell the truth? How do I know I ain't always getting a game? Hey? How do I know?"

To the indifferent people whose windows opened on the air-shaft there came the sound of a girl's low sobbing, while into it at times burst wildly the hoarse bitterness and rage of the man's tone. A grim thing is a Tenderloin air-shaft.

Swift arose and paused his harangue for a moment while he lit a cigarette. He puffed at it vehemently and scowled, black as a storm-god, in the direction of the sobbing.

"Come! Get up out of that," he said, with ferocity. "Get up and look at me and let me see you lie!"

There was a flurry of white in the darkness, which was no more definite to the man than the ice-floes which your reeling ship passes in the night. Then, when the gas glared out suddenly, the girl stood before him. She was a wondrous white figure in her vestal-like robe. She resembled the priestess in paintings of long-gone Mediterranean religions. Her hair fell wildly on her shoulder. She threw out her arms and cried to Swift in a woe that seemed almost as real as the woe of good people.

"Oh, oh, my heart is broken! My heart is broken!"

But Swift knew as well as the rest of mankind that these girls have no hearts to be broken, and this acting filled him with a new rage. He grabbed an alarm clock from the dresser and banged her heroically on the head with it.

She fell and quivered for a moment. Then she arose, and, calm and dry-eyed, walked to the mirror. Swift thought she was taking an account of the bruises, but when he resumed his cyclonic tirade, she said: "I've taken morphine, Swift!"

Swift leaped at a little red pill box. It was empty. Eight quarter-grain pills make two grains. The Suicidal Purpose was distinctly ahead of the Alarm Clock. With great presence of mind Swift now took the empty pill box and flung it through the window.

At this time a great battle was begun in the dining-room of the little flat. Swift dragged the girl to the sideboard, and in forcing her to drink whisky he almost stuffed the bottle down her throat. When the girl still sank to the depths of an infinite drowsiness, sliding limply in her chair like a cloth figure, he dealt her furious blows, and our decorous philosophy knows little of the love and despair that was in those caresses. With his voice he called the light into her eyes, called her from the sinister slumber which her senses welcomed, called her soul back from the verge.

He propped the girl in a chair and ran to the kitchen to make coffee. His fingers might have been from a dead man's hands, and his senses confused the coffee, the water, the coffee-pot, the gas stove, but by some fortune he managed to arrange them correctly. When he lifted the girlish figure and carried her to the kitchen, he was as wild, haggard, gibbering, as a man of midnight murders, and it is only because he was not engaged in the respectable and literary assassination of a royal juke that almost any sensible writer would be ashamed of this story. Let it suffice, then, that when the steel-blue dawn came and distant chimneys were black against a rose sky, the girl sat at the dining-room table chattering insanely and gesturing. Swift, with his hands pressed to his temples, watched her from the other side of the table, with all his mind in his eyes, for each gesture was still a reminiscence, and each tone of her voice a ballad to him. And yet he could not half measure his misery. The tragedy was made of homeliest details. He had to repeat to himself that he, worn-out, stupefied from his struggle, was sitting there awaiting the moment when the unseen hand should whirl this soul into the abyss, and that then he should be alone.

The girl saw a fly alight on a picture. "Oh," she said, "there's a little fly." She arose and thrust out her finger. "Hello, little fly," she said, and touched the fly. The insect was perhaps too cold to be alert, for it fell at the touch of her finger. The girl gave a cry of remorse, and, sinking to her knees, searched the floor, meanwhile uttering tender apologies.

At last she found the fly, and, taking it, her palm went to the gas-jet which still burned weirdly in the dawning. She held her hand close to the flame. "Poor little fly," she said, "I didn't mean to hurt you. I wouldn't hurt you for anything. There now—p'r'aps when you get warm you can fly away again. Did I crush the poor little bit of fly? I'm awful sorry—honest, I am. Poor little thing! Why I wouldn't hurt you for the world, poor little fly——"

Swift was wofully pale and so nerve-weak that his whole body felt a singular coolness. Strange things invariably come into a man's head at the wrong time, and Swift was aware that this scene was defying his preconceptions. His instruction had been that people when dying behaved in a certain manner. Why did this girl occupy herself with an accursed fly? Why in the name of the gods of the drama did she not refer to her past? Why, by the shelves of the saints of literature, did she not clutch her brow and say: "Ah, once I was an innocent girl"? What was wrong with this death scene? At one time he thought that his sense of propriety was so scandalized that he was upon the point of interrupting the girl's babble.

But here a new thought struck him. The girl was not going to die. How could she under these circumstances? The form was not correct.

All this was not relevant to the man's love and despair, but, behold, my friend, at the tragic, the terrible point in life there comes an irrelevancy to the human heart direct from the Wise God. And this is why Swift Doyer thought those peculiar thoughts.

The girl chattered to the fly minute after minute, and Swift's anxiety grew dim and more dim until his head fell forward on the table and he slept as a man who has moved mountains, altered rivers, caused snow to come because he wished it to come, and done his duty.

For an hour the girl talked to the fly, the gas-jet, the walls, the distant chimneys. Finally she sat opposite the slumbering Swift and talked softly to herself.

When broad day came they were both asleep, and the girl's fingers had gone across the table until they had found the locks on the man's forehead. They were asleep, and this after all is a human action, which may safely be done by characters in the fiction of our time.

The "Tenderloin" As It Really Is

Many requiems have been sung over the corpse of the Tenderloin. Dissipated gentlemen with convivial records burn candles to its memory each day at the corner of Twenty-eighth street and Broadway. On the great thoroughfare there are 4,000,000 men who at all times recite loud anecdotes of the luminous past.

They say: "Oh, if you had only come around when the old Haymarket was running!" They relate the wonders of this prehistoric time and fill the mind of youth with poignant regret. Everybody on earth must have attended regularly at this infernal Haymarket. The old gentlemen with convivial records do nothing but relate the glories of this place. To be sure, they tell of many other resorts, but the old gentlemen really do their conjuring with this one simple name—"the old Haymarket."

The Haymarket is really responsible for half the tales that are in the collections of these gay old boys of the silurian period. Some time a man will advertise "The Haymarket Restored," and score a clamoring, popular success. The interest in a reincarnation of a vanished Athens must pale before the excitement caused by "The Haymarket Restored."

Let a thing become a tradition, and it becomes half a lie. These moss-grown columns that support the sky over Broadway street corners insist that life in this dim time was a full joy. Their descriptions are short, but graphic.

One of this type will cry: "Everything wide open, my boy; everything wide open! You should have seen it. No sneaking in side doors. Everything plain as day. Ah, those were the times! Reubs from the West used to have their bundles lifted every night before your eyes. Always somebody blowing champagne for the house. Great! Great! Diamonds, girls, lights, music. Well, maybe it wasn't smooth! Fights all over Sixth avenue. Wasn't room enough. Used to hold over-flow fights in the side streets. Say, it was great!"

Then the type heaves a sigh and murmurs: "But now? Dead—dead as a mackerel. The Tenderloin is a graveyard. Quiet as a tomb. Say, you ought to have been around here when the old Haymarket was running."

Perchance they miss in their definition of the Tenderloin. They describe it as a certain condition of affairs in a metropolitan district. But probably it is in truth something more dim, an essence, an emotion—something superior to the influences of politics or geographies, a thing unchangeable. It represents a certain wild impulse, and a wild impulse is yet more lasting than an old Haymarket. And so we come to reason that the Tenderloin is not dead at all and that the old croakers on the corners are men who have mistaken the departure of their own youth for the death of the Tenderloin, and that there still exists the spirit that flings beer bottles, jumps debts and makes havoc for the unwary; also sings in a hoarse voice at 3 A.M.

There is one mighty fact, however, that the croakers have clinched. In the old days there was a great deal of money and few dress clothes exhibited in the Tenderloin. Now it is all clothes and no money. The spirit is garish, for display, as are the flaming lights that advertise theatres and medicines. In those days long ago there might have been freedom and fraternity.

—

Billie Maconnigle is probably one of the greatest society leaders that the world has produced. Seventh avenue is practically one voice in this matter.

He asked Flossie to dance with him, and Flossie did, seeming to enjoy the attentions of this celebrated cavalier. He asked her again, and she accepted again. Johnnie, her fellow promptly interrupted the dance.

"Here!" he said, grabbing Maconnigle by the arm. "Dis is me own private snap! Youse gitaway f'm here an' leggo d' loidy!"

"A couple a nits," rejoined Maconnigle swinging his arm clear of his partner. "Youse go chase yerself. I'm spieling wit' dis loidy when I likes, an' if youse gits gay, I'll knock yer block off—an' dat's no dream!"

"Youse'll knock nuttin' off."

"Won't I?"

"Nit. An' if yeh say much I'll make yeh look like a lobster, you fresh mug. Leggo me loidy!"

"A couple a nits."

"Won't?"

"Nit."

Blim! Blam! Crash!

The orchestra stopped playing and the musicians wheeled in their chairs, gazing with that semi-interest which only musicians in a dance hall can bring to bear upon such a scene. Several waiters ran forward, crying "Here, gents, quit dat!" A tall, healthy individual with no coat slid from behind the bar at the far end of the hall, and came with speed. Two well-dressed youths, drinking bottled beer at one end of the tables, nudged each other in ecstatic delight, and gazed with all their eyes at the fight. They were seeing life. They had come purposely to see it.

The waiters grabbed the fighters quickly. Maconnigle went through the door some three feet ahead of his hat, which came after him with a battered crown and a torn rim. A waiter with whom Johnnie had had a discussion over the change had instantly seized this opportunity to assert himself. He grappled Johnnie from the rear and flung him to the floor, and the tall, healthy person from behind the bar, rushing forward, kicked him in the head. Johnnie didn't say his prayers. He only wriggled and tried to shield his head with his arms, because every time that monstrous foot struck it made red lightning flash in his eyes.

But the tall, healthy man and his cohort of waiters had forgotten one element. They had forgotten Flossie. She could worry Johnnie; she could summon every art to make him wildly jealous; she could cruelly, wantonly harrow his soul with every device known to her kind, but she wouldn't stand by and see him hurt by gods nor men.

Blim! As the tall person drew back for his fourth kick, a beer mug landed him just back of his ear. Scratch! The waiter who had grabbed Johnnie from behind found that fingernails had made a ribbon of blood down his face as neatly as if a sign painter had put it there with a brush.

This cohort of waiters was, however, well drilled. Their leader was prone, but they rallied gallantly, and flung Johnnie and Flossie into the street, thinking no doubt that these representatives of the lower classes could get their harmless pleasure just as well outside.

The crowd at the door favored the vanquished. "Sherry!" said a voice. "Sherry! Here comes a cop!" Indeed a helmet and brass buttons shone brightly in the distance. Johnnie and Flossie sherried with all the promptitude allowed to a wounded man and a girl whose sole anxiety is the man. They ended their flight in a little dark alley.

Flossie was sobbing as if her heart was broken. She hung over her wounded hero, wailing and making moan to the sky, weeping with the deep and impressive grief of gravesides, when he swore because his head ached.

"Dat's all right," said Johnnie. "Nex' time youse needn't be so fresh wit' every guy what comes up."

"Well, I was only kiddin', Johnnie," she cried, forlornly.

"Well, yeh see what yeh done t' me wit'cher kiddin'," replied Johnnie.

They came forth cautiously from their alley and journeyed homeward. Johnnie had had enough of harmless pleasure.

However, after a considerable period of reflective silence, he paused and said: "Say, Floss, youse couldn't a done a t'ing t' dat guy."

"I jest cracked 'im under d' ear," she explained. "An' it laid 'im flat out, too."

A complacence for their victory here came upon them, and as they walked out of the glow of Seventh avenue into a side street it could have been seen that their self satisfaction was complete.

—

Five men flung open the wicket doors of a brilliant cafe on Broadway and, entering, took seats at a table. They were in evening dress, and each man held his chin as if it did not belong to him.

"Well, fellows, what'll you drink?" said one. He found out, and after the ceremony there was a period of silence. Ultimately another man cried: "Let's have another drink." Following this outburst and its attendant ceremony there was another period of silence.

At last a man murmured: "Well, let's have another drink." Two members of the party discussed the state of the leather market. There was an exciting moment when a little newsboy slid into the place, crying a late extra, and was ejected by the waiter. The five men gave the incident their complete attention.

"Let's have a drink," said one afterward.

At an early hour of the morning one man yawned and said: "I'm going home. I've got to catch an early train, and——"

The four others awoke. "Oh, hold on, Tom. Hold on. Have another drink before you go. Don't go without a last drink."

He had it. Then there was a silence. Then he yawned again and said: "Let's have another drink."

They settled comfortably once more around the table. From time to time somebody said: "Let's have a drink."

—

Yes, the Tenderloin is more than a place. It is an emotion. And this spirit seems still to ring true for some people. But if one is ever obliged to make explanation to any of the old croakers, it is always possible to remark that the Tenderloin has grown too fine. Therein lies the cause of the change.

To the man who tries to know the true things there is something hollow and mocking about this Tenderloin of to-day, as far as its outward garb is concerned. The newer generation brought new clothes with them. The old Tenderloin is decked out. And wherever there are gorgeous lights, massive buildings, dress clothes and theatrical managers, there is very little nature, and it may be no wonder that the old spirit of the locality chooses to lurk in the darker places.

In the "Tenderloin"

The waiters were very wise. Every man of them had worked at least three years in a Tenderloin restaurant, and this must be equal to seven centuries and an added two decades in Astoria. Even the man who opened oysters wore an air of accumulated information. Here the science of life was perfectly understood by all.

At 10 o'clock the place was peopled only by waiters and the men behind the long bar. The innumerable tables represented a vast white field, and the glaring electric lamps were not obstructed in their mission of shedding a furious orange radiance upon the cloths. An air of such peace and silence reigned that one might have heard the ticking of a clock. It was as quiet as a New England sitting room.

As 11 o'clock passed, however, and time marched toward 12, the place was suddenly filled with people. The process was hardly to be recognized. One surveyed at one moment a bare expanse of tables with groups of whispering waiters and at the next it was crowded with men and women attired gorgeously and plainly and splendidly and correctly. The electric glare swept over a region of expensive bonnets. Frequently the tall pride of a top hat—a real top hat—could be seen on its way down the long hall, and the envious said with sneers that the theatrical business was booming this year.

Without, the cable cars moved solemnly toward the mysteries of Harlem, and before the glowing and fascinating refrigerators displayed at the front of the restaurant a group of cabmen engaged in their singular diplomacy.

If there ever has been in a New York cafe an impulse from the really Bohemian religion of fraternity it has probably been frozen to death. A universal suspicion, a thing of so austere a cast that we mistake it for a social virtue, is the quality that generally oppresses us. But the hand of a bartender is a supple weapon of congeniality. In the small hours a man may forget the formulae which prehistoric fathers invented for him. Usually social form as practised by the stupid is not a law. It is a vital sensation. It is not temporary, emotional; it is fixed and, very likely, the power that makes the rain, the sunshine, the wind, now recognizes social form as an important element in the curious fashioning of the world. It is as solid, as palpable as a fort, and if you regard any landscape, you may see it in the foreground.

Therefore a certain process which moves in this restaurant is very instructive. It is a process which makes constantly toward the obliteration of the form. It never dangerously succeeds, but it is joyous and frank in its attempt.

—

A man in race-track clothing turned in his chair and addressed a stranger at the next table. "I beg your pardon—will you tell me the time please?"

The stranger was in evening dress, very correct indeed. At the question, he stared at the man for a moment, particularly including his tie in this look of sudden and subtle contempt. After a silence he drew forth his watch, looked at it, and returned it to his pocket. After another silence he drooped his eyes with peculiar significance, puffed his cigar and, of a sudden, remarked: "Why don't you look at the clock?"

The race-track man was a genial soul. He promptly but affably directed the kind gentleman to a place supposed to be located at the end of the Brooklyn trolley lines.

And yet at 4:30 A.M. the kind gentleman overheard the race-track man telling his experience in London in 1886, and as he had experiences similar in beauty, and as it was 4:30 A.M., and as he had completely forgotten the incident of the earlier part of the evening, he suddenly branched into the conversation, and thereafter it took ten strong men to hold him from buying a limitless ocean of wine.

—

A curious fact of upper Broadway is the man who knows everybody, his origin, wealth, character and tailor. His knowledge is always from personal intercourse, too, and, without a doubt, he must have lived for ten thousand years to absorb all the anecdotes which he has at the tip of his tongue. If it were a woman, now, most of the stories would be weird resurrections of long-entombed scandals. The trenches for the dead on medieval battle fields would probably be clawed open to furnish evidence of various grim truths, or of untruths, still more grim. But if, according to a rigid definition, these men are gossips, it is in a kinder way than is usually denominated by the use of the word. Let a woman once take an interest in the shortcomings of her neighbors, and she immediately and naturally begins to magnify events in a preposterous fashion, until one can imagine that the law of proportion is merely a legend. There is one phrase which she uses eternally. "They say——" Herein is the peculiar terror of the curse. "They say——" It is so vague that the best spear in the world must fail to hit this shadow. The charm of it is that a woman seldom relates from personal experience. It is nearly always some revolving tale from a hundred tongues.

But it is evident in most cases that the cafe historians of upper Broadway speak from personal experience. The dove that brought the olive branch to Noah was one of their number. Another was in Hades at the time that Lucifer made his celebrated speech against the street-lighting system there. Another is an ex-member of the New Jersey Legislature. All modes, all experiences, all phases of existence are chronicled by these men. They are not obliged to fall back upon common report for their raw material. They possess it in the original form.

A cafe of the kind previously described is a great place for the concentration of the historians. Here they have great opportunities.

"See that fellow going there? That's young Jimmie Lode. Knew his father well. Denver people, you know. Old man had a strange custom of getting drunk on the first Friday after the first Thursday in June. Indian reservation near his house. Used to go out and fist-fight the Indians. Gave a twenty-dollar gold piece to every Indian he licked. Indians used to labor like thunder to get licked. Well, sir, one time the big chief of the whole push was trying to earn his money, and, by Jove, no matter what he did, he couldn't seem to fix it so the old man could lick him. So finally he laid down flat on the ground and the old man jumped on him and stove in his bulwarks. Indian said it was all right, but he thought forty dollars was a better figure for stove-in bulwarks. But the old man said he had agreed to pay twenty dollars, and he wouldn't give up another sou. So they had a fight—a real fight, you know—and the Indian killed him.

"Well, that's the son over there. Father left him a million and a half. Maybe Jack ain't spending it. Say! He just pours it out. He's crushed on Dollie Bangle, you know. She plays over here at the Palais de Glace. That's her now he's talking to. Ain't she a peach. Say? Am I right? Well, I should say so. She don't do a thing to his money. Burns it in an open grate. She's on the level with him, though. That's one thing. Well, I say she is. Of course, I'm sure of it."

In the meantime others pass before the historian's watchful vision, and he continues heroically to volley his traditions.

—

The babble of voices grew louder and louder. The heavy smoke clouds eddied above the shining countenances. Into the street came the clear, cold blue of impending daylight, and over the cobbles roared a milk wagon.

Stephen Crane in Minetta Lane

Minetta Lane is a small and becobbled valley between hills of dingy brick. At night the street lamps, burning dimly, cause the shadows to be important, and in the gloom one sees groups of quietly conversant negroes with occasionally the gleam of a passing growler. Everything is vaguely outlined and of uncertain identity unless indeed it be the flashing buttons and shield of the policeman on post. The Sixth avenue horse cars jingle past one end of the Lane and, a block eastward, the little thoroughfare ends in the darkness of MacDougal street.

One wonders how such an insignificant alley could get such an absurdly large reputation, but, as a matter of fact, Minetta Lane, and Minetta street, which leads from it southward to Bleecker street, were, until a few years ago, two of the most enthusiastically murderous thoroughfares in New York. Bleecker street, MacDougal street and nearly all the streets thereabouts were most unmistakably bad, but when the Minettas started out the other streets went away and hid. To gain a reputation in Minetta Lane, in those days, a man was obliged to commit a number of furious crimes, and no celebrity was more important than the man who had a good honest killing to his credit. The inhabitants for the most part were negroes and they represented the very worst elements of their race. The razor habit clung to them with the tenacity of an epidemic, and every night the uneven cobbles felt blood. Minetta Lane was not a public thoroughfare at this period. It was a street set apart, a refuge for criminals. Thieves came here preferably with their gains, and almost any day peculiar sentences passed among the inhabitants. "Big Jim turned a thousand last night." "No-Toe's made another haul." And the worshipful citizens would make haste to be present at the consequent revel.

As has been said, Minetta Lane was then no thoroughfare. A peaceable citizen chose to make a circuit rather than venture through this place, that swarmed with the most dangerous people in the city. Indeed, the thieves of the district used to say: "Once get in the Lane and you're all right." Even a policeman in chase of a criminal would probably shy away instead of pursuing him into the Lane. The odds were too great against a lone officer.

Sailors and any men who might appear to have money about them, were welcomed with all proper ceremony at the terrible dens of the Lane. At departure, they were fortunate if they still retained their teeth. It was the custom to leave very little else to them. There was every facility for the capture of coin, from trap-doors to plain ordinary knock-out drops.

And yet Minetta Lane is built on the grave of Minetta Brook, where, in olden times, lovers walked under the willows of the bank, and Minetta Lane, in later times, was the home of many of the best families of the town.

A negro named Bloodthirsty was perhaps the most luminous figure of Minetta Lane's aggregation of desperadoes. Bloodthirsty, supposedly, is alive now, but he has vanished from the Lane. The police want him for murder. Bloodthirsty is a large negro and very hideous. He has a rolling eye that shows white at the wrong time and his neck, under the jaw, is dreadfully scarred and pitted.

Bloodthirsty was particularly eloquent when drunk, and in the wildness of a spree he would rave so graphically about gore that even the habituated wool of old timers would stand straight. Bloodthirsty meant most of it, too. That is why his orations were impressive. His remarks were usually followed by the wide lightning sweep of his razor. None cared to exchange epithets with Bloodthirsty. A man in a boiler iron suit would walk down to City Hall and look at the clock before he would ask the time of day from the single-minded and ingenuous Bloodthirsty.

After Bloodthirsty, in combative importance, came No-Toe Charley. Singularly enough, Charley was called No-Toe solely because he did not have a toe to his feet. Charley was a small negro and his manner of amusement was not Bloodthirsty's simple way. As befitting a smaller man, Charley was more wise, more sly, more round-about than the other man. The path of his crimes was like a corkscrew, in architecture, and his method led him to make many tunnels. With all his cleverness, however, No-Toe was finally induced to pay a visit to the gentlemen in the grim gray building up the river.

Black-Cat was another famous bandit who made the Lane his home. Black-Cat is dead. It is within some months that Jube Tyler has been sent to prison, and after mentioning the recent disappearance of Old Man Spriggs, it may be said that the Lane is now destitute of the men who once crowned it with a glory of crime. It is hardly essential to mention Guinea Johnson. Guinea is not a great figure. Guinea is just an ordinary little crook. Sometimes Guinea pays a visit to his friends, the other little crooks who make homes in the Lane, but he himself does not live there, and with him out of it there is now no one whose industry in unlawfulness has yet earned him the dignity of a nickname. Indeed, it is difficult to find people now who remember the old gorgeous days, although it is but two years since the Lane shone with sin like a new head-light. But after a search the reporter found three.

Mammy Ross is one of the last relics of the days of slaughter still living there. Her weird history also reaches back to the blossoming of the first members of the Whyo gang in the old Sixth ward, and her mind is stored with bloody memories. She at one time kept a sailor's boarding house near the Tombs prison, and accounts of all the festive crimes of that neighborhood in ancient years roll easily from her tongue. They killed a sailor man every day, and pedestrians went about the streets wearing stoves for fear of the handy knives. At the present day the route to Mammy's home is up a flight of grimy stairs that is pasted on the outside of an old and tottering frame house. Then there is a hall blacker than a wolf's throat and this hall leads to a little kitchen where Mammy usually sits groaning by the fire. She is, of course, very old and she is also very fat. She seems always to be in great pain. She says she is suffering from "de very las' dregs of de yaller fever."

During the first part of a reporter's recent visit, old Mammy seemed most dolefully oppressed by her various diseases. Her great body shook and her teeth clicked spasmodically during her long and painful respirations. From time to time she reached her trembling hand and drew a shawl closer about her shoulders. She presented as true a picture of a person undergoing steady, unchangeable, chronic pain as a patent medicine firm could wish to discover for miraculous purposes. She breathed like a fish thrown out on the bank, and her old head continually quivered in the nervous tremors of the extremely aged and debilitated person. Meanwhile her daughter hung over the stove and placidly cooked sausages.

Appeals were made to the old woman's memory. Various personages who had been sublime figures of crime in the long-gone days were mentioned to her, and presently her eyes began to brighten. Her head no longer quivered. She seemed to lose for a period her sense of pain in the gentle excitement caused by the invocation of the spirits of her memory.

It appears that she had had a historic quarrel with Apple Mag. She first recited the prowess of Apple Mag; how this emphatic lady used to argue with paving stones, carving knives and bricks. Then she told of the quarrel; what Mag said; what she said; what Mag said; what she said. It seems that they cited each other as spectacles of sin and corruption in more fully explanatory terms than are commonly known to be possible. But it was one of Mammy's most gorgeous recollections, and, as she told it, a smile widened over her face.

Finally she explained her celebrated retort to one of the most illustrious thugs that had blessed the city in bygone days. "Ah says to 'im, Ah says: 'You—you'll die in yer boots like Gallopin' Thompson—dat's what you'll do. You des min' dat, honey! Ah got o'ny one chile an' he ain't nuthin' but er cripple, but le'me tel' you, man, dat boy'll live t' pick de feathers f'm de goose dat'll eat de grass dat grows over your grave, man!' Dat's what I tol' 'im. But—lan' sake—how I know dat in less'n three day, dat man be lying in de gutter wif a knife stickin' out'n his back. Lawd, no, I sholy never s'pected noting like dat."

These reminiscences, at once maimed and reconstructed, have been treasured by old Mammy as carefully, as tenderly, as if they were the various little tokens of an early love. She applies the same back-handed sentiment to them, and, as she sits groaning by the fire, it is plainly to be seen that there is only one food for her ancient brain, and that is the recollection of the beautiful fights and murders of the past.

On the other side of the Lane, but near Mammy's house, Pop Babcock keeps a restaurant. Pop says it is a restaurant and so it must be one, but you could pass there ninety times each day and never know that you were passing a restaurant. There is one obscure little window in the basement and if you went close and peered in, you might, after a time, be able to make out a small dusty sign, lying amid jars on a shelf. This sign reads: "Oysters in every style." If you are of a gambling turn of mind, you will probably stand out in the street and bet yourself black in the face that there isn't an oyster within a hundred yards. But Pop Babcock made that sign and Pop Babcock could not tell an untruth. Pop is a model of all the virtues which an inventive fate has made for us. He says so.

As far as goes the management of Pop's restaurant, it differs from Sherry's. In the first place, the door is always kept locked. The wardmen of the Fifteenth precinct have a way of prowling through the restaurant almost every night, and Pop keeps the door locked in order to keep out the objectionable people that cause the wardmen's visits. He says so. The cooking stove is located in the main room of the restaurant, and it is placed in such a strategic manner that it occupies about all the space that is not already occupied by a table, a bench and two chairs. The table will, on a pinch, furnish room for the plates of two people if they are willing to crowd. Pop says he is the best cook in the world.

When questioned concerning the present condition of the Lane, Pop said: "Quiet? Quiet? Lo'd save us, maybe it ain't! Quiet? Quiet?" His emphasis was arranged crescendo, until the last word was really a vocal explosion. "Why, disher' Lane ain't nohow like what it uster be—no indeed, it ain't. No, sir! 'Deed it ain't! Why, I kin remember when dey des was a-cuttin' an' a-slashin' 'long yere all night. 'Deed dey was! My—my, dem times was diff'rent! Dat dar Kent, he kep' de place at Green Gate Cou't—down yer ol' Mammy's—an' he was a hard baby—'deed, he was—an' ol' Black-Cat an' ol' Bloodthirsty, dey was a-roamin' round yere a-cuttin' an' a-slashin' an' a-cuttin' an' a-slashin'. Didn't dar' say boo to a goose in dose days, dat you didn't, less'n you lookin' fer a scrap. No, sir!" Then he gave information concerning his own prowess at that time. Pop is about as tall as a picket on an undersized fence. "But dey didn't have nothin' ter say to me! No, sir! 'Deed, dey didn't! I wouldn't lay down fer none of 'em. No, sir! Dey knew my gait, 'deed, dey did! Man, man, many's de time I buck up agin 'em. Yes, sir!"

At this time Pop had three customers in his place, one asleep on the bench, one asleep on the two chairs, and one asleep on the floor behind the stove.

But there is one man who lends dignity of the real bevel edged type to Minetta Lane and that man is Hank Anderson. Hank of course does not live in the Lane, but the shadow of his social perfections falls upon it as refreshingly as a morning dew. Hank gives a dance twice in each week, at a hall hard by in MacDougal street, and the dusky aristocracy of the neighborhood know their guiding beacon. Moreover, Hank holds an annual ball in Forty-fourth street. Also he gives a picnic each year to the Montezuma Club, when he again appears as a guiding beacon. This picnic is usually held on a barge and the occasion is a very joyous one. Some years ago it required the entire reserve squad of an up-town police precinct to properly control the enthusiasm of the gay picnickers, but that was an exceptional exuberance and no measure of Hank's ability for management.

He is really a great manager. He was Boss Tweed's body servant in the days when Tweed was a political prince, and anyone who saw Bill Tweed through a spy-glass learned the science of leading, pulling, driving and hauling men in a way to keep the men ignorant of it. Hank imbibed from this fount of knowledge and he applied his information in Thompson street. Thompson street salaamed. Presently he bore a proud title: "The Mayor of Thompson street." Dignities from the principal political organization of the city adorned his brow and he speedily became illustrious.

Hank knew the Lane well in its direful days. As for the inhabitants, he kept clear of them and yet in touch with them according to a method that he might have learned in the Sixth ward. The Sixth ward was a good place in which to learn that trick. Anderson can tell many strange tales and good of the Lane and he tells them in the graphic way of his class. "Why, they could steal your shirt without moving a wrinkle on it."

The killing of Joe Carey was the last murder that happened in the Minettas. Carey had what might be called a mixed-ale difference with a man named Kenny. They went out to the middle of Minetta street to affably fight it out and determine the justice of the question. In the scrimmage Kenny drew a knife, thrust quickly and Carey fell. Kenny had not gone a hundred feet before he ran into the arms of a policeman.

There is probably no street in New York where the police keep closer watch than they do in Minetta Lane. There was a time when the inhabitants had a profound and reasonable contempt for the public guardians, but they have it no longer, apparently. Any citizen can walk through there at any time in perfect safety unless, perhaps, he should happen to get too frivolous. To be strictly accurate, the change began under the reign of Police Captain Chapman. Under Captain Groo, the present commander of the Fifteenth precinct, the Lane has donned a complete new garb. Its denizens brag now of its peace, precisely as they once bragged of its war. It is no more a bloody lane. The song of the razor is seldom heard. There are still toughs and semi-toughs galore in it, but they can't get a chance with the copper looking the other way. Groo has got the poor old Lane by the throat. If a man should insist on becoming a victim of the badger game, he could probably succeed upon search in Minetta Lane, as indeed, he could on any of the great avenues, but then Minetta Lane is not supposed to be a pearly street in Paradise.

In the meantime, the Italians have begun to dispute possession of the Lane with the negroes. Green Gate Court is filled with them now, and a row of houses near the MacDougal street corner is occupied entirely by Italian families. None of them seems to be overfond of the old Mulberry Bend fashions of life, and there are no cutting affrays among them worth mentioning. It is the original negro element that makes the trouble when there is trouble.

But they are happy in this condition, are these people. The most extraordinary quality of the negro is his enormous capacity for happiness under most adverse circumstances. Minetta Lane is a place of poverty and sin, but these influences cannot destroy the broad smile of the negro, a vain and simple child but happy. They all smile here, the most evil as well as the poorest. Knowing the negro, one always expects laughter from him, be he ever so poor, but it was a new experience to see a broad grin on the face of the devil. Even old Pop Babcock had a laugh as fine and mellow as would be the sound of falling glass, broken saints from high windows, in the silence of some great cathedral's hollow.

Adventures of a Novelist

[*The headline above Crane's report in the September 20, 1896, edition of the New York* Journal *read:*
ADVENTURES OF A NOVELIST
BY STEPHEN CRANE
THE DISTINGUISHED AUTHOR'S NARRATIVE OF HOW HE SOUGHT "MATERIAL" IN REAL LIFE IN THE "TENDERLOIN" AND FOUND MORE THAN HE BARGAINED FOR.]

This is a plain tale of two chorus girls, a woman of the streets and a reluctant laggard witness. The tale properly begins in a resort on Broadway, where the two chorus girls and the reluctant witness sat the entire evening. They were on the verge of departing their several ways when a young woman approached one of the chorus girls, with outstretched hand.

"Why, how do you do?" she said. "I haven't seen you for a long time."

The chorus girl recognized some acquaintance of the past, and the young woman then took a seat and joined the party. Finally they left the table in this resort, and the quartet walked down Broadway together. At the corner of Thirty-first street one of the chorus girls said that she wished to take a car immediately for home, and so the reluctant witness left one of the chorus girls and the young woman on the corner of Thirty-first street while he placed the other chorus girl aboard an uptown cable car. The two girls who waited on the corner were deep in conversation.

The reluctant witness was returning leisurely to them. In the semi-conscious manner in which people note details which do not appear at the time important, he saw two men passing along Broadway. They passed swiftly, like men who are going home. They paid attention to none, and none at the corner of Thirty-first street and Broadway paid attention to them.

The two girls were still deep in conversation. They were standing at the curb facing the street. The two men passed unseen—in all human probability—by the two girls. The reluctant witness continued his leisurely way. He was within four feet of these two girls when suddenly and silently a man appeared from nowhere in particular and grabbed them both.

The astonishment of the reluctant witness was so great for the ensuing seconds that he was hardly aware of what transpired during that time, save that both girls screamed. Then he heard this man, who was now evidently an officer, say to them: "Come to the station house. You are under arrest for soliciting two men."

With one voice the unknown woman, the chorus girl and the reluctant witness cried out: "What two men?"

The officer said: "Those two men who have just passed."

And here began the wildest and most hysterical sobbing of the two girls, accompanied by spasmodic attempts to pull their arms away from the grip of the policeman. The chorus girl seemed nearly insane with fright and fury. Finally she screamed:

"Well, he's my husband." And with her finger she indicated the reluctant witness. The witness at once replied to the swift, questioning glance of the officer, "Yes; I am."

If it was necessary to avow a marriage to save a girl who is not a prostitute from being arrested as a prostitute, it must be done, though the man suffer eternally. And then the officer forgot immediately—without a second's hesitation, he forgot that a moment previously he had arrested this girl for soliciting, and so, dropping her arm, released her.

"But," said he, "I have got this other one." He was as picturesque as a wolf.

"Why arrest her, either?" said the reluctant witness.

"For soliciting those two men."

"But she didn't solicit those two men."

"Say," said the officer, turning, "do you know this woman?"

The chorus girl had it in mind to lie then for the purpose of saving this woman easily and simply from the palpable wrong she seemed to be about to experience. "Yes; I know her"—"I have seen her two or three times"—"Yes; I have met her before——" But the reluctant witness said at once that he knew nothing whatever of the girl.

"Well," said the officer, "she's a common prostitute."

There was a short silence then, but the reluctant witness presently said: "Are you arresting her as a common prostitute? She has been perfectly respectable since she has been with us. She hasn't done anything wrong since she has been in our company."

"I am arresting her for soliciting those two men," answered the officer, "and if you people don't want to get pinched, too, you had better not be seen with her."

Then began a parade to the station house—the officer and his prisoner ahead and two simpletons following.

At the station house the officer said to the sergeant behind the desk that he had seen the woman come from the resort on Broadway alone, and on the way to the corner of Thirty-first street solicit two men, and that immediately afterward she had met a man and a woman—meaning the chorus girl and the reluctant witness—on the said corner, and was in conversation with them when he arrested her. He did not mention to the sergeant at this time the arrest and release of the chorus girl.

At the conclusion of the officer's story the sergeant said, shortly: "Take her back." This did not mean to take the woman back to the corner of Thirty-first street and Broadway. It meant to take her back to the cells, and she was accordingly led away.

The chorus girl had undoubtedly intended to be an intrepid champion; she had avowedly come to the station house for that purpose, but her entire time had been devoted to sobbing in the wildest form of hysteria. The reluctant witness was obliged to devote his entire time to an attempt to keep her from making an uproar of some kind. This paroxysm of terror, of indignation, and the extreme mental anguish caused by her unconventional and strange situation, was so violent that the reluctant witness could not take time from her to give any testimony to the sergeant.

After the woman was sent to the cell the reluctant witness reflected a moment in silence; then he said:

"Well, we might as well go."

On the way out of Thirtieth street the chorus girl continued to sob. "If you don't go to court and speak for that girl you are no man!" she cried. The arrested woman had, by the way, screamed out a request to appear in her behalf before the Magistrate.

"By George! I cannot," said the reluctant witness. "I can't afford to do that sort of thing. I—I——"

After he had left this girl safely, he continued to reflect: "Now this arrest I firmly believe to be wrong. This girl may be a courtesan, for anything that I know at all to the contrary. The sergeant at the station house seemed to know her as well as he knew the Madison square tower. She is then, in all probability, a courtesan. She is arrested, however, for soliciting those two men. If I have ever had a conviction in my life, I am convinced that she did not solicit those two men. Now, if these affairs occur from time to time, they must be witnessed occasionally by men of character. Do these reputable citizens interfere? No, they go home and thank God that they can still attend piously to their own affairs. Suppose I were a clerk and I interfered in this sort of a case. When it became known to my employers they would say to me: 'We are sorry, but we cannot have men in our employ who stay out until 2:30 in the morning in the company of chorus girls.'

"Suppose, for instance, I had a wife and seven children in Harlem. As soon as my wife read the papers she would say: 'Ha! You told me you had a business engagement! Half-past two in the morning with questionable company!'

"Suppose, for instance, I were engaged to the beautiful Countess of Kalamazoo. If she were to hear it, she would write: 'All is over between us. My future husband cannot rescue prostitutes at 2:30 in the morning.'

"These, then, must be three small general illustrations of why men of character say nothing if they happen to witness some possible affair of this sort, and perhaps these illustrations could be multiplied to infinity. I possess nothing so tangible as a clerkship, as a wife and seven children in Harlem, as an engagement to the beautiful Countess of Kalamazoo; but all that I value may be chanced in this affair. Shall I take this risk for the benefit of a girl of the streets?

"But this girl, be she prostitute or whatever, was at this time manifestly in my escort, and—Heaven save the blasphemous philosophy—a wrong done to a prostitute must be as purely a wrong as a wrong done to a queen," said the reluctant witness—this blockhead.

"Moreover, I believe that this officer has dishonored his obligation as a public servant. Have I a duty as a citizen, or do citizens have duty, as a citizen, or do citizens have no duties? Is it a mere myth that there was at one time a man who possessed a consciousness of civic responsibility, or has it become a distinction of our municipal civilization that men of this character shall be licensed to depredate in such a manner upon those who are completely at their mercy?"

He returned to the sergeant at the police station, and, after asking if he could send anything to the girl to make her more comfortable for the night, he told the sergeant the story of the arrest, as he knew it.

"Well," said the sergeant, "that may be all true. I don't defend the officer. I do not say that he was right, or that he was wrong, but it seems to me that I have seen you somewhere before and know you vaguely as a man of good repute; so why interfere in this thing? As for this girl, I know her to be a common prostitute. That's why I sent her back."

"But she was not arrested as a common prostitute. She was arrested for soliciting two men, and I know that she didn't solicit the two men."

"Well," said the sergeant, "that, too, may all be true, but I give you the plain advice of a man who has been behind this desk for years, and knows how these things go, and I advise you simply to stay home. If you monkey with this case, you are pretty sure to come out with mud all over you."

"I suppose so," said the reluctant witness. "I haven't a doubt of it. But I don't see how I can, in honesty, stay away from court in the morning."

"Well, do it anyhow," said the sergeant.

"But I don't see how I can do it."

The sergeant was bored. "Oh, I tell you, the girl is nothing but a common prostitute," he said, wearily.

The reluctant witness on reaching his room set the alarm clock for the proper hour.

In the court at 8:30 he met a reporter acquaintance. "Go home," said the reporter, when he had heard the story. "Go home; your own participation in the affair doesn't look very respectable. Go home."

"But it is a wrong," said the reluctant witness.

"Oh, it is only a temporary wrong," said the reporter. The definition of a temporary wrong did not appear at that time to the reluctant witness, but the reporter was too much in earnest to consider terms. "Go home," said he.

Thus—if the girl was wronged—it is to be seen that all circumstances, all forces, all opinions, all men were combined to militate against her. Apparently the united wisdom of the world declared that no man should do anything but throw his sense of justice to the winds in an affair of this description. "Let a man have a conscience for the daytime," said wisdom. "Let him have a conscience for the daytime, but it is idiocy for a man to have a conscience at 2:30 in the morning, in the case of an arrested prostitute."

The officer who had made the arrest told a story of the occurrence. The girl at the bar told a story of the occurrence. And the girl's story as to this affair was, to the reluctant witness, perfectly true. Nevertheless, her word could not be accounted of any value. It was impossible that any one in the courtroom could suppose that she was telling the truth, save the reluctant witness and the reporter to whom he had told the tale.

The reluctant witness recited what he believed to be a true accounting, and the Magistrate discharged the prisoner.

The reluctant witness has told this story merely because it is a story which the public of New York should know for once.

Note on the Text

This edition of Stephen Crane's New York writings includes Crane's "Bowery Tales," *Maggie* and *George's Mother*, along with other tales and sketches written by Crane while a journalist in New York in the 1890s. The first published editions of *Maggie* (1893, self-published by Crane), and *George's Mother* (1896) are generally regarded to be truest to Crane's intentions; these editions are reproduced here. For the remaining New York writings, this edition follows the authoritative *Works of Stephen Crane,* Volume VIII ed. Fredson Bowers (University Press of Virginia), with kind permission of the publisher.

COMMENTARY

HAMLIN GARLAND

STEPHEN CRANE

WILLIAM DEAN HOWELLS

HAMLIN GARLAND

["Maggie"] is a work of astonishingly good style. It deals with poverty and vice and crime also, but it does so, not out of curiosity, not out of salaciousness, but because of a distinct art impulse, the desire to utter in truthful phrase a certain rebellious cry. It is the voice of the slums. It is not written by a dilettante; it is written by one who has lived the life. The young author, Stephen Crane, is a native of the city, and has grown up in the very scenes he describes. His book is the most truthful and unhackneyed study of the slums I have yet read, fragment though it is. It is pictorial, graphic, terrible in its directness. It has no conventional phrases. It gives the dialect of the slums as I have never before seen it written—crisp, direct, terse. It is another locality finding voice.

It is important because it voices the blind rebellion of Rum Alley and Devil's Row. It creates the atmosphere of the jungles, where vice festers and crime passes gloomily by, where outlawed human nature rebels against God and man.

The story fails of rounded completeness. It is only a fragment. It is typical only of the worst elements of the alley. The author should delineate the families living on the next street, who live lives of heroic purity and hopeless hardship.

The dictum is amazingly simple and fine for so young a writer. Some of the works illuminate like flashes of light. Mr. Crane is only twenty-one years of age, and yet he has met and grappled with the actualities of the street in almost unequalled grace and strength. With such a *technique* already at command, with life mainly *before him,* Stephen Crane is to be henceforth reckoned with. "Maggie" should be put beside "Van Bibber" to see the extremes of New York as stated by two young men. Mr. Crane need not fear comparisons so far as *technique* goes, and Mr. Davis will need to step forward right briskly or he may be overtaken by a man who impresses the reader with a sense of almost unlimited resource.

From *The Arena,* June 1893

STEPHEN CRANE

As far as myself and my own meagre success are concerned, I began the battle of life with no talent, no equipment, but with an ardent admiration and desire. I did little work at school, but confined my abilities, such as they were, to the diamond. Not that I disliked books, but the cut-and-dried curriculum of the college did not appeal to me. Humanity was a much more interesting study. When I ought to have been at recitations I was studying faces on the streets, and when I ought to have been studying my next day's lessons I was watching the trains roll in and out of the Central Station. So, you see, I had, first of all, to recover from college. I had to build up, so to speak. And my chiefest desire was to write plainly and unmistakably, so that all men (and some women) might read and understand. That to my mind is good writing. There is a great deal of labor connected with literature. I think that is the hardest thing about it. There is nothing to respect in art save one's own opinion of it. . . .

The only thing that deeply pleases me in my literary life—brief and inglorious as it is—is the fact that men of sense believe me to be sincere. "Maggie," published in paper covers, made me the friendship of Hamlin Garland and W. D. Howells, and the one thing that makes my life worth living in the midst of all this abuse and ridicule is the consciousness that never for an instant have those friendships at all diminished. Personally I am aware that my work does not amount to a string of dried beans—I always calmly admit it. But I also know that I do the best that is in me, without regard to cheers or damnation. When I was the mark for every humorist in the country I went ahead, and now, when I am the mark for only 50 per cent of the humorists of the country, I go ahead, for I understand that a man is born into the world with his own pair of eyes, and he is not at all responsible for his vision—he is merely responsible for his quality of personal honesty. To keep close to this personal honesty is my supreme ambition. There is a sublime egotism in talking of honesty. I, however, do not say that I am honest. I merely say that I am as nearly honest as a weak mental machinery will allow. This aim in life struck me as being the only thing worth while. A man is sure to fail at it, but there is something in the failure.

From a letter to John Northern Hilliard, January 1896(?), reprinted in *Stephen Crane: Letters,* 1960

WILLIAM DEAN HOWELLS

It is a long time since I have seen the once famous A Glance at New York, but I distinctly recall through the misty substance of some forty-five very faded years the heroic figures of the volunteer fireman and his friends, who were the chief persons of the piece. I do not remember the others at all, but I remember Mose, and Sikesy, and Lize. Good and once precious fragments of literature linger in my memory, as: " 'Mose,' says he, 'git off o' dem hose, or I'll swat you over der head wid de trumpet.' And I didn't get off o' der hose, and he did swat me over der head wid der trumpet." Other things have gone, but these golden words remain with me.

I

It is interesting to note that the first successful attempt to represent the life of our streets was in dramatic form. Some actor saw and heard things spoken with the peculiar swagger and whopperjaw utterance of the b'hoy of those dreadful old days, when the blood-tubs and the plug-uglies reigned over us, and Tammany was still almost purely American, and he put them on the stage and spread the poison of them all over the land, so that there was hardly anywhere a little blackguard boy who did not wish to act and talk like Mose.

The whole piece was painted with the large brush and the vivid pigments of romanticism, and yet the features many long years later when Mr. Harrigan came to the study of our low life in his delightful series of plays. He studied it in the heyday of Irish supremacy, when Tammany had become almost purely Celtic, and he naturally made his heroes and heroines Irish. The old American b'hoy lingered among them in the accent and twist of an occasional barkeeper, but the brogue prevailed, and the highshouldered sidelong carriage of the Americanized bouncer of Hibernian blood.

The treatment, however, was still romanticistic, though Mr. Harrigan is too much of a humorist not to return suddenly to nature, at times from the most exalted regions of "imagination." He loves laughing and making laugh, and that always saved him when he was in danger of becoming too grand, or fine, or heroic. He had moments when he was exactly true, but he allowed himself a good many friendly freedoms with the fact, and the effect was not always that of reality.

It seemed to me that so far as I could get the drift of a local drama in German which flourished at one of the East Side theatres a winter ago, that the author kept no more faithfully to life than Mr. Harrigan, and had not his sublime moments of absolute fidelity. In fact, the stage is almost as slow as criticism to perceive that there is no other standard for the arts but life, and it keeps on with the conventional in motive even when the matter is honest, apparently in the hope that by doing the stale falsehood often enough it will finally affect the witness like a fresh verity. It is to the honor of the stage, however, that it was first to recognize the value of our New York low life as material; and I shall always say that Mr. Harrigan, when he was not over-powered by a tradition or a theory, was exquisitely artistic in his treatment of it. He was then true, and, as Tolstoi has lately told us, to be true is to be moral.

II

The fiction meant to be read, as distinguishable from the fiction meant to be represented, has been much later in dealing with the same material, and it is only just beginning to deal with it in the spirit of the great modern masters. I cannot find that such clever and amusing writers as Mr. Townsend, or Mr. Ralph, or Mr. Ford have had it on their consciences to report in the regions of the imagination the very effect of the life which they all seem at times to have seen so clearly. There is apparently nothing but the will that is wanting in either of them, but perhaps the want of the will is the want of an essential factor, though I should like very much to have them try for a constant reality in their studies; and I am far from wishing to count them out in an estimate of what has been done in that direction. It is only just to Mr. Stephen Crane, however, to say that he was first in the field where they made themselves known earlier. His story of Maggie, a Girl of the Streets, which has been recently published by the Appletons, was in the hands of a few in an edition which the author could not even give away three years ago; and I think it is two years, now, since I saw George's Mother, which Edward Arnold has brought out, in the manuscript.

Their present publication is imaginably due to the success of the Red Badge of Courage, but I do not think that they will owe their critical acceptance to the obstreperous favor which that has won. As pieces of art they are altogether superior to it, and as representations of life their greater fidelity cannot be questioned. In The Red Badge of Courage there is a good deal of floundering, it seems to me. The narration repeats itself; the effort to imagine, to divine, and then to express ends often in a huddled and confused effect; there is no repose, such as agony itself assumes in the finest art, and there is no forward movement. But in these other books the advance is relentless; the atmosphere is transparent; the texture is a continuous web where all the facts are wrought with the unerring mastery of absolute knowledge. I should say that The Red Badge of Courage owed its excellence to the training the author had given himself in setting forth the life he knew in these earlier books of later publication. He learned to imagine vividly from seeing clearly.

There is a curious unity in the spirit of the arts; and I think that what strikes me most in the story of Maggie is that quality of fatal necessity which dominates Greek tragedy. From the conditions it all had to be, and there were the conditions. I felt this in Mr. Hardy's Judge, where the principle seems to become conscious in the writer; but there is apparently no consciousness of any such motive in the author of Maggie. Another effect is that of an ideal of artistic beauty which is as present in the working out of this poor romance as in any classic fable. This will be foolishness, I know, to the foolish people who cannot discriminate between the material and the treatment in art, and who think that beauty is inseparable from daintiness and prettiness, but I do not speak to them. I appeal rather to such as feel themselves akin with every kind of human creature, and find neither high nor low when it is a question of inevitable suffering, or of a soul struggling vainly with an inexorable fate.

My rhetoric scarcely suggests the simple terms the author uses to produce the effect which I am trying to report again. They are simple, but always most graphic, especially when it comes to the personalities of the story: the girl herself, with her bewildered wish to be right and good; with her distorted perspective; her clinging affections; her hopeless environments; the horrible old drunken mother, a cyclone of violence of vulgarity; the mean and selfish lover, a dandy tough, with his gross ideals and ambitions; her brother an Ishmaelite from the cradle, who, with his warlike instincts beaten back into cunning, is what the b'hoy of former times has become in our more strenuously policed days. He is indeed a wonderful figure in a group which betrays no faltering in the artist's hand. He, with his dull hates, his warped good-will, his cowed ferocity, is almost as fine artistically as Maggie, but he could not have been so hard to do, for all the pathos of her fate is rendered without one maudlin touch.

So is that of the simple-minded and devoted and tedious old woman who is George's mother in the book of that name. This is scarcely a study at all, while Maggie is really and fully so. It is the study of a situation merely: a poor, inadequate woman, of a commonplace religiosity, whose son goes to the bad. The wonder of it is the courage which deals with persons so absolutely average, and the art that graces them with the beauty of the author's compassion for everything that errs and suffers. Without this feeling the effects of his mastery would be impossible, and if it went further or put itself into the pitying phrases it would annul the effects. But it never does this; it is notable how in all respects the author keeps himself well in hand. He is quite honest with his reader. He never shows his characters or his situations in any sort of sentimental glamour; if you will be moved by the sadness of common fates you will feel his intention, but he does not flatter his portraits of people or conditions to take your fancy.

In George and his mother he has to do with folk of country origin as the city affects them, and the son's decadence is admirably studied; he scarcely struggles against temptation, and his mother's only art is to cry and to scold. Yet he loves her, in a way, and she is devotedly proud of him. These simple country folk are contrasted with simple city folk of varying degrees of badness. Mr. Crane has the skill to show how evil is greatly the effect of ignorance and imperfect civilization. The club of friends, older men than George, whom he is asked to join, is portrayed with extraordinary insight, and the group of young toughs whom he finally consorts with is done with even greater mastery. The bulldog motive of one of them, who is willing to fight to the death, is most impressively rendered.

From "New York Low Life in Fiction,"
New York World, July 26, 1896

Reading Group Guide

1. Taking the writings in this volume together, discuss the picture of slum life in turn-of-the-century New York that Crane gives us. What are some of its defining features? How is poverty reflected in the lives of Bowery dwellers?

2. Reflect on the continuities and differences between the characters in Crane's two Bowery Tales, "Maggie" and "George's Mother." For instance, how does Jimmie compare to George Kelcey?

3. How does "Maggie, a Girl of the Streets" speak to the constraints imposed by gender conventions? What choices are available to Maggie? Why does she go with Pete? Why is she driven from her mother's house?

4. Alcohol figures centrally in Crane's depiction of poverty and "low life," from the status that accrues to Pete because of his job as bartender, to the powerful hold of alcohol over the lives of the poor in general. Discuss Crane's depiction of alcohol in his New York writings.

5. Critics have praised Crane's style—especially in "Maggie, a Girl of the Streets," with its stark, minimal style—as breaking with nineteenth-century literary conventions, and in many ways anticipating major fea-

tures of subsequent American writing. What makes Crane's writing unique and innovative?

6. In his emphasis on the realistic depiction of the inexorable effects of outside forces—social and natural—on the lives and destinies of individual characters, Crane is often described as a literary naturalist. Is this an apt description? Discuss naturalism in relation to Crane's New York writings, and the relationship of Crane's work to that of other writers (like Dreiser and Norris) usually associated with the term.

THE MODERN LIBRARY EDITORIAL BOARD

Maya Angelou
•
Daniel J. Boorstin
•
A. S. Byatt
•
Caleb Carr
•
Christopher Cerf
•
Ron Chernow
•
Shelby Foote
•
Stephen Jay Gould
•
Vartan Gregorian
•
Charles Johnson
•
Jon Krakauer
•
Edmund Morris
•
Joyce Carol Oates
•
Elaine Pagels
•
John Richardson
•
Salman Rushdie
•
Arthur Schlesinger, Jr.
•
Carolyn See
•
William Styron
•
Gore Vidal

MODERN LIBRARY IS ONLINE AT WWW.MODERNLIBRARY.COM

MODERN LIBRARY ONLINE IS YOUR GUIDE TO CLASSIC LITERATURE ON THE WEB

THE MODERN LIBRARY E-NEWSLETTER

Our free e-mail newsletter is sent to subscribers, and features sample chapters, interviews with and essays by our authors, upcoming books, special promotions, announcements, and news.

To subscribe to the Modern Library e-newsletter, send a blank e-mail to: **sub_modernlibrary@info.randomhouse.com** or visit **www.modernlibrary.com**

THE MODERN LIBRARY WEBSITE

Check out the Modern Library website at **www.modernlibrary.com** for:

- The Modern Library e-newsletter
- A list of our current and upcoming titles and series
- Reading Group Guides and exclusive author spotlights
- Special features with information on the classics and other paperback series
- Excerpts from new releases and other titles
- A list of our e-books and information on where to buy them
- The Modern Library Editorial Board's 100 Best Novels and 100 Best Nonfiction Books of the Twentieth Century written in the English language
- News and announcements

Questions? E-mail us at **modernlibrary@randomhouse.com**. For questions about examination or desk copies, please visit the Random House Academic Resources site at **www.randomhouse.com/academic**

"While Leonard excels at low-life suspense, he's also a master fiction writer whose gift for dialogue and cunningly meandering plots any novelist would envy."

—*San Francisco Examiner & Chronicle*

"Roundly satisfying. . . . Chili Palmer . . . is a vintage Leonard hero. . . . A perfect resolution puts punch in the title and will keep readers smiling for days." —*Publishers Weekly*

"Leonard does crime fiction better than anyone since Raymond Chandler." —*Plain Dealer* (Cleveland)

"Vintage Leonard. . . . Ranks among his best."

—*Palm Beach Post*

"Leonard is the best in the business: His dialogue snaps, his characters are more alive than most of the people you meet on the street, and his twisting plots always resolve themselves with a no-nonsense plausibility." —*Newsday*

"Wonderful. . . . Astonishing. . . . Leonard understands Hollywood perfectly." —*New York Times*

"His books defy classification. . . . What Leonard does is write fully realized novels, using elements of the classic American crime novel and populating them with characters so true and believable you want to read their lines aloud to someone you really like." —*Dallas Morning News*

"Leonard is tops in his field. . . . In Leonard's sleazy world you always meet interesting characters."

—*Times-Picayune* (New Orleans)

"Clever, entertaining . . . and for anyone not yet hooked, a good place to start." —*Boston Globe*

Books by Elmore Leonard

FICTION

Djibouti
Comfort to the Enemy and Other Carl Webster Stories
Road Dogs
Up in Honey's Room
The Hot Kid
The Complete Western Stories of Elmore Leonard
Mr. Paradise
When the Women Come Out to Dance
Tishomingo Blues
Pagan Babies
The Tonto Woman & Other Western Stories
Cuba Libre
Out of Sight
Riding the Rap
Pronto
Rum Punch
Maximum Bob
Killshot
Freaky Deaky
Touch
Bandits
Glitz
LaBrava
Stick
Cat Chaser
Split Images
City Primeval
Gold Coast
Gunsights
The Switch
The Hunted
Unknown Man No. 89
Swag
Fifty-Two Pickup
Mr. Majestyk
Forty Lashes Less One
Valdez Is Coming
The Moonshine War
The Big Bounce
Hombre
Last Stand at Saber River
Escape from Five Shadows
The Law at Randado
The Bounty Hunters

NONFICTION

Elmore Leonard's 10 Rules of Writing

GET SHORTY

ELMORE LEONARD

HARPER

NEW YORK • LONDON • TORONTO • SYDNEY

HARPER

This book is a work of fiction. The characters, incidents, and dialogue are drawn from the author's imagination and are not to be construed as real. Any resemblance to actual events or persons, living or dead, is entirely coincidental.

GET SHORTY. Copyright © 1990 by Elmore Leonard, Inc. All rights reserved. Printed in the United States of America. No part of this book may be used or reproduced in any manner whatsoever without written permission except in the case of brief quotations embodied in critical articles and reviews. For information address HarperCollins Publishers, 10 East 53rd Street, New York, NY 10022.

HarperCollins books may be purchased for educational, business, or sales promotional use. For information please write: Special Markets Department, HarperCollins Publishers, 10 East 53rd Street, New York, NY 10022.

First Harper Torch edition published 2002.

First Dark Alley edition published 2005.
First Harper paperback published 2011.

Designed by Daniel Lagin

Library of Congress Cataloging-in-Publication Data
is available upon request.

ISBN 978-0-06-212025-0

14 15 RRD 10 9 8 7 6 5 4 3

For Walter Mirisch,
one of the good guys

1

WHEN CHILI FIRST CAME TO MIAMI BEACH TWELVE YEARS ago they were having one of their off-and-on cold winters: thirty-four degrees the day he met Tommy Carlo for lunch at Vesuvio's on South Collins and had his leather jacket ripped off. One his wife had given him for Christmas a year ago, before they moved down here.

Chili and Tommy were both from Bay Ridge, Brooklyn, old buddies now in business together. Tommy Carlo was connected to a Brooklyn crew through his uncle, a guy named Momo, Tommy keeping his books and picking up betting slips till Momo sent him to Miami, with a hundred thousand to put on the street as loan money. Chili was connected through some people on his mother's side, the Manzara brothers. He worked usually for Manzara Moving & Storage in Bensonhurst, finding high-volume customers for items such as cigarettes, TVs, VCRs, stepladders, dresses, frozen orange juice. . . . But he could never be a made guy himself because of tainted blood, some Sunset Park Puerto Rican on his father's side, even though he was raised Italian. Chili didn't care to be made anyway, get into all that bullshit having to do with respect. It was bad enough having to treat these guys like they were your heroes, smile when they made some stupid remark they thought was funny. Though it was pretty nice, go in a restaurant on 86th or Cropsey Avenue the way they knew his name, still a young guy then, and would bust their ass to wait on him. His wife Debbie ate it up, until they were married a few years and she got pregnant. Then it was a different story. Debbie said with a child coming into their lives he had to get a regular job, quit associating with "those people" and bitched at him till he said okay, all *right,* Jesus, and lined up the deal with Tommy Carlo in Miami. He told Debbie he'd be selling restaurant supplies to the big hotels like the Fontainebleau and she believed him—till they were down here less than a year and he had his jacket ripped off.

This time at Vesuvio's, they finished eating, Tommy said he'd see him at the barbershop—where they had a phone in back—turned up the collar of his Palm Beach sport coat for whatever good it would do him and took off. Chili went in the checkroom to get his jacket and all that was in there were a couple of raincoats and a leather flight jacket must've been from World War Two. When Chili got the manager, an older Italian guy in a black suit, the manager looked around the practically empty checkroom and asked Chili, "You don't find it? Is not one of these?"

Chili said, "You see a black leather jacket, fingertip length, has lapels like a suitcoat? You don't, you owe me three seventy-nine." The manager told him to look at the sign there on the wall. WE CANNOT BE RESPONSIBLE FOR LOST ARTICLES. Chili said to him, "I bet you can if you try. I didn't come down to sunny Florida to freeze my ass. You follow me? You get the coat back or you give me the three seventy-nine my wife paid for it at Alexander's."

So then the manager got a waiter over and they talked to each other in Italian for a while, the waiter nervous or he was anxious to get back to folding napkins. Chili caught some of what they were saying and a name that came up a few times, Ray Barboni. He knew the name, a guy they called Bones he'd seen hanging out at the Cardozo Hotel on the beach. Ray Bones worked for a guy named Jimmy Capotorto who'd recently taken over a local operation from a deceased guy named Ed Grossi—but that was another story. The manager said to the waiter, "Explain to him Mr. Barboni borrow the coat."

The waiter, trying to act like an innocent bystander, said, "Somebody take his coat, you know, leave this old one. So Mr. Barboni put on this other coat that fit him pretty good. He say he gonna borrow it."

Chili said, "Wait a minute," and had the waiter, who didn't seem to think it was unusual for some asshole to take a jacket that didn't belong to him, explain it again.

"He didn't take it," the waiter said, "he borrow it. See, we get his coat for him and he return the one he borrow. Or I think maybe if it's your coat," the waiter said, "he give it to you. He was wearing it, you know, to go home. He wasn't gonna keep it."

"My car keys are in the pocket," Chili said.

They both looked at him now, the manager and the waiter, like they didn't understand English.

"What I'm saying," Chili said, "how'm I suppose to go get my coat if I don't have the keys to my car?"

The manager said they'd call him a taxi.

"Lemme get it straight," Chili said. "You aren't responsible for any lost articles like an expensive coat of mine, but you're gonna find Ray Bones' coat or get him a new one. Is that what you're telling me?"

Basically, he saw they weren't telling him shit, other than Ray Bones was a good customer who came in two three times a week and worked for Jimmy Cap. They didn't know where he lived and his phone number wasn't in the book. So Chili called Tommy Carlo at the barbershop, told him the situation, asked him a few times if he believed it and if he'd come by, pick him up.

"I want to get my coat. Also pull this guy's head out of his ass and nail him one."

Tommy said, "Tomorrow, I see on the TV weather, it's gonna be nice and warm. You won't need the coat."

Chili said, "Debbie gave me it for Christmas, for Christ sake. I go home, she's gonna want to know where it's at."

"So tell her you lost it."

"She's still in bed since the miscarriage. You can't talk to her. I mean in a way that makes any fuckin sense if you have to explain something."

Tommy said, "Hey, Chil? Then don't fuckin tell her."

Chili said, "The guy takes my coat, I can't ask for it back?"

Tommy Carlo picked him up at the restaurant and they stopped by Chili's apartment on Meridian where they were living at the time so he could run in and get something. He tried to be quiet about it, grab a pair of gloves out of the front closet and leave, but Debbie heard him.

She said from the bedroom, "Ernie, is that you?" She never called him Chili. She called him honey in her invalid voice if she wanted something. "Honey? Would you get my pills for me from the sink in the kitchen and a glass of water, please, while you're up?" Pause. "Or, no—honey? Gimme a glass of milk instead and some of those cookies, the ones you got at Winn-Dixie, you know the chocolate chip ones?" Dragging it out in this tired voice she used since the miscarriage, three months ago. Taking forever now to ask him what time it was, the alarm clock sitting on the bed table a foot away if she turned her head. They had known each other since high school, when he'd played basketball and she was a baton twirler with a nice ass. Chili told her it was three-thirty and he was running late for an appointment; bye. He heard her say, "Honey? Would you . . ." but he was out of there.

In the car driving the few blocks over to the Victor Hotel on Ocean Drive, Tommy Carlo said, "Get your coat, but don't piss the guy off, okay? It could get complicated and we'd have to call Momo to straighten it out. Okay? Then Momo gets pissed for wasting his time and we don't need it. Right?"

Chili was thinking that if he was always bringing Debbie her pills, how did they get back to the kitchen after? But he heard Tommy and said to him, "Don't worry about it. I won't say any more than I have to, if that."

He put on his black leather gloves going up the stairs to the third floor, knocked on the door three times, waited, pulling the right-hand glove on tight, and when Ray Bones opened the door Chili nailed him. One punch, not seeing any need to throw the left. He got his coat from a chair in the sitting room, looked at Ray Bones bent over holding his nose and mouth, blood all over his hands, his shirt, and walked out. Didn't say one word to him.

ERNESTO PALMER GOT THE NAME CHILI ORIGINALLY because he was hot-tempered as a kid growing up. The name given to him by his dad, who worked on the docks for the Bull Line when he wasn't drinking. Now he was Chili, Tommy Carlo said, because he had chilled down and didn't need the hot temper. All he had to do was turn his eyes dead when he looked at a slow pay, not say more than three words, and the guy would sell his wife's car to make the payment. Chili said the secret was in how you prepped the loan customer.

"A guy comes to see you, it doesn't matter how much he wants or why he needs it, you say to him up front before you give him a dime, 'You sure you want to take this money? You're not gonna put up your house or sign any papers. What you're gonna give me is your word you'll pay it back so much a week at interest.' You tell him, 'If you don't think you can pay at least the vig every week when it's due, please don't take the fuckin money, it wouldn't be worth it to you.' If the guy hesitates at all, 'Well, I'm pretty sure I can—' says anything like that, I tell him, 'No, I'm advising you now, don't take the fuckin money.' The guy will beg for it, take an oath on his kids he'll pay you on time. You know he's desperate or he wouldn't be borrowing shylock money in the first place. So you tell him, 'Okay, but you miss even one payment you're gonna be sorry you ever came here.' You never tell the guy what could happen to him. Let him use his imagination, he'll think of something worse. In other words, don't talk when you don't have to. What's the point?"

It was the same thing getting his coat back. What was there to say?

So now it was up to Ray Bones. If getting his nose busted and his teeth pushed in pissed him off he'd have to do something about it. Some things you couldn't prevent. Tommy Carlo told him to get lost for a while, go fishing in the Keys. But how was he going to do that with Debbie an invalid, afraid to take a leak she might see blood?

He imagined different ways Ray Bones might try for him. Eating at Vesuvio's, look up, there's Bones pointing a gun. Or coming out of the barbershop on Arthur Godfrey Road where they had their office in back. Or, no—sitting on one of the chairs while he's shooting the shit with Fred and Ed, which he did sometimes when there weren't customers in the place. That would appeal to Ray Bones, with his limited mentality: the barbershop was here and it was the way guys had gotten hit before, like Albert Anastasia, that Ray Bones would know about. Chili said shit, went over to S.W. Eighth Street and bought a snub-nosed .38 off a Cuban. "The famous Smit and Wayson model *treinta y ocho.*"

It happened when Chili was in the backroom office making entries in the collection book. Through the wallboard he heard Fred say, "Paris? Yeah, I been there plenty of times. It's right offa Seventy-nine." Ed saying, "Hell it is, it's on Sixty-eight. It's only seventeen miles from Lexington." Fred saying, "What're you talking about, Paris, Kentucky, or Paris, Tennessee?" Then a silence, no answer to the question.

Chili looked up from the collection book, listened a moment to nothing, opened the desk drawer and got out the .38. He aimed it at the open doorway. Now he saw Ray Bones appear in the back hall, Bones in the doorway to the office, his face showing surprise to see a gun aimed at him. He began firing the big Colt auto in his hand maybe before he was ready, the gun making an awful racket, when Chili pulled the trigger and shot him in the head. The .38 slug creased Ray Bones, as it turned out, from hairline to crown, put a groove in his scalp they closed up at Mt. Sinai with more than thirty stitches—Chili hearing about it later. He pried two slugs out of the wall and found another one in the file cabinet he showed Tommy Carlo.

Tommy called Momo and Momo got in touch with Jimmy Cap, taking the situation to the table, so to speak, discuss whether Ray Bones had been shown disrespect by an associate from another crew, or was it his own fault he got shot. Otherwise it could get out of hand if they let it go, didn't make a judgment. The two bosses decided this coat thing and what came out of it was bullshit, forget it. Jimmy Cap would tell Ray Bones he was lucky he wasn't dead, the guy's wife had given him the coat for Christmas for Christ sake. That was the end of the incident, twelve years ago, except for one unexpected event that came out of it right away, and something else that would happen now, in the present.

The unexpected event was Debbie walking out on Chili, going home to Bay Ridge to live with her mother over a clothing store.

It happened because during the discussion period Momo called Chili to get his side—as a favor to Tommy Carlo, otherwise he would never have spoken to him directly—and

Debbie listened in on the extension. All Momo told Chili was to cut out the schoolyard bullshit, grow up. But that was enough for Debbie to know Chili was still connected. She went so far as to get out of bed to keep after him, wanting to know what he was doing with Momo and "those people," becoming screechy about it until finally he told her, so he was working for Momo for Christ sake, so what? Thinking it would shut her up and he'd get the silent treatment for about a month, which he could use. But instead of that she became hysterical, telling him, "That's why I had the miscarriage, I knew it. I *knew* you were back in that life and the baby knew it from me *and didn't want to be born!*"

What? Because its dad was operating a quick-loan business? Helping out poor schmucks that couldn't get it from a bank? How did you talk to a woman who believed an unborn kid would know something like that? He tried. He told her she ought to see a doctor, get her fuckin brain looked at. Debbie's last words to him, she said, "You think you're so smart, let's see you get a divorce, big shot." In other words she would pass up alimony and live with her mother over a clothing store to prevent his ever remarrying. Debbie, too dumb to realize the world had changed with rock and roll and the pill, believed it would keep him from ever getting laid again.

Chili, from then until now, went with a succession of women, some on a serious basis, some not. There was one named Rose, a bartender, who lived with him a few years. One named Vera, a go-go dancer he fell in love with, but he couldn't stand other guys watching her and they broke up. He took out women who were waitresses, beauticians, sales clerks at Dadeland Mall, would take them to dinner and a movie, sometimes to bed. There was a singer named Nicole he liked a lot, but her whole life seemed to be rock and roll and he never knew what she was talking about. Chili liked women and was comfortable with them without putting on any kind of act. He was who he was and they seemed to go for him. What some of the women didn't go for was seeing so many movies, practically every time they went out. They would get the feeling he liked movies more than he did them.

The other thing that came out of the coat incident, now twelve years later, happened right after they got word about Momo, shot dead as he left a restaurant on West 56th in Manhattan, and Tommy Carlo went to attend the funeral. The day after that Chili had a couple of visitors come in the shop looking for him, a big colored guy he had never seen before and Ray Bones.

"THEY CUT STRAIGHT HAIR IN THIS PLACE," BONES ASKED Chili, "or just fags?"

Times changed. Fred and Ed were gone and a couple of guys named Peter and Tim were doing hair of either sex in an art deco backstage-looking setup, light bulbs around rose-colored mirrors. They were okay. They had Chili combing his hair straight back, no part, like Michael Douglas in *Wall Street*.

Chili had changed too in the past dozen years, tired of showing respect to people he thought were assholes. Momo had been okay, but guys in his crew would come down to Miami on vacation and act like hard-ons, expecting him and Tommy to show them around, get them broads. Chili would tell the hard-ons, "Hey, I'm not your pimp," and they'd give Tommy a bad time because he was Momo's nephew and had to go along. The result of this situation, Chili was phasing himself out of the shylock business, only handling a few regular customers now who didn't give them any trouble. He was also doing midnight car repossessions for small loan companies and some collection work for local merchants and a couple of Las Vegas casinos, making courtesy calls. He had chilled down a few more degrees too.

Still, he couldn't help saying to Ray Bones, "The way you're losing your hair, Bones, you oughta let these guys style what you have left, see if they can cover up that scar. Or they can fit you with a rug, either way."

Fuck him. Chili knew what was coming.

There weren't any customers in the shop. Ray Bones told Peter and Tim to go get a coffee. They left making faces and the big colored guy backed Chili into a barber chair, telling him, "This man is the man. You understand what I'm saying? He's Mr. Bones, you speak to him from now on."

Chili watched Mr. Bones go into the back hall toward the office and said to the colored guy, "You can do better'n him."

"Not these days," the colored guy said. "Not less you can talk Spanish."

Bones came out with the collection book open, looking at all the names of who owed, the amounts and due dates in a green spiral notebook. He said to Chili, "How you work it, you handle the spics and Tommy the white people?"

Chili told himself it was time to keep his mouth shut.

The colored guy said, "The man's talking to you."

"He's outta business but don't know it," Bones said, looking up from the book. "There's nothing around here for you no more."

"I can see that," Chili said. He watched Bones put his nose in the book again.

"How much you got working?"

"About three and a half."

"Shit, ten grand a week. What'd Momo let you have?"

"Twenty percent."

"And you fucked him outta what, another twenty?"

Chili didn't answer. Bones turned a page, read down the entries and stopped.

"You got a miss. Guy's six weeks over."

"He died," Chili said.

"How you know he died, he tell you?"

Ray Bones checked the colored guy to get some appreciation, but the guy was busy looking at hair rinses and shit on the counter. Chili didn't give him anything either. He was thinking he could kick Mr. Bones in the nuts if he came any closer, then get up and nail him. If the big colored guy would leave.

"He got killed," Chili said, "in that TransAm jet went down in the Everglades."

"Who told you?"

Chili got out of the chair, went in the back office and returned with a stack of *Miami Heralds.* He dropped them on the floor in front of Bones and got back in the chair.

"Help yourself. You find him on the list of victims, Leo Devoe. He's Paris Cleaners on Federal Highway about 124th Street."

Bones nudged the stack of newspapers with a toe of his cream-colored perforated shoes that matched his slacks and sport shirt. The front page on top said "TransAm Crash Kills 117." Chili watched Bones toe his way through editions with headlines that said "Winds Probed in Crash" . . . "Windshear Warning Was Issued" . . . "Nightmare Descends Soon After Farewells" . . . getting down to a page of small photographs, head shots, and a line that read, "Special Report: The Tragic Toll."

"His wife told me he was on the flight," Chili said. "I kept checking till I saw, yeah, he was."

"His picture in here?"

"Near the bottom. You have to turn the paper over."

Bones still wasn't going to bend down, strain himself. He looked up from the newspapers. "Maybe he took out flight insurance. Check with the wife."

"It's your book now," Chili said. "You want to check it out, go ahead."

The colored guy came over from the counter to stand next to the chair.

Ray Bones said, "Six weeks' juice is twenty-seven hunnerd on top of the fifteen you gave him. Get it from the guy's wife or out of your pocket, I don't give a fuck. You don't hand me a book with a miss in it."

"Payback time," Chili said. "You know that coat? I gave it to the Salvation Army two years ago."

"What coat?" Bones said.

He knew.

The colored guy stood close, staring into Chili's face, while Bones worked on the Michael Douglas hairdo, shearing off a handful at a time with a pair of scissors, telling Chili it was to remind him when he looked in the mirror he owed fifteen plus whatever the juice, right? The juice would keep running till he paid. Chili sat still, hearing the scissors snip-snipping away, knowing it had nothing to do with money. He was being paid back again, this time for reminding Ray Bones he had a scar that showed white where he was getting bald. It was all kid stuff with these guys, the way they acted tough. Like Momo had said, schoolyard bullshit. These guys never grew up. Still, if they were holding a pair of scissors in your face when they told you something, you agreed to it. At least for the time being.

Chili was still in the chair when the new-wave barbers came back and began to comment, telling him they could perm what was left or give him a moderate spike, shave the sides, laser stripes were popular. Chili told them to cut the shit and even it off. While they worked on him he sat there wondering if it was possible Leo Devoe had taken out flight insurance or if the wife had thought about suing the airline. It was something he could mention to her.

But what happened when he dropped by their house in North Miami—the idea, see what he could find out about any insurance—the wife, Fay, stopped him cold. She said, "I wish he really was dead, the son of a bitch."

SHE DIDN'T SAY IT RIGHT AWAY, NOT TILL THEY WERE out on the patio with vodka and tonics, in the dark.

Chili knew Fay from having stopped by to pick up the weekly four-fifty and they'd sit here waiting for Leo to get home after a day at Gulfstream. Fay was a quiet type, from a small town upstate, Mt. Dora, not bad looking but worn thin in her sundress from working at the cleaner's in that heat while Leo was out betting horses. They'd sit here trying to make conversation with nothing in common but Leo, Chili, every once in a while, catching her gaze during a silence, seeing her eyes and feeling it was there if he wanted it. Though he couldn't imagine Fay getting excited, changing her expression much. What did a shy woman stuck with a loser think about? Leo would appear, strut out on the patio and count the four-fifty off a roll, nothing to it. Or he'd come shaking his head, beat, saying he'd have it tomorrow for sure. Chili never threatened him, not in front of the woman and embarrass her. Not till he left and Leo would know enough to walk him out to his car parked by the streetlight. He'd say, "Leo, look at me," and tell him where to be the next day with the four-fifty. Leo was never to blame: it was the horses selling out or it was Fay always on his back, distracting him when he was trying to pick winners. And Chili would have to say it again, "Leo, look at me."

He owed for two weeks the night he didn't come home. Fay said she couldn't think where Leo could be. The third week she told him Leo was dead and a couple weeks after that his picture was in the paper.

This visit sitting on the patio, knowing Leo was not going to appear, strutting or otherwise, the silences became longer. Chili asked what she planned to do now. Fay said she didn't know; she hated the drycleaner business, being inside. Chili said it must be awful hot. She said you couldn't believe how hot it was. He got around to asking about life insurance. Fay said she didn't know of any. Chili said, well . . . But didn't move. Fay didn't either. It was dark, hard to see her face, neither one of them making a sound. This was when she said, out of nowhere, "You know what I been thinking?"

Chili said, "Tell me."

"I wish he really was dead, the son of a bitch."

Chili kept still. Don't talk when you don't have to.

"He's called me up twice since going out to Las Vegas and since then I haven't heard a goddamn word from him. I know he's there, it's all he ever talked about, going to Las Vegas. But I'm the one stuck my neck out, I'm the one they gave the money to, not him. I'm talking about the airline company, the three hundred thousand dollars they gave me for losing my husband." Fay paused to shake her head.

Chili waited.

She said to him on that dark patio, "I trust you. I think you're a decent type of man, even if you are a crook. You find Leo and get me my three hundred thousand dollars back if he ain't spent it, I'll give you half. If he's hit big we split that, or whatever he has left. How's that sound as a deal?"

Chili said, "That's what you been thinking, huh? Tell me why the airline thinks Leo got killed if he wasn't on the flight."

"His suitcase was," Fay said, and told Chili everything that happened.

It was a good story.

2

HARRY ZIMM BELIEVED IF HE KEPT HIS EYES CLOSED and quit listening that sound coming from somewhere in the house would stop and pretty soon they'd go back to sleep.

But Karen wouldn't leave it alone. He heard her say, "Harry?" a couple of times, maybe not sure if she was hearing something or not. Then, *"Harry—"* still a whisper but putting more into it. This time when he didn't answer she gave him a poke in the back, hard. "Harry, God damn it, somebody's downstairs."

They hadn't slept in the same bed on a regular basis in over ten years, not since they had lived together, and Karen still knew when he was faking. The only other time, in this same bed, was right after she and Michael were divorced and Michael, a star by then, gave Karen the house. There was no way to hide from her. So he rolled over and there she was in her Lakers T-shirt, sitting up on her side of the king-size bed, a soft white shape in the dark, a little porcelain doll.

"What's wrong?"

"Be quiet and listen."

A tough little porcelain doll under that loose T-shirt.

"I don't hear anything." It was true, he didn't at the moment.

"I thought at first it might be Miguel," Karen said. "My houseman. But he's visiting his mom in Chula Vista."

"You have a houseman?"

"Miguel does everything, cleans the house, takes care of the outside . . . *There,*" Karen said. "If you can't hear that, Harry, you're deaf."

He wanted to ask her how old Miguel was and what he looked like. Miguel . . . and thought of Michael, her former, now a superstar. Michael had lived here and slept in this bed. He wondered if Miguel ever got in it with her. Karen was closing in on forty but still a knockout. She kept in shape, had given up dope for health food, switched from regular cigarettes to low-tar menthols.

"Harry, don't go to sleep on me."

He said, "Have I ever done that?" Was quiet for a moment and said, "You have any idea what that is?"

"Those are *voices,* Harry. People talking!"

"Really?"

"On television. Somebody came in and turned the TV on."

"You sure?"

"Listen, will you?"

Harry raised his head from the pillow, going along, hearing a faint monotone sound that gradually became voices. She was right, two people talking. He cocked his head in the bedroom silence and after a moment said, "You know who the one guy sounds like? Shecky Greene."

Karen turned her head, a slow move, to give him a look over the shoulder. "You're still smashed, aren't you?" Judging him, but the tone not unsympathetic, a little sad.

"I'm fine."

Maybe half in the bag but still alert, with a nice glow. The headache would come later if he didn't take something. He must have put away half the fifth of Scotch earlier, down in the study where the TV was on, while he told Karen about his situation, his thirty years in the picture business on the brink. He was about to become either a major player or might never be heard from again. And she sat there listening to him like a fucking Teamsters business agent, no reaction, no sympathy. He thought of something else and said:

"Maybe, you know how you go downstairs in the morning sometimes you see pictures cockeyed on the wall? You're thinking, This is some hangover, wow. Then you see on the news there was an earthquake during the night over near Pasadena someplace. Not a big one, like a four-point-two. You know? Maybe it's something like that, an atmospheric disturbance turned on the TV."

Karen was listening, but not to him, staring at the bedroom doorway, pitch-dark out there, her nice slim back arched.

"Or maybe it's only the wind," Harry said.

That got her looking at him again because she knew the line, intimately. From *Grotesque, Part Two,* one of his highest grossing pictures. The maniac's up on the roof ripping out shingles with his bare hands; inside the house the male lead with all the curly hair stares grimly at the ceiling as Karen, playing the girl, says to him, "Maybe it's only the wind." She hated the line, refused to say it until he convinced her it was okay, it worked.

"I love your attitude," Karen said. "What do you care if somebody broke in, it's not your house."

"If you think somebody broke in, why don't you call the police?"

"Because I don't intentionally allow myself to look stupid," Karen said, "if I can help it. Not anymore."

The way she kept staring at him, over the shoulder, was a nice angle. The dark hair against pale skin. The lighting wasn't bad either, Karen backlit with the windows behind her. It took at least ten years off her age, the tough little broad a sweet young thing again in her white T-shirt. She was telling him now, in a thoughtful tone, "When I came upstairs, you stayed to finish your drink."

"I didn't turn the TV on."

"You said you wanted to watch a few minutes of Carson."

She was right. "But I turned it off."

"Harry, you can't be sure what you did."

"I'm positive."

Yeah, because he had turned it off the moment he thought about getting in bed with Karen instead of sleeping in the guest room: the idea, start talking again, work on her sympathy . . .

"I used the remote control thing and laid it on the floor," Harry said. "You know what could've happened? The dog came in and stepped on it, turned the TV back on."

"I don't have a dog."

"You don't? What happened to Muff?"

"Harry, are you going down, or you want me to?"

He wanted her to but had to be nice, obliging, to have any hope of using her.

Getting out of bed his boxer shorts hiked up on him and he had to work them down, get the elastic band under his belly. Karen thought he was fat.

In the study, earlier, he had told her about the story he'd optioned that could change his life, an original screenplay: no fiends or monsters, this one straight-up high-concept drama. He told her he was taking it to a major studio and Karen said, "Oh?" He told her—making it sound like an afterthought—yeah, and guess who read the script and flipped over it? Michael. No kidding, loves it. Her ex, and she didn't say a goddamn word, not even "Oh?" or make a sound. She stared at him, smoking her cigarette. He told her he did have a few problems. One, getting past Michael's agent, the prick, who refused to let Michael take a meeting with him. And, there was some sticky business to clean up that involved money, naturally, not to mention getting out from under his investors, a couple of undesirables who'd been financing him. Which he did mention, in detail. This was his career on the launch pad, about to either fly or go down in flames; and Karen sat there letting the ice melt in her drink, blowing menthol smoke at him. Didn't comment outside of that one "Oh?" or ask one question, not even about Michael, till he was through and she said, "Harry, if you don't lose thirty pounds you're going to die." Thanks a lot. He told her he was glad he stopped by, find out all he had to do to save his ass was join Vic Tanny.

"Harry? What're you doing?"

"I'm putting my shirt on."

He moved to a window to be moving, doing something while he worked on the goddamn buttons.

"Is that okay? So I don't catch cold? But I'm not gonna get all dressed for some friend of yours thinks he's funny."

"Friends don't break in, Harry, they ring the bell."

"Yeah? What about stoned they might."

Karen didn't comment; she was clean now, above it. Harry looked out the window at the backyard, overgrown around the edges, a tangle of plants and old trees surrounding the lawn and the pale oval shape of the swimming pool. It looked full of leaves.

"Does Miguel skim the pool? It needs it."

"Harry—"

He said, "I'm going," and got as far as the door. "If somebody broke in, how come the alarm didn't go off?"

"I don't have an alarm."

"You have it taken out?"

"I never had one."

That's right, it was the house in Westwood, where Karen had lived with him. She'd come in, forget to touch the numbers to turn it off . . . Marlene had the alarm system now and the house that went with it. He had married Marlene, his director of development, after Karen left to marry Michael.

Then when both marriages ended at about the same time he told Karen it was a sign, they should get back together. Karen said she didn't believe in signs. Which was a lie, she read her horoscope every day. Marlene was married to a guy who at one time ran production at Paramount and was now producing TV sitcoms, one of them a family with a Chihuahua that could talk. Tiny little dog with a tiny little fake Puerto Rican accent. Why chew look hat me like dat? The dog always fucking up. He was thinking of Karen in the Westwood house instead of this one, her own place, a semi-French château high up in Beverly Hills, above the lights of L.A. Built in the late twenties for a movie star and passed on to others.

From the doorway he said to Karen, "Why chew make me do thees?"

"Because I'm a girl," the pale figure on the bed answered, "and you're bigger than I am. A lot."

Harry moved down the curved staircase in his shirt and boxer shorts, the monotone sound of voices becoming more distinct; he could hear words now and what sounded like audience response, the volume turned up to be heard on the second floor. He believed it was the Letterman show. The tile in the foyer was cold on his bare feet. Mexican tile now and primitive art, hardwood floors except in the study, all the fat comfortable slipcovered furniture from Michael's time gone. And yet there were pictures of him in the study, among the dozens of photographs of movie people and movie posters covering the paneled walls.

He crossed to the study, the door open partway, dark inside except for the glow from the big thirty-two-inch Sony. There, David Letterman talking to someone—not Shecky, it wasn't his voice.

Harry couldn't see the desk, where he and Karen had sat with the bottle of Scotch, schmoozing, Karen telling him she was reading a script she might do. Oh, really? Want to get back into it, huh? Great. Biding his time until finally making his presentation: here is my tremendous opportunity, but here are the problems. Pause. Waiting then for her to say, Maybe I can help. No, she tells him he ought to lose weight.

Still, there was hope. Asking him to spend the night was a good sign. Looking after him, saying he was in no condition to drive. It meant she cared. Though not enough to let him sleep with her when he suggested it, as kind of a trip down memory lane. Spunky Karen said, "If you think nostalgia's going to get you laid, forget it." He could take the guest room or a cab. Fine, sleeping with her wasn't that important anyway; they were back on familiar ground with one another. When he did slip into her bed, later, Karen said, "I mean it, Harry, we're not going to do anything."

But, she didn't kick him out.

So he felt pretty good pushing open the door to the study, telling himself there was no one in here. If there was it would be one of Karen's friends, no doubt stoned, some bit-part actor thinking he was funny. Okay, he'd nod to the guy very nonchalantly, turn the TV off and walk out.

Moving into the glow from the big Sony now, most of the room dark, he saw David Letterman talking to Paul Shaffer, his music guy, the two of them acting hip. Harry felt his bare feet in the warm carpeting. Felt himself jump and said, "Jesus Christ!" as Letterman and Paul Shaffer vanished, the screen going to black in the same moment the desk lamp came on.

A guy Harry had never seen before was sitting there, hunched over a little, his arms resting on the desk. A guy in black. Dark hair, dark eyes, that lean, hard-boned type. A guy in his forties.

He said, "Harry Zimm, how you doing?" in a quiet tone of voice. "I'm Chili Palmer."

3

HARRY PRESSED A HAND AGAINST HIS CHEST. HE SAID, "Jesus, if I have a heart attack I hope you know what to do," convinced the guy was a friend of Karen's, the way he was making himself at home, the guy staring at him out of those deep-set dark eyes but with hardly any expression.

He said, "Where you been, Harry?"

Harry let his hand slide down over his belly, taking his time, wanting to show he had it together now, not the least self-conscious, standing there without his pants on.

"Have we met? I don't recall."

"We just did. I told you, my name's Chili Palmer."

The guy speaking with some kind of East Coast accent, New York or New Jersey.

"Tell me what you been up to."

Harry still had a mild buzz-on that made him feel, not exactly reckless, but not shy either.

"You mean what am I doing here?"

"You want, you can start with that."

He didn't appear upset or on the muscle. But if he had a key to get in—Harry assuming that—the guy was closer to Karen than just a friend, Karen maybe going in for rough trade now.

Harry said, "I'm visiting, that's all. I'm up in the guest room, I hear the TV. . . . You turned it on?"

The guy, Chili, kept staring, not saying anything now. Typecast, he was a first or second lead bad guy, depending on the budget. Hispanic or Italian. Not a maniac bad guy, a cool bad guy with some kind of hustle going. But casual, black poplin jacket zipped up.

The answer came to Harry and he said, "You're in pictures, right?"

The guy smiled. Not much but enough to show even white teeth, no doubt capped, and Harry was convinced of it. The guy was an actor friend of Karen's and she was in on it—the reason she was so anxious to get him down here—setting him up for this bullshit audition. The guy scares hell out of you to prove he can act and you give him a part in your next picture.

"Did you stop to think what if I had a heart attack?"

The guy didn't move, still doing the bit, no expression, very cool.

He said, "You look okay to me, Harry. Come over here and sit down. Tell me what you been up to."

The guy wasn't bad. Harry took one of the canvas director's chairs by the desk, the guy watching him. He knew how to stare without giving it much. The angle was nice too: the guy lean and dark, the bottle of Scotch, the ice bucket and the glasses he and Karen had left, in the foreground. Harry raised one hand and passed it over his thinning hair. He could feel it was losing its frizz, due for another permanent and touch-up, add some body and get rid of the mousy gray trying to take over. The guy had a full head of dark hair, as that type usually did, but close-cropped so you could see the shape of his head, like a skull. It was a nice effect.

He said, "Harry, you looking at me?"

Harry brought his hand down. "I'm looking at you."

"I want you to keep looking right here, okay?"

"That's what I'm doing," Harry said, going along. Why

not? The guy was from Brooklyn or the Bronx, one of those. If he was putting it on he had it down cold.

"Okay, so tell me what's up."

He was good, but irritating.

"I don't have a script," Harry said, "so I don't know what you're talking about. *Okay?*"

"You don't have a script," Chili said. "How about, you happen to have a hunnerd and fifty big ones on you?"

Harry didn't answer.

"You're not saying nothing. You remember being in Vegas November twenty-sixth of last year, at Las Mesas?"

It was starting to sound real. "I go to Vegas, that's where I stay, at Mesas," Harry said. "Always have, for years."

"You know Dick Allen?"

"Dick Allen's a very dear friend of mine." It still could be a script, something Karen put together. "How far you want to go with this?"

The guy gestured, his hands limp, very natural.

"We're there, Harry. You signed markers for a hunnerd and a half, you're over sixty days past due and you haven't told anybody what the problem is."

It wasn't a script.

Harry said, "Jesus Christ, what're you, a collector? You come in here, walk in the house in the middle of the fucking night? I thought you were some actor, au*dition*ing, for Christ sake."

The guy raised his eyebrows. "Is that right?" He seemed about to smile. "That's interesting. You thought I was acting, huh?"

"I don't believe this," Harry said. "You break in the house to tell me I owe on some *markers*? I know what I owe. So what? I go to Mesas I get comped, the whole shot. I got a credit line for as much as I owe—and they send you here to *collect*?" Harry felt an urge to move, do something.

He pushed up out of the chair to look down at the guy, get an advantage on him. "We'll see about this," Harry said, picked up the phone and punched the 0. "Operator, how do I get Las Vegas Information?" He listened a moment and hung up.

Chili said, "Lemme give you some advice, okay?"

Harry looked up, the phone in his hand again, about to punch the number.

"You don't want to act like a hard-on you're standing there in your undies. You know what I'm saying? You got enough to handle. You got the markers and you got another outstanding debt if I'm not mistaken. What you wanta do, Harry, is use your head, sit down and talk to me."

It stopped him. "What outstanding debt?"

"Put the phone down."

"I want to know what you're talking about," Harry said, getting a peeved tone now, indignant, "outside of what I owe at Mesas, which they know I'm good for."

"They know you're good up to your last trip. After that, as they say, nobody knows nothing." Chili waited.

Harry hung up the phone. He felt the chair against his bare legs and sat down.

"A marker's like a check, Harry . . ."

"I know what a marker is."

"They don't want to deposit yours and have 'em bounce, insufficient funds, or they find out the account's closed. That's embarrassing. So your customer rep, your very dear friend Dick Allen's been calling, leaving messages on your machine, but you never get back to him. So basically, you want to know why I'm here—I don't actually work for Mesas, but Dick Allen asked me as a favor would I look you up. Okay, I come to L.A., try your apartment, your office, you're not anywhere around. So I contact some people I know of, get a few leads—"

"What people?"

"You have high blood pressure, Harry? You oughta lose some weight."

"*What* people?"

"You don' know 'em, some people I was put in touch with. So I start calling around. I call here, Karen tells me she hasn't seen you. So we talk, I ask her if this's the Karen Flores used to be in the movies. Yes, it is. Well, how come I haven't seen you? . . . I remember her in *Grotesque* with the long blond hair. I start to think, this is where I'd come if I was Harry Zimm and I want to stay off the street."

"You think I'm hiding out?"

"What're you getting excited about?"

"I don't like the insinuation, I'm hiding."

"Well, that's up to you, what you like or what you don't. I called your former wife, the one in Westwood? She goes, 'I hope you're a bill collector and you find the cheapskate.' "

"You have fun talking about me? Jesus," Harry said, "that broad used to work for me. She's supposed to know the business, but apparently has no idea what I was going through at the time." His gaze moved to the bottle of Scotch thinking of Marlene, who liked her booze, also thinking he wouldn't mind having one.

"You're not looking at me, Harry."

"Why do I have to keep looking at you?"

"I want you to."

"You gonna get rough now, threaten me? I make good by tomorrow or get my legs broken?"

"Come on, Harry—Mesas? The worst they might do is get a judgment against you, uttering a bad check. I can't imagine you want that to happen, man in your position."

"I've won there and I've lost," Harry said, staying with the peeved tone. "They carry me and I always pay what I owe. But now all of a sudden they're worried I'm gonna stiff 'em?

Why? They don't give you a credit line of a hundred and a half unless they know you're good for it."

"What's that, Harry?"

"You heard me."

"What I heard," Chili said, "your credit line's an even hunnerd and they gave you the extra fifty TTO, this trip only, 'cause you had front money, that cashier's check for two hunnerd thousand, right? Four hours later, the night's still young, it's all gone, the two you rode in on and the hunnerd and a half. It can happen to anybody. But now a couple months go by, Dick Allen wonders if there's a problem here, if Harry Zimm was playing with scared money. He says you never put down more than ten on a basketball game in your life. You come in this time and drop the whole load, like you're not doing it for fun."

"I didn't have to twist any arms. I told 'em what I wanted to put down and they okayed it."

"Why not? It's your money."

"They tell you what game it was and the point spread? Lakers and the Pistons, in Detroit. Which happens to be where I grew up. Now I'm out here I follow the Lakers, had seats up to last year. Not down there with Jack Nicholson, but they weren't bad seats. You don't recall the game?"

"I mighta read about it at the time. What was the spread?"

The guy showing interest. It picked Harry up.

"The sports book line had the Pistons by three and a half. The bad boys from Motown over the glamor boys from showtown."

"You live here," Chili said, "but you like the Pistons. I can understand that. I don't live in New York anymore, I'm in Miami, but I still follow the Knicks, put a few bucks on 'em now and then. Even though it's been years."

"I don't happen to bet that way," Harry said, "emotionally. I like the Pistons this time 'cause they're at home, twenty thousand screaming fans on their ass. Also the fact they beat the Lakers four zip in the finals last year."

He had the guy's attention; no question about it, waiting to hear about a basketball game that was played more than two months ago.

"You know how I bet it?"

"You went with the Pistons and the Lakers won."

"I went with the Pistons," Harry said, "and the Pistons won."

Right away Chili said, "The point spread."

Harry sat back in the director's chair. "The Pistons by three and a half. The score was one-oh-two to ninety-nine. They won and I lost."

Now Chili sat back. "That was close. You almost did it."

The guy showing sympathy. Good. Harry wanted him to get up now, shake hands and leave. But the guy was staring at him again.

"So then you go through your credit line playing black-jack," Chili said, "chasing what you lost, going double-up to catch up. But when you have to win, Harry, that's when you lose. Everybody knows that."

"Whatever you say," Harry said, tired of talking about it. He yawned. Maybe the guy would take the hint.

But Chili kept at it. He said, "You know what I think? You went in the hole on some kind of deal, so you tried to bet your way out. See, I don't know anything about your business, Harry, but I know how a guy acts when he's facing a payment he has to make and he doesn't have it. You get desperate. I know a guy put his wife out on the street, and she wasn't bad looking either."

"You don't know anything about my business," Harry said, showing some irritation, "but you don't mind sticking your nose in it. Tell Dick Allen I'll cover the markers in the next sixty days, at the most. He doesn't like it, that's his problem. First thing in the morning," Harry said, "I'm gonna call him, the prick. I thought he was a friend of mine."

Harry paused, wondering whether or not he should ask the guy how he got in the house, and decided he didn't want to know. The guy says he broke a window—then what? Harry waited. He was tired, irritable, not feeling much of a glow. He said, "We gonna sit here all night or what? You want me to call you a cab?"

The guy, Chili, shook his head. He kept staring, but with a different kind of expression now, more thoughtful, or maybe curious.

"So you make movies, huh?"

"That's what I do," Harry said, relieved, not minding the question. "I produce feature motion pictures, no TV. You mentioned *Grotesque,* that happened to be *Grotesque, Part Two* Karen Flores was in. She starred in all three of my *Slime Creatures* releases you might've seen."

The guy, Chili, was nodding as he came forward to lean on the desk.

"I think I got an idea for one, a movie."

And Harry said, "Yeah? What's it about?"

4

AT FIRST, ALL KAREN HEARD WAS HARRY'S SIDE OF whatever was going on. As soon as she came out of the bedroom she heard his voice, Harry saying, *"Jesus Christ!"* and it gave her goose bumps standing in her T-shirt and panties, one hand on the railing that curved around the open upstairs landing. Her eyes held on the foyer, directly below: dark except for a square of light on the floor, coming out of the study. A few minutes passed. Karen was about to step back into the bedroom to call the police when she heard Harry's voice again, Harry saying, *"What people?"* and then repeating it, *"What people?"* With an edge this time, Harry acting tough. A good sign. He wouldn't use that tone with a burglar. Little Harry Zimm, with his perm, his frizzed hair, loved to act tough. But then Karen began to wonder if Harry could be talking to himself. Harry into the Scotch again.

What people?

Meaning the people he wanted to get out from under, his investors, the undesirables. Harry trying to convince himself there was no problem.

What people?

As if to say, What, those guys? Seeing if he could make the mess he was in seem trivial.

It was possible. He used to talk to himself sometimes

when he was loaded, or rewriting dialogue in a script, look at the line and recite it to her aloud, when they were living together. She liked the idea of Harry boozing, trying to reassure himself. She liked it a lot better than thinking someone had broken in and was still in the house. Harry talking to himself made sense.

Until his voice, raised, came out of the study again.

"You heard me."

Karen listened, holding on to the railing.

That was it. *You heard me.* Then silence.

Would he say that to himself? She didn't think so. Unless he was acting out his own kind of scene, imagining what he would like to tell his money guys. *You heard me.* Harry hating to be controlled, especially by outsiders, people not in the movie business. Harry called investors a necessary evil. Talking to him earlier he had sounded okay . . .

But looked awful.

In the past ten years he'd become a fat little sixty-year-old guy with frizzy hair. The same guy she once thought was a genius because he could shoot a ninety-minute feature in ten days and be looking at a workprint two weeks later . . .

Harry doing the first of the *Slime Creatures* in Griffith Park when she read for him in bra and panties, he said to give him an idea of her figure, and she got the part. Karen asked him if he did horror or T and A and Harry explained to her the philosophy of ZigZag Productions. "Zig for the maniac, escaped lunatic and dope-crazed biker pictures." No vampires or werewolves; she would never get bitten or eaten. "Zag for the ones featuring mutations fed on nuclear waste, your slime people, your seven-foot rats, your maggots the size of submarines. But there's nothing wrong with showing a little skin in either type picture." She told him if he was talking about full frontal nudity, forget it, she didn't do porn, hard or soft. If she had to go to bed with him, okay, one time only, but it would have to be an awfully good part. Harry acted insulted. He said, "You ought to be ashamed of yourself, I'm old enough to be your uncle. But I like your spunk and the way you talk. Where you from, somewhere in Texas?" She told him he was close, Alamogordo, where her dad was a rocket man and her mom was in real estate. Karen told him she left to study drama at New Mexico State, but since coming here had done nothing but wait on tables. Harry said, "Let's hear you scream." She gave him a good one and he gave her a big smile saying, "Get ready to be a star."

Karen was slimed to death within twenty minutes of her first appearance on the screen.

Michael, who had also read for a part and was turned down, told her she was lucky, not have to hang around the set. It was where she first met Michael, when they were casting *Slime Creatures* fifteen years ago, saw him a few other times after, but they didn't seriously get it on until Michael was a star and she was living with Harry . . . tired of it, saying mean things and arguing by that time, picking at dumb lines that had never bothered her before. Like the one Harry threw at her in bed, out of nowhere . . .

"Maybe it's only the wind."

Knowing she'd remember it.

Instead of giving him a look, she should have said, "What're you up to, Harry? What can I do for you?"

Make him come out and say it instead of trying to take her down memory lane. It was so obvious. Harry wanted her to use her influence with Michael to set up a meeting. But wanted it to be her idea, happy to do him this favor because she owed him, theoretically, for putting her in pictures, making her a ZigZag Productions star.

But it was weird—hearing that line again.

When she first read it she said to Harry, "You've got to be kidding." It was his line, he was always rewriting, sticking in additional dialogue. Harry said, "Yeah, but it works. You hear the roof being torn off, you look up and say to the guy, 'Maybe it's only the wind.' You know why?"

"Because I'm stupid?"

"Because you want it to be the wind and not that fucking maniac up there. It may sound stupid, but what it does, it gives the audience a chance to release nervous laughter."

"At my expense," Karen said.

And Harry said, "You going to sulk? It's entertainment, babe. It's a put-on, the whole business of making pictures. You ever catch yourself taking it seriously you're in trouble."

Karen recited the line. It got a laugh and a picture that cost four hundred thousand to make grossed over twenty million worldwide. She told Harry it was still schlock. He said, "Yeah, but it's my schlock. If it doesn't make me famous, at least it can make me rich."

She might ask Harry in the morning, "Who's taking it seriously now?" Harry dreaming of a twenty-million-plus production he'd never get off the ground. And a star he'd never sign. With or without her help.

She might ask him, "Remember I told you last night about a picture I've been offered?" After a seven-year layoff. She had expected Harry to at least be curious, show some interest. "You remember I wanted to talk about it and all you said was 'Yeah? Great'?"

Now she was the one taking it seriously, standing on the upstairs landing in her T-shirt . . . listening, beginning to see the stairway and the foyer below as a set.

It would be lighted to get eerie shadows and she would have on a see-through nightie rather than a T-shirt. She hears a sound and calls out softly, "Harry? Is that you?" She starts down the stairs and stops as a shadow appears in the foyer, a moving shadow coming out of the study. She calls again, "Harry?" in a stupid, tentative voice knowing goddamn well it isn't Harry. If it's a Zig shadow, now the maniac appears, looks up, sees her. A Zag shadow is followed by a gross, oversized mutation. Either one, she stands there long enough to belt out a scream that will fill movie theaters, raise millions of goose bumps and make Harry a lot of money.

Karen cleared her throat. It was something she always did before the camera rolled. Cleared her throat and took a deep breath. She had never screamed for the fun of it because it wasn't fun. After only three takes—Harry's limit—her throat would be raw.

The house was so quiet.

She was thinking, Maybe do one, hang it out there for about five beats. See what happens.

And in almost the same moment heard Harry's voice coming from the study.

"We gonna sit here all night?"

Now she heard a faint murmur of voices, Harry's and another voice, but not the words, Harry carrying on a conversation with someone who had walked in her house, or broken in. You could take that seriously. Now she heard Harry's voice again, unmistakably Harry.

"Yeah? What's it about?"

Those familiar words.

A question she heard every day when they were living together and Harry got her involved in story development because he hated to read. *What's it about?* Never mind a script synopsis, coverage to Harry meant giving him the plot in three sentences, fifty words or less.

Karen went back through the bedroom to the bathroom and turned the light on. She stared at herself in the mirror as she took a minute to run a comb through her hair.

What's it about? . . . It's what Hollywood was about. Somebody making a pitch.

5

WHILE THEY WERE STILL IN THE OTHER ROOM, THE STUDY, getting ready to come out here, Harry said to him, "You're Chili? . . . I don't think I caught your last name."

Chili told him it was Chili Palmer and saw Harry give him that look. Oh? Like he was wondering what the name was before somebody changed it.

They were in the kitchen now. It was as big as the kitchen in the Holmhurst Hotel, Atlantic City, where he had washed dishes a couple of summers when he was a kid, back before they tore the place down to make a parking lot. The fifth of Dewar's, what was left of it, and a tray of ice were on the butcher-block table. There were all kinds of pots and pans hanging from a rack right above them. He saw Harry, who was sitting at the end of the table facing the door to the hall, look up as he was about to take a drink and stop.

Harry said, "Karen?" sounding surprised. He took the drink then and said, "Karen, say hello to Chili Palmer. Dick Allen sent him. You remember Dick, at Mesas? Chili, this is Karen Weir."

"Flores," Karen said.

"That's right," Harry said, "you changed it back."

Chili had been telling his movie idea until this interruption, which he didn't mind at all, a chance to meet Karen Flores. He sat with his arms resting on the table, looking past his shoulder now at Karen in the doorway, the hall behind her dark. She looked smaller in real life than in movies, about five-two and no more than ninety-nine pounds. She was still good looking, but where was all the blond hair? And the boobs he remembered as big ones for her slim figure. He nodded, saying to her, "Karen, it's a pleasure. How you doing?"

She didn't say anything, looking at him as if trying to figure out if she knew him. Or she was giving him a pose, standing there with her arms folded in a Los Angeles Lakers T-shirt that came down just past her crotch and was like a little minidress on her. Middle of the night, never saw him before in her life—she could be on the muscle without showing it. Her legs were nice and tan.

Harry was telling her, "Chili's the one called you the other day. He says just from talking to you on the phone he had a feeling I'd show up here sooner or later. You imagine that?"

Harry seemed in a better mood since coming out here to get ice and they sat down with their drinks, Harry more talkative. Listening to the movie idea he kept sticking his own ideas in.

Chili straightened, touched the front of his jacket to smooth it down. He thought of getting up but now it was too late. He liked the way Karen kept looking right at him without appearing nervous or emotional, putting on any kind of act. No, this was her. Not anything like Karen the screamer facing the maniac with a butcher knife or seven-foot rats or giant ticks gorged on human blood. He liked her hair, the way it was now, thick and dark, hanging down close to one eye. He noticed how thin her neck was and took a few more pounds off, got her down to around ninety-five. He figured she was now up in her thirties, but hadn't lost any of her looks to speak of.

"He's telling me an idea for a movie," Harry said. "It's not bad, so far." He motioned with his glass. "Tell Karen, let's see what she thinks."

"You want me to start over?"

"Yeah, start over." Harry looked at Karen again. "Why don't you sit down, have a drink?"

Chili watched her shake her head.

"I'm fine, Harry."

He liked her voice, the quiet way she spoke. She was looking at him again, curious, doing a read.

"How did you get in the house?"

"The door from the patio, in back."

"You broke in?"

"No, it was open. I mean it wasn't locked."

"What if it was?"

That was a good question. He didn't have to answer it though, Harry saying, "He works for Dick Allen. Got sent here to check up on me."

Karen said, "Oh," and nodded. "That makes it all right to walk in my house."

Chili didn't say anything. He liked the way she was handling it. If she was pissed off you couldn't tell.

"He knew I was gonna turn up here," Harry said, "just from talking to you on the phone."

"Why, what did I say?"

"Something about your voice. It was a feeling he had, a hunch. You want to hear his idea?"

Chili watched her. His feeling now was Karen'd say no and tell him to get the hell out of her house. But she didn't say anything. Or Harry didn't give her a chance.

"It's about a guy," Harry said, "who scams an airline out of three hundred grand. Go on, tell her."

"You just did."

"I mean the way you told it to me. Start at the beginning, we see how the story line develops."

"Well, basically," Chili said, "this guy owes a shylock fifteen thousand, plus he's a few weeks behind on the vig, the interest you have to pay, on account of he doesn't have it. The guy runs a dry cleaner's but spends everything he makes at the track."

Chili could see Harry ready to cut in and let him.

"You understand what he means," Harry said. "The guy borrowed money from a loan shark. It's the kind of situation, you don't pay you get your legs broken."

"Or the guy thinks he could get 'em broken," Chili said. "You have to understand the loan shark's in business the same as anybody else. He isn't in it looking for a chance to hurt people. He's in it to make money. You go to him, you understand that, you're gonna pay him every week. You don't like that idea, you don't have any business going to him."

Karen said, "Yeah?" Telling him to go on.

"But you don't make your payments," Harry said, "you can get your legs broken, or worse."

"It can happen," Chili said, looking at Karen, "but it's not, you know, the usual way. Maybe once in a while you hear about it."

"If the guy doesn't think it's gonna happen to him," Harry said, "you don't have a story. That's the only reason he gets on the plane, he's scared to death, he's running for his life."

"That's right," Chili said, "the guy's scared. I just meant he wouldn't necessarily get his legs broken in that kind of situation, a few weeks behind. The guy doesn't know any better, so he gets on the plane."

"This's Miami," Harry said. "He's going to Vegas. He's got a few bucks and he's thinking maybe it's his only chance."

"He gets on the plane," Chili said, watching Karen's eyes come back to him, "ready to go, and the plane sits there at the gate, doesn't move. They announce over the PA there's some kind of mechanical problem, they'll be there maybe an hour, but keep your seats in case they get it fixed sooner. The guy's nervous, in no shape to just sit there, sweat it out. So he gets off the plane, goes in the cocktail lounge and starts throwing 'em down, one after the other. He's in there when the plane takes off . . ."

"Without him," Harry said. "The guy's so out of it he doesn't even know it's gone."

"That's right," Chili said. "As a matter of fact, he's still in the cocktail lounge when he hears people talking about a plane crash. But the shape he's in, he doesn't find out right away it's the plane he was on. It didn't gain altitude on account of something to do with the wind and went down in the Everglades, the swamp there, and exploded. Killed everybody aboard, a hunnerd and seventeen people counting the crew. Then when the guy finds out it was his flight, he can't believe it. If he'd stayed on that plane he'd be dead. Right then he knows his luck has changed. If everybody thinks he's dead he won't have to pay back the fifteen or what he owes on the vig, four and a half a week. He'd be saving himself a pile of dough."

Karen was about to say something, but Harry beat her.

"Not to mention saving his ass."

She said to Chili, "The interest is four hundred and fifty a week on fifteen thousand?"

"That's right. Three percent."

"But a week," Karen said. "That's a hundred and fifty percent a year."

"A hunnerd and fifty-six," Chili said. "That's not too bad. I mean some'll charge you more'n that, go as high as six for five on a short-term loan."

He watched her shrug without unfolding her arms.

"What the guy does," Chili said, "is look in the *Herald* for his name on the list of victims. See, the way the plane exploded and went down in the swamp, they're not only having trouble identifying bodies, they can't find 'em all. Or a lot of 'em, they find like just parts of bodies, an arm . . . Others, they're burned beyond recognition. So when the guy doesn't see his name in the paper right away, he has his wife call the airline and say her husband was on that flight. What they do, they bring her out to the airport where they're identifying bodies and going through personal effects, whatever wasn't burned up. See, the guy's bags were on the plane. Oh, the bodies they keep in refrigerated trucks right there in the hangar. They don't show the wife any bodies, they tell her to get her husband's dental chart from his dentist. She says Leo hasn't been to a dentist for as long as they're married. The guy's name is Leo, Leo Devoe."

Karen moved to lean against the doorjamb and Chili noticed she was barefoot. He wondered if she wore anything under that T-shirt she slept in.

"So what the wife does, she identifies stuff from Leo's bags. Tells 'em what to look for and there it is, his monogrammed shirts, what kind of razor he used, things only she would know about. So Leo's identified and gets his name in the paper. A couple days go by, people from the airline come to see the wife, tell her how sorry they are and all and offer her a settlement, the amount based on what he would've earned operating the dry cleaner's the rest of his life. Leo had some kind of trouble with his kidneys, so they were giving him about ten years."

"Yeah, but wait," Harry said. "The best part, the guy hadn't even thought about a settlement, he's so happy to get out from under the shylock. All of a sudden he realizes he can sue the airline, go for at least a million. It's the loser's grandiose dream, see, but now he's pressing his luck . . ."

Karen said, "How much is the wife offered? . . ."

Chili started to tell her as Harry said, "Three hundred grand, and they take it, money in the hand, babe. The guy has his wife cash the check and he takes off for Las Vegas with the dough. Gets there, he's supposed to call her, tell her when to come out . . . Wait, he does call her a couple of times."

"Twice," Chili said. "Basically stringing her along."

"After that, nothing," Harry said. "She never hears from him again. Meanwhile, the guy's hot. Runs the three hundred grand up to almost half a million . . ."

"He comes to L.A.," Chili said, and stopped as Harry raised his hand.

"It drives the guy nuts, he's winning but can't tell anybody who he is. You show in a back story his motivation, his desire to be famous, pal around with celebrities, the headliners doing the big rooms. Now he's got the dough to buy his way in, mix with celebs and he can't resist the temptation. Even if it means he's liable to be revealed as a fraud, and very likely shot dead by the shylock, he makes up his mind to go for it. Where else but Hollywood. That wouldn't be a bad title, *Go for It.*" Harry said all this to Karen. Now he looked at Chili again. "So, he comes to L.A. . . ."

"I don't know about his wanting to meet celebrities," Chili said, "that's something new. But, yeah, he comes to L.A. Then, after that, I don't know what happens."

He saw Karen waiting. She seemed patient, moved only that one time. He turned his head to see Harry looking at him, Harry saying after a moment, "That's it? That's your great idea for a movie?"

"I said I had an idea, that's all."

"That's half a movie, with holes in it." Harry looked at Karen. "Maybe forty minutes of screen time."

Karen said, "How did you know Harry was here?"

Like that, getting back to it.

"His car's in the garage," Chili said.

"You called, that was four days ago. How did you know he'd be here this evening?"

"I've been stopping by. See if there's a gray '83 Mercedes around with ZIGZAG on the license plate."

"So you walked in. What if all the doors were locked?"

"I would've rung the bell."

"Hey, it's okay," Harry said. "The guy's a friend of Dick Allen's. He's not gonna take anything."

"It might be okay with you," Karen said. "What you're doing, Harry, you're bringing your dirty laundry into my house and I don't want it."

Chili felt she was going to keep talking but Harry moved in saying he should've rung the bell. Why didn't he? Chili said he wanted to surprise him, catch him with his pants down, so to speak. A little humor there. Nobody laughed though or even smiled. Karen asked, what if she had called the police? Chili told her Harry would've explained to them it was okay, just like he explained it to her now. She stared at him and he stared back at her until Harry told him, well, anyway, he had the beginning of an idea but it was full of holes.

"In the first place," Harry said, "it's not believable the wife would get a settlement that fast. From an in*sur*ance company? Without them checking her out?"

"They did," Chili said. "I didn't tell you all the details, how nervous she was about it and all."

"Harry doesn't realize it's a true story," Karen said.

They were both looking at her now.

"That Miami flight that went down in the Everglades, it was on the news every day for about a week, covering the investigation, interviews with witnesses, relatives of the victims from around here . . . Harry was busy."

Chili caught the tone. So she knew about Harry's problems, but wasn't exactly crying over them.

Harry was squinting, as if to get his memory to work, saying, "Yeah, on the news . . ." and then turning to Chili. "That's where you got the idea."

"Part of it, yeah."

"And you made up the rest."

"No, it's all true, Harry, everything I told you."

This got him squinting again. Chili could see his mind working. He expected to hear from Karen, but Harry was staying with it.

"The part about the shylock?"

"Everything."

"Wait a minute. You're not the guy, are you?"

Chili said, "You mean Leo?" shaking his head. It was getting good.

"You wouldn't be talking to me if you were."

"I'm not the guy, Harry."

Again he expected Karen to jump in and say something as Harry started thinking, looking up at the pots and pans before getting an idea.

"You know the wife?"

"Yeah, I know her. Fay."

Harry seemed to like that. It got him hunched over the table. "You're related to her. Wait—you're her brother."

Chili shook his head, not giving him any help.

"But you're a close friend. She asked you to help her find her husband."

"I talked to her, that's all."

Chili waited. Harry was still thinking of it as a movie instead of real life. You could see him going over the story in his head, trying to come up with the answer. Staring at his glass now to see if it was in there.

Harry said, "Okay, the guy goes to Vegas . . ." Then stopped and looked at Chili. "How's the wife know for sure that's where he went?"

"Take my word for it."

"Okay, he's in Vegas," Harry said, "he can't trust anybody . . . So he uses an assumed name. Right?"

"Larry Paris."

"How do you know?"

"Trust me."

"Okay, he starts gambling, gets hot right away . . . Wait a minute, you made that part up. The guy *doesn't* win. That's it—he not only doesn't win, he blows the entire three hundred thou, gets into Mesas for a chunk of dough and they send you to find him."

Now he was back to real life, putting in things he knew, but still making it sound like a movie. Chili felt like saying to him, See? Not a bad idea, huh? At least so far. But Harry was still talking.

"It's what you do, working for the casino. It's why you're here tonight."

"You're close," Chili said, "but you're coming at it wrong. I'm looking for the guy, yeah, but it wasn't the casino sent me. They asked would I look *you* up, that's all."

"Which I resent," Harry said, "and believe me Dick Allen's gonna hear about it."

"Okay, but getting back," Chili said, watching the way Harry was staring at him, still interested, "where you think I fit in the picture?"

Karen said, "Harry, for God's sake," sounding bored.

They both looked over at her, Harry saying, "What's the matter?"

"He's the shylock," Karen said.

She was staring at him again as Harry said, "Is that right, that's what you do for a living?"

"What I did up till recently," Chili said, still looking at Karen. "After I get done here I'll think about what I'm gonna do next."

Karen straightened, where she was leaning against the doorjamb. "With your experience," she said to Chili, "you could always become an agent. Right, Harry?"

"Yeah, that's what we need," Harry said, "more agents."

Still looking at Chili she said, "Well, if I don't see you again . . ." gave him kind of a shrug and walked away, left them.

"She's upset," Harry said.

"You think so?"

She didn't seem upset to Chili; he thought she had it together, handled it just right.

"You should've rung the bell," Harry said, hunching over the table. "But getting back for a minute—it was the guy's wife told you where he went, huh?"

"Yeah, Fay. She felt it was her money more'n it was his," Chili said. "So she offers me half of whatever I bring back, if I find Leo and he has any of it left."

"You didn't mention this before."

"You said keep it simple."

"But what it does," Harry said, "it adds a whole new dimension to the story. So you went to Las Vegas but didn't find him. The guy stayed a jump ahead of you."

"No, I found him," Chili said, and paused.

Harry, waiting, seemed more interested now than he did before.

"You want to hear about what happened in Vegas?"

6

THE NEXT EVENING AFTER THE VISIT WITH FAY HE WAS in Las Vegas, checked into the Golden Nugget and on the phone with Benny Wade, the man in charge of collections at Mesas. Chili knew him well enough to call his house, tell him he was in town looking for a Leo Devoe and didn't have much time, a couple of days . . .

"Never heard of him."

Chili said to Benny somebody must know of a flashy kind of guy comes to town with three hundred grand. Benny said high rollers left their money at home and played on credit; this guy sounded like a runaway, the kind dreams of making a score and then flying down to Rio by the sea-o.

"Can you check for me? I'll do you one gratis."

"That's what I like to hear. Where are you?"

"The Nugget, downtown."

"What's the matter with Mesas? Give you casino rate."

"The Strip," Chili said, "you have to get a cab to go anywhere. Here, you walk out the door you're in Vegas."

Right there out the window, the Pioneer, Binion's, Sassy Sally's, all the grind joints, hot slots, discount prime ribs, keno, bingo, race and sports book . . . cleaning and pressing While-U-Wait . . .

"Downtown, you get it out of your system, why you're here, in less'n twenty-four hours."

"Not to mention it's cheaper," Benny said. "You could stay in your room, watch TV, you want to save money. Or you could've stayed home."

"I wouldn't be here," Chili said, "if I didn't have to find this guy. He took a walk, so the new management tells me he pays or I do."

Benny said, "Let me get on it. Leo Devoe?"

"Yeah, but listen, he could be using a different name," Chili said, looking at While-U-Wait in red neon down on the street. "You don't score with Devoe, try Paris. It's the name of his dry-cleaning place."

Chili wasn't going to get dressed up but changed his mind, put on a dark suit and tie, white shirt—so he wouldn't look like a tourist—a giant neon cowgirl watching him through the window. The suit picked him up, made him feel like going out, find some broad to have dinner with him, nice bottle of wine . . . He was studying himself in the mirror, smoothing his short hair forward to lie flat, wondering why people didn't like to get dressed up anymore, when Benny Wade called back.

"You ought to put down some bets tonight, you're lucky. Did you know that?"

"I try to be."

"There's a Larry Paris keeps changing hotels, moving up the Strip. Stayed a few nights at the Trop, left and went to the Sands, the Desert Inn, Stupak's Vegas World. Currently he's appearing right up the street from you, at the Union Plaza."

"So is 'Nudes on Ice,' " Chili said, feeling himself getting more into a Vegas mood. "How's he doing?"

"Nobody knows. He didn't apply for a credit line anywhere he stayed."

"Not with a phony name. It must be the guy."

"I mentioned 'Larry Paris' and the night manager at Stupak's knew right away who I meant. He said Mr. Paris rented a bodyguard to carry his cash. They do that, pay some local stiff ten bucks an hour, try and impress you."

"That's Leo," Chili said. "He must think he died and went to heaven."

Benny Wade said he sounded like the kind you'd find shooting craps, where you can draw a crowd. Check the dice tables at the Plaza.

It made sense, but didn't take into account this was Chili's lucky night. He went downstairs, walked across that flowery Nugget carpeting and there was Leo playing roulette, a lady's game, Leo betting numbers while his bodyguard, a guy who looked like a young dressed-up weight lifter, held his briefcase.

CHILI STOOD AWAY FROM THE TABLE, BEHIND LEO AND a little to one side. Two women in their thirties, wearing party dresses but not too attractive, were across the table from Leo, who was trying to get something going. He'd shake his head at their betting one chip at a time, saying you had to take risks if you wanted to score big. Leo was playing what they called the action numbers, 10 through 15 and 33, the numbers scattered evenly around the wheel. His chips were a shade of green to match his outfit, but there was no way to tell what the chips were worth or how much he was betting. The two women were playing with blue and pink chips. A lot of color at the table, Leo looking like the Easter bunny in a pale green sport coat with gold buttons, an open pink shirt with one of those high Hollywood collars, Leo's face hunched in there behind sunglasses, hair slicked back. Chili watched the wheel spin and stop. The house won. As the two women walked away Leo told them the dinner offer was still on. They said thanks anyway and turned to each other rolling their eyes. Leo watched them go, the poor little dry cleaner trying to be a high roller. The bodyguard, a young guy with shoulders that filled his suit, was opening the briefcase now. He brought out a stack of 100's in a paper strap and handed it to Leo, the dealer waiting. Leo tore the strap, wet his thumb and counted out twenty bills he passed to the dealer, who gave Leo his stack of twenty green chips. So he was betting a hundred a spin on each of the seven action numbers, looking for a hit that would pay him 35 to 1. Chili watched. Leo hit and put three chips on each number, his idea of a system. He hit again, collecting over ten grand, tried three chips again on the seven numbers and lost. Now he went back to betting a hundred on each and was covering the numbers when Chili walked up behind him, said, "Look at me, Leo," and Leo spilled his chips. The dealer looked over.

Leo, getting himself ready, didn't turn right away. When he came around he was adjusting his sunglasses over a casual expression that showed just enough surprise—a guy who scams three hundred thousand ready to put on whatever kind of act was needed—though all he managed to say was "Well, well . . ." The bodyguard, with his build and his hair shorter than Chili's, stepped in to put his hand on Leo's shoulder.

Chili said, "What's this guy do, Leo, stop traffic you want to cross the street?"

"Well, this is a surprise," Leo said, "believe me. What're you doing here?"

"I'm collecting," Chili said. "Twenty grand even."

Leo pushed his sunglasses up on his nose. He seemed to be squinting, puzzled. "I owe you twenty? How you figure that?"

"Expenses," Chili said, "and a late charge I'm adding on."

The young weight lifter had his eyes narrowed, giving Chili his ten-bucks-an-hour bodyguard look.

"Mr. Paris, is this guy bothering you?"

Leo waved him off. "It's okay, Jerry." Still looking at Chili. "I was gonna call you, it slipped my mind. Listen, when I'm through here we'll have a drink, I'll write you a check." Turning to the table he said, "It's good seeing you, Chil," and began picking up his chips.

"You'll write me a check," Chili said. "You serious? Leo, look at me, I'm talking to you."

"I'm busy at the moment," Leo said, studying the table layout. "Okay? You mind?"

He was serious.

It didn't make sense till Chili began to think about it, staring at Leo's shoulders rounded inside that sporty green jacket, his sprayed hair hanging over the Hollywood collar, and said, "Lemme ask you something, Leo."

"You heard Mr. Paris," the ten-dollar bodyguard said. "He don't want to talk to you."

"Okay, you ask him," Chili said, watching Leo reach over the table to cover his action numbers. "Does he think I just happened to run into him . . ." He saw Leo begin to straighten, bringing his arm in. "Or I knew where to look?"

Leo turned from the table. The old Leo once again, Leo the loser. He took the case from the bodyguard.

"How much you want?"

"What you owe me. I'm not into extortion, Leo. I will give you one piece of advice you can take any way you want. Call Fay. And I mean tonight, soon." He felt the bodyguard start to move in and said to him, "Keep out of this. There's no problem." Now the bodyguard didn't know what to do. Leo was bringing a stack of currency from the briefcase. "We're old friends," Chili said to the bodyguard. "I knew him when."

Leo handed him the currency saying, "Fay told you, huh?"

"What'd you expect?" Chili said, looking hard at Leo, wondering what was going on in the little dry cleaner's head. "What're you doing, Leo? You nuts or something? Can you tell me?"

Leo raised his face, sunglasses shining in the light. "What am I *doing*? You kidding? I'm doing what I never dreamed in my whole life I'd ever have a chance to. That's what I'm doing."

The dealer, watching them with his arms folded, said, "We have a problem here, gentlemen? I can get the floorman."

BENNY WADE TOLD HIM ON THE PHONE TO GO IN THE door next to the cage, the cashier's window, take a left at the hard count room, go down past the coffeemaker and the Xerox machine and you're there. Benny came out from behind his computer terminal—gray-haired, easygoing, not at all what Chili thought an ex-FBI agent should look like. He didn't act like a guy who'd once been a hard-on in wing tips, either.

"So you found him."

"I found him," Chili said, "then lost him again."

"You told me on the phone you collected."

"I did. I wanted to see him about something else. He was suppose to call his wife last night—it's a long story. I talked to her and found out he never called, so I wanted to see him again. This morning I go over the Plaza, he's gone, checked out."

"Maybe he's back on the Strip."

"No, he left, went to L.A."

"Let me see what we have there," Benny said, sat down at the computer and began tapping keys. "Yeah, one of Dick Allen's customers, guy owes us a hundred and fifty K, over sixty days. You want to talk to Dick? I mean if you're going to L.A."

"Yeah, why not."

Benny sat there staring at him. "You found this guy Leo and collected. But you don't seem too happy about it. What's the matter?"

"I don't know if I told you, I had my ass in a crack when I came here."

"You mentioned it in passing."

"It's still there," Chili said. "You remember your saying to me last night I was lucky, should lay down some bets?"

"Don't tell me the rest," Benny said, "I don't want to feel responsible."

"I'm not blaming you, I'm the one did it."

"Okay then, how much you lose?"

"What I collected, less some change."

7

"YOU KNOW WHY IT DOESN'T WORK?" HARRY SAID. "I mean even before I find out you don't know how it ends. There's nobody to sympathize with. Who's the good guy? You don't have one."

Chili said, "The shylock's the good guy." Sounding surprised.

Harry said, "You kidding me? The shylock's the heavy in this. Leo's the victim, but we don't give a shit about him either. You don't have a good guy, you don't have a girl in it, a female lead . . . you have a first act, you're partway into the second.

Chili said to him, "I guess I better tell you about my coat getting ripped off and this guy named Ray Bones I shot one time and wants to pay me back."

Harry said, "Jesus Christ." He said, "Yeah, I think you better."

THEY WERE STILL IN THE KITCHEN, THREE A.M., drinking coffee now and smoking Chili's cigarettes till he ran out and Harry found a pack of Karen's menthols.

"That's everything?" Harry said.

"Pretty much."

"You have scenes that appear to work, but don't quite

make it," Harry said, wanting to know more about this guy without encouraging him too much. "The one in the casino, for example, at the roulette table. You don't do enough with the bodyguard."

"Like what?"

"The scene," Harry said, "that type of scene in a picture, should build a certain amount of tension. The audience is thinking, Jesus, here it comes. They know you're a tough guy, they want to see how you handle the bodyguard."

"Yeah, well in real life," Chili said, "you start something in a casino, you get thrown out and told don't come back. What I didn't mention, the next day it was the bodyguard, Jerry, told me Leo got on a flight to L.A. I had to find him first, check the different companies rent out bodyguards."

"You have to threaten him?"

"You want me to say I beat him up," Chili said, "this guy bigger'n I am. What I did, I took him out to breakfast. I even asked him how Leo did. Jerry goes, 'Oh, not too bad. I put him on that airplane with four hundred fifty-four thousand dollars, that's all.' "

"Why would he tell you that?"

"The kid was dying to tell me, it made him feel important. It's like saying you know where a movie star lives, being on the in."

Harry said, "I know where all kinds of movie stars live. It doesn't do a thing for me."

Chili said, "Yeah? I wouldn't mind driving past some of their homes sometime."

"You know who used to live right here? Cary Grant."

"No shit. In this house?"

"Or it was Cole Porter, I forget which."

Harry was lighting another one of Karen's menthols, tired, getting a headache now, but staying with it.

"So you have no idea where Leo is, other than he's in L.A."

"I don't even know that for sure. Fay, his wife, still hasn't heard. I called her again, she gave me a name to check, some broad she knows Leo met at a dry-cleaners' convention. It's why I'm staying at the motel over on Ventura Boulevard. It's near Hi-Tone Cleaners, the broad's place, but she's out of town. I'm hoping she's with Leo and they'll be back sometime."

"Say you find him, then what?"

Chili didn't answer right away and Harry waited. He saw the guy himself having far more possibilities than his idea for a movie.

"There are different ways I could go with it," Chili said. "Basically, you might say it's the wife's money. It was paid to *her*."

"Basically," Harry said, "it's the airline's money. That doesn't bother you?"

"Bother me—I didn't cop it, they did."

"Yeah, but you're talking about going halves with the wife."

"No, I said that's what she offered. I never said anything else about it. There might even be a few things, Harry, I haven't told you."

Starting to get cagey on him.

Harry had to think a moment, go at it another way. He said, "The plot thickens, huh? You have a girl in it now, even though she doesn't do much. See, it gets better the more details you give me. So you're at the roulette table, he pays off his debt . . . You didn't discuss the wife?"

"He realized I must've talked to her. That's what brought him back to earth."

"I mean you didn't say anything about basically it was her money."

"It looked like management was gonna get involved, so I left. But I told him, yeah, he better call her."

"So then you took the twenty gees in your hot little hands," Harry said with some pleasure, "and blew it."

"I dropped a little over seventeen," Chili said, "before my brain started working again. But the thing that got me about Leo, he looks me right in the eye and goes, 'When I'm through here I'll write you a check.' Like he's telling me he'll do it when he has time, so get off my back. This dry cleaner, been on the hook to us for years, talking to me like that. I couldn't believe it."

Harry said, "He must've thought you ran into him by accident."

"Yeah, like I don't know he's suppose to be dead. But what I'm talking about, *he* knows he's six weeks behind on the vig. That has to be right in the front of his head. But what's he do, he cops an attitude on me. I couldn't believe it. He comes on to me like there was no way I could touch him."

"It made you mad," Harry said.

"The more I thought about it, yeah. At the time, it surprised me. I never saw him act like that before. Then after, I got pretty mad thinking about it."

"That kind of attitude," Harry said, "is called delusions of grandeur, or, trying to play the power game. Having the bodyguard carry his bag was the tip-off. Out here it's very common. You see it in actors—guy making a hundred grand a picture gets lucky, his next one turns out to be a hit and his price goes up to a million. Pretty soon he's up to several million a picture plus a cut of the gross. He's the same schmuck who made it on his tight pants and capped teeth, but now all of a sudden he knows everything there is about making pictures. He rewrites the script or has it done. He tells the director how he's gonna play his part, and if he doesn't like the producer he has him barred from the set. But directors, producers, anybody can play the power game, especially agents. You keep score by getting so many points for being seen with the right people, driving a Ferrari or a Rolls, what table you get at Spago or The Ivy, what well-known actress blew you on location, how many of your phone calls to the real power players in town are returned, all that kind of bullshit."

Harry paused. He was getting off the track, wasting time.

"But when Leo tried to play the game, you pulled it out from under him. That was pretty neat, it's a good scene."

Harry paused again and was aware of the refrigerator humming in the silence. It was too bright in here, uncomfortable and his head ached. He didn't want to move, though. Not now.

"I like the coat story, too, you mentioned. It plays, but would work better if it wasn't a flashback. What it does, though, it shows you know how to handle yourself in that kind of situation. I imagine in your line of work there were other times . . ."

"I'm out of that now."

"But there were times, right, you had to get tough? Say one of your customers stopped paying?"

"They always paid," Chili said. "Oh, I've smacked guys. Smacking was common, just an open-hand smack. I'm talking to a guy trying to get my money, he looks away and I smack him in the face. 'Hey, you look at me when I'm fuckin talking to you.' Like that, get their attention. See, the kind of people we were dealing with, a lot of 'em thought they were tough guys, you know, from the street, guys that were basically hustlers, thieves, or they were into drugs. We had them besides the legit people, who ordinarily didn't give us any trouble, always paid on time. I think what you're getting at, Harry, you have the same attitude as some of the legitimate people I did collection work for. Like a car dealer, or a guy runs a TV store . . . They're carrying a deadbeat, they want you to get the money and they don't care how, break his fuckin legs. That's the first thing they think of, come up with that statement. I say to 'em, 'How's he gonna pay you he's in the hospital?' They don't think of that. They want a piece of the guy *and* their money."

Harry said, "Well, you've been in some tight spots. The business with Ray Bones—that's a good name for a character. I meant to ask you, you weren't arrested for shooting him that time?"

"Bones had the idea of doing me on his own," Chili said. "He told the cops it happened out on the street, an unknown assailant come up to him. He still wants to do me, it's on his mind."

"And you still have to pay him?"

"Yeah, only we have a different arrangement now. I talked to Tommy Carlo on the phone. . . . You have to know Tommy, his personality, he gets along with everybody. Jimmy Cap I mentioned, Capotorto? He always liked Tommy. But he has to go along with Ray Bones up to a point, Ray's his guy. So Jimmy Cap says split what the dead guy owes, me and Tommy, fuck the running vig, a flat eight grand each and that's it, forget it."

"You spoke to Tommy," Harry said, leaning over the table on his arms. "So now he knows Leo's still alive."

"Did I say that?"

Harry sat back again, questions popping in his mind along with the headache, but wanting to appear relaxed, the producer showing a certain amount of interest in a story.

"So you didn't happen to mention it to him," Harry said and grinned at the deep-set eyes staring at him. "You want Leo Devoe for yourself."

"What I *don't* want," Chili said, "is Ray Bones finding out. Tommy, he'd think it's pretty funny, this dry cleaner taking an airline. He'd swear he wouldn't tell a soul, but I know he would. So why put him in that position?"

"But you still have Ray Bones to think about."

Chili moved his shoulders. The deep-set eyes didn't change.

"You gonna pay him?"

"Maybe, when I get around to it."

"What if he comes looking for you?"

"It's possible. The guy's got a one-track mind."

"Have you been involved in any shootings since Ray Bones?"

Chili's eyes moved and he seemed to be thinking about it or trying to remember, looking off for a moment.

"Well, there was one time, it was when me and Tommy were running a club in South Miami, a guy came in looking for another guy, not me, but I was in the way."

"What happened?"

"Nothing. He shot the guy and left."

Now Harry paused. Chili Palmer had been sent to him from heaven, no question about it.

"You were running a club?"

"Belonged to Momo. We had entertainment, different groups'd come in; catering mostly to the younger crowd."

Harry had the next question ready.

"You pack a gun?"

Chili hesitated. "Not really."

"What does that mean?"

"Not ordinarily. Maybe a few times I have."

"You ever been arrested?"

"I've been picked up a few times. They'd try to get me on loan-sharking or a RICO violation—you know what I mean? Being in what they call a racketeering kind of activity, but I was never convicted, I'm clean."

"Racketeering, that covers a lot of ground, doesn't it?"

"What do you want to know?"

Harry hesitated. He wasn't sure.

"Why don't you get to the point, Harry? You want me to do something for you, right?"

8

HERE WAS A MAN HAD MADE FORTY-NINE MOVIES AND named a bunch of them earlier, when he was making coffee. Chili remembered having seen quite a few. The one about the roaches—guy turns on the kitchen light, Christ, there's a fuckin roach in there as big as he is. He had seen some of the *Grotesque* movies, about the escaped wacko who'd been in a fire and was pissed off about it. The one about the giant ticks trying to take over the earth. The one about all the people in this town getting scalped by an Indian who'd been dead over a hundred years, *Hairraiser* . . . Forty-nine movies and he looked more like a guy drove a delivery truck or came to fix your air-conditioning when it quit, a guy with a tool kit. When he'd gone over to the range to get the coffee in his shirt and underwear showing his white legs, skinny for a fat guy, he looked like he should be in detox at a booze treatment center. Chili had seen loan customers in this shape, ones that had given up. Harry's mind seemed to be working okay, except all of a sudden he wasn't as talkative as before.

"Tell me what you're thinking, Harry."

Maybe he didn't know how to say it without sounding like a dummy.

"Okay, you want me to help you out in some way," Chili said. "How do I know—outside of your asking me questions here like it's a job interview. I happened to mention—we were in the other room—I said when I came out here I talked to some people and you kept saying 'What people?' having a fit. You remember that? Well, they were a couple lawyers I was put in touch with. I told you I talked to Tommy Carlo . . ."

Harry was listening but making a face, trying to understand everything at once.

"What's he got to do with it?"

"I go to your apartment, your office on Sunset, ZigZag Productions, you're not either place and nobody knows where you are. So I call Tommy, now in tight with Jimmy Cap, and ask him, see if he can get me a name out here, somebody that knows somebody in the movie business. Tommy calls back, says, 'Frank DePhillips, you're all set.' You ever hear of him?"

Harry shook his head.

"Don't go to sleep on me, okay?"

"I got a headache, that's all. Who's Frank DePhillips?"

"He's to some part of L. A. what Jimmy Cap is to South Miami. But I don't meet with him, he's on a level only talks to certain people. I meet with one of his lawyers down at the courts, criminal division. Young guy, he comes running out of a courtroom loaded down with papers and shit, looks at me, says, 'What do you want?' Fuckin lawyers, they're always rushing around the last minute. I remind him Mr. DePhillips set this up, also I happen to represent one of the biggest casinos in Vegas. That gets me about two minutes of his time. He says, 'I'll see what I can do. Gimme a phone number.' I tell him I'll call him, otherwise I'd never hear. Also I don't want him to know I'm staying at this dump on Ventura. Two days later I meet him and another lawyer in a restaurant in a hotel that's Japanese. I mean the entire hotel, not just the restaurant, a Japanese hotel right in the middle of downtown L.A."

Harry said, "Yeah, the Otani."

"Right by the city hall. These two lawyers eat there all the time. I watch 'em dig into the raw fish, suck up bowls of noodles . . . The noodles weren't bad. So this other lawyer gives me addresses and phone numbers, yours and anybody you ever been intimate with on a single sheet of paper. He says, 'You're not the only one looking for old Harry Zimm,' and mentions your investors have been trying to find you for two months. I said, 'Oh, what's the problem?' Guy says, 'It looks like Harry skipped with two hunnerd thousand they put in one of his movies.' "

Harry was shaking his head. He looked worn out.

"That doesn't surprise me. This town loves rumors, everybody knows everything, just ask them. My investors have been trying to find me for two months? I spoke to them, it wasn't more than two weeks ago."

Chili said, "You mention the Piston–Lakers game?"

Harry said, "Look, these guys came to me originally, I mean before. They already put money in two of my pictures and did okay, they're happy. Which you can't say about most film investors, the ones that want to be in show biz, get to meet movie stars and they find out, Christ, it's a high-risk business."

Harry was easing into it, watching his step.

Chili said, "Yeah? . . ."

"These guys already know movie stars, celebrities; they run a limo service. So they come in on another participation deal—this was back a few months ago when I was planning what would be my next picture. About a band of killer circus freaks that travel around the country leaving bodies in their wake. The characters, there's a seven-hundred-pound fat lady who wouldn't fit through that door, has a way of seducing guys, gets them in her trailer—"

Chili said, "Harry, look at me," and waited to see his watery eyes in the kitchen light, frizzed hair standing up.

"You're trying to tell me how you fucked up without sounding stupid, and that's hard to do. Let's get to where you're at, okay? You blew their two hunnerd grand on a basketball game and you haven't told 'em about it. Why not?"

"Because they're not the type of guys," Harry said, "would take it with any degree of understanding or restraint."

"They scare you."

"What'd I just say?"

"I'm not sure. You want to say something to me, Harry, say it, don't beat around the bush."

"Okay, they scare me. I keep thinking the first thing they'd do is break my legs."

"You got that on the brain. What's the second thing?"

"Or they'd have it done—you don't know these guys. They're not exactly financial types."

"Harry, I prob'ly know 'em better than you do. What you're telling me," Chili said, "they got more out on the street than limos. They're dealing, huh? Selling dope to movie stars and using you to launder their dough. Put it in a Harry Zimm production, take it out cleaned and pressed."

Chili waited.

Harry eased back. The chair creaked and that was the only sound.

"You don't know or you don't want to or you're not saying," Chili said. "But from what you tell me, that's what it sounds like."

He smiled, wanting Harry to relax.

"You have my interest aroused. I wouldn't mind knowing more about these guys, if they're real hard-ons or they're giving you a buncha shit. Or what their connections are, if they have any. But what I want to know first," Chili said, "is why you took their two hunnerd grand to Vegas, put yourself in that kind of a spot. I mean if you're scared of these guys to begin with . . ."

"I had to," Harry said, sounding pretty definite about it. "I've got a chance to put together a deal that'll change my life, make me an overnight success after thirty years in the business. . . . But I need a half a million to get it started."

"A movie," Chili said, wanting to be sure.

"A blockbuster of a movie."

"You don't want to ask your limo guys?"

"I don't want them anywhere near it," Harry said. "It's not their kind of deal, it's too big." Harry was hunching over the table again. "See, what happened . . . This's at the time I'm getting *Freaks* ready for production. I've got a script, but it needs work, get rid of some of the more expensive special effects. So I go see my writer and we discuss revisions. Murray's good, he's been with me, he wrote all my *Grotesque* pictures, some of the others. He's done I don't know how many TV scripts, hundreds. He's done sitcoms, westerns, sci-fi, did a few *Twilight Zones* . . . Only now he can't get any TV work 'cause he's around my age and the networks don't like to hire any writers over forty. Murray has kind of a drinking problem, too, that doesn't help. Likes the sauce, smokes four packs a day . . . We're talking—get back to what I want to tell you—he happens to mention a script he wrote years ago when he was starting out and never sold. I ask him what it's about. He tells me. It sounds pretty good, so I take the script home and read it." Harry paused. "I read it again, just to be sure. My experience, my instinct, my *gut,* tells me I have a property here, that with the right actor in the starring role, I can take to any studio in town and practically write my own deal. This one, I know, is gonna take on heat fast. The next day I call Murray, tell him I'm willing to option the script."

"What's that mean?"

"You pay a certain amount to own the property for a year, take it off the market. It's an option to buy. I paid Murray five hundred against twenty-five thousand if I exercise the option, then another twenty-five at the start of principal photography."

"That doesn't sound like much."

"It's an old script, been shopped around."

"Then why do you think you can get it made?"

"Because on the other hand it's so old it's new. The kid studio execs they have now had just come into the world when Murray wrote it."

"So you don't buy it," Chili said, "till you know you have a deal. Is that right?"

"Or raise the money independently," Harry said, "which is the way I prefer to go. You retain control. But with the actor I have in mind, I know I'm looking at a twenty-million-dollar picture, minimum, and that means going to one of the majors. Otherwise I wouldn't go in a studio to take a leak."

"You're so sure it's a winner," Chili said, "what's the problem?"

"I told you, I need a half a million to get started," Harry said. "See, the guy I want is the kind of star not only can act, he doesn't mind looking bad on the screen. Tight pants and capped teeth won't make it in this one. If I could get Gene Hackman, say, we'd be in preproduction as I speak. But Gene's got something like five pictures lined up he's committed to, I checked."

Chili thought of his all-time favorite. "What about Robert De Niro?"

"Bobby De Niro is possibly the finest actor working today, right up there with Brando. But I don't quite see him for this one."

"Tom Cruise?"

"Wonderful young actor, but that's the problem, he's too young for the part. I'll have to show you my list, the ones I've considered are at least good enough and the right age. Bill Hurt, Dreyfuss, who happens to be hot at the moment, Pacino, Nicholson, Hoffman . . . Dustin I saw as a close second choice."

"Yeah? Who's your first?"

"Michael Weir, superstar."

Chili said, "Yeah?" surprised. He said, "Yeah, Michael Weir," nodding then, "he's good, all right. The thing I like about him, he can do just about anything, play a regular person, a weirdo . . . He played the mob guy in *The Cyclone* that turned snitch?"

"One of his best parts," Harry said.

Chili was nodding again. "They shot that in Brooklyn. Yeah, Michael Weir, I like him."

"I'm glad to hear it," Harry said.

"He's a different type than your usual movie star. I think he'd be good," Chili said, even though he didn't know how to picture Michael Weir in this movie, whatever it was about. "Have you talked to him?"

"I took a chance, sent the script to his house." Harry sat back, brushing a hand over his frizzy hair. "I find out he not only read it, he flipped, absolutely loves the part."

"You found out—he didn't tell you himself?"

"Remember my saying I need half a mil? I have to deposit that amount in Michael's name, in a special escrow account before he'll take a meeting with me. This is his fucking agent. You have to put up earnest money to show you're serious, you're not gonna waste his time."

"That's how it's done, huh? Make sure you can handle it."

"It's how this prick does it, his agent. He says, 'You know Michael's price is seven million, pay or play,' That means if he signs and for any reason you don't go into production, you still have to pay him the seven mil. You make the picture, it's released, and now he gets ten percent of the gross. Not the net, like everybody else, the fucking gross. Hey, but who cares? He loves the script."

"How'd you find out?"

"From the guy who's cutting the picture Michael just finished, the film editor. We go way back. In fact, I gave him his start on *Slime Creatures.* He calls, says Michael was in the cutting room with the director, raving about a script he had with him, *Mr. Lovejoy,* how it's the best part he's read in years. The cutter, the friend of mine, doesn't know it's my property till he notices *ZigZag Productions* on the script. He calls me up: 'You're gonna do one with Michael Weir? I don't believe it.' I told him, 'Well, you better, if you want to cut the picture.' I don't know yet who I want as my director. Jewison, maybe. Lumet, Ulu Grosbard . . ."

Chili said, "What's it called, *Mr. Lovejoy*?"

"That's Murray's title. It's not bad when you know what it's about."

Chili was thinking it sounded like a TV series, *Mr. Lovejoy,* about this faggy guy raising a bunch of kids of different nationalities and a lot of that canned laughter. He wondered if they got people to come into a studio, told them to go ahead, laugh, and they recorded it, or if they told them jokes. He remembered a TV program about how movies were made that showed people kissing their hands, the sound of it being recorded to go in a love scene the hand kissers were watching on a screen. Movies were basically fake. The sounds in a fight scene weren't anything like what you heard nailing some guy in the mouth. Like the fight scenes in the *Rocky* movies, Stallone letting some giant asshole pound him, he'd be dead before the end of round one. But there were good movies too, ones that had the feeling of real life . . .

Harry was saying once he had a development deal at a studio, that would satisfy Mesas, they'd quit bothering him. Harry saying now if he could get to Michael Weir through Karen he wouldn't need to raise the half a mil . . .

Wait a minute. "What?"

"You knew she was married to Michael at one time."

"Karen? No . . ."

"Four years, no kids. This is the house they lived in till Michael walked out on her."

"No, I didn't know that," Chili said. "So you want her to call him, set up a meeting?"

"That's all—put in a good word."

"They get along okay?"

"They never see each other. But he'd do it, I know."

"Then what's the problem? She won't ask him?"

"I haven't asked *her,*" Harry said. "If I did, I'm pretty sure she'd turn me down. See, but if she thinks about it a while and it becomes her idea, then she'd do it."

"I don't follow."

"That's 'cause you don't know actors," Harry said, "the way their minds work. Karen can't just call Michael up cold and ask him. She wasn't even that talented—aside from having that chest, you might've noticed, which I think is what made her a fantastic screamer. But, she still has that actor mentality. Karen would have to *feel* the situation. First, she has to want to do it as a favor to me . . ."

"For putting her in your movies."

"Yeah, and she lived with me too. Then, she has to have a certain attitude when she calls Michael, feel some of the old resentment. *He* walked out on *her,* so he owes her the courtesy of a positive response. You understand?"

"You and Karen lived together?"

"Three and a half beautiful years. So for old times' sake Karen lays a guilt trip on Michael and I get a free meeting with him."

"Will she do it?"

"She's lying in bed at this moment thinking about it."

"It sounds like a long way around to get there," Chili said, taking his time. He couldn't see Karen living with this guy, even if he wasn't fat then. He could see her with Michael Weir. He said to Harry, "Well, if she doesn't want to help you for some reason, maybe I could talk to Michael, get you your meeting."

Harry said, "How? Threaten him?"

"I'm serious," Chili said. "I think I could get next to him, talk about that movie he was in, *The Cyclone*."

"How would you do that?"

"You want to discuss Michael Weir or Leo the dry cleaner? All that dough he's carrying around? Came here with four hundred and fifty thousand . . ."

Harry wasn't saying a word now.

"You're thinking," Chili said, "what if I was to put you next to the dry cleaner. Ask him what he'd rather do, invest his dough in a movie or give it back to the airline and do some time."

Harry squirmed around in his chair saying, "It did cross my mind."

He reached for the pack of cigarettes and tore it open to get at the last one.

"Except I know it would bother you," Chili said, "the idea of using money Leo got the way he did."

Harry said, "Well, you take my investors, if you want to get technical," tapping the cigarette on the table, fooling with it, "or any investors. You don't ask where their money comes from."

"Which brings us to the limo guys," Chili said. "You want 'em to leave you alone, be patient. The time comes to do the *Freaks* movie, okay, you'll give 'em a call. But right now you're into something doesn't concern them."

Harry looked like he was afraid to move, hanging on every word.

"See, what I could do is talk to the limo guys along those lines," Chili said, "make the point in a way they'd understand it."

He reached over to take the cigarette from Harry's fingers. "You gonna smoke this?"

"No, it's yours."

Harry struck a match to light it.

"What would you say?"

"I'd tell 'em it's in their best interest, till you're ready for 'em, to stay the fuck off your back. Isn't that what you want?"

"You don't know these guys."

"It's up to you, Harry."

Chili watched Harry's gaze follow a stream of smoke. Harry the producer, with his forty-nine horror movies and his frizzy hair, looking at the offer. His gaze came back to Chili, his expression tired but hopeful.

"What do you get out of this?"

"Let's see how we get along," Chili said. "I'll let you know." He thought of something that had been on his mind and said to Harry, "The seven-hundred-pound broad that seduces guys in her trailer—what exactly does she do?"

KAREN FELT THE BED MOVE BENEATH HARRY'S WEIGHT. Lying on her side she opened her eyes to see digital numbers in the dark, 4:12 in pale green. Behind her Harry continued to move, settling in. She watched the numbers change to 4:13.

"Harry."

"Oh, you awake?"

"What's going on?"

"It's late—I felt you wouldn't mind if he stayed over."

"Harry, this isn't your house."

"Just tonight. I put him in the maid's room."

"I don't have a maid's room."

"The one back by the kitchen?"

There was a silence.

"I don't get it."

"What?"

"This guy—what're you doing?"

"He's got some ideas, gonna help me out."

"Harry, the guy's a crook."

"So? This town he should fit right in."

Harry rolled away from her, groaning in comfort.

" 'Night."

There was a silence, the house quiet.

"Harry?"

"Yeah."

"What's going on?"

"I told you."

"You want me to call you a cab? You and your buddy?"

She felt Harry roll back toward her.

9

CHILI ASKED HARRY IF HE LIKED TO SLEEP IN. HE SAID, "If you're gonna sleep in and I have to sit around waiting, forget it. Anything I can't stand is waiting for people."

Harry acted surprised. He said it was only ten after ten. "I got back in bed and Karen wanted to talk."

That stopped Chili.

He wanted to know if Harry was putting him on or what. He couldn't imagine Karen letting this fat guy get in bed with her. But there was no way to find out if it was true.

He said, "Well, she was up, no problem. She dropped me off to get my car. I come back and have to sit here another hour."

Harry said the limo guys never got to their office before ten-thirty eleven anyway. Then they'd discuss for about an hour where they were going to have lunch and take off. He said it didn't matter what time you went to see the limo guys, you always had to wait.

Chili said, "Harry, we don't go see them. They come see us. You want to make the call or you want me to?"

NOW THEY WERE IN HARRY'S OFFICE: UPSTAIRS IN A two-story building that was part of a block of white storefronts, on Sunset Boulevard near La Cienega. Harry turned on lights, wall sconces in the shape of candles against dark paneling, raised venetian blinds behind his big desk stacked with folders, magazines, scripts, papers, unopened mail, hotel ashtrays, a brass lamp, a clock, two telephones . . .

"Remember *77 Sunset Strip* on TV? Edd Kookie Byrnes, the parking attendant always combing his hair?"

Harry nodded out the window.

"They used a place right across the street for exteriors. I used to stand here and watch 'em shoot. Efrem Zimbalist, Jr., and Roger Smith were the stars, but the one you remember is Kookie."

"I wanted blond hair just like his, with the pompadour," Chili said. "I was about ten." He watched Harry staring out the window. "What about the script?"

"That's right," Harry said, "you haven't read it."

"I don't even know what it's about."

Going through the pile on his desk, Harry said he hadn't been in the office much lately and his girl, Kathleen, had left him to work for the guy that owned the building, a literary agent who'd been working in Hollywood over fifty years. Had lunch at Chasen's every day, or he'd call and have them deliver. Scallops and creamed spinach. Go down the hall right now—Harry bet that's what he'd be eating, scallops and spinach. "I asked him one time what type of writing brought the most money and the agent says, 'Ransom notes.' "

"What about the script, Harry?"

The guy's mind was wandering all over the place. In the car on the way here, Harry had started talking about *Mr. Lovejoy,* the story, but was barely into it when he said, "The famous Trocadero once stood right there," and the ride to the office became a tour of Sunset Strip, Harry pointing out mostly where places used to be. Schwab's drugstore. Ciro's, known for movie-star bar fights, now the Comedy Store. A restaurant that was once John Barrymore's guesthouse. The Garden of

Allah, where movie stars used to shack up, now a bank and a parking lot. The Chateau Marmont was still there—look at it—home on and off to Jean Harlow, Greta Garbo, Howard Hughes, where John Belushi checked out. Harry wide-awake, but off into Old Hollywood. Then telling what it was like when hippies took over the Strip, little broads in granny dresses, traffic bumper to bumper. "By the time you got from Doheny to here, you were stoned on the marijuana fumes." Chili reminded him the limo guys were coming at noon and Harry said, "Oh . . . yeah."

He poked through the clutter on his desk till he came to several *Mr. Lovejoy* scripts. "Here it is."

Chili picked one up, the first time he'd ever held a movie script in his hands. He had no idea what it would look like. It wasn't as thick as he thought it would be, less than an inch of pages between red covers, *ZigZag Productions* printed in gold on the front with speedlines coming off the lettering, the way they showed cars moving in a comic strip. Chili opened the script about in the middle, studied the way the page was set up and began to read, not understanding the first word he saw but kept going.

INT. LOVEJOY'S VAN—DAY

Ilona sits behind the wheel watching the corner bar across the street. Behind her, Lovejoy is getting his video camera ready for action.

ILONA

How long's he been in there?

LOVEJOY

(glancing at his watch)
Seventeen and a half minutes.

ILONA

I wish he'd hurry up.

LOVEJOY

(focusing camera)

We have to be patient. But sooner or later . . .

ILONA

There he is!

LOVEJOY

(quietly)

I see him.

EXT. CORNER BAR—CLOSE ON ROXY—DAY

Roxy hooks his thumbs in his belt, looks about idly. Gradually his gaze moves to the van and holds.

INT. LOVEJOY'S VAN—DAY

Ilona reacts, hunching down behind the wheel.

ILONA

He sees us!

LOVEJOY

No, he's walking to the car. Ilona, this could be it!!!

Chili looked up from the script. "What's he doing, following the guy?"

"Read it," Harry said. "It's a grabber."

Chili closed the script, laid it on the desk where he stood between a pair of fat red-leather chairs, old and cracked. He said to Harry, "We better get ready," placing his hands on the chairs. "Make sure they sit here, not over on the sofa." He saw Harry tugging at the string to lower the venetian blinds. "Leave 'em up, we want the light in their eyes. I'll be at the desk . . . But don't introduce me, let it go, just start talking. You're gonna be here." Chili stepped back from the chairs. "Behind 'em when they sit down."

"They'll be looking at you," Harry said. "They don't know who you are."

"That's right, they're wondering, who's this guy? You don't tell 'em. You're on your feet the whole time. You say, 'Well, I'm glad you assholes stopped by, so I can set you straight.' "

"You're kidding, right?"

"It's up to you. You're talking, relaxed, you stroll around to where you are now—all you tell 'em is the movie's been postponed. Say, till next year, if you want. But don't tell 'em why or what you're doing."

"They won't like it."

"They don't have to. Just do what I tell you," Chili said. "Okay, now the two guys. The one in charge is Ronnie? . . ."

"Ronnie Wingate. That's the name of the company, Wingate Motor Cars Limited, on Santa Monica."

Harry was poking around the desk again, straightening it up. Or nervous, feeling a need to be doing something.

"Ronnie, I think of as a rich kid who never grew up. He's from Santa Barbara, real estate money, came to Hollywood to be an actor but didn't make it. He thinks he knows the business because his grandfather was a producer at Metro at one time. Now he's after me to give him a part, wants to play one of the freaks."

"Why's he scare you?"

"I don't trust him, he's unstable. He's close to forty, he acts like a burned-out teenager."

"Maybe that's what he is."

"He has a gun in his office. He'll take it out and start aiming it around the room while he's talking to you. With one eye closed, going 'Couuu,' making that sound, you know, like he's shooting."

"What kind of gun?"

"I don't know, an automatic."

"And the other one, Bo Catlett?"

It was a familiar name. When Chili first heard it he thought of an all-star jazz drummer by the name of Catlett.

"He doesn't say much," Harry said. "The only time he opened up, I happened to mention I was raised in Detroit and started out there doing movies for the car companies. Catlett said, 'Yeah? I went to high school in Detroit. Loved it, like home to me.' I told him I couldn't get out of there fast enough. He said, 'Then you don't know it.' Other times he'd call me Mr. De-troit. He might be Chicano or some kind of Latin, I'm not sure, but he has that look. Ronnie mentioned once Catlett had been a farm worker, a migrant, and a lot of them I know are Chicano. He's tall, dresses up . . . You see Ronnie, the boss, he looks like he's going out to cut the grass, Catlett will have a suit and tie on. In fact, almost always. Dresses strictly Rodeo Drive."

"Bo Catlett," Chili said. The one he was thinking of was Sid Catlett. Big Sid.

"Ronnie, sometimes he'll call him Cat. He'll say, 'Hey, Cat, what do you think?' But you know Ronnie's already made up his mind." Harry came away from the desk. "I have to go down the hall."

"You nervous, Harry?"

"I'm fine. I gotta go to the bathroom, that's all."

He walked out and Chili moved around behind the desk to sit in the creaky swivel chair and look over Harry's office, his world, old and dusty, his shelves of books and scripts, his photos on the wall above the sofa: Harry with giant bugs, Harry shaking hands with mutants and maniacs, Harry and a much younger Karen with blond hair, Harry holding her by the arm. He didn't look too bad in the pictures. It got Chili thinking about them in bed together. It didn't make sense. There was no way, with her looks, she could be that hard up. This morning when he walked in the kitchen . . .

KAREN WAS HAVING A CUP OF COFFEE, READING THE paper. Dressed up, ready to leave. Purse and a movie script on the table. She said good morning and asked if he slept okay. Karen could be one of those people who acted more polite when they were pissed off. Chili poured a cup and sat down with her, saying he woke up and forgot where he was for a minute. Karen started reading the paper again and he felt stupid, wanting to start over. She had on a neat black suit, no blouse under it, pearl stud earrings in her dark hair, some eye makeup. Her eyes were brown. She had a nice clean look and smelled good, had some kind of perfume on.

"I'm sorry about walking in your house last night," Chili said, thinking she'd pass it off and that would be it.

But she didn't. Karen put the paper down saying, "What do you want me to tell you, it's okay? I'm glad you're here?"

Giving it back to him, but sounding like she was asking a simple question. She wasn't anything like most of the women he was used to talking to. They would've said it in a real sarcastic tone of voice.

"I have a hunch," she said now, "if the patio door was locked you would've broken in, one way or another."

He kept looking at her mouth, done in a light shade of lipstick. She had small white teeth, nice ones. He said, "I was never much into breaking and entering."

Karen said, "But you've always been a criminal, haven't you?" With the cool look and quiet voice, daring him. That's what it seemed like.

So he took it to her saying he had pulled a few holdups when he was a kid and didn't know better, hijacked freight, truckloads of merchandise and hustled it for a living, associated with alleged members of organized crime, but never dealt narcotics; telling her he'd been arrested, held over at Rikers Island, but never convicted of anything and sent to prison. "Okay, I was a loan shark up till recently and now I'm in the movie business," Chili said. "What're you doing these days?"

"I'm reading for a part," Karen said.

She took her coffee cup to the sink, came back to the table and picked up her purse and the script. Chili asked if she could give him a lift down to Sunset—he'd left his car there, back of a store. Karen said come on.

It wasn't until they were in her BMW convertible, winding down the hill past million-dollar homes, she started to come out of herself and communicate. He asked where she was going. Karen said to Tower Studios. She said she hadn't worked in seven years, didn't have to, but the head of production at Tower had offered her a part. Chili asked if it was a horror movie. A mistake. Karen gave him a look saying she hadn't screamed since leaving ZigZag and was never going to scream again, even in real life. Chili had noticed the title on the cover of the script, *Beth's Room.*

"What's it about?"

This was what opened her up.

"It's about a mother-daughter relationship," Karen said, already with more life in her tone, "but different than the usual way it's handled. The daughter, Beth, leaves her yuppie husband after a terrific fight and comes home to live with her mom, Peggy."

"Which one're you?"

"The mom. I was in high school when I had Beth and now she's twenty-one. I did get married but the guy, the father, took off right after. So for the next twenty years I devoted my life to raising Beth, working my tail off—but that's all in the back story, it's referred to. The picture opens, I'm finally living my own life. I own a successful art gallery, I have a boyfriend, an artist, who's a few years younger than I am . . . and along comes Beth, wanting to be mothered. Naturally I'm sympathetic, at first, this is my baby . . ."

"She act sick?"

"She has migraines."

"I can hear her," Chili said. " 'Mom, while you're up, would you get me my pills off the sink in the kitchen?' "

Karen was staring at him. She looked back at the road and had to crank the wheel to swerve around a parked car.

" 'And bring me a glass of milk, please, and some cookies?' "

"Warm milk," Karen said, "with a half ounce of Scotch in it. Did you look at the script?"

"Never saw it before. The daughter, she have a whiney voice?"

"It could be played that way. It's a young Sandy Dennis part. You know who I mean?"

"Sandy Dennis, sure. The daughter blame the mom for her marriage going to hell?"

Karen gave him another look. "She accuses me of talking her into getting married before she was ready. And that, of course, adds to my sense of guilt."

"What'd you do you feel guilty about?"

"It's not anything I did. It's more . . . what right do I have to be happy when my daughter's miserable?"

"You know the kid's faking?"

"It's not that simple. You have to read it, see the way Beth works on me."

"You got a problem."

"Well, yeah, that's what the picture's about."

"I mean feeling guilty. I think what you oughta do, either give little Beth a kick in the ass or tell her go see a doctor, get her head examined."

"You don't get it," Karen said. "I'm her *mother.* I have to come to grips with my maternal feelings."

Turning off Doheny, Karen shot through an amber light to swing into the traffic crawling along Sunset.

"People have guilt trips laid on them all the time and they accept it, the guilt. It doesn't have to make sense, it's the way people are."

"Anywhere along here's fine," Chili said, thinking of times he had been asked if he was guilty and not once ever having the urge to say he was. Real-life situations, even facing prison time, were never as emotional as movies. Cops got emotional in movies. He had never met an emotional cop in his life. He liked the way Karen sideslipped the BMW through a stream of cars to pull up at the curb. He thanked her, started to get out and said, "What happens, the kid goes after your boyfriend and that's when you finally stand up to her?"

"You're close," Karen said.

WHAT HE LIKED BEST, THINKING ABOUT IT, WAS NOT SO much guessing the ending but the look Karen gave him when he did. The eye contact. For a moment there the two of them looking at each other in a different way than before. Like starting over. Karen broke the spell saying she had to run and he got out of her car.

Still looking at the photos on the wall he thought about taking a closer look at the ones Karen was in. Check out her eyes. See what they were like when she was a screamer with blond hair. Maybe later.

Right now Harry was saying, "Here we are."

Harry, in the doorway, stepping aside, the two limo guys coming into the office past him.

10

CHILI STAYED WHERE HE WAS, AT THE DESK. THE ONE he took to be Ronnie Wingate—and had been thinking of as the rich kid—glanced at him, that's all, then looked around the office saying, "Harry, what year is it, man?" with a lazy rich-kid way of talking. "We enter a time warp? I feel like I'm back in the Hollywood of yesteryear." He was wearing a suede jacket so thin it was like a second shirt, with jeans and running shoes, sunglasses resting in his rich-kid hair he hadn't bothered to comb.

The other one, Bo Catlett, was an opposite type, tall next to Ronnie and put together in a tan outfit, suit, shirt and tie all light tan, a shade lighter than his skin. But what was he? From across the room he looked like the kind of guy who came from some island in the Pacific Ocean you never heard of. Ronnie kept moving as he looked at the photos over the sofa, his motor running on some chemical. Now Harry was waving his arm, inviting them to sit in the red chairs facing the desk.

Chili watched Catlett coming first, saw the mustache now and the tuft of hair beneath the lower lip and wondered what was wrong with Harry. The guy wasn't Latin or even from some unknown island out in the ocean. Up close he was colored. Colored and something else, but still colored.

Sitting down he said, "How you doing?"

That's what he was and what the other Catlett, the jazz drummer, was too. Chili said to him, "You any relation to Sid Catlett?"

It brought a smile, not much, but enough to make his eyes dreamy. "Big Sid, huh? No, I'm from another tribe. Tell me what brings you here."

"The movies," Chili said.

And Catlett said, "Ah, the movies, yeah."

Ronnie was seated now, one leg hooked over the chair arm, the leg swinging up and down on some kind of energy, his head moving too, as if plugged into a Walkman. Behind them Harry said, "This is my associate, Chili Palmer, who'll be working with me."

Harry already forgetting his instructions.

The limo guys nodded and Chili gave them a nod back. "I want to make sure there's no misunderstanding here," Harry said. He told them that despite rumors they might have heard, their investment in *Freaks* was as sound as the day they signed their participation agreement.

"Harry, are you making a speech?" Ronnie had his face raised to the ceiling. "I can hear you, but where the fuck are you, man?"

"What I been wondering," Catlett said in a quiet voice, looking at Chili, "is where he's been."

Ronnie said, "Yeah, where've you been? You called us once, Harry, in three months."

Harry came around from behind them to stand at one side of the desk, his back to the window, saying he'd been off scouting locations and interviewing actors in New York and his secretary had left without his knowledge to work for an agent, for Christ sake, Harry saying that was the kind of help you had to rely on these days, walked out, didn't even tell him.

Chili listened, not believing he was hearing all this.

Ronnie said, "Let's get the man a girl. Harry, you want one with big hooters or one that can type?"

Chili's gaze moved from Ronnie the fool to Bo Catlett the dude, the man composed, elbows on the chair arms, his fingertips touching to form a tan-skinned church, a ruby ring for a stained-glass window.

"The main thing I want to tell you," Harry said, "the start date for *Freaks* is being pushed back a little, a few months. We should be in production before the end of the year. . . . Unless because of unforeseen complications we decide it would be better to shoot next spring."

Chili watched Ronnie's leg, hanging over the chair arm, bounce to a stop.

"What're you telling us, Harry?"

"We have to put the start date off, that's all."

"Yeah, but why? Next spring, that's a whole year away."

"We'll need the prep time."

Ronnie said, "Hey, Harry? Bullshit. We have an agreement with you, man."

Chili raised his hand toward Harry.

"Wait a minute, okay? What we're talking about here—Harry, you're gonna make the movie, right. *Freaks?*"

Harry said, "Yeah," sounding surprised.

"Tell him."

"I just did."

"Tell him again."

"We're gonna make the picture," Harry said. He paused and said, "I've got another project to do first, that's all. One I promised this guy years ago."

Chili wondered if there was a way to shut Harry up without punching him in the mouth.

He saw Catlett watching him over the tips of his fingers while Ronnie fooled with his sunglasses, Harry telling them he'd be starting the other project any time now, a quickie, and as soon as it wrapped *Freaks* would go before the cameras.

There was a silence until Ronnie got up straighter in his chair and said, "I think what happened, you put our bucks in some deal that blew up in your face and now you're trying to buy time. I want to see your books, Harry. Show me where it is, a two with five zeroes after it in black and white, man. I want to see your books and your bank statements."

Chili said to the rich kid, "Hey, Ronnie? Look at me."

It caught him by surprise. Ronnie looked over. So did Bo Catlett.

Chili said, "You have a piece of a movie, Ronnie. That's all. You don't have a piece of Harry. You don't tell him what you want to see that has to do with his business, that's private. You understand what I'm saying? Harry told you we're doing another movie first, before we come along and do *Freaks*. And that's the way it's gonna be."

"Excuse me," Ronnie said, "but who the fuck are you?"

"I'm the one telling you how it is," Chili said. "That's not too hard, is it, figure that out?"

He watched Ronnie turn to Catlett, who hadn't moved or changed his expression much. Ronnie said, "Cat? . . ."

Chili watched Catlett now. He still couldn't understand how Harry missed seeing the guy was colored. He was light-skinned and his hair was fairly straight, combed over to one side, but that didn't mean anything. The color itself didn't mean anything either, Chili thinking the guy wasn't any darker than he was. Colored, but could you call him black? The guy was taking his time, giving the situation some thought.

When he spoke it was to Harry, Catlett asking, "What's this movie you're doing first?"

A simple enough question.

Chili said, "Harry, let me answer that."

He saw Catlett looking at him again.

"But first, I want to know who I'm talking to. Am I talking to you, or am I talking to him?" Meaning Ronnie.

He saw Catlett's expression change, not much, but something in the eyes, with that dreamy kind of half smile, that told Chili the man understood. The man saying now, "You can talk to me."

"That's what I thought," Chili said. "So let me put it this way. Outside of *Freaks,* it's not any of your fuckin business what we do."

Now it was between them, Chili giving the guy time but that's all, no way out for him except straight ahead or back off and the guy knew it too, looking at it and not moving a muscle, making up his mind . . .

Christ, when Harry stepped in, Harry reaching over the desk to pick up the script, Harry telling them, "This is the project, *Mr. Lovejoy.* I'm not trying to pull anything on you guys. This is it, right here." Harry blowing the setup and there wasn't a thing Chili could do about it.

He eased back in the chair and saw Catlett watching him with that dreamy half-smile again.

Ronnie was saying, *"Mr. Loveboy?"* reaching for the script. "What is it, Harry, a porno flick?"

Harry saying, "Love*joy,*" backing away, holding the script to his chest.

"Okay, but what's it about?"

"It's fluff, it's one I got involved in as a favor to a writer friend of mine. The guy's terminally ill and I owe it to him. Believe me, it's nothing you'd be interested in."

Ronnie said, "You think we go see the shit you turn out? Cat says he's seen better film on teeth." He looked at Catlett and said, "Right? I bet it's porno. Harry's lying to us."

Chili watched Catlett, the guy taking it all in, Harry telling them now the script was unreadable—holding it with both hands against his body—it needed all kinds of work. Catlett pushed out of the chair, in no hurry, and Chili had to look up to see his face, with that bebop tuft under his lip.

"I got an idea," Bo Catlett said to Harry. "Take our twenty points out of *Freaks* and put 'em in this other one, *Mr. Loverboy.* What's the difference."

"I can't do it," Harry said.

"You positive about that?"

"It's a different kind of deal."

"Okay." Catlett paused. "Then be good enough to hand us our money back."

"Why?" Harry said. "We have a deal, a signed agreement to do a picture I guarantee you is gonna get made."

"Take some time, think about our going into this other one," Catlett said. "Will you do that?"

"Okay, I'll think about it," Harry said. "I will."

"That's all we need to know, Harry. Till next time."

Chili watched Catlett look over before he turned—not long enough to be in each other's face, just a look—and walked out, Ronnie following after him.

NOW THEY WERE IN HARRY'S MERCEDES, CHILI NOT saying much for the time being: getting his thoughts together, deciding what kind of attitude he should have if he was going to stay in this deal: take it seriously or just go along and see what happens. So when Harry said, "That's where Lew Wasserman lives," Chili didn't ask who Lew Wasserman was. When Harry said, "There's where Frank Sinatra lives," Chili did look up, caught a glimpse of the house, but saw mostly Frank Sinatra's bushes, nice ones.

"You want to look at a star's home you can't even tell it's there," Harry said, "I'll take you past Bob Hope's place, over in Toluca Lake. You want to get a look at actual homes you can see, I'll show you where two of the Three Stooges used to live, also Joan Crawford, George Hamilton . . . Who else? The house Elvis Presley lived in when he was out here. It's in Bel Air. You know he made over thirty pictures and the only one I saw was *Stay Away, Joe*? A wonderful book they completely fucked up."

CHILI KEPT THINKING ABOUT RIGHT AFTER THE LIMO guys left saying to Harry, "What's wrong with you? What'd you tell 'em all your business for? Whyn't you do like I told you?"

Harry said, "What?" Acting surprised and then offended. "I had to tell 'em *some*thing."

"What'd we talk about, Harry, before? The way to handle it, you weren't gonna tell 'em shit. Isn't that right?"

"It didn't work out that way."

"No, 'cause you wouldn't shut up. You want these guys off your back, I tell you okay, here's how we do it. Next thing I know you're saying yeah, maybe they can have a piece of *Mr. Lovejoy.* I couldn't believe my fuckin ears."

"I said I'd think about it. What does that mean? In this business, nothing. I was buying time. All I have to do is hold 'em off till I make a deal at a studio."

"That's the difference between me and you," Chili said. "I don't leave things hanging. If I wanted Karen to talk to Michael I'd say, 'Karen, how about talking to Michael for me?' I told the limo guys it wasn't any of their fuckin business, period. They don't like it, that's too bad. What's the guy gonna do, Catlett, take a swing at me? He might've wanted to, but he had to consider first, who is this guy? He don't know me. All he knows is I'm looking at him like if he wants to try me I'll fuckin take him apart. Does he wanta go for it, get his suit messed up? I mean even if he's good he can see it would be work."

"He could've had a gun," Harry said.

"It wasn't a gun kind of situation. You don't pack, Harry, less you're gonna use it. You say Ronnie plays with his in the office. That told me something right there. Then, soon as I saw the colored guy, I knew he was the one in charge. I asked him—you heard me—he goes yeah, without coming right out and saying it. Ronnie's sitting there, he don't even know what I'm talking about."

"What colored guy?"

"Who do you think? Catlett. I don't know how you could've missed that. He lets the rich kid think he's the boss, but Catlett's pulling his strings. You don't see that?"

Harry said, "You think he's a black guy?" Sounding surprised again.

"I know he is. Harry, I've lived in Brooklyn, I've lived in Miami, I've seen all different shades and mixtures of people and listened to 'em talk and Catlett's a black guy with light-colored skin, that's all. Take my word."

"He doesn't talk like a black guy."

"What do you want him to say, Yazza, boss? He might be part South American," Chili said, "have some other kind of blood in him too, but I know he's colored."

They left the office talking about Catlett and the rich kid. Now they were in the car heading for Michael Weir's house, Chili wanting to get a good look at it, maybe let Harry drop him off and he'd stroll by. Harry said, "You see anybody out strolling? Not in this part of Beverly Hills. It's against the law to be seen on the street."

"THE ONE ON THE LEFT," HARRY SAID, "THAT'S WHERE Dean Martin used to live." Chili looked at the house without saying anything. "The one coming up—see the gate? Kenny Rogers rented that while he was having his new home built. You know what he paid a month? Fifty thousand."

"Jesus Christ," Chili said.

"Okay, right around the bend on the left, the one that looks like the place they signed the Declaration of Independence, that's Michael's house."

Coming up and now passing it: red brick with white trim behind a vine-covered brick wall and a closed iron gate. Through the bars Chili could see the drive curving up to the front door. He wondered if Michael Weir was in there at this moment.

"Why don't we ring the bell, see if he's home?"

"You don't get to see him that way, believe me."

"Go by again."

Harry nosed the Mercedes into a drive, backed around and came past the house saying, "Worth around twenty million, easy."

"It doesn't look that big."

"Compared to what, the Beverly Hills Hotel? It's twelve thousand square feet plus a tennis court, pool, cabana guesthouse and orange trees on three acres."

"Jesus Christ," Chili said. He could see the upper windows as they crept past the wall, the top part of a satellite dish in the side yard.

"There's no way you could sit in your car and watch the house," Harry said, "without attracting the police inside of two minutes. If you're thinking of waiting for him to come out."

"What's he do for fun?"

"His girlfriend lives with him. When he's not here, he's in New York. Has a place on Central Park West."

"I'd like to find out more about him," Chili said, "where he goes, so maybe I can run into him."

"Then what?"

"Don't worry about it. I got an idea."

"There was a piece on him, a cover story," Harry said,

"fairly recently in one of the magazines. About his career, his life. I remember there's a shot of him with his girlfriend. She was in entertainment, I think a singer with a rock-and-roll group when he met her. I wouldn't be surprised Karen has the magazine. I know she gets the trades, has stacks of 'em she keeps—I don't know why."

"I have to go back there anyway," Chili said, "pick up my car."

For a minute or so he was quiet, catching glimpses of the big homes through the trees and manicured shrubs, all the places so clean and neat and not a soul around, nobody outside. Not like Meridian Avenue, South Miami Beach. Not anything like Bay Ridge, Jesus, you had to go all the way over past the Veterans Hospital to Dyker Beach Park to find trees of any size.

He said to Harry, "You know the one Michael Weir was in, *The Cyclone*? When I saw it I recognized places on Bayview, Neptune Avenue, Cropsey. That's all close to my old neighborhood. I was in Miami then, but I heard some guys I know actually met him."

"Sure, every picture Michael's in," Harry said, "he researches the part, finds out exactly how he's supposed to play it. That's why he's so good. *The Cyclone,* he makes you believe he's a Mafia character."

"Well, basically, yeah, he sounded okay," Chili said. "What I couldn't believe, they would've let him in, the kind of simple asshole he was. Or let him get away after, a snitch? He would've ended up with his dick in his mouth. I don't mean to say there aren't assholes in those different crews, they're full of assholes. I just mean the particular kind of asshole he was in the movie."

"If he played a Mafia character," Harry said, "then I guarantee you he talked to some of them."

"Tommy would know," Chili said. "Tommy Carlo. I could call him and double-check."

"For what?"

"I'd like to know. Me and Tommy were both in Miami when they were making the movie, but he'd remember it. It was at the time we were running the club for Momo. Tommy was the one booked the different groups'd come in. Made him feel he was in the entertainment world."

"Well, if you want," Harry said, "call him from Karen's."

"What if she's not home? We just walk in?"

"It didn't bother you before."

"That was different. I'm not gonna bust in."

"If the patio door was open last night," Harry said, "it's still open. Karen's never been good at locking doors, closing windows when it rains, putting her top up . . ."

"When you were living together?"

"Anytime. She'd come in, forget to shut off the alarm system. Then the company that put it in calls and you have to give them an identifying code, three digits, that's all. But Karen could never remember the numbers. Pretty soon the cops pull up in the drive . . ."

"Harry, if Karen sets up Michael for you, what does she get?"

"She already got it." Harry said, "Me. I made her a movie star. She wasn't too bad, for that kind of picture. There aren't any lines that run more than ten words. Now she's reading for a part . . . Hasn't worked in seven years, she wants to get back in it. I don't know why—Michael set her up for life."

"Beth's Room," Chili said.

"What?"

"Beth's Room. That's the name of the movie she's gonna be in."

Harry gave him a quick glance. Looking at the road again he said, "I'll bet you a hundred bucks she doesn't get the part."

[illegible] in Miami
[illegible]
[illegible]
[illegible]
[illegible]

[illegible]

[illegible]

[illegible] school [illegible]
[illegible]

[illegible]

[illegible]

11

BO CATLETT LIKED TO CHANGE HIS CLOTHES TWO OR three times a day, get to wear different outfits. In less than two hours he was meeting friends at Mateo's in Westwood, so he had dressed for dinner before driving out to the airport.

Seated now in the Delta terminal, across the aisle from the gate where the mule from Miami would arrive by way of Atlanta, Catlett had on his dove-gray double-breasted Armani with the nice long roll lapel. He had on a light-blue shirt with a pearl-gray necktie and pearl cuff links. He had on light-blue hose and dark-brown Cole-Haan loafers, spit-shined. The loafers matched the attaché case next to him on the row of seats. Resting on the attaché case was a Delta ticket envelope, boarding pass showing—for anyone who might think he was sitting here with some other purpose in mind. Anyone who might think they recognized him from times before. Like that casual young dude wearing the plaid wool shirt over his white T-shirt, with the jeans and black Nikes.

Catlett liked to watch people going by, all the different shapes and sizes in all different kinds of clothes, wondering, when they got up in the morning if they gave two seconds to what they were going to wear, or they just got dressed, took it off a chair or reached in the closet and put it on. He could pick out the ones who had given it some thought. They weren't necessarily the ones all dressed up, either.

The young dude in the jeans and the wool shirt hanging out, he'd given that outfit some thought. A friendly young dude, said hi to the ladies behind the airline counter and they said hi back like they knew him.

Catlett wondered if the Bear had noticed that.

The Bear, having shown himself once, like reporting in, was around someplace: the Bear in a green and red Hawaiian shirt today with his baby girl.

Ninety-nine percent of the people in L.A. did not know shit about how to dress or seem to care. Nobody wore a necktie. They'd wear a suit and leave the shirt open. Or the thing now, they'd button the shirt collar, wearing it with a suit but no tie, and look like they'd just come off the fucking reservation. Ronnie Wingate, not knowing shit either, said, "Why wear a tie if you don't have to?" Like not wearing it was getting away with something. He had told Ronnie one time, "I use to dress just like you when I was a child and didn't know better." Living in migrant camps, moving from Florida to Texas to Colorado to Michigan, out here to California, the whole family doing stoop labor in hand-me-down clothes.

He said to Ronnie Wingate, "You know what changed my whole life?" Ronnie said what and he told him, "Finding out at age fourteen, not till then, I was part black."

Asshole Ronnie saying, "Negro?"

"Black. And if you're part, man, you're all."

Finding it out in a photograph the time he and his mother and three sisters went to visit his grandmother about to die; drove all the way to Benson, Arizona, from Bakersfield and his grandma got out her old pictures in an album to show them. The first ones, her own grandparents in separate brownish photos. An Indian woman in a blanket. (He had been told about having some Warm Springs Apache Indian blood, so this fat woman in the blanket came as no surprise.) It was the next photo that knocked him out. A black guy in the picture, no doubt about it. But not just any black guy. This one had a fucking sword, man, and sergeant stripes on his uniform. He was a U.S. Cavalryman, had served twenty-four years in the Army and fought in the Civil War when he was fifteen years old and was wounded at a place called Honey Springs in Missouri. Across the bottom of the photo it said: *Sgt. Bo Catlett of the 10th, Fort Huachuca, Arizona Territory, June 16, 1887.* And was signed by a man named *C. S. Fly.*

He asked could he have the photo and his grandma gave it to him.

"I think it was the sword did it," Catlett said to Ronnie that time. "I kept thinking about it a year until now *I* was fifteen. You understand the significance of what I'm saying? I changed my name from Antonio to Bo Catlett, left the camps for good and took off for Detroit to learn how to be black."

Asshole Ronnie didn't get it. "Detroit?" Even sucking on his base pipe didn't get it or ever would, 'cause the man would always be from Santa Barbara and never know shit about Detroit, about Motown, about Marvin Gaye . . .

Catlett spotted the Bear in his Hawaiian shirt, the Bear coming along carrying his three-year-old baby, cute little girl licking an ice-cream cone, dripping it on the Bear's shirt. The Bear looked this way without making eye contact, turned his head toward the young dude in the wool shirt and back this way again, wiping his little girl's mouth with a paper napkin, the Bear playing he was big and dumb but a nice daddy.

A voice just then announced the Atlanta flight was on the ground and would be at the gate in a few minutes.

Catlett got his mind ready. He'd been told the mule coming with the product this trip was a Colombian dude he had met one time before by the name of Yayo. Like so many of those people a mean little Colombian dude, but no size on him to speak of, going maybe one-thirty. They saw that movie *Scarface* and turned into a bunch of Al Pacinos doing Tony Montana. Only they didn't know how. They maintained a level of boring meanness that was like an act they put on. It made him think of the man sitting at Harry Zimm's desk, Chili Palmer, in his black jacket zipped up, not looking like any kind of movie producer or sounding like them either, full of shit. Chili Palmer maybe could be a mule, except he was bigger than any Colombian and looked at you different. Didn't put it on so heavy. Chili Palmer was quiet about it but came right at you, wanting to get it done. Catlett was thinking he could put the Bear in front of Mr. Chili Palmer, see if the man behaved the same way, gave the Bear that look . . .

The Bear and his baby girl were among the people by the gate now. Passengers were coming out of the ramp from the plane. The way it was set up, Yayo would have his ticket envelope in his hand, the envelope with a baggage claim check stapled inside. He'd lay the envelope on the trash container right there, not stick it down in, and keep coming. The Bear would step over, pick up the envelope and take off with his little girl to the baggage claim area. There it was happening . . .

And now Yayo was looking straight ahead coming through the people waiting—Catlett seeing them from behind moving aside to give this ignorant bean picker who looked like he'd never been in an airport before the right of way. That's what he reminded Catlett of, a migrant picker dressed for Saturday night in a clean starched shirt and khakis too big for him. Ignorant man, didn't know shit. Look at him being cool looking this way, coming over now.

As Yayo reached him Catlett said, "Don't say nothing to me. Turn around and act like you're waiting for somebody suppose to meet you."

"The *fock* you talking about?" Yayo hitting the word hard,

the way Tony Montana did. "They nobody know me here, man. Give me the focking case."

"Ain't in the case. Now turn around and be *look*ing," Catlett said. "You got eyes on you. Man over to your right in the blue wool shirt hanging out . . . The other way, *derecho*."

Catlett hunched over to rest his arms on his thighs, the seat of Yayo's khakis hanging slack before him, Yayo between him and the dude in the wool shirt now.

"That's a federal officer of some kind, most likely DEA. He moves his leg look for the bulge. You savvy bulge? Something stuck to his ankle, underneath his pants. His backup piece . . . *Hey.* Try it without looking right at him if you can."

Come out here you should always take some pills first, keep your blood pressure cool.

"You know he's there, now forget about him. While you wondering where your relatives are, suppose to meet you, I'm getting up. Gonna leave you and walk over to the cocktail lounge. After I'm gone, you sit down in this same seat I'm in. You feel something under your ass it's the key to a locker where your money is. But before you go open the locker you look around good now, understand? You don't want any guys have bulges on their ankles watching you. Take your time, go have a snack first. You know what a snack is?"

Yayo turned his head to one side. "You suppose to give me the focking money yourself."

Catlett got up, adjusted his dove-gray double-breasted jacket, smoothing the long roll lapel. He said, "Try to be cool, Yahoo," turning to pick up the ticket envelope and attaché case. "I was to hand you this fulla money we'd be speed-cuffed before we saw it happen. Do it how I told you and have a safe trip home. Or as you all say, *vaya con Dios,* motherfocker."

Down in Baggage Claim, Catlett stood away from the Bear and his little girl waiting at one of the carousels, the Bear looking at the numbers on the claim check that told him which bag coming out of the chute would have ten keys of cocaine in it. Seventeen thousand a key this month, a hundred and seventy grand waiting in the locker, the money plus some product they were returning: a whole key stepped on so many times it was baby food. No problem if Yayo was careful, looked around before he opened the locker. The trouble with this business, you had to rely on other people; you couldn't do it alone. Same thing in the movie business, from what Catlett had seen, studying how it worked. The difference was, in the movie business you didn't worry about somebody getting turned to save their ass and pointing at you in court. You could get fucked over in the movie business all kinds of ways, but you didn't get sent to a correctional facility when you lost out. The movie business, you could come right out and tell people what you did, make a name. Instead of hanging out on the edge, supplying highs for dumbass movie stars, you could get to where you hire the ones you want and tell 'em what to do; they don't like it, fire their ass. It didn't make sense to live here if you weren't in the movie business. High up in it.

The Bear came away from the carousel carrying his little girl and a Black Watch plaid suitcase. Catlett followed them outside, through the traffic in the covered roadway that was like an underpass to one of the islands where people were waiting for shuttles in daylight. The little girl said, "Hi, Bo," to Catlett coming up to them.

Catlett, smiling, said, "Hey, Farrah. Hah you, little honey bunny? You come see the big airplanes?"

"I been on airplanes," Farrah said. "My daddy takes me to Acapulco with him."

"I know he does, honey bunny. Your daddy's good to you, huh?"

Little Farrah started to nod and the Bear nuzzled her clean

little face with his beard saying, "This here's my baby sweetheart. Yes her is. Arn'cha, huh? Arn'cha my baby sweetheart?"

"Man, you gonna smother the child." Catlett raised the little girl's chin with the tips of his fingers. She seemed tiny enough to get lost in that shaggy beard, one tiny hand hanging on to it now, her tiny body perched on the Bear's arm. The Bear was going to fat but had taught bodybuilding at one time, worked as a movie stuntman and had choreographed fight scenes. Catlett thought of the Bear as his handyman.

"You know that place they use to shoot *77 Sunset Strip*?"

"Yeah, up by La Cienega."

"Harry Zimm's office is right across the street, white building, you see venetian blinds upstairs. I need to get in there, pick up a movie script. If you could meet me there tonight, open the door . . ."

"You want, Bo, I'll go in and get it."

"No, you do the B part and I do the E."

"I know that," Farrah said in her tiny voice. "A, B, E, C, D."

Catlett was smiling again. "Hey, you a smart little honey bunny, ain'cha?"

"Yes her is," the Bear said.

12

CHILI REACHED TOMMY CARLO AT THE BARBERSHOP BUT didn't get a chance to talk about *The Cyclone* and Michael Weir.

Tommy said, "I been wanting to call you, but you didn't gimme a number. Ray Bones is looking for you. He's got some kind of bug up his ass, can't sit still. He kept after Jimmy Cap about he wants to go to L.A. till Jimmy tells him to go ahead and fuckin go, he's tired hearing about it."

Chili was at the desk in Karen's study, the chair swiveled so that his back was to Harry, across the room. Harry was sitting on the floor; he had the cabinet in the bookcase open and was going through magazines.

Chili said, "You hang out with Jimmy Cap now?" keeping his voice low.

"I happen to be by there when they're talking, I notice Bones, how he's acting."

"You pay him the eight yet?"

"Fuck no, he'll get it when he gets it. Chil, it doesn't have nothing to do with money, you know that. I hate to say I fuckin told you, but I did. I told you, don't start nothing with him that time."

"You said don't say nothing, and I didn't."

"No, you broke his fuckin nose instead."

Talking about something that had happened twelve years ago, still hanging over him. "The guy only has room in his brain for one thing," Chili said, "that's the problem, he's a fuckin idiot."

"He don't like the way you talk to him. You ever showed him any kind of respect at all, he wouldn't be on your ass."

"I should've hit him a half-inch lower that time, with the thirty-eight. You think he's coming out, uh?"

"I know he is. He asked me where you're staying. I told him I didn't know. I still don't."

"When's he coming?"

"He never said, but I think the next couple days."

Getting into the kid stuff again and sounding stupid, hearing himself, Jesus, like he was reverting, talking like those hard-ons sitting around their social clubs.

"Wait a minute," Chili said. "How's he know I'm here?"

"I told him you went out to Vegas on a collection job and they sent you to L.A."

"What'd you tell him that for?"

"He already knew it. I don't know how unless—did you talk to the dry cleaner's wife since you're out there? What's her name, Leo's wife? I know Bones went to see her and maybe she mentioned it. This was yesterday."

"Tommy? What makes you think I told Fay I was going to Vegas?"

"I don't know—it musta been something Bones said. I just assumed."

"I'll call you back," Chili said, hung up and dialed information to get the number of Paris Cleaners in North Miami. Fay answered the phone. Chili asked her how she was doing. He was going to take his time, ease into it, but Fay started talking right away, sounding anxious to tell him.

"A man came to see me said was a friend of yours? He asked had I spoken to you since Leo was killed and I said yes,

I had. He asked what it was we talked about. I said oh, nothing in particular, and he hit me with his fist. I have a black eye and my jaw hurts something awful, I try to eat on that side? It might be broken. When I get off I think I'll go the doctor's and see about it."

"Fay? You told him what we talked about?"

"He asked had I given you any money and then, yeah, he made me tell him. If I didn't he was all set to beat me up."

"I mean, you told him Leo was alive?"

"I had to."

"And about the money, the settlement?"

"He went through my things and found the letter from the airline the check come in."

"Fay, what else did you tell him?"

"That's all."

"What about the woman Leo knows out here, Hi-Tone Cleaners?"

"Oh. Yeah, I might've mentioned her, I forget."

That meant she did. Chili was pretty sure.

"I was kinda groggy from him hitting me."

"There was nothing you could do, Fay."

She said, "I guess now everybody's gonna know about Leo, what he did."

"No, I think just us three," Chili said. "The guy won't tell anybody. I think what he'll do is try and find Leo, get the money for himself."

Fay said, "Well, how are you doing otherwise? Are you coming back here sometime?"

Chili gave her Karen's number, hung up and called Tommy Carlo at the barbershop.

"Tommy, did Bones say anything to Jimmy Cap about Leo?"

"Not that I heard. Why?"

"Only that he was gonna come looking for me?"

"That's what he said."

"He didn't tell you anything, I mean about Leo?"

"Like what?"

"Nothing," Chili said. "Listen . . ." and asked about Michael Weir and the time he was in Brooklyn making the movie.

Tommy said yeah, he knew guys talked to him personally, had Michael Weir to their club, one on 15th corner of Neptune, another place on 86th Street. Yeah, they shot scenes in Bensonhurst, Carroll Gardens, on the bridge, the Bush Terminal docks, the amusement park . . . "That movie, you know, was from a book called *Coney Island,* but Michael Weir had it changed, he didn't like the title. He said to call it *The Cyclone* and they did."

"The Cyclone," Chili said, "the roller coaster."

"Yeah, the roller coaster. You remember the movie? Michael Weir, he's Joey Corio, he's running the fuckin roller coaster in the beginning part, before he gets in with the guys and he's made. So the guys call him Cyclone. 'Hey, Cyc, how you doing?' You don't remember that?"

Chili looked up to see Harry coming to the desk with a stack of magazines. "I'll talk to you later," Chili said, paused, lowered his voice then as he said, "Tommy? Find out when's he coming out. I'll call you," and hung up.

"Michael's in every one of these," Harry said, dropping the magazines on the desk. "Recent ones in *American Film* and *Vanity Fair,* about the picture he just finished, called *Elba.* This one, there's a cover story. Everything you ever wanted to know about him. There's a picture of Karen in there and also his present live-in."

Chili picked up the magazine, *Premiere,* to see Michael Weir full face, almost life-size, grinning at him. The guy had to be up in his late forties but looked about thirty-five. Not bad looking, thick dark hair he wore fairly long, kind of a big nose. There was that Michael Weir twinkle in his eyes, Michael telling his many fans he was basically a nice guy and didn't put on any airs. It said next to the picture in big letters, MICHAEL WEIR, and under it, smaller, WILL THE REAL ONE PLEASE STAND UP?

"He's got a big nose," Chili said. "I never noticed that before."

"Prominent," Harry said.

"It's big," Chili said, opening the magazine to the cover story, a full-page color shot of Michael in a faded work shirt and scruffy jeans, wearing black socks with his Reeboks. See? Just a regular guy who happened to make seven million every time he did a movie. Chili started to tell Harry his observation in a dry tone of voice, but caught himself in time.

What was he putting Michael Weir down for? He didn't even know the guy.

He had that fuckin Ray Bones on his mind now, that was the problem, and he was taking it out on this actor who happened to have a big nose and liked scruffy jeans.

The beginning of the article, on the opposite page, had for a title over it, WEIR(D) TALES. On the next two pages were more pictures of Michael, Michael in different movies, Michael in *The Cyclone* holding a gun and looking desperate, Michael with Karen—there she was—still a blonde.

Chili turned the page, looked at more pictures, still thinking about Ray Bones, realizing Bones would check out the woman at Hi-Tone Cleaners and if he didn't find her he'd use his connections, talk to the lawyers that ate raw fish, and next he'd be coming this way to check out Harry Zimm. That fuckin Bones, all he did was mess things up.

"Here's the one he's living with now," Harry said over Chili's shoulder as he turned the page. "Nicki. She's a cutie, except for all that hair, a rock-and-roller. They met at Gazzarri's, on the Strip. Nicki was performing with some group."

"You know what?" Chili said, looking at a color shot of

Michael and Nicki by a limo, both in black leather jackets. "I think I know her. There was a girl with a group we used quite a few times at Momo's . . . Only her name was Nicole."

"That's close," Harry said. He ran his finger down a column of the story. "Here. She's twenty-seven, born in Miami. Performed with different groups . . . she's a singer."

"So's Nicole," Chili said, "but her hair's a lot blonder and she's older." He picked up the phone and dialed the back room of the barbershop.

Tommy said, "I talk to you more in L. A. 'n when you're here."

"There was a group we had at Memo's about seven eight years ago, the girl singer's name was Nicole?"

"Sure, Nicole. Man, I wanted to jump her so bad."

"She had blond hair, almost white?"

"Yeah, but not necessarily. I meant to tell you," Tommy said, "we talking about Michael Weir? Nicole lives with him. Only now she's Nicki."

"You sure it's the same one?"

"I just read about her, putting together a group. She was out of music for a while."

"How old would Nicole be, thirties?"

"Around there, thirty-four."

"This one's twenty-seven."

"Hey, Chil, it's the same broad, take my word."

"What's the name of the group?"

"Prob'ly 'Nicki.' I'll check, see what I can find out."

Chili gave him Karen's number and hung up. He said to Harry, "I was right, I know her."

Harry said, "Yeah, but does she know you?"

NOW THEY WERE HAVING A DRINK WHILE THEY LOOKED at magazines, Chili learning facts about Michael Weir: that he had three homes, three cars, three ex-wives, a dirt bike he rode in the desert, liked to play the piano, cook, didn't smoke, drank moderately . . . That he had appeared in seventeen features he was willing to talk about . . . That while grips and gaffers loved him, directors and writers "were not that enchanted by Michael's tendency to trample indifferently on their prerogatives; but since he was arguably a genius . . ."

Karen walked in on them in her neat black suit, looking good, calm, but maybe putting it on, and Chili learned a little more about her and about the movie business. Karen said, "Nothing's changed in ten years—you know it?" Harry raised his glass saying, "And it never will. Let me guess what happened. No, first tell me who was there." Chili, at the desk, became the audience, looking from one to the other.

Karen: "You know Warren Hurst?"

Harry: "Never heard of him."

Karen, looking at their drinks: "He's one of the production V.P.'s, a new guy. I don't think he'll last."

Harry, as Karen picked up Chili's drink, took a big sip and handed him the glass: "Who else?"

Karen: "Elaine Levin . . ."

Harry: "No—what's she doing at Tower?"

Karen: "Harry, she runs production. Don't you read?"

Harry: "What, the trades? I've missed a few lately." To Chili: "This's good. Elaine Levin, a few years ago was selling cosmetics . . ."

Karen, lighting a cigarette: "She was at UA and then Metro nine years."

Harry: "Okay, but before that she was at an ad agency in New York, right? Elaine comes up with an idea for a cosmetic she calls 'Bedroom Eyes'—you put it on you increase your chances of getting laid. The head of a major studio says to her, 'Honey, if you can sell that shit you can sell movies.' Next thing you know she's a vice-president of production."

Karen: "Elaine started in marketing."

Harry: "And how long was she there? That's what I'm talking about, before they moved her into production, this broad that sold eye makeup?"

Karen: "Harry, everybody used to do something else. What about when you were Harry Simmons making slide films, *How to Load a Truck*?" To Chili: "Did you know Zimm wasn't his real name?"

Harry: "The only thing I wasn't sure of, should Zimm have one *m* or two? Hey, but I was always a filmmaker, behind the camera. These people that run the studios, they're lawyers, former agents. They're strictly money guys."

Karen: "What are you, Harry?"

Harry: "They wouldn't even *see* movies, I'm convinced, they didn't have a screening room on the lot. That's why with few exceptions I've remained independent. You know that song Old Blue Eyes does, 'I did it my way'? . . ."

Karen: "But now you're going to a studio."

Harry: "I have no choice. But you know which one? Tower, I just decided. Play the power game with Bedroom Eyes, see if she's any good. Get in there and compete with all the ass kissers and bottom feeders, all the no-talent schmucks that constellate around the studio execs who don't know what they're doing either. All trying to figure out what the public wants to see. How about teenagers from outer space?"

Karen: "It's been done."

Harry: "Well, I got a property I *know* is gonna go into release. We open on a thousand screens we'll do over ten mil the first weekend. You oughta read it, see what I'm talking about. Why Michael would be the perfect Lovejoy. Karen? One phone call, I'm in business."

Chili watched her stub the cigarette out in the ashtray, maybe giving herself time to think. Harry said, "I'm gonna be optimistic, okay?" Karen didn't answer and Harry, after a moment, brought it back to where they had started.

"You haven't told us what happened at the meeting."

"I thought you wanted to guess."

"Okay. They liked what you did and'll let you know."

"I didn't read. I turned down the part."

"I thought you wanted to do it."

"I changed my mind," Karen said, and walked out.

"You know what happened," Harry said to Chili. "They told her don't call us, we'll call you, and she won't admit it." Harry paused to sip his drink. "I'm serious about going to Tower." He paused again. "I'll wait'll Karen's in a better mood and lay the script on her."

"I thought," Chili said, "I was gonna read it."

"What'd you bring, one copy?"

Chili thought about it and said, "I'm going back to the motel, get cleaned up and check out, find someplace over here to stay. Lemme have the key to your office, I could stop on the way back, pick up a script for myself. How would that be?"

KAREN, STILL IN THE NEAT BLACK SUIT, WAS AT THE kitchen table pouring a Coke. Chili watched her from the doorway—where she had stood last night in the Lakers T-shirt.

"Can I ask you a question?" She looked up at him and he said, "Why'd you change your mind?"

"About the part? I can't say I was dying to do it."

Karen looked down to pour some more Coke in the glass, careful that it didn't foam over. Chili got ready to say well, maybe he'd be seeing her sometime, when she looked up at him again.

"I probably would've taken it though. But during the meeting I got into what we were talking about this morning, my feeling guilty? You know . . ."

Chili said, "Why you let the daughter walk all over you."

"Yeah, I questioned that, and the answer I got, it's what

the audience expects, it's what they want to see. I said, but if I'm not stupid, if I realize in the end I'm being used, why don't I realize it right away? Warren goes, 'But if you did, Karen, we wouldn't have a movie, would we?' In this tone. You know, like I'm an idiot. It really pissed me off. I said well, if that's the way you want to do it, I'll see you."

"They try to talk you into it?"

"Elaine did, in a way. I got the feeling the studio forced the script on her and she has to go with it. She said, well, the story isn't exactly a great idea—she knows—but it's involving, reflective, has resonance, a certain texture—those are all story department words. I said, 'Yeah, and lines no one would say except in a movie.' Warren goes, 'But that's what it is, Karen, a movie.' Elaine stared at him without saying a word, like she was thinking, Where did I get this guy? You have to understand, there are movie lines and there are movie lines that work. Bette Davis comes out of a cabin, walks up to a guy on the porch, gives him a flirty look and says, 'I'd kiss you but I just washed my hair.' I love it, because it tells you who she is and you have to like her. But some of the stupid lines I've had to deliver . . ."

Chili said, "You want to get back into it, don't you?"

"I know I'm better than what I used to do. In Harry's movies I was always the bimbo. I walked around in a tank top and those fuck-me pumps with stiletto heels till it was time to scream. Harry kills me, he says don't ever take this business seriously, and he's the most serious guy I know. He puts studio people down—the main reason, because he'd love to run a major studio." Karen nodded saying, "If he ever did, he might not be bad. The cheapskate, I know he'd save them money." She started to smile, just a little, saying, "Another one of my favorite Bette Davis lines: 'He tried to make love to me and I shot him.' "

Chili smiled with her. He said, "I was thinking, you know

what you could do? Make a deal with Harry. You'll call Michael if he'll give you a part in the movie, a good one."

Karen said, "You're kidding," but kept staring at him until finally she said, "In the first place Michael will never do the picture—"

"Harry told me he loves it, he flipped."

"Michael is known for his flipping. He flips over a script, and then when the time comes to make a deal, he flips out. But what I started to say, Michael would never make the picture with Harry, he doesn't have the track record. It would not only have to be a big-name producer, Michael would also demand script, director and cast approval, and he'd get it."

Chili watched her finish pouring the Coke.

"You haven't answered my question."

"Which one?"

"You want to get back into it, don't you?"

"I'm thinking about it," Karen said. "I'll let you know."

13

CHILI WONDERED IF LEO WAS ATTRACTED TO SWEATY women in sundresses. Across the counter from him in Hi-Tone Cleaners on Ventura, Studio City, Annette looked kind of damp, clammy. She was on the heavy side, needed to fix her blond hair, but wasn't too bad looking. It was seven P.M. The help had left and Annette was closing up when Chili walked in, timing it to be the last customer. He gave his name, Palmer.

Annette stood looking through an alphabetical file on a turntable. "You don't have your receipt?"

"No, I don't," Chili said. He didn't have a pair of pants here, either, but that's what he told Annette he'd brought in. "They're light gray."

She said, "Are you sure? I don't see no Palmer in the file." She said *fahl* with the same kind of accent Fay had. Chili wondered what Leo gained trading for this one. Outside of about twenty-five pounds and those big round jugs in her brown-print sundress. He told her he'd brought the pants in yesterday and needed them since he was leaving tomorrow for Miami. Annette said, "Taking a vacation?" Chili told her no, it was where he lived. She said, "Oh?" showing a certain amount of interest.

Chili had on his dark-blue muted pinstripe, a blue shirt

with a tab collar and rust-colored tie. He appeared reasonable about his pants, not too concerned; he told her if she couldn't find them it was no big deal, and smiled, easy to get along with.

"Well, if you're sure," Annette said, nice about it because he was, "I can check, see if there's a pair of pants without a ticket on them." She stepped over to the conveyor loaded with clothes hanging in clear plastic covers, reached up and pressed a button. The conveyor started moving, bringing the clothes past her before it circled and returned them to the back part of the shop. Annette said, "I think you're gonna have to help me out here."

Chili walked around behind the counter to stand next to her. He looked at clothes going past for a minute before saying, "I've seen you someplace. . . . You weren't by any chance in Vegas last week."

Annette had her hand raised to the button, so she could stop the conveyor if they saw his pants. She looked past her bare shoulder at him and he could tell she was smiling, even though he couldn't see her mouth. She said, "No, but I was in Reno. How about that?"

"Getting a divorce?" Kidding with her.

"I took care of that 'fore I come out here. Got rid of excess baggage. No, this fella I was with took me."

"I hope your luck was better than mine. I dropped a bundle and it wasn't my laundry," Chili said, getting into it, showing Annette what a nice simple guy he was.

She told him she only played the slots and did okay. "But would you believe the fella I was with lost over a hundred thousand dollars and it didn't even bother him?"

"Jesus," Chili said, looking from the cleaning going by to Annette. "Guy must be loaded, drop that much and not worry about it."

"His philosophy is you win some, lose some."

"I guess that's as good a way to look at it as any."

"He's from Miami, Florida, too, originally."

"Yeah, what's his name?"

"I doubt you'd know him."

"He move out here?"

"I'm trying to get him to. He spends the whole day out to Santa'nita, loves the racetrack."

"You don't lose it as fast betting the horses."

"Oh, he wins, don't worry about that. You know the state lottery in Florida?"

"Yeah? He won that?"

"He won, I mean, big. But soon as his wife found out . . . His wife—listen to this. She's divorcing him at the time, but then when she finds out about the money she wants half as part of the settlement. He said the hell with that noise and took off."

"I don't blame him," Chili said.

"Changed his name, too. The wife never even played the lottery herself. But soon as he won, oh, now she wants in on it. Larry said he'd burn the money before he'd give her any."

"I imagine he's doing what he never dreamed of in his life," Chili said. "Right up there on top." He turned his head to look at Annette's bare shoulder and blond hair, dark strands of it combed up from her neck and held with a plastic comb. He said, "Your friend knows how to pick winners," waited for Annette to look at him and gave her a nice smile. "Why don't you shut this place down and we'll go have a drink."

"What about your pants?"

"I got other pants. Come on, let's do it."

"Gee, I'd like to," Annette said, "but I have to get cleaned up and meet my fella. He gets back from Santa'nita we meet at his ho-tel, have a drink in the Polo Lounge and go on out for dinner."

"Sounds good."

"You been there, haven't you?"

"Where's that?"

"The Polo Lounge, in the Beverly Hills Hotel? It's late now—the best time's around six, you see all kinds of celebrities in there."

"Is that right?"

"I've seen movie stars right at the next table."

"You have? Like who?"

Annette said, "Let's see," and thought about it staring at the clothes going by. She pressed the button to stop the conveyor. "I can never think of their names, after. There was one, he played in a western use to be on TV. What was his name? . . . They give you, with your drinks they give you corn chips with that guacamole dip? No charge. You see men, they have a phone brought to their table and you actually hear them talking about movies they're gonna make and what stars'll be in them. It's exciting to hear it, movie stars being mentioned like they're just, you know, regular people."

"I'll have to stop by there," Chili said, "maybe next time I come out. The Beverly Hills Hotel, that's where your friend stays, huh?"

"He has a suite costs him four hundred a night. Living room, bedroom, a balcony you can sit out on . . ."

"Sounds good. Listen, I was thinking," Chili said, "your friend's wife, she could have somebody looking for him, hire somebody." He watched Annette giving it some thought. "In case anybody comes by asking about him . . ."

"I'll just say I never heard of him."

"Yeah, except if the person happens to know you're an old friend maybe."

"I see what you mean," Annette said, giving it some more thought. "Just say he hasn't been here then."

Chili moved back around the counter telling her not to

worry about his pants, he said those things happened. He was anxious to get going, stop and have a bite to eat before taking that canyon road, full of hairpin turns, back over the mountain to Beverly Hills. For a moment he wondered what the mountain was called and thought of asking Annette, but changed his mind and was almost to the door when she said, "I remember who it was now, the movie star? Doug McClure."

Chili paused to say, "Oh," nodding.

"He was so close," Annette said, "I could've touched him."

HE WONDERED IF MAYBE THE LIGHTS OUTSIDE THE Sunset Marquis had been left over from Christmas: little pinpoint lights in the trees along the front, on both sides of the canopy that came out from the entrance. It was a slick place, only three stories hidden away in a lot of foliage down the hill from Sunset Boulevard—outdoor dining and the pool right in the middle, in a courtyard. Harry had recommended it and made the reservations, saying it used to be popular with rock groups and guys whose wives had kicked them out of the house for one reason or another. What Chili had in 325 was a two-hundred-buck suite with windows facing apartment balconies about fifty feet away; but that was okay, he wouldn't be looking out much. There was a phone in the bedroom, another one on the counter separating the living room from the kitchenette. Chili got the number of the Beverly Hills Hotel. When he asked for Larry Paris, the operator said just a moment, she'd connect him, Chili wondering how the little drycleaner had ever come this far as dumb as he was, going to the track every day and living in a four-hundred-dollar suite Chili would bet couldn't be any nicer than this one. It had an oriental look to it, maroon lamps shaped like pagodas. He let it ring till the operator came back on to say Mr. Paris's room was not answering. Chili had no intention of speaking to him anyway. He hung up and phoned Tommy Carlo at home, six P.M. in Miami.

"How about Nicole?"

"You mean Nicki," Tommy said. "I got hold of the guy use to be her manager through the booking service. You remember him? Marty, little guy with hair down to his ass?"

"Yeah, sorta."

"He's the A and R guy for a record company in Los Angeles, scouts new talent. He says Nicki's getting ready for a gig at Raji's on Hollywood Boulevard. She's been rehearsing there, putting a new band together and that's prob'ly where you'll find her. Raji's on Hollywood Boulevard. I think Marty said east of Vine, you got it?"

Chili was making notes on the Sunset Marquis pad by the phone. "Yeah. What about Bones? When's he coming?"

"I don't know any more'n I told you already."

"You find out anything, call me, okay?"

Chili gave him the number and said, "I'll see you."

"When?" Tommy said.

It stopped him.

Chili said, "I don't know, I may be going into the movie business, see what it's like."

Now it sounded like Tommy was stopped. "What're you talking about? You wanta be a movie star?"

"I'm no actor. I'm talking about producing."

"How you gonna do that? You don't know shit about making movies."

"I don't think the producer has to do much," Chili said. "The way it is here, this town, it goes out in all directions with all kinds of shit happening. You know what I mean? Like there's no special look to the place. Brooklyn, you got streets of houses are all exactly the same. Or Brooklyn in general, you know, has a bummed-out look, it's old, it's dirty. . . . Miami has a look you think of stucco, right? Or high-rises on the beach. Here, wherever you look it's something different. There homes'll knock your eyes out, but there's a lot of cheap shit, too. You know what I mean? Like Times Square. I think the movie business is the same way. There aren't any rules—you know, anybody saying this's how you have to do it. What're movies about? They're all different, except the ones that're just like other movies that made money. You know what I'm saying? The movie business, you can do any fuckin thing you want 'cause there's nobody in charge."

Tommy said, "Hey, Chil, you know what I think?"

"What?"

"You're fulla shit."

HE SAT DOWN ON THE SOFA TO RELAX FOR A WHILE IN his new surroundings with the oriental look, turned on the TV and punched remote control buttons to see what they had out here. . . . As many Spanish programs as Miami . . . The Lakers playing Golden State . . . *Shane.* He hadn't seen *Shane* in years. Chili got low in the sofa, his feet on the glass coffee table, and watched from the part where Shane beats the shit out of Ben Johnson for calling him sody pop to where he shoots Jack Wilson, practically blows him through the wall. It was almost real the way the guns went off in that movie, loud, but still not as loud as you heard it in a room, shooting a guy in the head just a little too high, and now the guy was coming out here.

Chili left his rented Toyota in the hotel garage, hiked up Alta Loma the half block to Sunset and had to stop and catch his breath from the climb, out of shape, before walking along Sunset till he was opposite white storefronts across the street. It was dark, a stream of headlights going by. He stood waiting for a break in the traffic, his gaze on the white building, and began to wonder why a light was on in Harry's office. He was pretty sure it was Harry's, the wide window with the venetian blinds. Maybe the cleaning woman was in there.

Chili jogged across the wide street, let himself in and climbed the stairs to ZigZag Productions, dark except for a light at the end of the hall. It was Harry's office, but not a cleaning woman who looked up from the desk as Chili entered.

It was the colored limo guy, Bo Catlett, wearing glasses and with a movie script open in front of him.

Catlett said, "This ain't bad, you know it? This *Mr. Lovejoy.* The title's for shit, but the story, man, it takes hold of you."

14

CHILI WALKED TOWARD THE DESK THINKING HE'D better nail the guy right away, not say a word, hit him with the phone, wrap the cord around his neck and drag him out. Except the guy had not busted the door, jimmied the lock, he wasn't robbing the place, he was sitting there with his glasses on reading a script. The guy telling him now, "I started reading, I couldn't put it down. I'm at the part—let's see, about fifteen pages to go—Lovejoy's coming out of court with his sister, can't believe what's happened to him." Chili reached the red leather chairs facing the desk, the guy saying, "I want to know how it ends, but don't tell me." Saying, "Yeah, I can see why Harry's dying to do it."

The guy talking about the script, but saying to Chili at the same time, Let's see how cool you are.

Chili sat down in one of the red leather chairs. He unbuttoned the jacket of his pinstripe suit to get comfortable and said, "I don't like the title either."

For a moment he saw that dreamy look in the man's eyes, almost a smile.

"You understand I knew Harry was lying," Catlett said. "I'm talking about his saying this wasn't any good, but holding on to it, man, like you have to break his fingers to get it from him." Catlett paused. "I'm explaining to you what I'm doing here. Case you think I come to rob the place, rip off any this dusty old shit the man has."

Chili said, "No, I'd never make you as a burglar, not with that suit you have on. It tells me what you do—when you're not taking people for rides in your limo."

"It's funny, I was thinking along the same line," Catlett said. "Guys in your business you don't see dressed up much anymore, but you have a nice suit of clothes on."

"You mean the movie business," Chili said.

There was that little slow gleam in Catlett's eyes again, showing understanding, maybe appreciation.

"Movie people don't dress up either, 'cept the agents. You see an agent duded up it means he's taking a serious meeting someplace, at a studio or a network. Or he wants you to think it's what he's doing. Or the older crowd at Chasen's, in the front room, they dress up. But I'm talking about your *main* business, working for the Italians."

"Yeah? How you know that?"

"Man, listen to you. You street, same as me, only we from different sides of it," Catlett said. "See, the first thing I wonder about I see you, I ask myself, What's this man Chili Palmer doing here? Is he'n investor? Harry called you his associate, but what does that mean? I never heard your name spoken in the business or read it in *Variety* or *The Reporter* or anyplace. I kept thinking till it came to me. It's wiseguy money financing *Lovejoy* and Frank DePhillips, the man, put you here to look out for Harry, see he doesn't mess up or keep people like myself from bothering him."

"You're part right," Chili said.

"Part or mostly?"

"You know DePhillips?"

"Enough about him."

"Then you oughta know if I worked for a guy like DePhillips," Chili said, "we wouldn't be talking. I would've thrown you out that window by now. I don't work for him and I don't work for Harry, either. It's what he said, I'm his associate."

Catlett slipped his glasses off. "You must bring something heavy to the deal."

"That's right, me," Chili said, and watched the man's smile come all the way, showing goldwork on his teeth.

Catlett said, "But no special talent, huh? Walk in off the street and become a film producer. You the financial or the creative side?"

"Don't worry about it."

"Can I ask you—how 'bout your lead? Who you see for Lovejoy?"

"We're getting Michael Weir."

"Hey, shit, come on. How you gonna do that?"

"I put a gun right here," Chili said, touching the side of his head, "and I tell him, 'Sign the paper, Mikey, or you're fuckin dead.' Like that."

"I wonder," Catlett said, "would that work. Man, it would simplify dealing with movie stars. They get temper'mental on you, lay the piece alongside their head. 'Get back to work, motherfucker.' Yeah, Michael Weir, he'd be good. You got anybody else?"

"We're working on it."

"You know who I see for Al Roxy? Harvey Keitel. The man could do it with his eyes closed. But you know who else? Morgan Freeman. You know who I mean?"

Chili said, "Yeah, Morgan Freeman. But he's a colored guy."

"Where's it say in the script he's white? Color is what the part needs, man, somebody to do it has some style. The way it is now Ronnie could do it, play himself, a cracked-out asshole. You also what you need is a good woman part, get some love in it. The only women you have now, you have Lovejoy's sister, on his ass all the time, and you have that whore friend of Roxy's, but she's only in two scenes."

Chili was trying to think of the name of the girl in the one page of the script he'd read. Not Irene . . .

"You know what I'm saying? A good juicy woman part."

Chili gave him a nod, still trying to think of the girl's name.

"You have Lovejoy smelling his flowers, right. So what you need is a woman different than he is to come along and help him out. Like, say, Theresa Russell, man. Or the one, what's her name? Greta something . . ."

"Greta Scacchi," Chili said.

"That's the one. That's how you pronounce it, huh, Skacky? I never knew that. I heard Scotchy, I never heard Skacky."

"You're hearing it now," Chili said.

"Sexy woman. You can go either way, Greta or Theresa Russell," Catlett said. "Take Roxy's friend the whore and make her more important. You understand? Like he beats up on her, so she goes to Lovejoy, tells him something important will help him out, just about the time he's thinking of giving up."

Chili remembered the girl's name in the script. "There's Ilona."

"What about her?"

"Get something going there."

"With Il*ona*? You know how old Ilona is?"

Chili got out a cigarette and lit it. He felt the guy watching him. "Yeah, she's young."

"She's sixteen," Catlett said, "same age as Lovejoy's kid, Bernard, she calls Bernie."

"I was thinking you could make her older."

The guy kept staring at him.

"You do that, you lose her telling things to Lovejoy about

his own son he don't know about, when he thought he was so close to the boy." Catlett paused a moment and said, "Have you *read* this?"

"Part of it, yeah."

"*Part* of it?" Catlett said, sitting back in Harry's creaky chair. "You know what it's about?"

"I know Lovejoy's following this other guy . . ."

There was a silence, not long, Chili and Catlett looking at each other until Catlett said, "Al Roxy, the one he's following around, killed his kid."

"Killed him—how?"

"Ran over him with his car. On his way home drunk, hits the kid crossing the street and keeps going. It's right in front of Lovejoy's flower shop. He sees it happen and almost goes to pieces right there, his boy laying dead. Before this we know Lovejoy's wife left him and all he has is this boy. The boy and his flower business, that's his whole life."

Chili didn't say anything.

He hadn't read the script, so the guy was telling him about it and it seemed okay. Why not? Saying now there was a witness who got the license number . . .

"So the cops pick up Roxy, he says he didn't know he hit anybody. It's the next day, so there's no way to tell he was drinking, but they have evidence, find some blood on his car matches up . . . Anyway, Roxy's lawyer does a job on the court and all the man gets is his license suspended, can't drive a car for six months. Lovejoy, he's at the court hearing, can't believe it. That's *all*? The motherfucker kills my kid and that's all he gets? That's what he's thinking, but see, the man is too . . . well, he's too timid to come out and say anything. After it's over Roxy says to Lovejoy, 'Tough break. But the kid shouldn't have run out in the street.' Or, 'The kid should have watched where he was going.' Something like that."

"What's Roxy do?" Chili said. "I mean, what kind of work?"

"He runs a body shop. You know, bump and paint. Does good too. This is in Detroit it takes place, Harry's hometown, though he don't have a fondness for the city like I do. I lived there nine years."

A question popped into Chili's mind.

"You ever do time?"

The guy started to smile, then let it go.

"I been bound over, but no jail time, no."

"So what happens?"

"Lovejoy gets it into his head Roxy, sooner or later, is gonna drive his car, this Cadillac. So what Lovejoy does, he takes his florist delivery van and changes it over. Paints out the name, has peepholes cut in the sides and gets in there with a video camera. He's gonna stay on Roxy every time the man shows himself. The minute he ever drives off in a car, Lovejoy is gonna have it on tape and show it to the cops."

"Ilona helps him out?"

"She drives him after school and they talk about Bernard, the kid. See, but now he's letting his business go to hell and his sister gets on him. Her and her husband, this big asshole that's always giving Lovejoy a hard time. It's good the way it starts out, but then it gets slow in the middle. You see Roxy, what he's doing. Likes to drink, likes to gamble, but you don't see him do anything so bad you get the idea the man's dangerous. You know what I'm saying? Like if Lovejoy gets too close and Roxy sees what he's doing, Lovejoy could get taken out. What I was thinking was if Lovejoy finds out the man's got some kind of crooked deal going."

"Using his place as a chop shop," Chili said. "Buys hot cars, cuts 'em up and sells the parts."

"Yeah, that's the kind of thing. Then get the woman in it, she's the one tells Lovejoy what the setup is."

"He catch the guy driving or not?"

"Yeah, he catches him, videos the man driving down the road. Catches him the last day he's gonna do this."

"The guy doesn't see him?"

"Never suspects a thing. So Lovejoy puts it on him, shows his tape to the cops. They pick up Roxy, there's a court hearing and what you suppose he gets? His license taken away again, this time for a year. Lovejoy is right back where he started only worse. He gets sued by Roxy for annoying him, invading his privacy, different other legal shit and the court decides in favor of Roxy. Lovejoy has to pay him a hundred thousand in damages. Coming out of court his sister is calling him a fool, saying now you have to sell your business and you got nothing. That's where I ended off." Catlett picked up the script. "With, yeah, fifteen pages to go."

Chili said, "You don't know how it ends? Take a look."

"I don't cheat, look at the end when I read something. But it's good, huh? What would you do," Catlett said, "you were Lovejoy?"

"I know guys," Chili said, "would cut Roxy in half with a chain saw."

"Yeah, but what would you do?"

"I'd have to think about it."

"I'd shoot the man in the head," Catlett said. "Set him up and do it."

"You like to think you would," Chili said. "Take a look, find out." Chili reached over, picked up one of the red-covered scripts from the desk and opened it. "What page you on?"

Catlett was looking at his script. "Ninety-two. They come out of the courthouse, his sister's on his ass. Then the brother-in-law, Stanley, gets on him."

Chili found the page, began to read:

EXT. COURTHOUSE—DAY

ANGLE ON Lovejoy's van pulling up in front. Ilona gets out, her expression distraught as she looks up and sees:

REVERSE—ILONA'S POV

Lovejoy and Helen coming out of the courthouse followed closely by Stanley. Helen is already speaking as they pause at the top of the stairs.

ANGLE ON LOVEJOY, HELEN AND STANLEY

Lovejoy sees Ilona, a wistful smile touches his face.

HELEN

You're so smart, aren't you? Now you have nothing, and you brought it all on yourself.

STANLEY

If you're thinking of coming to us for help, forget it.

Lovejoy turns to Stanley with a level gaze.

LOVEJOY

I wouldn't dream of it, Stanley. Besides, you both have your own problems.

STANLEY

(scowling)
What're you talking about?

LOVEJOY

Being married to each other.
(starts down the stairs)
Have a nice day.

ANGLE ON ILONA, WATCHING

As Lovejoy approaches and we hear Stanley CALL after him.

STANLEY (O.S.)

No more Sunday dinner at our house, Roger!

Lovejoy gives Ilona a wry grin.

LOVEJOY

At least some good has come of this.

They get in the van and drive off.

Chili looked at Catlett turning pages, skimming through the script. "I think when Stanley opens his mouth Lovejoy oughta pop him and walk away, not say a fuckin word."

"That's 'cause you don't know the man," Catlett said, turning another page. "Next, you see him alone in his flower shop watering some plants, thinking what he should do. The man likes working here and now he's gonna lose it. Next, you see him in the van again, going by Roxy's place."

Chili turned pages to catch up, came to a scene, Roxy—it looked like Roxy was having a party.

"Inside the office there," Catlett said, "Roxy's celebrating his putting it to Lovejoy, having drinks with his friends . . . Now you see Lovejoy in the van parked across the street, waiting, but we don't know what for. Looking like he's doing some more thinking . . . Back to Roxy, he's getting drunk, say he wants everybody to come out to his place on the lake . . . Now Lovejoy is listening to symphony music on the radio, still in the van . . . Roxy, inside the office, is now getting ugly, has a fight with the woman wants to take him home."

Chili turned some more pages. "What's I-N-T?"

"Interior," Catlett said. "Inside. Roxy goes out . . ."

"What's P-O-V?"

"Point of view. Lovejoy's P-O-V, like he's seeing it when Roxy comes out and gets in his Cadillac. Drives off—now we looking at the Cadillac through Lovejoy's windshield, following him."

Both Chili and Catlett turned a page.

"He's got the video camera with him," Chili said. "He's gonna get Roxy driving again."

"That's what he's doing," Catlett said.

"Roxy spots him."

"I could see that coming."

"He makes a sudden U-turn."

For several moments they both read in silence.

"I knew it," Catlett said. "He's on Lovejoy's ass now."

Chili kept quiet, reading the scene:

EXT. CITY STREETS—NIGHT

ANGLES ON the Cadillac chasing the van through traffic, squealing around corners, narrowly missing cars at intersections, the Cadillac sideswiping a parked car.

INTERCUT

Roxy at the wheel of the Cadillac, recklessly determined.

Lovejoy in the van, glancing at mirror apprehensively.

EXT. INTERSECTION—NIGHT

Quiet, little traffic, then none. Until suddenly the van comes around the corner and ducks into an alley. We SEE the rear lights go off. Now the Cadillac takes the corner and flies past the alley. After SEVERAL BEATS the van backs out, proceeds at a normal pace.

EXT. LOVEJOY'S FLOWER SHOP—NIGHT

The van arrives and parks at the curb across the street. Lovejoy gets out slowly, exhausted. As he starts across the street:

HEADLIGHTS POP ON

down the block. We hear an engine ROAR. And now a car, the Cadillac, is hurtling toward Lovejoy in the middle of the street, frozen in the highbeam of the headlights, *in the exact spot where his son was killed.*

Catlett said, "Hmmmm," sitting back, finished.

Chili said, "Wait," still reading, "don't say nothing." He was on the second to last page of the script.

INTERCUT

Roxy hunched over the steering wheel, wild-eyed.

Roxy's POV—to see Lovejoy through windshield.

CLOSE ON Lovejoy standing in the street.

REVERSE—Lovejoy's POV—car hurtling toward him.

Roxy's POV as Lovejoy suddenly bolts for the flower shop.

EXT. FLOWER SHOP—NIGHT

AN ANGLE—on the Cadillac swerving after Lovejoy, who dives out of the way just in time.

INT. CADILLAC—CLOSE ON ROXY

His look of horror as he sees:

THROUGH THE WINDSHIELD

The plate glass front of the flower shop suddenly in front of him.

INT. FLOWER SHOP (SLOW-MOTION SEQ.)—NIGHT

The Cadillac crashes through the plate glass, plows across the store interior to smash into the refrigerated showcase and come to a dead stop.

INT. FLOWER SHOP—ANOTHER ANGLE—NIGHT

Lovejoy enters, cautiously approaches the Cadillac, looks in to see:

ROXY IN CADILLAC

His bloody countenance among flowers, plants, the man obviously dead.

Chili turned to the last page. Now the cops are there, lot of activity. Medics come out with Roxy in a body bag. Lovejoy watches, depressed, looks up. There's Ilona. Ilona takes him aside and "with wisdom beyond her years" tells him it's over and a few other things about flowers, saying, "Besides, making things grow is your life." *Besides*—they used that word all the time in movies, but you hardly ever heard it in real life.

Catlett said, "Well?"

Chili looked up, closing the script.

Catlett said, "Didn't shoot him, like he should have."

"He didn't do *any*thing," Chili said. "The guy gets killed, yeah, but what's Lovejoy do?"

Catlett came up in the chair to lean on the desk.

"He makes it happen."

"What, he planned it? He dives out of the way to save his ass, that's all."

"What you don't understand," Catlett said, "is what the movie is saying. You live clean, the shit gets taken care of somehow or other. That's what the movie's about."

"You believe that?"

"In movies, yeah. Movies haven't got nothing to do with real life."

Chili was about to argue with him, but changed his mind and said, "I don't like the ending."

Catlett eased back again. "You want to change it?"

Chili didn't answer, looking at the ZigZag script cover, opening it then and looking at the title page.

MR. LOVEJOY

An Original Screenplay
by
MURRAY SAFFRIN

The title was the first thing that ought to be changed. And the guy's name. Murray Saffrin was better than Lovejoy.

"You don't care for the ending," Catlett said, "and I don't like the middle part. I'm thinking what we could do is fix it. You hear what I'm saying? Get some heat in it. Make the people's hands sweat watching it. You and me, we could do it. It's our kind of shit we talking about here. Like the action Roxy's into you mentioned, doing stolen cars."

"Fix up the girl's part," Chili said. An idea came to him and he said, "We might even be able to get Karen Flores."

Catlett looked up at him. "Karen Flores . . ."

"She's been out of movies a few years, but she's good."

Catlett said, "Karen Flores, I know that name . . ."

"Change the ending," Chili said, "so Lovejoy's the one makes it happen, he isn't just standing there."

"We could do all that," Catlett said, "you and me, sit down and write the script over where it needs it."

Chili opened the script again, flipped through a few pages looking at the format. "You know how to write one of these?"

"You asking me," Catlett said, "do I know how to write down words on a piece of paper? That's what you do, man, you put down one word after the other as it comes in your head. It isn't like having to learn how to play the piano, like you have to learn notes. You already learned in school how to write, didn't you? I *hope* so. You have the idea and you put down what you want to say. Then you get somebody to add in the commas and shit where they belong, if you aren't positive yourself. Maybe fix up the spelling where you have some tricky words. There people do that for you. Some, I've even seen scripts where I *know* words weren't spelled right and there was hardly any commas in it. So I don't think it's too important. You come to the last page you write in 'Fade out' and that's the end, you're done."

Chili said, "That's all there is to it?"

"That's all."

Chili said, "Then what do I need you for?"

HE HEARD THE ELEVATOR AS HE WAS OPENING THE door to 325, looked down the hotel hallway and saw Karen coming toward him, Karen in a loose-fitting white shirt and gray slacks. Chili pushed the door open and waited, two copies of *Lovejoy* under his arm.

"I was in the bar when you came in," Karen said. "I thought you saw me." He shook his head saying no, but was glad to see her now, motioning Karen to go in. She said, "Well, I read it." He followed her into the living room, the pagoda lamps still on, and dropped the scripts on the counter. A light on the phone was blinking on and off.

"You want to check your messages?"

"I can do it later," Chili said. "Sit down, make yourself comfortable. I want to hear what you think."

He took off his suitcoat as Karen went over to a fat chair next to the sofa.

"You read the script . . ."

"I could play the sister," Karen said, "and wear sensible shoes. That would be a switch."

Chili moved to the sofa, folding his suitcoat.

"I don't see you doing that one, the sister."

He laid the coat next to him as he sat down.

"But there isn't anything else, as it stands, you'd want to do."

"I wasn't really looking for a part."

"There could be a good one though. I got some ideas."

Karen said, "You do, huh?"

Looking at Karen he could see the phone on the counter above her, the message light blinking on and off. It would have to be Tommy, something about Bones maybe, or Nicki. He began telling Karen how he thought the script needed to be fixed, change the whore to make it a bigger part: how she helps Lovejoy out and pretty soon they have something going.

"The hooker and the florist," Karen said.

"You wouldn't have to be a hooker exactly."

"Mousse my hair and chew gum? Why don't you check your messages?"

"I can wait."

"You've read the script?"

"Not all of it, but I know what it's about."

"You and Harry'll make a great team. Has he read it?"

"He bought it, he must've."

"You sure? Harry used to have someone else read for him. Then he'd skim it if he thought he was going into production."

"He told me he read it twice."

"This one he might've. You like the idea?"

"Basically, yeah, except what I mentioned. The part I read, the ending, I didn't like 'cause it's a letdown. You know what I mean? Lovejoy's just standing there."

"What do you think he should do?"

"Well, if he's the star he's the one ought to make it happen. Get some action going that's his idea." She kept looking at him and he said, "I don't like the title either."

"Harry thinks he needs you," Karen said, "but he can't pay you anything, he's broke."

Chili said, "I know exactly how much he doesn't have."

"So what do you get out of it?"

"You came here to ask me that?"

She said, "I want to know," staring at him the way she did last night. It wasn't the old dead-eyed look exactly, but it wasn't bad.

"I like movies," Chili said. "I help Harry make one, I'll find out what you have to do outside of have an idea and raise the money. That doesn't sound too hard. I was in the money business and I get ideas all the time."

She looked so serious he had to smile at her.

"Then I'll do one, make a movie and put you in it."

He glanced at the message light on the phone flashing on and off.

Karen was still watching him.

She said, "I took your advice and made a deal with Harry.

Not to act in it. The way I see it, if I save Harry a half million by setting him up with Michael, I should have a piece of the action. I told him I want co-producer."

"What'd Harry say?"

"Harry would agree to anything. But I said I'd only do it if he can get a studio to put *Lovejoy* into development. So the first thing he has to do is sell the idea to Tower. That's where he wants to take it. He thinks he can handle Elaine Levin."

"What do you think?"

"If Elaine doesn't like the idea, Harry's not going to sell her on it. If she likes it, it could get made, with or without Michael."

Chili said, "The script still needs to be fixed."

"You know that," Karen said, "and you haven't even read it."

He watched her lean over to push out of the chair, then pause and toss her head as she looked at him again, her hair falling away from her eyes—and remembered Karen doing it with blond hair, giving the guy in the movie the same look.

She said, "This might work. You never know."

HE ASKED THE OPERATOR FOR HIS MESSAGES. SHE SAID, "Just a minute." He waited. She came back on saying, "A Karen Flores called. She didn't leave a message." The operator sounded Latin. "A Mr. Zimm called. He'll talk to you tomorrow." That was it.

Later on, watching *Taxi Driver* on TV, Chili kept thinking of the way Karen had looked at him and wondered if she was telling him something and if he should've asked her to stay and have a drink. But then when Robert De Niro shaved his hair into a Mohawk, Chili started thinking of Ray Bones, even though Ray Bones didn't have a Mohawk or look anything like Robert De Niro. Maybe it was all those guns De Niro had, wanting to shoot somebody.

15

CATLETT LIVED WAY UP IN THE HOLLYWOOD HILLS where you could see the lights of L.A. spread out in kind of a grid and hear coyotes yipping in the dark. Here were all these modern homes built on stilts hanging over the sides of cliffs and there were still wild animals running around free. Catlett, barefoot, wearing a white silk bathrobe, stood at the rail of his deck, nothing below it for about twelve stories to where faint voices were coming from a lit-up swimming pool, a bright little square of light blue down there in the night, a girl laughing now, a nice sound . . . while the Bear told about the Colombian mule, Yayo the yoyo, dumb son of a bitch, still out at the airport.

"Thinks they have him spotted."

"He call you?" Catlett said, his voice quiet. "How'd he know to do that?"

"He called Miami and they gave him our service number," the Bear said. "The service calls me and I call the yoyo at LAX. He says the focking guy you told him was a fed left, but two more focking guys just like him took his place. With those focking gones on their legs."

"Irritable, huh?"

"Making sounds like he's coming loose on us."

"Yeah, that's how those people are."

"He makes a run at the locker they'll grab him. Then you have to think," the Bear said, "pissed as he is, he could give us up too."

"Out of meanness," Catlett said, "or making a plea deal. You suppose you could go get him?"

"That's what I was thinking. Tell him the airport's too hot right now."

"I appreciate it," Catlett said.

"You want me to take him anyplace special?"

"I don't care, long as you get him out."

"I could take him home."

"Yeah, but don't let him go near Farrah, hear? How's the child?"

"Cute as a bug."

Catlett said, "Bear? Something else that's pressing. This man Chili Palmer, staying at the Sunset Marquis. I wonder you could do a read on him for me."

"Chili Palmer," the Bear said.

"Thinks he's mean. I wouldn't mind you ran into him. See if he's real."

"I could do that."

Catlett said, "Shit, everything at once. I also need to know where Harry Zimm's been hanging out. Put a limo on him"—Catlett starting to grin—"tail the motherfucker in a white stretch."

The Bear said, "I best take care of Yayo first," and left.

It was cool out on the deck, Catlett wearing just the thin robe, but felt good, some stars out and that clear sound of voices in the dark, the girl laughing again. People with style knowing how to live. It looked like they might be skinny-dipping down there, couple of pink shapes in the blue-lit square. Coyotes watching them from the bushes . . . Young coyote asks his daddy, What's that looks like a pussy over there? And his daddy says, It's what it is, boy. They might even be movie people, work either side of the camera, it didn't make any difference. They were the kind of people he wanted to associate with in his life, not have to fool with fools like Yayo anymore. Even if you had to watch your step in the movie business, keep from getting fucked over, at least the ones doing it had some style. Chili Palmer had it in his own way, *something*, but it was hard to put your finger on it. Chili Palmer looked like a mob guy and talked like one—not a movie mob guy, a real one—though he could maybe play one in a movie. He had the bullshit to make it work, if the camera didn't scare him. Ask him what did he bring to Harry's deal and he says, "Me." Catlett had to smile, by himself out on his deck and starting to shiver with cold, he had to smile at the man's bullshit. "Me." Or was it confidence he had in himself? Either way, it could work for him. And then saying what he did, if writing a script was so easy, saying, "What do I need you for?" He did know a few things about movies, who Morgan Freeman was and how to say Greta Scacchi's name, without looking like he'd know such things. He let you think he'd read the script but didn't get sassy when he got caught—no, he listened to it told, wanting to know. That showed confidence, too, didn't it? The man out in the open with himself. Maybe less bullshit about him than you think. Even though he looked and talked like a mob guy and those guys would bullshit you to death.

Catlett felt himself close to something here and said it out loud to hear it. "You close. You know it? You close." Thinking, Chili Palmer might know something about movies. Then saying out loud, "But you know more."

Time to quit thinking and start doing. Yeah.

Not let anything stand in the way. No.

Not Chili Palmer, not anybody.

RONNIE SAID, "I HAVE TO MAKE ALL THE DECISIONS around here? Why don't you decide for a change. It's not that hard, Cat. You want to go to Mateo's? The Ivy? You want to go to Fennel? Drive out to Santa Monica? Or we can run across the street to the Palm, I don't give a shit. But we have to eat, right?"

"I don't know," Catlett said, "do we?"

Give him a hard one like that, mess up his head.

"You have anything has to be done around here?"

There wasn't much that looked like business on Ronnie's desk. It stayed neat, his girl Marcella in the other office doing the scheduling and billing.

Ronnie said, "Not that I know of."

Catlett didn't have a desk. He sat across from Ronnie looking at Ronnie's cowboy boots up on the desk, ankles crossed, Ronnie low in his big chair, down behind there somewhere.

"Well, I know you got three cars out working. You got to pick up the producer coming in from New York, and later on the rock group that likes the white stretch. I know that much," Catlett said, "and I barely work here."

Ronnie said, "You know that, but you can't tell me where you want to have lunch. Hey, how about Chinois? The curried oysters with salmon pearls, mmmmm."

Catlett said, "How about Spago?" acting innocent, knowing they didn't serve lunch, and got a mean look from Ronnie. The last time they went there the woman tried to seat them over on the other side of the open kitchen and Ronnie went berserk, told her, "My fucking Rolls is in the front row outside and you want to put us in *back*?" The man had a point. You sat at the right tables if you expected to be recognized in this town. Ronnie's trouble was nobody remembered him.

Next, Catlett heard Ronnie's desk drawer open and saw Ronnie's automatic come edging out of the V between his crossed cowboy boots and heard Ronnie making gunfire sounds, *couuu, couuu,* the little guy playing with his Hardballer .45, a pistol ten inches long. *Couuu,* pretending he was shooting that lady maître d' at Spago.

"Put it away."

"I'm not pointing it at you."

"Ronnie?"

"Shit."

"In the drawer."

"I wouldn't mind somebody trying to rip us off," Ronnie said. "You know what this would do to a guy?"

"I know I'm not ever having lunch with you no more you don't put that thing away." Catlett waited, hearing the drawer slide open and close. "You have a delivery to make, don't you? Down to Palm Desert?"

"You want to take it?"

"They your friends, not mine."

Four years of this shit, being the buddy of an idiot. Earlier, when Catlett came in, he told Ronnie they were having trouble with Yayo and Ronnie said, "Which one's Yayo?" Four years retained on the books as Marketing Consultant, which meant sitting here with Ronnie deciding where to eat. Then having the martini lunches and watching him get shitfaced on those see-throughs. It meant going to Ronnie's parties with all the glitter twits. Watching Ronnie have his nose bleeds about every day. Put up with all that shit, it was still better than running a dope house or sitting in a boiler room selling fake bonds over the phone. Better than managing a string of bitchy ladies, better than thinking up the everyday kinds of hustles to get by . . . But not better than being in the movie business. He hadn't mentioned to Ronnie he'd read *Mr. Lovejoy* or said anything about it since their meeting with Harry. From now on it wouldn't be any of Ronnie's business.

"Hey, Cat? How about Le Dôme? We haven't been there in a while."

THEY GOT A NICE TABLE ON THE AISLE IN THAT MIDDLE section and Catlett waited for Ronnie to relax with his extra-dry martini before telling him he should take a rest. "You going down to Palm Desert anyway, why don't you stay awhile, take a month off, man, and ease out, share your toot with some nice young lady. You been working too hard."

Get the motherfucker out of his hair while he set up making his move.

Back in the office of Wingate Motor Cars Limited, past closing time and the help gone, Catlett sitting at Ronnie's desk starting to make plans, he got a call from the Bear.

"This guy's driving me nuts."

"Where you at?"

"Home. We were out at Universal—you know the studio tour? It's like Disneyland."

"You took Yayo?"

"I forgot I promised Farrah. Yeah, so I brought the yoyo along. All the guy does is bitch and say fock, in front of my little girl. I gotta dump him somewhere."

"Bring him by," Catlett said, "I'll talk to him."

STANDING AT THE WINDOW CATLETT WATCHED THE Bear's blue Dodge van come off Santa Monica, out of traffic and into the drive. By the time Catlett made his way through the offices and the reception room to the garage, the steel overhead door was coming down to seal off street sounds, Yayo was out of the van and the Bear, his Hawaiian shirt today full of blue and yellow flowers, was coming around the front end. There was one limo parked in the garage, the white stretch reserved for the rock group, and Catlett's car, a black Porsche 911.

He was in his shirtsleeves, a striped shirt with a tab collar, tie in place—had put it on thinking of Chili's shirt last night; it had looked pretty sharp.

Yayo could use a clean shirt and a shave, comb his hair, Yayo giving him the Tony Montana look with the lip curl. A man that didn't know how dumb he was.

"You have a nice time, Yayo?"

The little Colombian mule started out in Spanish before switching over to English, saying, "I tell this guy I want my focking money or you in trouble, man, believe me."

"There's no pleasing him," the Bear said, fooling with his beard. "I took his picture standing with this cutout of *Magnum P.I.*? Tom Selleck, looks real as can be. All he does is bitch."

Yayo turned enough to tell the Bear, "You think you funny. Is that it?"

"I took him to the *Miami Vice* Action Spectacular . . ."

"Man, it was shit."

"It opens," the Bear said, "here come Crockett and Tubbs on jet skis. It's like a movie set. You know, some shacks at the edge of the water, we're in the grandstand watching. The voice-over says, 'They have ruffled some feathers in flamingo land and the band of smugglers have a dynamite surprise waiting for them.' It's all low-grade special effects, but the tourists eat it up."

"It was all shit," Yayo told Catlett.

"He kept talking like that," the Bear said, "saying fock in front of my little girl."

Catlett frowned, a pained look. "He did?"

"Man wouldn't shut his mouth."

"Listen to me," Yayo said. "I wan' to leave this place, go home. Wha' you have to do, get the money and give it to me. Or give me some other money."

"I gave you the key," Catlett said. "That's all you need, and some patience."

Yayo had that lip curled saying, "I don't wan' no focking key. I wan' the money."

Catlett stood with his fingers shoved into his pockets. He shrugged saying, "Give it some time, pretty soon there won't be nobody watching you."

Yayo pointed a finger at him. He said, "Okay, man, I tell you something. I go the airport and open that focking locker. They bus' me, I tell them I come to get something for *you*, tha's all I know."

Catlett said, "Tha's all you know, huh? Wait here a minute, Yayo, I be back directly."

He left them: went back to Ronnie's office and got Ronnie's big AMT Hardballer .45 auto out of the center desk drawer and racked the slide, knowing Ronnie kept the piece loaded. Catlett walked through offices and the reception room to the garage, closed the door behind him and extended the Hardballer's long barrel at Yayo, walking up to within ten feet of the man. Yayo didn't move. The Bear didn't either.

Yayo cocked his head then and put his hands on his hips, giving Catlett a Tony Montana pose.

"The fock you doing with that?"

Catlett said, "I'm taking you out, Yayo," and shot him in the chest, the gun going off loud—man, it was loud—but didn't buck as much as Catlett expected. No, looking down at Yayo on the cement floor now among oil stains, arms flung out, eyes stuck wide open, he'd put that hole right where he'd aimed.

"Dead focking center, man."

"I get the feeling," the Bear said, "you done this before."

"Not in a while," Catlett said.

16

THE WAY CHILI FOUND OUT LEO THE DRY CLEANER'S room number at the Beverly Hills Hotel, he wrote *Larry Paris* on an envelope, handed it to the girl at the front desk and watched her stick the envelope in the mail slot for 207. It looked like 207, but he wasn't sure. So he used a house phone, around the corner by the entrance to the famous Polo Lounge, and asked for 207. The operator tried it, came back to say she was sorry, Mr. Paris wasn't answering. Chili, friendly because he was getting somewhere, told the operator Mr. Paris was probably still out at the track giving his money away. Ha ha. To double-check, Chili stepped into the Polo Lounge and ordered a Scotch at the bar.

He didn't see Leo or Leo's friend Annette waiting or Doug McClure or any faces he recognized from the silver screen. The room was crowded, six P.M., people at booths and little round tables, most of them probably tourists looking for movie stars. Harry said if anybody here even halfway resembled a star the rest of the tourists would say, "There's one. Isn't that, you know, he was in . . ." and some guy from out of town would have a few minutes of fame he'd never know about. Harry said there were guys in the picture business had their secretaries call them here; they get paged, everybody sees the phone brought to the table and then watch the schmuck talking to his secretary like he was making a deal and knew personally all the names he was dropping. Harry said the trouble with Hollywood, the schemeballs worked just as hard as the legit filmmakers.

The limo guy, Catlett, struck Chili as that type wanted to be seen. Looked good in his threads, sounded like he knew what he was talking about—the type of guy if he wasn't dealing drugs would be into some other kind of hustle. There were guys like him Chili knew by name in Miami, all five boroughs of New York and parts of Jersey. They gave you that stuff about having something in common, being from the street but different sides of it. You had to watch your back with guys like Catlett. Keep him away from Harry.

Earlier today Harry had called from his apartment on Franklin to say he'd come home to change but would be going right back to Karen's. "You know what I did? Asked her to come on the project as associate producer and she jumped at it." Chili was learning a little more about Harry every time the guy opened his mouth. "Karen dropped off the script at Tower and we're waiting to hear when Elaine can see us. Miss Bedroom Eyes. Listen to this. Elaine doesn't even take pitch meetings, but she'll do it for Karen. I'm telling you, bringing my old screamer aboard was a stroke of genius." Chili asked him, shouldn't the script be rewritten first, fixed up? Harry said, "What's wrong with it?" Chili told him point by point what he thought and Harry said, "Yeah, Karen mentioned that. It needs a polish, that's all. I'll cover that at the meeting. Don't worry about it."

Okay, for the time being he'd forget about *Lovejoy* and concentrate on Leo the dry cleaner, find him and get him out of town before Ray Bones showed up. Chili watched a waiter serving a tray of drinks, thinking he could sit here and get smashed and never even see Leo. Leo gets back, cleans up and goes out again without ever coming in here. It was watching the waiter with the drink order that gave Chili an idea, a way to get into Leo's suite.

He ordered a bottle of champagne, paid his tab and told the bartender he wanted the champagne put in room 207 right away, before his buddy got back, so it would be a surprise. The bartender acted like this was done all the time. Chili finished his drink and took the stairway to the second floor. Room 207 was right there, at an open center point where halls went off in three different directions, the wallpaper in the halls big green plants, or they might be palm-tree branches. About ten minutes later a room service waiter arrived with the champagne in a bucket and two glasses on a tray. Chili hung back by the stairway till the waiter had the door open, then moved fast to walk in right behind him saying, "Hey, I'm just in time," and handed the guy a ten-dollar bill.

THREE CIGARETTES AND A COUPLE GLASSES OF CHAMpagne later, he heard the key in the lock and watched the door open.

Leo came in wearing a sporty little plaid hat cocked on the side of his head. Leo still playing the high roller, not even dragging after all day at the track, not looking over this way either, going straight for the Chivas on the desk and having one out of the bottle, ahhh, before pulling a fat wad of cash out of his jacket, tossing it on the desk like it was change from the cab fare and then taking the jacket off, the shirt too, it was coming off, Leo getting down to his undershirt hanging on bony shoulders, but not touching the hat, the sporty hat stayed, Leo thinking he must look good in it or the hat brought him luck, Leo in his four-bills-a-day hotel suite having another swig from the bottle.

"You got no class."

The poor guy didn't move.

Not till Chili said, "Look at me, Leo."

Watching him now reminded Chili of the time in Vegas, Leo pinned to the roulette table, no escape, and finally coming around to say, "How much you want?" Leo the loser, no matter how much he won. Leo came around this time with the same hopeless look, but didn't say anything.

He was taking in the scene. Chili in his pinstripe, on the sofa. The champagne on the coffee table. But what caught Leo's eye and held his attention was sitting next to the champagne. His briefcase. The same one the bodyguard had carried for him in Vegas.

"I wouldn't think you're that dumb," Chili said, "leave over three hunnerd grand in the closet, underneath the extra blanket, but I guess you are."

For a second there Leo looked surprised. "I didn't know where else to keep it. Where would you?"

The guy was serious.

"You're here a while, what's wrong with a bank?"

"They report it to the IRS."

"You don't open an account, Leo, you put it in a deposit box. Dip in whenever you want."

He watched Leo nodding in his sporty hat and undershirt, thinking it over, what to do the next time he scammed an airline. Jesus, he was dumb.

"You been losing, huh?"

"I'm up twelve grand today."

"From when? You left Vegas with four-fifty."

"Who told you that?"

"Now you're down to three-ten in the briefcase. You must've cooled off quite a bit in Reno."

"Who says I was in Reno?"

The poor guy kept trying.

"Your friend Annette," Chili said.

Leo narrowed his eyes and stared, trying hard to fake who

he was. He raised his preshaped plaid hat and recocked it, see if that would help. No, there was nothing dumber than a dumb guy who thought he was a hotshot. You did have to feel a little sorry for him . . .

Till he said, "It was Fay, wasn't it, told you about Annette. She tell you my whole life history, for Christ sake?"

"I wouldn't let her if she tried," Chili said. "Why I'm here, Leo, basically, is to save your ass."

"How? By taking my money?"

"You can keep what you won today. That's yours."

"It's *all* mine," Leo said. "You don't have any right to it." Starting to whine. "You're some friend."

"No, I'm not your friend, Leo."

"I'll say you aren't. Come in and ruin my life. Why are you doing this to me? I paid you what I owed."

"Sit down, Leo."

Leo had to think about it, but he did. Went to the deep chair facing the coffee table, sat down and stared at his briefcase.

Chili said, "I don't know how you stayed in business, Leo, you're so fuckin dumb. Or how you ever got this far. But now you're through. I'm gonna explain to you why and I hope you're not too dumb you don't understand what I'm saying. Okay?"

So Chili laid it out, told how Ray Bones was now in the picture and the kind of guy Bones was, the reason Leo and Annette would have to disappear or else risk serious injury. That seemed simple enough, a no-option kind of situation.

Leo thought about it a minute and said, "Well, I'm not going home."

Look how his mind worked.

"I don't care where you go, Leo."

"I mean back to Fay."

"That's up to you."

"After what she did to me?"

"You aren't only dumb, Leo, you're crazy."

Leo thought about it another minute and said, "I don't see any difference who takes the money, you or this other guy. Either way I'm cleaned out."

"Yeah, but there different ways of getting cleaned out," Chili said. "Ray Bones'll take everything you have—"

"What—you won't?"

"Leo, listen to me. When I say everything, I mean even that sporty hat if he wants it. Your watch, that pinkie you have on . . . and then he'll hit you with some kind of heavy object if he doesn't shoot you, so you won't tell on him. I won't do that," Chili said, "take your jewelry or hurt you. You have three-ten in the case, right? I'm gonna take the three hundred you scammed off the airline, but the rest of it, the ten grand? I'm gonna borrow that and pay you back sometime."

He knew Leo wouldn't understand what he meant, Leo squinting at him now.

"You take all my money, but you're borrowing part of it?"

"At eighteen percent, okay? And don't ask me no more questions, I'm leaving," Chili said.

He picked up the briefcase as he rose from the sofa and Leo came up out of his chair.

"You're saying you want me to *loan* you the ten grand?"

"I'm not asking you, Leo. What I'm saying is I'm gonna pay you back."

"I don't understand."

"You don't have to. Let's leave it at that."

"Yeah, but how're you gonna pay me?"

Chili was moving toward the door. "Don't worry about it."

"I mean you won't know where I am. I don't even know where I'll be."

"I'll find you, Leo. You leave a trail like a fuckin caterpillar." Chili reached the door and opened it.

Leo saying now, "Wait a minute. What's this eighteen-percent-a-year shit? You want to borrow ten, the vig's three bills a week. You hear me?" Chili crossing the hall toward the stairway, shaking his head, Leo yelling after him, "Fifteen for the vig plus the ten, that's twenty-five big ones you go a whole year, buddy! You hear me?"

Chili stopped. He turned around. As he started back he saw Leo's scared look just before he slammed the door shut. Jesus, he was dumb.

17

HE THOUGHT RAJI'S WOULD BE A COCKTAIL LOUNGE with entertainment, a Hollywood nightspot. It turned out to be a bar with pinball machines and video games making a racket, also a counter where you could buy Raji's T-shirts, in case you wanted to show you had actually come in here. Sometimes it was hard to keep an open mind. Chili, in his pinstripe suit, nice tie, wondered if any regular people came here or just these kids trying to look like heroin addicts. He said to one of them, "How come there's no sign out in front?"

The kid said, "There isn't?"

He said to the kid, "I see they have Yul Brynner in the sidewalk outside."

Part of Hollywood's famous Walk of Fame, the names of 1,800 show-biz celebrities inlaid in stars.

The kid said, "Who's Yul Brynner?"

Chili said to the bartender, a young guy who looked normal, "How come there's no sign out in front?" The bartender said it was down temporarily while they reinforced the building against earthquakes. Chili asked him how come there weren't any barstools? The bartender said it was a stand-up kind of place: A and R guys from the record companies didn't like to sit down, they'd catch a group and then come back upstairs to have their conversation, where you could hear yourself think. He told Chili Guns N' Roses had been signed out of here. Chili said no shit and asked if Nicki was around. There were "Nicki" posters by the entrance. The bartender said she was downstairs but wouldn't be on for a couple hours yet.

"You in records?"

"Movies," Chili said.

He had never made it with Nicki or even tried, but she still ought to remember him. The idea, get her to ask him to drop by the house, say hello to Michael and he'd take it from there. Get next to him. *Look at me, Michael.* See what happens.

Chili went downstairs to an empty room with a bar and a few tables, hearing a band tuning up, hitting chords. It reminded him of bands at Momo's cranking up, doing sound checks, setting those dials just right, then blasting off loud enough to blow out the windows and he'd wonder what all that precision adjusting was for. Maybe they said they were reinforcing the place against earthquakes, but it was to keep the rockers from shaking the walls down, and that's why they played in the basement here: the bandstand through an archway in a separate room that was like a cave in there and maybe would hold a hundred people standing up.

There were four guys, three with guitars and a guy on the drums. He didn't see Nicki anywhere, just these four skinny guys, typical rock-and-roll assholes with all the hair, bare arms tricked out with tattoos and metal bracelets, all of them with that typical bored way they had. Looking over at him now standing in the archway, but too cool to show any interest. Some dickhead in a suit. Chili stared back at them thinking, Oh, is that right? Any you assholes want to be in the movies? No chance. They were turned toward each other now, one of them, with wild blond hair sticking out in every direction, talking as the others listened. Now the blond-haired one was looking over this way again, saying, "Chil?" The middle one.

Christ, it was Nicole, Nicki. They all looked like girls—that's why he thought she was a guy.

"Nicki? How you doing?"

He should've spotted her, the skinny white arms, no tattoos. Nicki handed her guitar that had a big bull's-eye painted on it to one of the guys and was coming over now, Nicki in black jeans that were like tights on her and, Christ, big work boots, smiling at him. Chili put his arms out as she raised hers, high, and saw dark hair under there in the sleeveless T-shirt, Nicki saying, "Chili, Jesus!" glad to see him and it was a nice surprise, knowing she meant it. Now she was in his arms, that slender body tight against him, arms around his neck giving him a hug, hanging on, while he kept thinking of her armpits, the dark tufts under there like a guy's, though she certainly felt like a girl. Nicki let go but kept grinning at him, saying, "I don't believe this." Then saying over her shoulder to the guys, "I was right, it's Chili, from Miami. He's a fucking gangster!"

The way they were looking at him now—he didn't mind her saying it.

"That's your new band, huh? They as good as the one you used to have?"

Nicki said, "What, at Momo's? Come on, that was techno-disco pussy rock. These guys *play.*" She took him by the arm over to a table, telling how she met them in the parking lot of the Guitar Center, standing there with their Marshall stacks, and couldn't believe her luck 'cause these kids could play speed riffs as good as—"You know the kind Van Halen did on 'Eruption' and every metal freak in the world copied? . . . No, you don't. What am I talking about? Eight years ago you were still into Dion and the Belmonts, all that doo-wop shit."

" 'I'm just a lonely teenager,' " Chili said.

"Right, and 'I Wonder Why.' Who do you listen to now?"

"Guns N' Roses, different ones." He had to think fast. "Aerosmith, Led Zeppelin . . ."

"You're lying. Aerosmith, that's who I was listening to in Miami, way back when. I'll bet you're a Deadhead, you dig that California acid Muzak."

"Let's have a cigarette," Chili said, sitting at the table with her now. "I wasn't sure you'd recognize me."

"You kidding? You're the only guy at Momo's didn't try to jump me."

"It crossed my mind a few times."

"Yeah, but you didn't make a big deal about it, like Tommy! I had to beat him off with a stick." She reached across the table to put her hand on his. "What're you *doing* here anyway?"

"I'm making a movie."

"Come on—"

"And you live with a movie star."

"Michael, yeah." She didn't sound too happy about it. She didn't sound unhappy either. Glancing at her watch, Nicki said, "He's gonna stop by. You want to meet him?"

Just like that.

"Yeah, I wouldn't mind."

"Michael won't stay for the performance, too many people. Crowds scare the shit out of him, like he's afraid he'll get mobbed."

"Sure, the guy's a star. Not only that, he can act."

"I know," Nicki said, "he's incredible. His new one, *Elba*? It isn't out yet—I caught some of the dailies when they were shooting. You see Michael, he *is* Napoleon. He doesn't play him, I mean he *is* this fucking military genius, man, this little guy . . ." She drew on her cigarette looking toward the bandstand. "I have to get back."

"How'd you meet him?"

"At a performance. I was with a metal group, Roadkill? They're still around. They try to sound like Metallica, straight-ahead rock with a lot of head banging. I had to fucking sing and throw my hair at the same time, only it was shorter then so I had to wear extensions. I remember thinking—this was about a year and a half ago—if only I was a light-skinned black chick I could make it on my voice, not have to do this shit."

"Michael saw you perform . . ."

"I guess he was in a particular mode at the time." Nicki tapped her cigarette over the ashtray, maybe giving it some thought. "Sees me up there thrashing, this chick in geekwear, shitkickers, hair under my arms . . . He still won't let me shave. I guess I fill some need. He works, I work and in between we kick back. We do drugs, but not all the time. I wouldn't call either of us toxic. We play tennis, we have a screening room, a satellite dish, twelve TV sets, seventeen phones, a houseman, maids, a laundress, gardeners, a guy who comes twice a week to check out the cars . . . But where am I really? Down in a basement with a sticky floor and three guys barely out of Hollywood High. I feel like I'm their mother."

"Why don't you get married?"

"You mean to Michael? I don't think I would even if he asked me."

"Why not?"

"What's the point? It's not like, wow, I'd be making it, something I've always wanted. You get married, then what? All it does is fuck up your life, especially marrying an actor. Look at Madonna . . . No, don't. I don't have all that underwear going for me. I'm a rock-and-roll singer and that's it, man, nothing else." She looked off toward the bandstand. "Listen, I have to go. But when Michael comes, I'll introduce you."

"Yeah, I wouldn't mind talking to him, he has time."

"You want him to do a movie?"

"We're thinking about it."

"Good luck." Nicki stubbed out her cigarette before looking up at him again. "We're gonna open tonight, play around with the Stones' 'Street Fighting Man.' What do you think?"

With that innocent straight face, putting him on.

It took Chili four seconds to find the album cover and the title in his mind from twenty years ago, the concert recorded live at the Garden and Tommy playing the record over and over, Tommy at the time stoned on the Stones.

Chili said, straight-faced back to her, "From *Get Yer Ya-Ya's Out,* huh? That one?"

It got Nicki smiting at him, looking good, those nice blue eyes shining. She said, "You're a cool guy, Chil, without even trying."

THEY'D START A NUMBER, RACE INTO IT AND STOP AND Nicki would play part of it over on her bull's-eye guitar, slower, smoother, and then one of the guitar players would pick it up, imitating, give a nod and the drummer would kick them off again. They might be good—Chili couldn't tell. Hearing a line of music by itself, when Nicki showed them how, it sounded okay, but all of them playing together came out as noise and was irritating.

Thinking of that album cover again, he seemed to recall a guy in an Uncle Sam hat jumping up in the air with a guitar in each hand. He liked the Rolling Stones then, back in the hippie days, all the flakes running around making peace signs. It made him think of the time they grabbed this hippie, dragged him into Tommy Carlo's cousin's barbershop and zipped all his fuckin hair off with the clippers. He thought of that and started thinking of Ray Bones again and Leo the dry cleaner, his calling Leo dumb for leaving three hundred grand in a hotel-room closet, and where was it now? Under his bed at the Sunset Marquis. He'd check, make sure Leo and Annette had taken off, just to be on the safe side. Later tonight he'd call Fay, tell her to look for three hundred big ones coming by Express Mail. Put it in one of those containers they gave you at the post office. He'd hang on to the extra ten grand. Maybe pay off Ray Bones, get that out of the way, or maybe not. But the three hundred, basically, was Fay's. Let her do whatever she wanted with it. Two to one she'd tell a friend of hers about it and pretty soon the suits would come by, knock on the door, flash their I.D.'s . . .

He wondered what would've happened if he'd brought Fay with him to Vegas . . .

And realized he was thinking of it as a movie again, the way he had told it to Harry and Karen, but seeing new possibilities, getting the woman, Fay, into the story more, looking at it the same way he had looked at *Lovejoy* and saw what was needed. Fay comes to L.A. with him . . .

Except it wouldn't be *him,* it would be an actor, Jesus, like Robert De Niro playing the shylock. And for Fay . . .

Karen. Why not? Karen even had kind of a you-all accent, though it wasn't as downhome as the way Fay talked. Okay, now, by the time they get to L.A. they realize they're hot for each other and aren't even sure they want to find her husband, Leo, except he's got all that fuckin dough. Do they want it? They know somebody who does, Ray Bones, he's coming after them and he'll kill for that money.

It didn't sound too bad.

You have Leo pulling the scam on the airline in the opening . . .

Or, no, you start with the shylock and Fay waiting for Leo to come home from the track, while actually he's out at the airport getting smashed and the jet takes off without him and goes down in the swamp, blows up.

So you have the shylock, basically a good guy, a former shylock, played by Bobby De Niro. You have Karen Flores making her successful comeback as Fay . . . She wouldn't have a sweaty job, she could be something else, an entertainer, a singer. You have Leo . . . You wouldn't have Harry in it or the limo guys—it wasn't a movie about making a movie—but you'd have Ray Bones in it. Leo would be a tough one to cast. Get an actor who could play a good sleazeball . . . It took Chili a moment to realize the room was quiet. Nicki and her guys were looking this way, but not at him. He looked over . . .

And saw Michael Weir.

It was, it was Michael Weir crossing the room from the stairs, giving Nicki a wave, the other hand in his pants pocket, baggy gray pants too long for him. Chili saw that as part of the whole picture, his first look at Michael Weir in person, white Reeboks too. But what caught and held his attention was Michael Weir's jacket. It was like the one left at Vesuvio's twelve years ago, that worn-out World War Two flight jacket nobody wanted. It was exactly like it. On a guy that made seven million bucks a movie.

Now Michael Weir had his hand raised to the band. Chili heard him say, "Hey, guys," and it was his voice, Chili recognized it from movies. Michael Weir was good at accents, but you could still tell his voice, kind of nasal. The cock-rockers gave him a nod, not too impressed, these young drop-outs with their hair and their guitars. Now it looked like Michael was joking around with them, doing the moonwalk and pretending he was strumming a guitar. He was good, but the guys still didn't seem impressed. Michael turned to Nicki and right away she grabbed his arm and Chili saw them coming this way, Nicki doing the talking, Michael Weir looking up and then Nicki looking up as she said, “Chil? I’d like you to meet Michael.”

Chili got to his feet, ready to shake hands with a superstar. What surprised him now was how short the guy was in real life.

18

IT TOOK CHILI A COUPLE OF MINUTES TO FIGURE MICHAEL Weir out. He wanted people to think he was a regular guy, but was too used to being who he was to pull it off.

The two of them sitting at the table now, Chili asked him if he wanted a drink. Michael, watching Nicki and her band through the archway, said yeah, that sounded like a good idea. Chili asked him what he wanted. Michael said oh, anything. Did he want Scotch, bourbon, a beer? Michael said oh, and stopped and said no, he'd like a Perrier. Still watching Nicki and the band. They hadn't started to play. Chili looked over at the bar, not open yet, thinking he'd have to go all the way upstairs to get the movie star his soda water. Right then Michael said, "They're a tough audience."

Chili noticed the movie star's expression, eyebrows raised, like he'd just heard some bad news but was more surprised than hurt.

"My Michael Jackson went right by them."

Oh—meaning his moonwalk routine. Chili said, "It looked good to me." It did.

"To do it right you put on a touch of eye makeup, white socks, the glove . . . I was a little off on the voice too, the baby-doll whisper?"

Chili said, "I couldn't hear that part."

"But I can understand it, guys like that, their attitude. It has to do with territorial imperative."

Chili said, "That must be it," feeling more at ease with the movie star, knowing a bullshitter when he met one. It didn't mean the guy wasn't good.

"I'm not certain why," Michael said, "but it reminds me of the one, the third-rate actor doing Hamlet?" Michael smiling with his eyes now. "He's so bad that before long the audience becomes vocally abusive, yelling at him to get off the stage. They keep it up until the actor, finally, unable to take any more, stops the soliloquy and says to the audience, 'Hey, what're you blaming me for? I didn't write this shit.' "

Now they were both smiling, Michael still doing his with his eyes, saying, "I could tell those kids I didn't invent Michael Jackson . . . someone else did." Chili wondering, if it doesn't bother him, why didn't he just drop it? Chili looking for the right moment to bring up *Mr. Lovejoy.*

He was ready to get into it, said, "Oh, by the way . . ." and Nicki's band kicked off, filling the room with their sound, and Michael turned his chair to face the bandstand through the archway. They were loud at first, but then settled down and it wasn't too bad, more like rhythm and blues than rock and roll. The beat got the tips of Chili's fingers brushing the table. Michael sat with his hands folded in his lap, his legs in the baggy pants stretched out in front of him, ankles crossed, the laces of one of his Reeboks loose, coming untied. He looked more like in his thirties than forty-seven. Not a bad-looking guy, even with the nose, Chili studying his profile. There was no way to tell if Michael liked the beat or not. Chili thought of asking him, but had the feeling people waited for the movie star to speak first, give his opinion and then everybody would say yeah, that's right, always agreeing. Like with Momo, the few times Chili saw him in the social club years ago, noticing the way the guys hung on to whatever Momo said. It was like you had to put kneepads on to talk to this man who never worked in his life.

Chili leaned into the table saying, "You might not remember, but we met one time before."

He gave the movie star time to look over.

"In Brooklyn, when you were making *The Cyclone,* that movie."

Michael said, "You know, I had a feeling we'd met. I couldn't quite put my finger on it, the occasion. Chil, is it?"

"Chili Palmer. We met, it was at a club on 86th Street, Bensonhurst. You dropped by, you wanted to talk to some of the guys."

"Sure, I remember it very well," Michael said, turning his chair around to the table.

"You were, I guess you were seeing what it was like to be one of us," Chili said, locking his eyes on the movie star's the way he looked at a slow pay, a guy a week or two behind.

"Yeah, to listen more than anything else."

"Is that right?"

"Pick up your rhythms of speech."

"We talk different?"

"Well, different in that the way you speak is based on an attitude," the movie star said, leaning in with an elbow on the table and running his hand through his hair. Chili could see him doing it on the screen, acting natural. "It's like ya tone a voice," the movie star said, putting on an accent, "says weah ya comin' from." Then back to his normal voice, that had a touch of New York in it anyway, saying, "I don't mean where you're from geographically, I'm referring to attitude. Your tone, your speech patterns demonstrate a certain confidence in yourselves, in your opinions, your indifference to conventional views."

"Like we don't give a shit."

"More than that. It's a laid-back attitude, but with an intimidating edge. Cut-and-dried, no bullshit. Your way is the only way it's going to be."

"Well, you had it down cold," Chili said. "Watching you in the movie, if I didn't know better I'd have to believe you were a made guy and not acting. I mean you *became* that fuckin guy. Even the fink part," Chili said, laying it on now. "I never met a fink and I hope to God I never do, but how you did it must be the way finks act."

The movie star liked that, starting to nod, saying, "It was a beautiful part. All I had to do was find the character's center, the stem I'd use to wind him up and he'd play, man, he'd play." The movie star nodding with Nicki's beat now, eyes half closed, like he was showing how to change into somebody else, saying, "Once I have the authentic sounds of speech, the rhythms, man, the patois, I can actually begin to think the way those guys do, get inside their heads."

Like telling how he studied this tribe of natives in the jungles of Brooklyn. That's how it sounded to Chili.

He said, "Okay, I'm one of those guys you mention. What am I thinking?"

The movie star put on an innocent look first, surprised. What? Did I say something? The look gradually becoming a nice-guy smile. He ran both hands through his hair this time.

"Don't get me wrong, I'm not saying an actual metamorphosis takes place, I become one of you. That wouldn't be acting. I had the opportunity one time, years ago, to ask Dame Edith Evans how she approached her parts and she said, 'I pretend, dear boy, I pretend.' Well, I'll get involved in a certain life, observe all I can, because I want that feeling of realism, verisimilitude. But ultimately what I do is practice my craft, I act, I pretend to be someone else."

"So you don't know what I'm thinking," Chili said, staying with it.

It got another smile, a tired one. "No, I don't. Though I have to say, I'm curious."

"So, you want to know?"

"If you'd like to tell me, yeah."

"I'm thinking about a movie."

"One of mine?"

"One we're producing and we want you to be in," Chili said, seeing the movie star's eyebrows go up, and one of the arms in the worn-out leather jacket, raising his hand as Chili tried to tell him, "It's one you already know about, you read."

But Michael wasn't listening, he was saying, "Wait. Time out, okay?" before lowering his arm and settling back. "I don't want to come off sounding rude, because I appreciate your interest and I'm flattered, really, that you'd think of me for a part. But, and here's the problem. My agent won't let me go anywhere near an independently financed production, I'm sorry."

Chili got to say, "It isn't that kind—" and the hand shot up again.

"My manager along with my agent, the business heads, they've made it our policy. Otherwise, I'm sure you can understand, I'd have pitches coming at me from independents day and night." The movie star shrugged, helpless, his gaze moving off to the band.

"You think I'm talking about wiseguy money," Chili said. "No way. This one's gonna be made at a studio."

It brought the movie star partway back.

"I'm not connected to those people anymore. Not since I walked out of a loan-shark operation in Miami."

That brought the movie star all the way back with questions in his eyes, sitting up, interested in the real stuff.

"What happened? The pressure got to you?"

"Pressure? I'm the one applied the pressure."

"That's what I mean, the effect that must've had on you. What you had to do sometimes to collect."

"Like have some asshole's legs broken?"

"That, yeah, or some form of intimidation?"

"Whatever it takes," Chili said. "You're an actor, you like to pretend. Imagine you're the shylock. A guy owes you fifteen grand and he skips, leaves town."

"Yeah?"

"What do you do?"

Chili watched the movie star hunch over, narrowing his shoulders. For a few moments he held his hands together in front of him, getting a shifty look in his eyes. Then gave it up, shaking his head.

"I'm doing Shylock instead of *a* shylock. Okay, what's my motivation? The acquisition of money. To collect. Inflict pain if I have to." Michael half-closed his eyes. "My father used to beat me for no reason . . . Take the money I earned on my paper route, that I kept in a cigar box . . ."

"Hold it," Chili said. "I was a shylock—what do I look like?"

"That's right, yeah," Michael said, staring at Chili, his expression gradually becoming deadpan, sleepy.

"You the shylock now?"

"Guy owes me fifteen large and takes off, I go after him," the movie star said. "The fuck you think I do?"

"Try it again," Chili said. "Look at me."

"I'm looking at you."

"No, I want you to look at me the way I'm looking at you. Put it in your eyes, 'You're mine, asshole,' without saying it."

"Like this?"

"What're you telling me, you're tired? You wanta go to bed?"

"Wait. How about this?"

"You're squinting, like you're trying to look mean or you

need glasses. Look at me. I'm thinking, You're mine, I fuckin own you. What I'm *not* doing is feeling anything about it one way or the other. You understand? You're not a person to me, you're a name in my collection book, a guy owes me money, that's all."

"The idea then," the movie star said, "I show complete indifference, until I'm crossed."

"Not even then. It's nothing personal, it's business. The guy misses, he knows what's gonna happen."

"How about this?" the movie star said, giving Chili a nice dead-eyed look.

"That's not bad."

"This's what I think of you, asshole. Nothing."

"I believe it," Chili said.

"I turn it on when I confront the guy."

"Yeah, but you haven't found him yet."

Chili watched the movie star wondering what he was supposed to do next, giving him a strange look, Chili wondering himself exactly what he was doing, except he could see it right there in his mind so he kept going.

"The guy took off for Las Vegas."

"How do I know that?" The movie star picking up on it.

"The guy's wife tells you."

Chili paused, the movie star waiting.

"Yeah?"

"The wife wants to go with you on account of her husband skipped with all her money . . . three hundred grand," Chili said, starting to roll and not seeing anywhere to stop, "they conned off an airline after this jet crashed the guy was supposed to be on but wasn't and everybody was killed."

The movie star was looking at him funny again.

"If the guy wasn't on the plane . . ."

"He was, but he got off just before it left and blew up. So his bag's on the plane, his name's on the passenger list . . ."

"The wife sues the airline," the movie star said, nodding. "This is a gutsy babe."

"Good looking too."

"The husband takes off with the money, plus he still owes me the fifteen large," Michael the shylock said, "and the wife and I take off after him. Go on. When do I meet up with the guy and give him the look?"

Chili had to think about it. Tell Michael what actually happened or what he thought would sound better?

"It's not that simple," Chili said. "You have to be careful. Leo, the husband, isn't much to worry about, outside of he could try and nail you from behind if you get close. But there's another guy that comes along, a hard-on you happen to owe money to. A mob guy. He knows about the three hundred grand and would like to take you out anyway, on account of a past situation."

This time when Chili paused, wondering how to get back to where this thing had started, the movie star said, "This actually happened, didn't it? It's a true story."

"Basically," Chili said.

"You're the shylock."

"I was at one time."

"So, did you find the guy? What's his name, Leo?"

"I found him," Chili said, "yeah."

That was a fact. But now he didn't know what else to say, or how he actually got this far into it.

"You understand, you're pretending you're a shylock."

"Yeah? Go on."

"I mean that's all we're doing. You wanted to see if you can think like a shylock, get in his head. So I gave you a situation, that's all."

"You're not going to tell me the rest?"

"At this point, basically, that has to be it."

Michael was giving him a strange look again: not so confused this time, more like he was figuring something out. He said, "Well, if you won't, you won't," and started to grin. "I don't know how long you've been in the business, but that was the most ingenious pitch I've ever had thrown at me, and I mean in my entire career. You got me playing the guy, the shylock, before I even realized it was a pitch. So now I have to read the script to find out what happens. Beautiful. Really, that was artfully done."

Chili said, "Well, actually . . ." The movie star had his head turned and was watching Nicki and her group wailing away. "Actually, what I started to mention, the movie we want you to be in is *Mr. Lovejoy.* We understand you read the script and like it . . . a lot."

Now he had to wait for this to make sense, give the movie star time to think about it. Michael said, *"Lovejoy,"* looking over again. "That's the one, the florist sees his boy run over?"

"And goes after the guy, to catch him driving his car."

"What production company was that?"

"ZigZag, Harry Zimm."

"That's right, the slime-people guy. I read for Harry when I first started working in features. I didn't get the part."

Chili said, "He turned you down? Come on."

"I wasn't Michael Weir then," Michael said.

He wasn't kidding either. It sounded strange.

"Anyway, we're going to Tower Studios with it," Chili said, and that got a smile from Michael.

He said, "You know what they say about Elaine Levin. She fucked her Rolodex to get where she is. But I'll tell you something, she didn't have to if she did. Elaine knows what she's doing. She made an awful lot of money for Metro up to the time they forced that disaster on her. Did you see it, *San Juan Hill*?"

"I liked it," Chili said.

"It wasn't a bad picture," Michael said. "It had the facts

right for once, the black troops saving Teddy Roosevelt's ass, but that didn't sell tickets and it was way overproduced. The picture cost more than the actual war, which hadn't been done to my knowledge since *A Message to Garcia* with John Boles. I remember a script called *Siboney,* the same war, I thought very seriously about doing. That was a fascinating period, the U.S. emerging as a world power, the enactment of the Monroe Doctrine, eminent domain . . . I might look at that script again, *Siboney.* That was where our troops landed in Cuba."

"Sounds good," Chili said, not having any idea what the guy was talking about. He tried to get back to *Lovejoy* with, "Listen, what we're thinking—"

But Michael was already saying, "The title does have a nice sound. Build the score around the song. Si-bo-ney, da da *da* da . . ."

Christ, now he was singing it, against the rock beat in the background.

"Da da *da* da, Si-bo-ney . . . It's an old piece but has all kinds of dramatic riffs in it. It can be stirring, romantic, militaristic. Someone like John Williams could score the ass off that picture."

Chili said, "What I wanted to mention . . ." and paused. The room was quiet again, the band finished with their number. "We're definitely gonna produce the movie at a studio."

Michael Weir nodded. But now he was getting up, looking over at Nicki raising her guitar strap over her head. He said, "I guess we're taking off. It was nice talking to you."

"You have to go, huh?"

"Nicki's waiting. We're going to duck out . . ."

"But you like *Lovejoy*?"

"I like the character, the guy, he has possibilities. But the way the plot develops it turns into a B movie by the time you're into the second act. Take a look at *The Cyclone* again, the way a visual fabric is maintained even while the metaphor plays on different levels, with the priest, with the mother . . . so that you never lose sight of the picture's thematic intent,"

Chili said, "Yeah, well, we're already making changes. Getting a girl in it, fixing up the ending . . ."

"Sounds good."

"Can we talk about it, you get a chance?"

"Anytime," Michael Weir said, moving away. "Call Buddy and we'll set something up."

"Buddy?"

"My agent," the movie star said. "Harry knows him."

CHILI OPENED THE DOOR TO 325 TO SEE THE MESSAGE light on the phone blinking on and off. He lit a cigarette before dialing the operator.

She said, "Just a minute." The one with maybe a Latin accent. She came back on saying, "A Mr. Zimm called. You have a meeting tomorrow, three P.M. at Tower Studios. He'll call you in the morning. Let's see. And a Mr. Carlo called. He said he was going out for the evening and to tell you . . . Mr. Barboni will arrive tomorrow on Delta Flight Eighty-nine at twelve-oh-five. You like me to repeat that?"

Chili told her thanks anyway.

19

CATLETT WAS THINKING MAYBE THE BEST WAY WOULD be if Lovejoy did have a gun and shot Roxy with it to get his satisfaction.

He was dressed casual today, white linen jacket over French blue India cotton, sitting in Ronnie's chair in Ronnie's office waiting for the Bear to come in and report, Marcella's radio playing Top 40 hits in the other office. There was no reason for her to come in here; Marcella was the kind you said hi to and bye to, you didn't chat with her.

The audience would like it: see Lovejoy open this old trunk of his, take out a big revolver and load it. Be dramatic, that part, except this was movies and the kind of good guy Lovejoy was couldn't just go out and shoot the bad guy—like you drive past a man's house was edging into your business and shoot him off his front steps. Or another time the man was sitting in his car, pull up next to him, *bam*. The way it was done in real life. The way soon as Yayo threatened him, bye-bye, Yayo, the mean little Colombian now two feet under the desert somewhere off U.S. 10. The Bear had said, "Never again. I don't clean up after, become an accessory." The Bear due here any minute now. Yayo's people in Miami had called asking where he was and Catlett told them, "I saw him take the bag from the locker. He never came back? You have any friends down in Old Mexico could look into it? Check out Acapulco? Ixtapa?" Something you could pull on those people one time only. Losing a hundred and seventy grand and a mule was worth a phone call; it ever happened again, they'd be out. Man, but that money and the stepped-on bag of product in the locker could come in handy for something else now, the way Catlett was looking at his future: his mind going from Lovejoy to Chili Palmer, but most of the time stuck on Chili Palmer and the need to get the man out of the picture.

THE BEAR BROUGHT FARRAH AND A VIDEO GAME THEY plugged into the TV, something to occupy the child while the Bear made his report.

"One, according to the plane ticket on his dresser he's C. Palmer. Flew here from Vegas and has an open return to Miami. Two, also on the dresser, an Express Mail receipt for a package he sent to a person by the name of Fay Devoe in Miami. Three, the label in his suit and a couple of sport coats are all a men's store in Miami. So what does that tell you?"

Catlett was watching the little girl playing Top Gun, three years old in a jet fighter, zapping bandits out of the sky. He said, "Look at that child."

"I mean what else does it tell you," the Bear said, "outside of he's from Miami?"

"Not what you're thinking," Catlett said. "That he's connected to Yayo? Uh-unh. He was here before Yayo, has nothing to do with product, or he'd have made some mention of it or let it slip. What else have you got to tell me?"

"The man has ten grand in casino bank straps, all hundreds."

"That's interesting."

"Laid out in the bottom of his suitcase."

"You take it?"

"I almost did."

"Anybody see you go in his room?"

"Come on."

"Just checking. What about Harry? You put somebody on him?"

"Harry showed up at his apartment yesterday afternoon, stayed about an hour and came out carrying a hanging bag. He drove to an address on La Collina in Beverly Hills, top of the street. I went over there later and spoke to a neighbor's maid walking the dog. For ten bucks, she says, 'Oh, that's a movie star lives there, Karen Flores.' "

"Man, I been trying to place that name. Sure, Karen Flores," Catlett said. "Was in some of Harry Zimm's pictures and some others after that, but never made it. That's where he's been hanging out?"

"It's where he was last night."

"That old man—I believe he's casting. Gonna get himself some of that. Say he'll give her a part in *Lovejoy* if she'll play Great Balls of Fire with him."

"What's Great Balls of Fire?"

"You never played it? You light your dick and the woman quick has to blow it out."

The Bear didn't say anything.

"Man, you don't ever smile, do you?"

"If I hear something funny."

"So—Karen Flores, yeah. The way she was built she could play the whore, except she be too old now. Less they want to do the part as an old whore. That wouldn't hurt nothing. Get Theresa or Greta for the new female lead." Catlett paused. He said, "Wait a minute," getting up straighter in Ronnie's cushy chair. "Karen Flores, she was married one time to Michael Weir. And Michael Weir's suppose to be in the movie."

He saw the Bear watching Farrah shooting down jets with that electronic wapping-zapping sound, hitting every one of them as they popped on the screen, the Bear urging her now, saying, "Get it, honey. Get that son of a bitch."

"You hear what I'm saying?" Catlett said. "Karen Flores, Michael Weir, and Harry's over at her house . . . The man wasn't lying, Harry's doing the picture with Michael Weir and, man, it's gonna be *big.* I had the feeling, you know it, ever since I noticed the way Harry was hanging on to that script. Like it was made of gold and you'd have to kill him to get it. I knew it without even reading it. Then when I did . . ."

The Bear was grinning, watching his little girl.

"There was two copies of the script and Chili Palmer took 'em both. Wouldn't even consider us getting together on it, the perfect team. Dumbass, hadn't even read it. And Harry took him as his associate? Bear, this is *my* chance. Chili Palmer's gonna have to wait on his, get in line. You listening to me?"

Not only listening the Bear was a jump ahead, saying, "I'm not taking any more trips to the desert. I told you that. Stick my neck out to help your career. You want to be a producer there's all kinds of deals in this town you can buy into."

Catlett said, "Not with Michael Weir on a twenty-million-plus production. This is a big big one. No mutated bugs, no bloodsucking geeks or kung-fu kind of Rambo assholes kicking the shit out of dress-extras, uh-unh. This's the big movie I've been looking to get in on."

"They all sound big," the Bear said, "at the talking stage."

Catlett said, "Bear, I drive limos now and then."

"I know that."

"Why—'cause I like to listen, hear all about the deals and shit happening. Hear who's hot and who's not. What names you can take to the bank this month. Learn what studio head is on his way out 'cause he pissed on a big producer's script. Learn who the hot agents are, what they're packaging, who's getting two hundred phone calls a day. Hear the agent tell the actor he's gonna pull out the guns, kill to make the deal, gonna take no fucking prisoners. Weekends, some of the agents and producers and studio execs, they're up in the Malibu hills playing war games with these CO_2 guns. Running around in the woods shooting paint bullets at each other. You hear what I'm saying? They talk about how they're gonna kill to make a deal. Then they go out and play with toy guns." Catlett grinned. "Shit, huh? You think I can't manage with people like that? Man, I've done it for real."

"I've played that game," the Bear said. "It's fun."

"And you've fallen off buildings and rolled cars and been in five hundred fights—in the movies. But you don't know what the real thing is like, do you? The ultimate deed. Shoot a man."

"How many have you?" the Bear said, not watching Farrah now, Farrah on her own.

"What's the difference, one or five, or ten? One and you're blooded," Catlett said, leaning on Ronnie's desk. "My first time, I was eighteen years old and had gone to Bakersfield to see my mother. Got out of school, picked up an Olds Cutlass, maroon, and drove there from Detroit. This day we're out for a ride, we stop at a gas station, my mother wanting to use the ladies' room. The gas station man told her no migrants could use it. Then he changed his mind, said okay. She's in there, he comes in and starts messing with her. She told me in the car, after. I drove back there, I said to the man, 'You disrespected my mother. I'd like you to apologize to her.' He start laughing and told us to get out. My mother was crying the whole time . . . I went back later on to have a talk with the man. He got ugly and I shot him."

"Eighteen years old," the Bear said. "Where'd you get the gun?"

"I had it. Brought it with me."

"But why'd you have it?"

"I was out of school, starting to look over career possibilities." Catlett smiled. "Way before I knew I wanted to be in the movie business."

"You killed a man 'cause he showed your mother disrespect?"

"He dissed me too. Said I must be one of those motherfuckers he'd heard about. I did him, got on the interstate and went back to Detroit. Oh, and I took his cash. I sent it to my mother."

"Show her," the Bear said, "what a sweet boy you are."

"I see her. She's living in Delano now, has friends there she doesn't want to leave. I bought her a house."

"I imagine," the Bear said, "not knowing any better, she's proud of you."

Catlett watched the Bear, rubbing his beard, look over toward the wapping-zapping sound of his child knocking jets out of the sky. A daddy proud of his little girl. It would be fun to have one of those of his own. Pick a good-looking woman with nice features and have one. Pick a woman wasn't a tighthead. He used to say he didn't deal in coal when he was running around with white women, but had changed his mind about that, since meeting some fine little sisters out here.

He said, "Bear? This man Chili Palmer, what you suppose he does?"

"Ten grand in his suitcase," the Bear said, "what do you think, he's a bank messenger?"

"He scored it at a casino, didn't he?"

"Whether he did or not," the Bear said, "the guy's into some kind of hustle."

"How do you know that?"

"I've done desk reads in this business," the Bear said, looking over, "where somebody wants to know, say, what this executive is up to. Like if he's about to leave with a property he hasn't told the studio about. They want to know if he might be negotiating someplace. I look at the man's telephone notes, play his recorder, see who's on his Rolodex, get to know him. This guy C. Palmer has got nothing that puts him with anybody or tells what he might be doing. He's too clean. The only thing he had written down on his note pad was 'Raji's, Hollywood Blvd. near Vine.' "

Catlett frowned. "*Ra*ji's? Man, that's a hard rock joint. You can tell looking at Chili Palmer he ain't into that metal shit. I might have to look into that one."

"I'll tell you one thing," the Bear said. "You shoot him, you'll never see me again."

Catlett started frowning again. "No, man, I don't want that on my conscience. Focking Yayo, that was different, he could've hurt us. And I mean both of us, right? You buried that monkey chaser you were protecting your own ass as much as mine. No, what I'm thinking . . . Bear, you listening?"

"I can hear you."

"We got the cash out the airport and the stepped-on bag that ain't worth shit. What I'm thinking, what if Chili Palmer went out there to pick it up?"

Catlett waited for the Bear to turn his head this way, the Bear nodding, seeing the picture.

"Yeah?"

"We even call the feds. Make that anonymous kind of phone-in tip they love to get. What would happen?"

"You'd be out a hundred and seventy grand."

"When they bust him, haul his ass off to jail."

"You don't care about the money?"

"We got stuff for it, didn't we? We're not out nothing."

"He'll tell the feds he was set up."

"I 'magine he will, but how's he gonna put it on *me*? I don't even know the man and there isn't anybody seen us together."

"Harry has."

"I can talk to Harry," Catlett said. "No, the trick will be getting Mr. Chili Palmer to go out to the airport and open that locker."

Find some way to work that or do it clean and quick, the way Farrah was zapping jets out of the sky.

Catlett said, "Man, she's gooood."

The Bear said, "That's my little ace."

RAY BONES CAME OFF THE DELTA FLIGHT TO FIND A young guy with more hair and gold jewelry than he needed holding a square of laundry cardboard that said MR BARBONE in black Magic Marker. The young guy's shirt was open halfway down, his sleeves turned up twice. He said, "Mr. Bar-bone? Welcome to L.A. I'm Bobby, your driver. Mr. De-Phillips asked me to extend you his best and be of help any way I can. You have a good flight?"

Bones said, "I hope you drive better than you fuckin spell. My name's Barboni, not Bar-bone."

Northbound from the airport on 405, Bones rode in the backseat of the Cadillac enclosed in dark glass. He commented on the traffic. "Shit, this isn't bad. Miami, we got bumper to bumper all day long." He asked Bobby the driver, "What's that over there?"

"Oil wells," Bobby said.

"They're ugly fuckin things. You got oil wells and freeways. You got smog . . ."

"You ever wanta go to the beach," Bobby said, "here's the freeway you take, we're coming to."

"I live in Miami Beach," Bones said, "and you want to show me a fuckin beach? The sun ever come out here, or you have this smog all the time? Jesus. Where's downtown at? I don't see it."

Four-oh-five to Santa Monica Boulevard to the Beverly

Hilton, Bobby telling Bones it was the home of Trader Vic's, if he liked Chinese. Bones said he hated it. They pulled up to the hotel entrance and got out.

"What do you have for me?"

Bobby opened the trunk, brought out Bones' luggage, one bag, went back in and came out with a black leather attaché case. "Compliments of Mr. DePhillips. The names and phone numbers are in here. The same ones that were given to your friend Mr. Palmer."

"What else?"

"It's in there too. Beretta three-eighty, a nice one."

"Gimme the car keys."

"I'm suppose to drive you."

"Frank DePhillips said extend me his best wishes and help me out any way I want, right?"

"Yeah . . ."

"So gimme the fuckin keys."

Bones handed the kid five bucks and told him to get a haircut.

20

IN THE CAR ON THE WAY OVER, HARRY TOLD CHILI AND Karen what to expect. "We'll sit down and start schmoozing about the business. Who got fired, divorced, had an abortion, entered a treatment center, moved back to New York, died of AIDS, came out of the closet . . . We'll get offered something to drink like Evian water or decaffeinated coffee and Elaine will ask if *Lovejoy* was inspired by a true story reported in the media—since you don't see that many original ideas that are original and weren't stolen from a book or a picture made forty years ago—and that's when I begin to ease into the pitch. I say, 'You know why you ask that, Elaine? Because *Lovejoy* is about life, about universal feelings of sorrow and hope. It's about redemption and retribution, the little guy's triumph over the system . . ."

Karen said, "Harry, you're full of shit."

He said, "If I'm wrong then I haven't made something like three hundred pitches in my career. You're talking to a distributor or studio execs, it's the same thing."

Karen said, "You haven't met Elaine Levin."

CHILI HAD HIS DARK PINSTRIPE SUIT ON, STRIPED SHIRT and conservative dark tie, walking into Elaine's office in the Hyman Tower Building on the Tower Studios lot, Hollywood, California. It wasn't like an office; it was like a big old-fashioned living room with a dining L, but unfinished, or as if all this furniture was in the wrong room. A dark-haired woman in her forties, wearing glasses down on her nose was sitting at a dining room table talking on the phone. She covered it with her hand as they came in and said, "Hi, I'll be right there. You want a soda, mineral water, some coffee?" She was from New York, no question. Karen gave her a wave saying thanks, but they just had lunch. Harry said to Chili, "What'd I tell you?" They sat down in the living room part, Chili next to Karen on a dull-green sofa that looked like an antique and felt like one, the seat round and hard. Harry was moving his butt around in a chair with a carved wood back and arms, trying to get comfortable. The floor and the walls were bare, no carpeting, no pictures or anything. As Chili was looking around Karen said, "Elaine's redecorating. All this stuff goes." Harry said, "Studio office, one week it's Old English, the next week art deco moderne. You know who makes out in this town, the interior designers. On account of turnover." Harry started pushing himself up and now Karen got up, so Chili did too as Elaine came over to them, her hand out.

She was smaller than Chili thought she'd be, maybe five-two in her stocking feet, which was the way she actually was, wearing a beige suit with the sleeves pushed up but no shoes. She wasn't bad looking though, even with that mop of hair all over the place, like she hadn't combed it in a week. Shaking Harry's hand she said, "Harry, I feel as if I know you. I've been a fan of yours ever since *Slime Creatures.* They remind me of so many people I know in the industry." Harry told Elaine he'd been following her career with interest ever since she broke in. Elaine turned to Chili and gave his hand a good grip as Karen introduced them and Elaine said, "My word, both the gentlemen in suits, I'm flattered. You should see the way most of them come in, like they do yard work and I guess some of them do, the writers, if they're not parking cars." Still holding on to his hand she said, "Chili Palmer, hmmmm," in the slow way she spoke. It surprised him, this offhand manner she had about her, talking a lot but in no hurry. Maybe her mind somewhere else. Not what he'd heard about dynamic women executives. Elaine sat down, now the four of them around a coffee table where there was a big ashtray loaded with butts. She brought a pack of cigarettes and a lighter out of her jacket saying, *"Mr. Lovejoy . . ."* and Chili got ready to take his first meeting at a movie studio.

HARRY: "WHAT HOOKED ME, ELAINE, IS THE THEME. Redemption and retribution, the little guy's triumph over the system."

Elaine: "Yeah . . . well, I'm as turned on by redemption and retribution, Harry, as anyone; but what's the system he triumphs over?"

Harry: "The legal system."

Elaine: "I don't see the ending exactly as a triumph. The man who killed his boy is dead, but Lovejoy would still owe—what is it, a hundred thousand to somebody, the guy's heirs?"

Harry: "We're revising the ending . . ."

Elaine: "Good."

Harry: "Roxy has brought Lovejoy to court, but the case is still pending when Roxy is killed. So Lovejoy keeps his flower shop, doesn't have to pay anything."

Elaine: "Uh-huh, yeah . . . But what about motivation? Why he goes after the guy with a video camera."

Harry: "*Why?* To see justice done."

Elaine: "But it isn't. The guy gets his license revoked again—so what?"

Harry: "What we plan to do as part of revising the ending,

is have Lovejoy do something to cause Roxy's death. I don't mean murder him, but not have Lovejoy just standing there either."

Elaine: "That gets us back to his motivation. I can't see this mingy florist becoming so vindictive."

Harry: "Who, Lovejoy?"

Elaine: "Even his name."

Harry: "We're thinking of changing it. No, but the idea—here's a guy you think is a schlub, right? But beneath that quiet exterior he's passionate, impulsive and extremely likable. Once you get to know him."

Elaine: "He's passionate? Who does he fuck?"

Harry: "You mean in the script?"

Elaine: "In his life. His wife left him—who does he sleep with. He's quiet, low-key, yeah, but does that mean he doesn't fuck?"

Chili couldn't believe he was hearing her say that. There were all kinds of movies where nobody got laid in them. Unless she meant it as something the guy did that you never saw. Like people in movies never went to the bathroom even though you know they would have to.

There was a pause, a silence right after Elaine spoke. And then Karen got into it.

Karen: "What he needs—what the story needs is for somebody to give him a kick in the ass, get him going. I'm thinking about a woman who's been abused by Roxy, knows his life, his habits, that he's into something illegal. And she also knows he's *driving*—that's it, when he's not supposed to. Otherwise where does Lovejoy get the idea to catch him at it? She goes to Lovejoy and lays it out. Let's get this son of a bitch. Catch him driving. What's the girl's name in the script, the hooker?"

Harry: "Lola."

Karen: "Lovejoy, Ilona, *Lola*—come on. Call her—I don't

know—Peggy. Working class but bright. From a big family she's had to help support. Worked all her life . . . Roxy's hobby is making porno films he shows to his friends. He gets Peggy stoned and shoots nude footage of her. She discovers it, burns the tape and he beats her up . . . This is the *kind* of situation I mean, not necessarily what will work best. But get her personally involved. Where does the video camera come from? It's Roxy's. She rips it off . . . You see what I'm getting at?"

Elaine: "You're on the right track."

Harry: "But then it's not Lovejoy's story, it's the girl's."

Karen: "It's a subplot. We're looking for motivation, what gets Lovejoy started."

Harry: "And I'm looking at a property, as it *is,* Michael Weir wants to do."

Elaine: "Oh, God. Michael."

Chili watched Elaine look over at Karen.

Harry: "Elaine, Michael read it and flipped. Why? Because it's about life. It's cosmic, it's about universal feelings and values. But he won't touch it if it isn't his story. You know that. Michael is bigger than the idea."

Elaine: "Mr. Indecisive, won't be pressured into making a commitment. I love him, but he's worse than Hoffman and Redford put together, and his price isn't even as high as theirs. You know what he does, don't you? He puts his writer on it and every few months or so they show up with a different version of the story. Then he'll bring a director, some guy who's in awe of Michael and if the picture's ever shot he'll make the mistake of allowing Michael in the cutting room. You go over budget, miss release dates and post-production goes on forever while Michael fine-tunes."

Harry: "And if you can get him, it's worth it."

Elaine: "Why don't you bring me a nice sci-fi/horror idea? Something original. No pissed-off teenagers or comic-book characters. Drama, if it's offbeat, quirky but real. I want to discover new actors, do something different."

Chili saw her looking at him over her glasses. She blew out a stream of cigarette smoke.

Elaine: "Mr. Palmer, what do you think of Michael Weir?"

"I think he's a great actor," Chili said, "and I think you could get him to do it. When I was talking to him last night he said he likes the character a lot." That got their attention. "He also likes the idea of putting a girl in it and fixing the ending, but he thinks it turns into a B movie in the second act."

Elaine: "He means whenever you cut away from him."

"I think he was talking mostly," Chili said, "about the visual fabric of the movie and the theme, what you're doing here, so it doesn't start to look like something else."

Elaine: "You know Michael?"

"I know the girl lives with him, Nicki. She introduced me." Harry was looking at him from across the coffee table, staring. Karen, on the sofa next to him, had her head turned to look right at him. "Speaking of the ending," Chili said, "I think if Lovejoy runs the guy over with his van the audience in the theater would get up and cheer."

Elaine: "The direct approach."

"Say he wants to do it," Chili said. "He starts out with every intention and then changes his mind. But it happens anyway, he runs the guy over and kills him and you don't know for sure if he meant it or it was an accident." He watched Elaine take her glasses off. She kept looking at him without saying anything.

Karen: "I kind of like that. Keep it ambiguous till the very end. Say he tells Peggy it was an accident and she believes him . . ."

Elaine: "But the audience still isn't sure."

Karen: "That's what I was thinking. Give them something to talk about after they walk out."

Elaine: "You mean leave the theater."

Karen, smiling: "Right." Still smiling: "Warren's idea—did he tell you?"

Chili placed the name, the studio exec Karen had mentioned who sounded like an asshole.

Elaine: "We talked about it briefly."

Karen: "Lovejoy videotapes a couple of robberies and becomes a surveillance expert?"

Elaine: "With Mel Gibson. We do sequels or sell it to a network for a series."

Harry: "So, the next step—"

Karen: "I thought he'd be here."

Elaine: "Warren's no longer with us. He's in Publicity."

Karen: "Oh."

Harry: "So, we know the script needs a little work, no problem. I'll give Murray our comments."

Elaine: "Which Murray is that?"

Harry: "Murray Saffrin, my writer."

Elaine: "Oh . . . Well, I'll tell you right now, I wouldn't have a chance with Murray Saffrin. Karen could take the script upstairs bareass and not sell Murray Saffrin."

Harry: "So I'll get somebody else."

Elaine: "It's your decision. I can give you a few names, writers I know would be acceptable, like . . ."

Chili listened to the names, not surprised he'd never heard of any of them. How many people knew who wrote the movies they saw?

Harry: "So we're talking development?"

Elaine: "Not till I have at least a treatment I know I can sell. It's still your project, Harry. Your decision, if you want to see how far we can run with it."

Harry: "You're saying I pay the writer. Any of the guys you mentioned, what's a rewrite gonna cost me?"

Elaine: "Depending on who you get, I would say anywhere from one-fifty to four, and a few points. Call their agents, see who's available and might want to do it."

Harry: "I love talking to agents, right next to having a case of hives. You don't think bringing Michael Weir deserves a development deal?"

Elaine: "Michael Weir signed, gagged and chained to a wall till you start shooting, I can take upstairs. I tell them Michael Weir likes the part . . . Yeah? What else is new? Harry, it's your decision, think it over. Karen, I wonder if you'd stay a few minutes. If the gentlemen wouldn't mind waiting . . ."

Chili got up with Harry. They started out.

Elaine: "Harry? What about romance among less than attractive people?"

Harry: *"Marty?"*

Elaine: "Beyond *Marty.*"

Harry: "The seven-hundred-pound broad who crushes her lovers to death when she climaxes?"

Elaine: "Call me, Harry, okay?"

THEY WAITED FOR KAREN IN HARRY'S CAR, PARKED next to a sound stage as big as a hangar, up the street from the Hyman Tower Building and the front gate. Chili half expected to see extras walking around in period costumes and military uniforms, the way you saw them in movies about movies, but there didn't seem to be anything going on. Harry, coming out of the building, kept asking about Michael Weir. And then what did he say? He really seemed interested? How was it left? Why didn't you call me last night? Why'd you wait till in the meeting? You trying to make points? All that. Chili said, "I think you ought to listen to what Elaine says about the guy. He doesn't sound too reliable." Getting in the car, the front seat, Chili said, "Last night I noticed he's a lot shorter than I thought."

Next, Harry started bitching about how studio people never come right out and say yes or no, they string you along. They put you in a high-risk position you can't afford to be in and say it's up to you.

It was hot in the car. Chili rolled down his window. "What'd she say a writer would cost?"

"Between one-fifty and four hundred thousand."

"Jesus Christ," Chili said, "just to fix it? That's what I thought she meant, but I wasn't sure. The writers do okay, huh?"

"It's the fucking agents ruining the business. Agents and the unions. But you know what? If I had the dough I'd hire one of those guys. That's how sure I am of this one."

Chili, not at all sure, didn't say anything.

"With a little luck, say if you were to run into your pal the dry cleaner," Harry said, "and could negotiate me a quick loan . . ."

Chili watched two young ladies walking up the middle of the studio street: long blond hair, miniskirts, a couple of Miss Californias.

"I found him, Harry."

Harry said, "Where?" jumping on it, twisting around in that tight space between the seat and the steering wheel.

"What's the difference where? I took the money off him and sent it to his wife."

"You didn't."

"Three hunnerd grand. I kept ten for Bones, if I decide to pay him."

"You had the money in your *hand*?"

"Take it easy, Harry." The guy looked like he might go berserk. "I didn't have to tell you, 'cause it isn't any your business, is it? But I did. Okay, so forget it."

"Three hundred thousand." Now he was shaking his head, still not looking too stable. "I don't know what good you're doing me."

"I don't raise money for you, Harry, that was never in the deal."

"What deal? I'd like to know what you do for me."

"You telling me you'd use Leo's money? Take a chance of him getting picked up—'cause he will, I know it. The first thing he'd do then is try and lay it on us, the whole con, and throw his wife in too."

Harry, staring straight ahead now, didn't say anything. He looked uncomfortable, his suit too tight for him.

CHILI GOT OUT AND HELD THE DOOR OPEN AS KAREN approached the car. He couldn't tell anything by her expression. When she got close to him, before ducking inside, she said, "The visual fabric of the theme? You might just make it, Chil."

He got in back. Harry started the car but didn't move, looking at Karen. "You want to tell me what that was about?"

"Elaine's going to call Michael," Karen said. "If he shows enough interest and you have the script revised, she'll put it into development."

"Fucking studios," Harry said, "they can't give you a simple yes or no, they have to intrigue it up. Why'd she tell you that and not me?"

"That wasn't why she asked me to stay," Karen said, and paused and said in a quieter tone, "Elaine offered me a job."

Harry squinted at her. "As what?"

"Production exec. Maybe vice-president in a year."

Harry said, "Jesus Christ, I don't believe it."

Chili reached over the seat to touch Karen's shoulder. He said, "Nice going," and just for a second she laid her cheek against his hand.

21

THE LAST PERSON CATLETT WOULD EVER IMAGINE HAVING a tender feeling toward was Marcella, the woman that kept the limo service going. But he had one today. Walked in from the garage through the working office where Marcella looked up from her computer to say, "Mr. Zimm has been trying to get hold of you," and Bo Catlett wanted to hug her.

He said, "You don't mean to tell me."

"He didn't leave a message. He'll call back."

"When?"

"I don't know, but he sure called a buncha times," this big doll in her pink outfit and pink-frame glasses said. Just then the phone rang on Marcella's desk. He watched her pick it up and say, "Wingate Motors Limited," dainty for a woman her size, the way she moved, the way she held her fifty-year-old head of golden hair. He had never noticed this before. Marcella said, "Yes, Mr. Catlett's here. Just a moment, please." Looked at him and nodded and this time he wanted to kiss her.

He took it in Ronnie's office, feet up on the desk, ankles crossed, looking at his shiny Cole Haan loafers as he said, "Harry, I was thinking of calling you, man. How you doing?"

Harry said just great. The way he always did, sitting on the other side of this desk times before, here to ask for investment money—oh, everything was just great—though he did happen to have a few points left over if they wanted in. A few points meaning half the budget for the movie. In financial shit up to his chin, no doubt as he was at this moment, Harry was just great.

"We got a deal going at Tower . . ."

"On *Mr. Lovejoy*?"

"They're extremely high on it."

"I hear you got Michael Weir."

"Boy, this town. Word gets around, doesn't it?"

"So how can I help you?"

"I'm looking for a little working capital."

"Like how much?"

"Couple hundred."

"What's wrong with using the money we put in *Freaks*?"

"That's in escrow, I can't touch it."

Meaning the man had spent it. So for the time being Catlett resigned himself to forget it. Move on to bigger things.

"You offering a participation in *Lovejoy*?"

"A small one, considering it's a twenty-million-dollar shoot, minimum. Maybe twenty-five."

"So we're talking about like one percent."

"Around there."

"Or less."

"Tell me what you want," Harry said. "Let's see if we can work it out."

Listen to him. Cool for a man who was desperate or wouldn't have picked up the phone. "I was about to call you, Harry."

"Is that right?"

"Tell you how much I like *Lovejoy*."

"You read it?"

"I think so much of it, man, I'm prepared to make you a deal you might not believe. But I also want to participate actively. You understand what I'm saying? I want to work on the movie with you, be part of it, man."

"I'd like to know where you got hold of a script."

"Harry, let's me and you meet someplace and have a drink. I'll tell you how you can put your hands on a hundred and seventy thousand and you won't have to give me any points or pay interest on it. You pay me back at your convenience. How's that sound?"

"You serious?" Harry said.

No mention now of the script.

"Where you want to meet?" Catlett asked him.

"I don't care," Harry said. "Where do you?"

After going around on that Catlett called the Bear, named a restaurant and asked him to be there in half an hour. When Catlett left, going out through the working office where Marcella the pink woman sat behind her computer, he wondered what it was like to go to bed with a woman you would never think of going to bed with, if it was different.

A MEXICAN IN A WHITE BUSBOY COAT AND CRUMMY-looking pants brought drinks to them on Karen's patio. She sounded different, so polite saying, "Thank you, Miguel. I'll see you tomorrow." The Mexican didn't say anything. He was bowlegged and had big gnarled hands on him. After Miguel went in the house Karen said, "Would you think he's only in his forties? He's been a migrant farm worker all his life. He came by one day asking to do yard work and I hired him as my houseman."

Chili sipped his drink and said, "Jesus, I don't think he put any tonic in this. It's good though."

"Miguel's learning," Karen said, and looked up at the trees. "It's nice out here, isn't it? This is my favorite time of the day."

She sounded different this evening. Neither of them said

anything for a minute or so, looking at the trees and the sky changing color. It reminded Chili a little of sitting with Fay as it got dark and they waited for Leo to come home; except Leo and Fay didn't have a swimming pool. He had thought they were waiting for Harry—the plan, to go out to dinner—till Karen said Harry had already stopped by. Changed his mind, made a phone call and left. Still upset about the meeting, among other things.

Chili took the "among other things" to mean him. "He doesn't think I'm doing anything for him."

Karen turned to look at him. "Are you?"

"What's he want? I'll do it."

"He wants Michael . . . But listen," Karen said, "the way Harry's acting, that's his personality. To help him, you first have to break through this barrier he sets up—doing it *his* way, the independent producer, nobody knows anything but him. His last three pictures might've broken even, but didn't do nearly as well as his early stuff. I tried to tell him. You know why? You haven't kept up. If you're going to do low budget exploitation you either have to go much heavier on the special effects, or you have to get outrageously campy, make pictures like *Assault of the Killer Bimbos, Surf Nazis Must Die, Space Sluts in the Slammer*—they're so bad they're fun. Or, you have to approach horror in a new and different way, like *Near Dark,* that I think is brilliant. A love story about a guy who falls for a vampire. But there's not one scene in a dark empty castle, the vampire dressed like Fred Astaire in white tie and tails. These are raunchy vampires; they roam around this flat, empty farmland out west in a station wagon looking for blood, hurrying to get what they need and stay out of the sun or they'll catch fire and burn up. It shows what it's really like to be a vampire," Karen said. "And I couldn't get Harry to go see it."

Chili sipped his vodka and not much tonic, glad Harry

wasn't here, comfortable in the cushioned patio chair, more impressed by Karen every time he talked to her. She wasn't anything like Fay, but she'd understand Fay and could play her in a minute.

"You know all that stuff," Chili said. "I don't mean just what movies are about, but other things, the business."

"I've been out here fifteen years and I pay attention," Karen said. "Harry's upset, and one of the reasons is my being offered a studio job. He said, 'I don't believe it,' because he still thinks of me as the girl he hired with nice tits and a great scream. My dad teaches quantum physics at a university and my mother's a real estate broker, has her own company and is incredibly successful; she has a super business mind. I'm not saying I follow after either one of them exactly, but I didn't come into the world on a bus to L.A. I have a background. I know more about the film industry now than Harry does because I keep up, I know what's going on and I have good story sense. Elaine knows that, it's why she wants to hire me."

"You gonna take the job?"

"I'm thinking about it," Karen said. "Meanwhile, poor Harry's off trying to raise money, so he can hire a writer . . ."

Chili paused, about to sip his drink.

". . . and get deeper in debt. That's where he went, to talk to his investors."

Chili said, "You mean the limo guys?"

"I know it's the same ones he's been trying to avoid. I said, 'Harry, you told me you've been dying to get out from under them,' and he said he didn't have a choice."

"He went to their office?"

"No, they're meeting somewhere . . . Tribeca, it's on Beverly Drive."

Chili put his drink down. "Can we have dinner there?"

Karen said, "If you'd like," and stared at him for maybe

ten seconds before she said, "Harry's a big boy," and continued to stare as if wanting him to say something. "Isn't he?"

Chili got up. He said, "You ready?"

THEY WERE IN THE BIG CORNER BOOTH UPSTAIRS AT Tribeca, Catlett, Harry, now the Bear sliding in and Catlett had to stop what he was saying to introduce his associate, this former movie stuntman, bodybuilder and health nut in the Hawaiian shirt. So what did the health nut do? Immediately dove into the bread basket and started eating rolls thick with butter, getting crumbs in his beard and all over the table in front of him. Now Harry, watching him, grabbed a roll for himself before they were gone. Harry was on his second Scotch, Catlett still sipping his ice-cold Pouilly-Fuissé. Harry had ordered the meatloaf, which Catlett liked the sound of, basic food, indicating the man was in a basic frame of mind and would not get tricky on him. Catlett had ordered the shrimp salad, not wanting to make this one his dinner; he'd have that later on at Mateo's with people he liked, some cute woman who'd laugh at his wit and bullshit. The Bear ordered a beer—another simple soul—and would eat later, at home.

So far Catlett had explained once again he'd give Harry one hundred and seventy thousand dollars, interest and point free, pay it back when you can, for the privilege of working on *Lovejoy* and learning from the expert how moving pictures were made. Fringe benefits would come up later. All he wanted, Catlett had mentioned this time, was some kind of small credit up on the screen, head gofer, anything, his friends would get a kick out of seeing. Now then . . .

"I told you it was your boy, didn't I, let me have the script?"

Harry didn't know who he meant. "My boy? . . ."

"Chili Palmer, from Miami, Florida."

"He gave it to you?"

"Loaned it. Was the other night in your office."

Harry said, "Well, you *say* you read it," not yet convinced.

"Ask me something."

"All right, what's Lovejoy's brother-in-law's name?"

"You mean Stanley? I was thinking it wouldn't be bad if something happened to Stanley, the way he gets on your nerves. Even though as Lovejoy says to his sis, her and Stan have their own problems, being stuck with each other."

Now the man couldn't have a doubt in his head, just questions.

"Why'd he show it to you?"

"I thought maybe you told him to."

"I sent him to pick up a script, that's all."

"Well, he called me, I went over. Man, I've been wondering why ever since. This town, you don't want to go showing your ideas around. I know of a guy left a script in one of the limos and the producer fired him. I thought that was heavy. The producer—I won't mention his name, one of the big power players—he said if the guy wasn't any more reliable than that he didn't want him around."

Catlett sipped his wine, giving Harry a minute to think about it and then took a shot saying, "I asked this Chili Palmer what his position was and he said you and him were partners, gonna produce the movie together. It surprised me, him coming in off the street and not knowing shit, you know, about the business. I noticed he didn't even know how to read a script, what some of the directions meant. In *fact,* he's talking about producing the movie with you, he hadn't even *read* it. Man, that didn't sound right to me."

Harry picked up his roll and took a bite out of it like he was eating an apple, crumbs dribbling down the front of him. The Bear, spreading butter on his, paused to watch this.

"I don't mean to sound like I'm sticking my nose in your business," Catlett said, going at him again, "and if you don't care to tell me, don't. It's just I'm curious to know what this Chili Palmer does for you."

"Not much," Harry said.

Good, starting to speak.

"He run errands for you?"

"He has different functions, you might say."

"Kind of a tough guy, huh? That was how he came on," Catlett said. "See, I suspected you had him around to do heavy work, deal with me and Ronnie, and that was something I couldn't get straight in my head. What would you need him for? Has Ronnie ever given you any trouble? I know I haven't. Ronnie might've shot off his mouth, but that's Ronnie. Man, he's from Santa Barbara and he's gonna let you know it. Anyway, Ronnie isn't in this deal—the one hundred and seventy thousand dollars I'm giving you as working capital in good faith. You're gonna find out, Harry, I know more about movies than most people in the business. You watch me."

Harry said, "When can I have the money?"

Getting right down to business. Never mind all the bullshit, huh? This was the meatloaf man.

"Whenever you want it, Harry. The money's in hundred dollar bills inside one of those jock bags, you know? In a locker at the airport, waiting to be picked up."

Harry looked at him. "The airport?"

"It was waiting out there on another deal, one that didn't go through you don't want to know about," Catlett said. "Or maybe you should know *some*thing about it. I don't want you to get in any trouble. It was money put there to make a buy, if you know what I mean."

Harry picked up his glass and took a drink on that one. "Yeah?"

But was still interested, look at that. Anxious.

"What I'm saying to you, Harry, you could go out there,

take the bag out of the locker and be on your way, nobody bother you. But you never know who's hanging around that airport."

"You mean cops," Harry said.

"Well, that's possible, yeah. Maybe Drug Enforcement individuals—I don't know. I was thinking more of other people in the product trade know buys are made out there, money changing hands. You understand what I'm saying? They the ones you have to watch out might rip you off. Like if you look, I don't mean like one of them, but kinda suspicious, you act nervous taking the bag out of the locker . . ."

"I don't know," Harry said, shaking his head.

Wanting it, you could tell, but afraid.

"It's what I'm saying, it's not the kind of thing you do," Catlett said. "That's why I was thinking you could send your boy, Chili Palmer. He gets hit on the head you aren't out nothing."

THEY TOOK CHILI'S RENTED TOYOTA, DOWN RODEO TO Wilshire to come back around on Beverly Drive. On the way he told Karen about going into a restaurant on Little Santa Monica when he first got here. Went in all dressed up and was put way in the back after waiting at the bar about an hour, while these people who looked like they'd been out camping would come in and get the empty front tables right away. He told her about the worn-out leather jacket Michael had been wearing.

"You buy them new like that," Karen said. "What did you think of him?"

Chili said he thought he was basically a nice guy, but it was hard to tell. "He was *on* most of the time. I think he has trouble being just himself."

"He do any imitations?"

"Michael Jackson."

"He used to do Howard Cosell constantly." She said, "You know it isn't easy being Michael Weir."

Chili didn't comment on that, thinking seven million ought to make it a *little* easier.

They were quiet and then she said, "What's Nicki like?"

"She's a rock-and-roll singer." He thought a moment and said, "She doesn't shave under her arms."

"Michael probably goes for that. He thinks he's earthy."

"You still like him?"

"I don't hold anything against him. He's Michael Weir . . . and he's great."

"You mean his acting."

"What'd you think I meant, in bed? In bed he was funny."

"Funny in what way?"

"He was *funny.* He said funny things."

For a few moments they were quiet again.

"He's a lot shorter than I thought."

"That's not his fault," Karen said.

Chili dropped her off in front of Tribeca, a storefront kind of café with the name on the plate glass, and drove up the street looking for a place to park.

THEY WEREN'T AT THAT OLD-TIME-LOOKING BAR OR anywhere on the main floor. Chili headed for the open stairway and started up. The place could be called the Manhattan or the Third Avenue, that's what it looked like, one of those typical overpriced New York bar-restaurants. The TriBeCa area, he thought of warehouses, buildings with lofts, but it was as good a name as any. He saw a railing along the upstairs, this end of it open, overlooking the bar. And he saw a guy standing near the top of the stairs, the guy a few steps down but not coming down, standing there waiting for him. A guy in a Hawaiian shirt with beef on him and a full reddish-brown beard.

Moving up the stairs Chili got a good look at the guy and his size. Now he saw Bo Catlett appear above the guy to stand on the top step, almost directly behind him, and Chili knew the guy wasn't going to move. He got within three steps of the guy and stopped, but not looking up now, not wanting to put himself in that awkward position, his head bent back. He was looking at the guy's waist now at eye level, where the Hawaiian shirt bloused out of the elastic band of the guy's blue pants, double-knit and tight on him.

Catlett's voice said, "I like you to meet my associate, the Bear. Movie stuntman and champion weight lifter, as you might've noticed. Picks up and throws out things I don't want."

Chili looked at the thickness of the guy's body, at red and gold hibiscus blossoms and green leaves on a field of Hawaiian blue, but wouldn't look at his face now. He knew they were hibiscus, because Debbie used to grow them on Meridian Avenue before she flipped out and went back to Brooklyn.

Now the guy was saying, "I know Chili Palmer. I know all about him."

The Bear sucking in his stomach and acting tough, his crotch right there in Chili's face. This guy was as nuts as Debbie. You could tell he had his stomach sucked in, because the waistband was creased where the guy's gut ordinarily hung over and rolled it, the pants as out of shape as this guy trying to give him a hard time. But Chili didn't look up.

Catlett said, "We think you ought to turn around and go back to Miami"

Chili still didn't look up. Not yet.

The Bear said, "Take your ten grand with you, while you still have it."

And Chili almost looked up—this guy as much as telling him he had been in his hotel room, nothing to it, saw all that dough and left it—but he didn't. Chili kept his eyes on the guy's waist and saw the stomach move to press against the elastic band, the guy still putting on his show but giving his gut a breather. Chili looked at the guy's crotch one more time before moving his gaze up through the hibiscus till he was looking at the guy's bearded face.

Chili said, "So you're a stuntman," with the look he'd use on a slow pay. "Are you any good?"

What the Bear did in that next moment was grin and turn his head to the side, as if too modest to answer and would let Catlett speak for him. It made the next move easier, the guy not even looking as Chili grabbed a handful of his crotch, stepped aside and yanked him off the stairs. The Bear yelled out of pain and fear and caught Chili's head with an elbow going by, but it was worth it to see that beefy guy roll all the way down the stairs to land on the main floor. Chili kept watching till he saw the guy move, then looked up at Catlett. "Not bad, for a guy his size."

KAREN SAW IT.

There was a scene like it in an Eastwood picture only Clint grabs the guy a little higher. The thug asks him where he thinks he's going. She couldn't remember if Clint had a line. He's going upstairs in a hotel to have it out with Bobby Duvall. Grabs the guy with one hand and in a Reverse you see him tumble down the stairs to crash at the bottom. It was a western.

Karen had left the table within moments of seeing Catlett stop at the top of the stairs with the bearded guy, the Bear, in front of him, a few steps below, and knew they were waiting for Chili and something was going to happen. As a film sequence it would work from her point of view if she represented a third party in the scene. Then another setup to get the effect of it on her face. But there would have to be close shots too of what was going on. His hand grabbing the guy's crotch. A tight close-up reaction shot of the guy's face. As he begins to scream cut to a Reverse to see him go down the stairs. Catlett was down there now. They were leaving, the guy looking back this way, but not Catlett. Karen watched from the upstairs railing, people from tables around her now asking what happened. Chili was coming past the ones at the top of the stairs. She heard him say, "I guess the guy fell." Now he was looking at her. He came over and she said, "What did he do to you?" Chili shook his head. He touched her arm and they moved through the tables to the corner booth where Harry was standing with his drink in his hand.

Harry said, "What was that all about?"

KAREN SAT AT ONE END OF THE ROUND BOOTH SO she'd have an angle on both of them at once and wouldn't have to turn her head looking from one to the other. She moved the shrimp salad that hadn't been touched away from her, and the half glass of white wine. Chili brushed bread crumbs away from his place. He would look over, wanting to include her at first, telling them Catlett and the bearded guy, the Bear, had broken into his hotel room and gone through his things. Telling it matter-of-factly, making the point: "These are the kind of people you're dealing with, Harry. They want me out of the way so they can have a piece of you." Nice irony. The ex-mob guy telling Harry to look out for the limo guys, they're crooks.

Harry had been acting strange ever since she arrived and he introduced her to Catlett and Catlett introduced her to his friend the Bear and they let her stand there a few minutes, Harry's broad, nothing more, while Catlett spoke to him and placed a key on the table next to Harry's meatloaf. Most of it and the baked potato eaten; he hadn't touched his green beans. When Catlett got up he smiled and touched her arm and said it was a pleasure. A good-looking guy, he reminded her of Duke Ellington, dressed by Armani or out of that place on Melrose, Maxfield's, wearing about two thousand dollars' worth of clothes.

The key wasn't on the table now.

Harry said to Chili, "You know what he is, you told me. So what? I need a hundred and a half, at least, and he's loaning it to me, no strings, I write any kind of agreement I want. All I have to do is pick up the dough. Okay? If you have a problem with him that's your problem. I don't."

It seemed that simple till Chili asked, "Is he giving you a check or cash?" and it got interesting. Harry said cash. He said it happened to be waiting right this moment in a locker at the airport. He said something about a business deal that didn't go through and Chili said, "Jesus Christ, the guy's setting you up. Don't you see that? You pulled out of their *Freaks* deal so he's teaching you a lesson. He's not giving you anything, Harry, he's paying you back." Harry said he didn't know what he was talking about and Chili said, "Harry, I could write a fuckin book on paybacks. You reach in that locker, you're gonna come out wearing handcuffs, I'm telling you."

Karen wished she could write some of it down.

Harry said, "Oh, is that right? I'm being set up? Then how come Catlett said I should send you out to get it, since you haven't done a fucking thing for me since you got into this?"

Karen watched Chili start to smile and for a moment it surprised her. Smiled and shook his head and said, "Harry, I was wrong, I'm sorry. You're not the one he wants to set up."

Harry was not the Harry she had known for fifteen years; he was too quiet. But pouty, acting offended, Harry realizing he was into something he couldn't handle—that was it—and afraid of looking dumb.

Chili said, "Give me the key. If it's there and I don't see a problem, I'll get it for you."

Karen watched Harry turn his head to look at Chili as though he had a choice and was appraising him, thinking it over.

She watched Chili shrug. He said, "It's up to you, Harry. But don't do it yourself, I'm telling you."

She watched Harry put his hand in his coat pocket and bring out the key. He didn't hand it to Chili, he laid it on the table between them. He said, "A hundred and seventy grand. I wonder if I'm ever gonna see you again."

HARRY LEFT AFTER THAT, WHICH WAS FINE WITH CHILI. He and Karen went downstairs to sit at the bar for one, not sure if they'd eat here or go someplace else. She was full of questions, asking about the limo guys and how they made their money. Then asking if he was going out to the airport later this evening. He told her he was thinking of waiting till tomorrow around noon, when there'd be a lot of people there.

Right after that was when Karen said, "Oh, I forgot to tell you. A friend of yours from Miami called the house."

"Tommy Carlo?"

"No that wasn't it. I wrote it down," Karen said. "Ray something. Ray Bar-bone? . . ."

22

THE WAY THE LOCKERS IN THE DELTA TERMINAL worked, you put in three quarters for twenty-four hours. If you expected to use the locker any longer than that, you left two bucks inside for each additional twenty-four hours and a locker attendant would come by and check the time and collect the money. Chili had to read the instructions, printed on each locker, twice before he figured it out. He did this before walking past the bank of lockers where C-018 was located, noticing the lockers on both sides of it had keys sticking out. He liked that as much as he liked all the travelers here today. This LAX, ten-thirty in the morning, was a busy airport.

Next thing he did was check the Arrivals monitor to see what flight he was waiting for if anybody should ask. The one that caught his eye was 83 from Newark, due in at twelve-forty. He imagined Debbie coming out of the gate carrying a makeup kit full of pills and with that pissed-off look she had. Hi, honey, how was the flight? It was awful. The food was awful, the stewardess was a snip and I have a headache. He seemed to be thinking of Debbie and his situation more, still married to her, since meeting Karen, even though he wasn't thinking of Karen in any serious way beyond—he wasn't sure what. The thing he liked about Karen, his past life and associations didn't seem to turn her on or off. She was natural with him, didn't put on airs. Also she was a knockout, she was smart, she was a movie star, or had been, and was starting to give him a certain look and call him Chil. All last night after the business with the stuntman, she had looked at him in a different way, he felt, than she did before. Like she wanted to know things about him. And she was quieter, even while asking a lot of questions, though she didn't ask if he was married or anything too personal. Dropping her off he thought she was going to ask him in. He believed she came close before changing her mind for some reason. Still looking at the Arrivals monitor he noticed Flight 89 from Atlanta up there, the one Bones had connected with from Miami and arrived on yesterday. Karen called him Ray Bar-bone, but didn't ask about him, so he didn't tell her what kind of pain in the ass this fuckin Bones was turning out to be: the way he kept showing up, Christ, for twelve years now, here he comes again, Bones the mob guy and playing it for all it was worth, but basically second-rate muscle, Bones could be handled. As long as he didn't have that big colored guy with him. Chili thinking he didn't need that one too, he already had a colored guy on his back, the dude. What was this? The first time in his life having trouble with colored guys.

In the gift shop Chili bought an L.A. Lakers T-shirt, purple and gold, and a black canvas athletic bag, a small one. The T-shirt went in the athletic bag inside the paper gift-shop bag. He looked around at the souvenirs, all the different kinds of mementos of Los Angeles, at the wall of books and magazines. There was a scruffy kid about eighteen who looked promising, checking out the skin magazines. Chili went up to him and said, "You want to make five bucks, take you two minutes?" The kid looked at him but didn't answer. "You go over to those lockers across the aisle there and put this in C-017." The kid still didn't say anything. "It's a surprise for my wife," Chili said. "But you have to do it quick, okay? While she's in the can." That sounded as if it made sense, so the kid said yeah, okay. Chili gave him the paper bag his purchases were in, a five-dollar bill and three quarters. The kid left and came back with a key that had C-017 on the round flat part of it.

What Chili didn't do was look around the terminal to see if he could spot any suits—the way in movies you saw them standing around reading newspapers. That was bullshit. Maybe you could spot them if you were out here all the time doing business. Maybe the limo guys could spot them and that's why the hundred and seventy grand was sitting untouched in the locker. Chili had no doubt it was there or this wouldn't be a setup. The suits grab you with something incriminating, with what they called "suspected drug money," or there could be more than cash in the locker, some dope, to make the bust stick. There was no sense in looking around, because if it was a setup Catlett would have called it in and the suits would be here dressed all kinds of ways watching locker No. C-018, here and there but not standing anywhere near the locker, so why bother looking?

What Chili did, he left the airport for a couple of hours: drove over Manchester Avenue where he found an Italian place and had a plate of seafood linguine marinara and a split of red. While he was here he wrote the Newark flight number and arrival time on a piece of Sunset Marquis notepaper. It seemed like a lot of trouble, the whole thing, but it was better to have a story just in case, not have to make one up on the spot.

By half past twelve he was back in the Delta terminal waiting at the gate where 83 was due to arrive at twelve-forty. It was on the ground at five past one. He watched all the passengers come off the plane and out through the gate till he was standing there by himself. Okay, he turned and walked down the aisle now to the bank of thirty-three lockers, three high, where C-018 was about in the middle. He looked both ways, taking his time, waiting till a group of people was passing behind him, giving him a screen, giving him just time enough to open C-017, grab the black athletic bag, leaving the gift-shop bag inside, and close the locker. He got about ten yards down the aisle, heading for daylight, when the black guy in the suit coming toward him stopped right in his path.

"Excuse me, sir. Would you come with me, please?"

Now there was a big guy in a plaid wool shirt next to him and another guy, down the aisle, talking on his hand radio. All of them out in the open now. The black guy had his I.D. folder open. They were Drug Enforcement. As Chili said, "What's wrong?" acting surprised. "What's this about?" The black guy turned and started off.

The one in the plaid shirt said, "Let's follow him and behave ourselves. What do you say?"

They took him to a door marked AUTHORIZED PERSONNEL ONLY the black guy opened with a key. It was bare and bright inside the office, fluorescent lights on. Nothing on the metal desk, not even an ashtray. There were three chairs, but they didn't ask him to sit down. The one in the plaid shirt told him to empty his pockets and place the contents on the desk, actually using the word *contents.* But that was as official-sounding as it got. Chili did as he was told acting bewildered, saying he thought they had the wrong person. The black guy opened his wallet and looked at the driver's license while the other one pulled the Lakers T-shirt out of the athletic bag and felt around inside. They glanced at each other without giving any kind of sign and the black guy said, "You live in Miami?"

"That's right," Chili said.

"What're you doing in Los Angeles?"

"I'm in the movie business," Chili said.

They glanced at each other again. The black guy said, "You're an investor, is that it?"

"I'm a producer," Chili said, "with ZigZag Productions."

"You have a card in here?"

"Not yet, I just started."

The one in the plaid shirt looked at the "contents" on the desk and said, "Is that everything?"

"That's it," Chili said. He watched the black guy pick up the note with the Newark flight number and arrival time written on it. Chili said, "I'd appreciate your telling me what this is about." He could act nervous with these guys without trying too hard.

"I got a John Doe warrant here," the one in the plaid shirt said. "I can strip-search you if I want."

"Pat him down," the black guy said.

"Why don't I strip-search him?"

"Pat him down," the black guy said.

Chili was starting to like the black guy, his quiet way, but couldn't say as much for the other one. The big guy in the plaid shirt put him against the wall, told him to spread his legs and did a thorough job going over him as the black guy asked what he was doing at the airport. Chili said he was supposed to meet his wife, but she wasn't on the flight. The black guy asked why, if he lived in Miami, his wife was coming from Newark? Chili said because they'd had a fight and she left him, went back to Brooklyn. He said he asked her to come out here, maybe with a change of scenery they could get back together and she said okay, but evidently changed her mind. He didn't mention it was twelve years ago she'd left him.

The black guy said, "Your wife a Lakers fan?"

"I am," Chili said. "I'm a fan of everything that's L.A. I love it out here." And looked over his shoulder to give the guy a smile.

The black guy said he could go. Then, when Chili was at the desk, asked him, "What was the number of the locker you used?"

Chili paused. "It was C . . . either sixteen or seventeen." He said, "Can I ask you—are you looking for a bomb? Something like that?"

"Something shouldn't be there," the black guy said.

"Why don't you get the attendant to open all the lockers and take a look? Maybe you'll find it."

"That's an idea," the black guy said. "I'll think about it."

"That's what I'd do," Chili said. "I'd make sure I got the right guy next time."

That was it. Time to collect his "contents" and his new bag and leave. He didn't like the way the black guy was looking at him.

23

CHILI DIDN'T SEE THE STUNTMAN UNTIL HE WAS UP ON the third level of the parking structure. There he was, the Hawaiian Bear, standing by the Toyota. So he must have been here all day. Walking up to him Chili said, "I don't know how I could've missed you with that shirt on. It's the same as the other one you had on only the hibiscus are a different color, right?"

The Bear didn't answer the question. He looked okay, no cuts or bruises showing from his fall down the stairs. He said, "So you didn't have the key with you."

Chili said, "You think I'd be standing here? You set somebody up and you want it to work, it has to be a surprise. Can you remember that?"

"You spotted them, huh?"

This guy was either dumb or he was making conversation.

"Who, the suits? If I know they're there, what's the difference which ones they are? Tell that colored guy you work for he blew it. Whose idea was it, yours or his?" The Bear didn't answer and Chili said, "Did you see it work in some movie you got beat up in? There's quite a difference between movies and real life, isn't there?"

Now Chili was making conversation. For some reason he felt sorry for this guy in his Hawaiian shirt.

"What movies were you in I might've seen?"

The Bear hesitated as if he might be thinking of titles. He wasn't though. He said, "I have to ask you for that key."

"What're you talking about?"

"The locker key."

"I know what one you mean," Chili said. "I can't believe what you're telling me. The setup didn't work so you want the key back?"

"Catlett says if you don't open the locker the deal's off."

"You serious?" Chili said. "This is how you guys do business? I can't believe you aren't dead."

The Bear kept staring but didn't say anything.

"Look," Chili said, "you know as well as I do there's no fuckin way I'm gonna give you the key, outside of you point a gun at my head. Then we might have something to talk about. Otherwise . . . I'd like you to step away from the car."

"I don't need a gun," the Bear said. "Where is it? If it isn't on you, it's around here someplace."

Chili shook his head, tired of this, but still feeling a little sorry for the guy. The Bear didn't seem to have his heart in it; he was going through the motions, doing what he was told. Chili looked off in kind of a thoughtful way, turned to the Bear again and kicked him in the left knee, hard. The Bear stumbled, hunching over. Chili grabbed him by the hair with both hands, pulled his head down and brought his knee up into the guy's face. That straightened him and now Chili hit him high in the belly as hard as he could, right under the rib cage. The Bear gasped and sucked air with his mouth open trying to breathe, helpless now and in pain. Chili took him by the arm saying, "Lie down on your back. Come on, if you want to breathe." He got the Bear down on the concrete, straddled his midsection and reached down to lift him up by the waist of his pants, the same blue ones he had on yesterday, telling him, "Take deep breaths through your mouth and let it out slow . . . That's it, like that."

Once the Bear was breathing okay, checking his teeth now, feeling his nose, Chili said, "Hey. Look at me," and got him to raise his eyes. "Tell your boss I don't ever want to see him again. He made a deal with Harry and a deal's a deal. I'm talking about if we get the dough out of the locker. We don't, then okay, there's no deal. But either way I don't want to see him coming around anymore. You understand? Will you tell him that?"

The Bear seemed to nod, closing and opening his eyes.

"What're you hanging around with a guy like that for? You were in the movies, right? A stuntman? What's he ever done he can talk about? The guy pimps you and you let him do it. You feel okay?"

"Not too bad," the Bear said.

"How 'bout when you went down the stairs?"

He touched his left thigh. "I think I pulled my quadriceps."

"If I was you," Chili said, "I'd quit that guy so fast. No, first I'd kick him down some stairs, let him see what it's like. Then I'd quit."

The Bear didn't say anything, but had a look in his eyes that maybe he was thinking about it.

"How many movies you been in?"

"About sixty."

"No shit," Chili said. "What're some of 'em?"

THE LOCKER KEY WAS DOWN ON THE FIRST LEVEL OF the parking structure, stuck in a crack where the pavement joined one of the concrete support posts. Chili made sure nobody was in sight before he picked it up.

Now he drove to the Avis lot to return the Toyota, walked over to National and took out a Cadillac Sedan de Ville, a black one. There was more to this than switching cars just in case. He felt he deserved a Cadillac. If he had one at home, he should have one out here. At least a Cadillac. Driving up

405 he began thinking that if somehow he got the cash out of that locker he'd tell Harry he wanted a ten percent commission on it, then turn in the Cadillac and lease a Mercedes or that expensive BMW. Karen said top agents and studio execs were driving BMWs now. She said a Rolls was too pretentious; low-key was in. Other things to remember: you don't "take a meeting" anymore, you say you have "a two-thirty at Tower." If a studio passes on a script, you don't say "they took a Pasadena." That was out before it was in. Like "so-and-so gives good phone." If they say it's "for a specialized audience" or it's "a cast-driven script," that's a pass. But what Elaine Levin gave *Lovejoy* was a "soft pass," which meant it was salvageable. There were a lot of terms you had to learn, as opposed to the shylock business where all you had to know how to say was "Give me the fuckin money." He'd call Karen later on, after he had a talk with Harry.

PULLING INTO THE PARKING AREA BENEATH THE SUNSET Marquis he wondered if he should switch hotels. He liked this one, though, a lot. The people here were friendly, relaxed. They gave you free shampoo, suntan lotion, moisturizing cream. The food was good. You could cook in your room if you wanted. There were ashtrays everywhere you looked. A Sunset Marquis ashtray right there by the elevator, if you forgot to take one from your room when you checked out.

Chili unlocked the door to 325 and stepped inside, not too surprised to see the message light on the phone blinking. That would be Harry dying to know how he made out, Harry becoming a nervous wreck lately. He'd tell Harry it was still possible to get the money, but it wasn't going to be easy. Show Harry, first, he still needed him, then straighten him out about the limo guys—stay away from them. Chili took off his suitcoat, turned to drape it over one of the chairs at the counter and saw that someone had been in here.

Not the maid, someone else. The maid hadn't come in yet to clean up the room. You could tell, the newspapers on the sofa, the ashtray by the phone . . .

What had caught his eye, the cupboard doors in the kitchenette were open. Not all the way, but not closed tight either, the way he'd left them. But the desk drawer, Chili noticed, was closed, and he had left that one open about an inch. He had set the drawers in the bedroom the same way, some open an inch or so, some closed—a little nervous about security after the Bear had come in and tossed the place and didn't leave one clue that he'd been here. This one who'd come in either didn't know how to cover his moves or didn't care. The Bear had left the ten grand in the suitcase in the bedroom closet, but this one was different, this guy . . .

Chili was about to go in there and thought, Wait a minute. What if the guy's still here? As he fooled with that idea, looking toward the hall where you went into the bathroom or turned right and two steps took you into the bedroom, he knew who it was. Bones. There was no doubt in his mind now, that fuckin Bones had been here. Or was still here. In the bedroom.

There was one way to find out, but he didn't want to walk in there, maybe surprise him, even though Bones, if he was there, would have heard him come in. Except that you couldn't tell what Bones might do, the guy being either too dumb or crazy to act in a normal way.

What Chili did, he called out, "Hey, Bones? I'm home." Waited maybe ten seconds watching the hall and there he was.

Bones appeared extending a pistol in front of him, some kind of bluesteel automatic. In the other hand he was holding a paper laundry sack you found in hotel closets. Chili didn't have to guess what was in it. His ten grand. Bones waved the pistol at him.

"Get over there, by the sofa."

"You don't need that," Chili said. "You want to sit down and talk, it's fine with me. Get this straightened out."

Chili turned his back on him, walked over to the sofa and sat down. He watched Bones come in the room to stand by the counter, by the suitcoat hanging on the chair, and began to see what was going to happen.

Bones had on a shitty-looking light-gray suit with a yellow sport shirt, the top button fastened. It might be the style out here, but Bones looked like a Miami bookmaker and always would. Jesus, and gray shoes.

"I gave up looking for the drycleaner," Chili said. "This place's all freeways, you can drive around forever and never leave town. How'd you get in here?"

"I told them at the desk I was you," Bones said. "I acted stupid and they believed me."

He came to the middle of the room, still pointing the gun, and held up the laundry sack.

"Where'd you get this?"

"Vegas. I won for a change."

Bones stared at him, not saying anything. Then swung the sack to drop it on a chair.

"Get up and turn around."

"What're you gonna do, search me?"

Chili got to his feet. Bones motioned with the gun and he turned to face the painting over the sofa that looked like a scene in Japan, misty pale green and tan ricefields, the sky overcast, not a lot going on there. He felt Bones lift his wallet out of his back pocket.

"You won the ten grand in Vegas?"

"That's where Leo went before he came here and I lost him."

"Las Vegas."

"Yeah, it's in Nevada."

"Then how come the straps on the ten grand say Harrah's, Tahoe? Can you explain that to me?"

There were figures in the painting he hadn't noticed, people way out in the field picking rice.

Chili said, "You sure it says that, Harrah's?"

He hadn't noticed any printing on the money straps either, or didn't remember.

"You're the stupidest fuckin guy I ever met in my life," Bones said. "Let's see what's in your pockets."

Chili shoved his hands in and pulled the side pockets out.

"What you should've done was told me the guy was alive and skipped, soon as you found out."

Chili heard the voice moving away. He looked over his shoulder to see Bones pulling his suitcoat from the back of the chair at the counter.

"Why would I do that?"

" 'Cause the guy's my customer now, stupid. His ass belongs to me."

Bones laid the pistol on the counter, held the suitcoat up with one hand and felt through it with the other. Chili waited for his expression to change. There—his eyes opening wider.

"What have we here?" Bones said. His hand came out of the coat with the locker key.

Chili sat down in the sofa again.

"Give me my cigarettes. They're in the inside pocket."

Bones threw the coat at him. "Help yourself." And held the key up to look at it. "C-oh-one-eight." Frowning now, putting on a show. "I wonder what this's for, a locker? Yeah, but where is it?"

Chili sat back to smoke his cigarette and let it happen.

"I checked a bag at the airport, when I came."

"Yeah? Which terminal?"

Chili hesitated. He said, "Delta," and it was done.

Bones said, "You found Leo, didn't you? . . . Took the poor asshole's money and put it in a locker, ready to go." Bones looked over. "Why haven't you left?"

"I changed my mind. I like it here."

"Well, there's nothing for you in Miami."

Bones was nervous or anxious, touching his thin strands of hair, his collar, making sure it was buttoned.

"How much's in the locker? Just out of curiosity."

Chili drew on his cigarette, taking his time. "A hunnerd seventy thousand."

"Jesus Christ, that drycleaner left with three hunnerd," Bones said. "I hadn't got here you would've pissed the rest of it away. You knew I was coming, right? That fuckin Tommy Carlo, I know he phoned you."

"Yeah, but he didn't know why. 'Less you told him about the drycleaner."

"I didn't tell him nothing."

"What about Jimmy Cap, you tell him?"

Bones paused. He said, "Look, there's no reason why you and I shouldn't get along. Forget all the bullshit going back to that time—I don't even remember how it started. You took a swing at me over some fuckin thing, whatever it was—forget it. You owe me eight grand, right? Forget that too. But, you don't say a fuckin word about this to anybody. It's strictly between you and I, right?"

"I get to keep the ten in the laundry bag," Chili said.

Bones had to think about that one.

"Look," Chili said, "I was gonna pay you the eight I owe you out of the ten. See, but now you tell me I don't have to. So . . ."

"So I take two out of it and we're square," Bones said. "How's that?"

"Sounds good to me," Chili said.

HE LOOKED UP THE NUMBER FOR THE DRUG ENFORCEMENT Administration in the phone book, dialed it and told the woman who answered he wanted to speak to the agent in charge. She asked what it was in regard to and he said a locker out at the airport, full of money.

A male voice came on saying, "Who's speaking, please?"

"I can't tell you," Chili said, "it's an anonymous call."

The male voice said, "Are you the same anonymous asshole, called last night?"

"No, this's a different one," Chili said. "Have you looked in that locker, C—oh-one-eight?"

There was a pause on the line.

"You're helping us out," the male voice said. "I'd like to know who this is."

"I bet you would," Chili said. "You want to chat or you want me to tell you who to look for? The guy's on his way out right now."

This DEA agent wouldn't give up. He said, "You know there's a reward for information that leads to a conviction. That's why I have to know who this is."

"I'll get my reward in heaven," Chili said. "The guy you want has a bullet scar in his head and is wearing gray shoes. You can't miss him."

24

"THIS WAS WARREN'S OFFICE," KAREN SAID, "BEFORE he was shipped off to Publicity. Warren Hurst, I think I mentioned him to you."

"Beth's Room," Chili said, sitting across from Karen at her big oak desk. "The one that said if you did it your way they wouldn't have a movie."

"You remember that."

She said it with that nice look in her eyes she had been using on him lately. Interested, letting him know she liked him. The only difference today, she had on glasses, round ones with thin black frames. She was telling him now the office decor was pre-Warren, he hadn't been here long enough to redecorate; that it wouldn't be bad in a men's club, but she wasn't going to touch it. "Not till I see if I get a vote here."

Chili said, "You don't fool around."

"What, taking the job? Why not?"

Karen's shoulders moved in the beige silk blouse, the little ninety-pounder behind the big executive desk.

"I think I'll be good at it if they let me. Look at the scripts."

She picked up one from a stack of about ten and moved it to another part of the desk.

"Elaine says all of them have spin in varying degrees. That means they're supposed to be good."

She picked up another one. "*Beth's Room,* still under consideration."

She picked up another and laid it down again.

"Elaine wants to know what I think."

"Tell her the truth."

"Don't worry."

"I got an idea spinning around."

"You told me about it."

As he said, "It's getting better," Karen's phone buzzed.

She picked it up. "Yeah?" Said, "Tell him I'll call him back," and looked at Chili as she hung up. "Harry. That's the third time today."

Chili said, "I have to call him too, tell him what happened."

And Karen said, "That's right, you were going out to the airport," her expression changing, her eyes losing that nice glow as they became serious. She took off her glasses as he told her about the DEA guys and hunched her shoulders leaning on the desk, looking right at him but maybe picturing it too, the scene. That was the feeling he had. He finished the part at the airport and she said, "You really did that?" sounding amazed. "So the money's still there?" He had to tell her about Bones then, and she listened to that part, every word of it, without blinking her eyes. When he finished she sat back in her chair for a moment thinking, still looking at him, then came forward again asking about Bones, who he was. So Chili had to take her all the way back to Vesuvio's and the leather coat.

This time when he finished Karen said, "He'll tell the DEA guys you set it up. Won't he?"

"If they get him," Chili said. "Yeah, Bones'll try to put it on me. If they come around looking and I get hauled in, I say I don't know what he's talking about."

"But they saw you there today," Karen said, "at the airport."

"Yeah, well, they'd still have to prove I put the money in

the locker and there's no way they can do that, 'cause I didn't. I never touched that locker. If I see I'm in too deep I can always give 'em Catlett. But I don't want to go through all that right now. Even if I didn't have to post a bond it would be annoying, the way they keep after you asking questions. So I checked out of the Marquis. Now I have to find another place."

She was giving him that amazed look again. "You're serious."

"Yeah, I tried the Chateau Marmont, see if I could get Jean Harlow's room, but they're full up. One thing I did, not knowing any better at the time, I told the DEA guys I was with ZigZag. They didn't write it down, so they might not remember it, and I didn't have a card to give them. But if they do, they'll look up Harry, try to find me that way."

"What Harry will have trouble accepting," Karen said, "you didn't get the money, not that you could go to jail."

"Yeah, I'll have to explain it to him. Once Bones found the key, the way his one-track mind works it was out of my hands. I had to let it happen."

"I'd like to have seen that," Karen said. She pushed out of her leather chair, came around the desk in a black skirt a few inches above her knees and leaned against the edge of the desk, close, looking down at him. He thought for a moment she was going to touch his face. She said, "I'll bet you have scars . . ."

"A few."

"I like your hair."

"That's another story I could tell you sometime."

She said, "Why don't you hide out at my house?"

"Sleep in the maid's room?"

She said, "We'll work something out."

THERE WAS A CERTAIN LOOK ABOUT THE MEXICAN GARdener that made Harry think of one of his maniacs: the little gnomelike one in *Grotesque Three* who took over after the original hideously disfigured maniac was burned to death in *Grotesque Two* and the picture went on to gross twenty million worldwide. The Mexican gardener coming this way across the lawn was bowlegged. Maybe that was it. *Grotesque Three* did almost eight million, which still wasn't bad. Or it was—of *course,* it was the shears the guy was carrying, the way he held them in front of him with both hands. The gnomelike maniac had used shears a lot.

Harry was on Karen's patio. Out here now as he kept moving, waiting for the phone to ring. Harry nodded to the Mexican approaching with the shears, wishing he'd point them down. "How are you?"

"Miss Flores isn' home."

"I know that," Harry said.

"She's at work."

"I know where she is," Harry said, "and she knows I'm here. It's okay, I'm a good friend of hers. We're amigos."

This Mexican, with his dark skin and big nose, reminded Harry of an Aztec figure carved in relief on a stone wall. It got Harry thinking about human sacrifices, a blood cult four centuries old, virgins into the volcano . . . like movie ideas presented to a studio. The Mexican was saying something.

"What?"

"I ask you want a drink."

"Do I want a drink—I thought you were the gardener."

"The houseman, Miguel. I do outside, inside, everything."

Harry said, "*You're* Miguel?" feeling a change in his mood, a sudden lift knowing Karen wasn't sleeping with her houseman, not this old guy and not that it made any difference, really, but he felt better in general and said, "Yeah, Miguel, let me have a Scotch, lot of ice."

FOUR TIMES NOW CATLETT HAD TRIED TO GET HOLD OF the Bear: phoning his house from home, from the limo office, from his Porsche coming here and now here, in the turn-around part of the driveway at Karen Flores's French-looking house. Still no answer, only the Bear's recorded voice: Leave a message if you want. The only thing good happening Catlett could see was Harry's old Mercedes parked there, and Harry was the reason he'd come. Catlett went up to the door and rang the bell, set his sunglasses on straight, smoothed down his double-breasted navy blazer he wore with a white cotton shirt open wide at the throat and cream-colored pants.

The door swung in and the man standing there startled him, flashed him back in his mind to migrant camps and hundreds of guys with round, tired shoulders just like this one. Catlett said, "Man, I haven't seen you since picking lettuce down the Imperial Valley. How you doing?" Found out this was Miguel the houseman and got taken out to the kitchen where his good friend Harry Zimm was sitting at the table with a drink, a bottle of Chivas Regal and a big pair of garden shears, the kind with ten-inch blades and wooden handles. Harry had that expectant look in his eyes, hoping for news.

"You hear anything?"

"I was about to ask you," Catlett said. "There's been plenty of time to do it."

He turned his head and there was Miguel the houseman asking what would he like to drink, this stoop-labor field hand, Catlett thinking Karen Flores must be a strange kind of lady.

"Let me have a glass of chilled white wine. Some Pouilly-Fuissé, you happen to have it in the house."

Harry said, "Well, I guess he ran with it."

Harry sounding tired out, depressed.

"Or, as I mentioned could happen if he wasn't careful," Catlett said, "somebody hit him on the head. Or, there's the chance he got busted."

"What he got was the money," Harry said. "I called his hotel. They said he checked out."

"He could've done that before."

"I spoke to him at ten this morning. He was just leaving."

"That's right, that's what I heard."

From the Bear, phoning as he tailed him, the Bear in communication up to that time.

"He didn't check out," Harry said, "till two-thirty this afternoon."

Catlett said, "Hmmmmm," to Harry, nothing to Miguel, noticing the man's broken fingernails, big knuckles, handing him the glass of wine; or when Miguel said he was leaving, going home, and walked out the back door to the garage.

Harry looked so depressed he seemed in a daze.

"I didn't think he'd do it. I said to him, 'I wonder if I'll ever see you again.' But I honestly thought I would."

Catlett sat down with Harry at the table wondering why, if Chili Palmer was going to run with it, he didn't take a flight out while he was at the airport. Why come back to the hotel? The Bear would have the answer if he could ever locate the Bear.

"Harry, you can't trust nobody like that, has those bad connections. This man come in off the street, nobody speaking for him, you don't know who he is."

"He was working for Mesas. I know the people there and they know him. They use him for collections."

"They know the guy that takes out the garbage too. Harry. How'd he find you right away if I couldn't?"

"Through Frank DePhillips."

"Man, what does that tell you? What you're saying to me right there?"

"I was staying here that night . . ."

"Yeah, with Karen?"

"We're in bed, we hear a noise. Voices. We listen awhile. It's the TV, downstairs. Karen says, 'But it can't just come on by itself.' I tell her, 'That's right, somebody had to push the button.' So I go down . . ."

"You have a gun?"

"Where do I get a gun? Karen doesn't own one. No, I went downstairs figuring it has to be somebody she knows. Some friend of hers probably stoned, thinks he's a riot. I walk in the study, the TV goes off—it was the Letterman show—the light comes on and there's Chili sitting at the desk."

"Chili Palmer," Catlett said, "yeah. Sneaky, huh? You should've known right then, just from the way he does things. Man breaks in the house . . ."

"The patio door was open."

"Yeah? Was there a sign on it, 'Come on in'? Harry, you walk in where you don't belong it's breaking and entering, whether you have to break in or not. Chili Palmer commits a felony against the law and you take him in, make him your partner."

"He isn't my partner," Harry said, and took a drink from his glass. "I don't know what he is."

That was okay as far as it went. But what Catlett wanted would be for Harry to kick and scream, call the man names. A no-good lying motherfucker would cover it. Harry though, for some reason, didn't seem all the way unsold yet on Chili Palmer. So Catlett reset his gold-frame sunglasses and went at him again saying, "The man robs you and you tell me you don't know what he *is*? If he managed to get his hands on the hundred and seventy thousand and took off with it . . . Harry, you paying attention?"

"Yeah, if he got it, what?"

"Or, if he messed up out there and *they* got it, but somehow or other they didn't get *him* . . . What I'm saying is either way, Harry, it was your money. You understand? Soon as I presented you with the key to the locker it was the same as giving you the money. So you the one he ripped off, huh?"

Harry was looking at him with a frown turning all of a sudden from worried to mean.

"You're saying I still owe it to you? A hundred and seventy grand I haven't even *seen?*"

It wasn't the point Catlett had intended to make. Yeah, but it was true. He opened his hands, helpless, and said to Harry, "Man, you owe me *some*thing."

KAREN HAD GIVEN HIM A KEY TO THE FRONT DOOR, IN case her houseman had already left.

Chili dropped his suitcase in the foyer, checked the study, the living room, then moved down the back hall to the kitchen. He knew Harry's car, could guess who the Porsche belonged to and got it right—Mr. Bo Catlett in the kitchen with Harry, Catlett looking this way through his hotdog sunglasses. It was in Chili's mind to grab a frying pan from the rack, go over the table with it and whop him across the head. Right now, not say a word. But he was no sooner in the kitchen Catlett was on his feet, Christ, holding a pair of shears in front of him. Chili said, "You knew I was coming, huh?" looking at the shears, the blades gunmetal, clamped together. "The Bear tell you?"

He wanted Catlett to answer, keep it between them and settle with this guy. But now Harry got into it, Harry again, ruining the moment.

"I don't know how many times I tried to call you," Harry said. "Where've you been?"

"Talking to federal agents," Chili said, still looking at Catlett. "DEA, the ones were waiting for me."

"They let you go?" Harry said.

"It didn't take too long."

Catlett said, "Uh-huh. Harry, you understand what he saying? If he was talking to federal agents, how come he's here talking to us?"

Chili said, "I didn't have the key on me."

Catlett said, "You didn't have the key . . ." and let his voice trail off. "All right, why would they pick you up then, if you didn't have the key?"

"They thought I opened the locker."

"But you didn't?"

"Ask the Bear, he saw it."

"Is that right? You talk to him?"

"After. He wanted me to give him back the key," Chili said, and watched Catlett take that and run with it.

"Sure, 'cause I told him, anything goes wrong, see if you can help out. Like take the key off your hands, case you get followed and picked up again they won't find it on you." Looking at Harry: "I told you it could happen, didn't I? That's why I said don't you go out there, send your man here." Looking at Chili again. "You know what I'm talking about. You experienced in shit where you have to keep your eyes open. Was I wrong? If you still have the key, what's the problem? Wait for it to cool and try again. Only be more careful next time."

Chili said, "That's all you have to say?"

Catlett frowned in his sunglasses. "I don't see what the problem is."

"I told you, they were waiting for me."

"You're the type they go for, man. I can't help it how you look."

This guy was not only sure of himself, he was starting to get cocky, insulting even. Chili fingered the button holding his double-breasted jacket closed. He said, "I'll make you a deal. If you can get out of here before I take my coat off, I won't clean the floor with you, get your yacht-club outfit all messed up."

Catlett shook his head, acting tired. He said, "Harry, you hear this?"

"Harry, stay out of it. This's between me and him," Chili said, undoing the button to let the jacket come open. He said to Catlett, "You have your choice."

"You don't know me," Catlett said, his voice quiet now. "You only think you do."

"I know if I wanted to," Chili said, "I could take those shears away from you and cut your nuts off. You want to stay around, take a chance?"

"I think the party's getting rough," Catlett said. "Harry, this make any sense to you?"

"It will, when I tell him how they knew I was coming," Chili said, holding the coat open now to slip it off his shoulders. "You want to add something to that? Ask me how I found out?"

Catlett shrugged, keeping whatever he felt about it to himself, behind his sunglasses. He said, "What's the difference? I'm not gonna get into it with you," and laid the shears on the table. "This kind of shit is not my style." He moved to the door saying, "Whatever is, huh, Harry? But you still need all kinds of money, don't you?" and walked out of the kitchen, into the hall.

Chili reached across the table to pick up the glass of wine, ice-cold on the tips of his fingers, and took a sip, Harry watching him.

"What it comes down to after all that, you didn't get the money."

Chili stood listening till he heard the front door close.

"There's more to it, Harry."

"But you still have the key?"

"There's a lot more to it," Chili said, pulling a chair out from the table.

TURNING OUT OF KAREN'S DRIVE, CATLETT WAS BUSY handling all the stuff flashing in his head at once. He had to talk to the Bear, find out before he did anything else what happened at the airport, where the key was, how Chili Palmer knew he was informed on unless he was lying, telling Harry stories now, except the only good thing about it was Harry needed money more than he needed Chili Palmer, but Chili Palmer still had to be removed from the situation. There was something else flashing in his head, that suitcase . . . And Catlett had to crank the wheel, quick, waking up to the BMW turning in directly in front of him. The cars came side by side, the windows going down, the woman's face in the BMW a bit higher than his. Catlett put his sunglasses up on his head. He smiled, seeing late sun reflected in her sunglasses, not smiling. He said, "Miss Flores, this is my pleasure. Harry Zimm might've mentioned my name to you, Bo Catlett?"

She kept looking, though her face didn't change.

So he said, "Can I tell you I've always been one of your biggest fans?"

Her face still didn't change as she said, "What're you doing here?"

He said, "I was with Harry," acting a little surprised on account of her tone. "We had a meeting."

Her face *still* didn't change, this time saying to him, "If I ever see you here again I'll call the police."

The BMW was there and then it wasn't and he was looking at shrubs. Man. Whatever the woman had heard about him couldn't have been too good. Like Chili Palmer had been talking to her. Already today, with everything going on he had taken the time. Came back from the airport, checked out of his hotel . . . And there was that other thing that had flashed in his head to think about, the black nylon suitcase sitting in her front hall by the door.

The suitcase hadn't been there before Chili Palmer came.

Checked out of the hotel and was moving in with Karen

Flores. Sure, the one he wanted in the movie as the girl. Checked out in case the DEA people wanted to look him up again and came here to hide. Which presented new possibilities, didn't it? Catlett drove down the hill thinking of some, deciding which one he might use. The one he liked best was the simplest. Shoot the motherfucker and have it done.

FOR A FEW MOMENTS HE WASN'T AWARE OF HER standing in the doorway.

Karen watched him sitting alone at the table. Saw the bottle of Scotch, the garden shears, saw him raise his glass of wine and take a sip. He had a cigarette going too. She watched him draw on the cigarette and raise his head to exhale a thin stream of smoke. Karen the camera again watching him, this guy who had told her in a matter-of-fact way federal agents might pick him up and he might have to post bond. . . . She wanted to know what happened while Catlett was here. Where was Harry and why the garden shears? She had questions to ask and something amazing to tell him—Chili Palmer in his pinstripe suit, tough guy from Miami. Not a movie tough guy, a real one. She kept watching him with her camera eye wondering if, real or not, he could be acting. If he was, he was awfully good.

"Not a worry in the world," Karen said.

He looked over. "Hey, how you doing?"

"You really aren't worried, are you?"

He said, "About what?"

And she had to smile because that was an act, the bland expression. But he wasn't serious about it, he was smiling now and that seemed natural.

"Where's Harry?"

"I think he's in the bathroom. He didn't say where he was going, but that'd be my guess."

She said, "Catlett was here? . . ."

"Yeah, did you see him?"

"I almost ran into him, on his way out."

"I think basically he's all the way out now," Chili said. "I explained the whole thing to Harry, told him if he ever saw the guy again he oughta have his brain looked at. Harry kept nodding, yeah, he understood, till I got to the part, Bones walking out with the locker key? He hasn't said a word to me since."

"He does that," Karen said, "he pouts."

She wondered again about the shears, but was more anxious to tell him the latest amazing development.

"Meanwhile, back at the studio, Elaine spoke to Michael . . ."

Right away Chili said, "Hey, where's Harry?" looking toward the door. "He's got to hear this."

"He wants to meet with *you,*" Karen said. "He didn't mention Harry."

She kept her eyes on Chili, who didn't say anything now, staring at her as she sat down across the table from him.

"You told Michael about the drycleaner and the shylock."

"That's what he wants to talk about?"

"And he told Elaine it was the best pitch he's ever heard. Now Elaine wants to hear it."

"Yeah, but it wasn't a pitch. He was pretending he was a shylock, wondering what it'd be like. So I gave him a situation, that's all."

"He wants to have dinner with you this evening, at Jimmy's. That is," Karen said, watching him, "if you can make it."

He said, "Is it a nice place?" with his bland look, eyebrows raised.

And she said, "You think it's funny. You *do.* But you're going to meet with him, aren't you?"

"It depends," Chili said. "Who pays?"

"You don't have a script. You have the beginning of an idea that doesn't go anywhere . . ."

"I've added to it. There's a girl in it now."

"Yeah—and what happens? What's the *story*?"

"You mean what's the theme? I'm still thinking about the visual fabric, as they say."

"I can't believe you're serious."

"The guy wants to talk—I know how to do that. But Harry has to be there too."

"Or you won't meet with him?"

"Why's it have to be like that? Get his permission. Harry comes along, he's there, right? What's Michael gonna do, tell him to leave? We'll talk about *Lovejoy,* bring it up, see what happens. If Michael says no, Harry'll have a chance to argue with him. He won't blame me if the guy doesn't want to do it."

"You're serious," Karen said.

"I don't see what's the big deal."

"Right, it's only a movie." She had to smile at him. "Fifteen years in Hollywood . . . I'd give anything to be there."

"You can come. Why not?"

She was shaking her head as Harry walked in and Chili said, "Michael called. He wants to meet."

"Well, it's about time," Harry said.

Karen shook her head again, this time slowly, in amazement. Harry, pouring himself a Scotch, didn't notice. But Chili did. He gave her his innocent look, with the eyebrows.

25

WHEN HE ASKED KAREN IF IT WAS A NICE PLACE HE WAS kidding and she never said, or told him who was supposed to pay. As soon as they walked in through the dark cocktail lounge area, Chili knew dinner for three would run at least a hundred bucks with wine.

He and Harry were taken to a table in the middle of the front section, eight-thirty, the restaurant crowded. Michael had made the reservation, but didn't show up till after nine. Then it took him about ten minutes to get to the table, stopping off to say hello to people sticking their hands out at him, Michael pleasant about it, smiling at everybody. Like Momo coming into a joint on 86th Street, getting the treatment. Only Momo would have a suit on, as most of the guys did here; Michael was wearing his World War Two flight jacket with a dark T-shirt under it.

As soon as he sat down at the table he looked at their drinks, ordered a Perrier and then started fanning the air in front of him.

"Would you guys mind terribly not smoking?"

Harry stubbed his cigarette out in a hurry saying of course not, he was trying to quit anyway. Chili took another drag on his and blew it out past the empty chair at the table, toward the entrance to the room where a little guy with dark shiny hair was standing there looking around as the maître d' hurried up to him, the maître d' giving him the same treatment he had given Michael, though the guy was not a movie star or Chili would have known him. Chili believed ninety percent of the guys in Hollywood had dark hair and looking around the room confirmed it. What he saw was a lot of hair, dark hair on the guys, different shades of blond hair on the women; older guys with younger women, girls, which was what he had expected. He observed this as Michael was saying that, according to a study he read, smokers exercised less than nonsmokers, were not as likely to use seat belts, were more prone to argue, missed work more often than nonsmokers, and were two-point-two times more likely to be dissatisfied with their lives, not to mention they were two-point-six times more likely to have bronchitis and emphysema.

Harry was saying, "They made a study, huh? Gee, that's interesting, I'd like to read it," as the mâitre d' was looking this way now and the little guy with the dark shiny hair was coming to the table. Chili noticed he had on a dark-gray shirt and tie with a dark-gray sport coat and light-gray pants that looked like pajamas. Drab colors, but the guy still had a shiny appearance. He pulled out the empty chair and sat down. A waiter tried to push his chair in and the guy waved him away, turning the chair and hunching toward Michael, his back to Chili. As this was happening Michael said, "Buddy—" sounding a little surprised.

So this was Michael's agent.

Buddy was supposed to know Harry, but didn't even glance at him. He started right in with, "They want you to take a meeting with this producer they keep talking about. You believe it? The guy's a fucking *writer.* I mean he writes *books,* not even screenplays, but he wants this broad as the producer. I never heard of this in my life."

"I want the property," Michael said.

"Don't worry about it, you'll get the property. I said to the guy's agent, 'The fuck *is* this, you trying to hold a gun to my head? We have to take the broad?' Which is out of the question. I said, 'What if there's no communication between she and Michael? What's she made, three pictures?' One did okay, the other two barely earned back negative costs."

"I want that book," Michael said.

"Michael, you'll get the book, soon as we get done with this pissing contest. If it was a director—yeah, I can understand he's got a producer he likes to work with. But this is a fucking *writer.* I said to his agent, 'Hey, Michael doesn't *have* to option this book, you know.' And the agent goes, 'And we don't have to sell it.' I go, 'Well, what the fuck is the guy writing for, he doesn't want to sell his work?' You ever hear anything like that?"

"You have to understand his motivation," Michael said. "A writer can spend years working on a book he isn't sure will ever sell. What makes him do it?"

"Money. The idea of hitting big," Buddy said. "Selling one to Michael Weir. What else? Look, what we do, we say okay to the meeting. The broad arrives, we ask her to wait a minute, be right with you. I call the guy's agent and I say, 'Do we have a deal? Come on, we have a deal or not? We don't have a deal, I'm sending the broad home.' Put it to them like that, I guarantee you within five minutes we'll have a deal."

Chili watched Michael playing with a book of matches that would never be used for lighting cigarettes, Michael saying, "How you handle it is up to you."

Buddy said, "I'll give you a call."

Getting up he seemed to notice Harry for the first time, Harry waiting to be recognized, Harry saying, "Buddy, how you doing?" The agent nodded, said yeah, great. Chili watched him glance this way now—like, what, another one? Where'd these guys come from? Michael didn't tell him. He said one more time he wanted that book. Buddy told him it was his, and left.

Harry said, "Well now . . ."

But there was something Chili wanted to know and he said to Michael, "What he mentioned to you there . . . You mind my asking—what if the other agent says okay, you got a deal? Then will you have the meeting with the woman, the producer?"

"I don't know, I suppose," Michael said, "we'd talk to her. I'm not really involved in this."

Harry said, "Chil, it has nothing to do with Michael."

And now Michael was nodding. "All it amounts to is a power play, the dance of the agents, circling each other for position."

"With the woman in the middle," Chili said, "not knowing what's going on. I was thinking she's sitting there like a hostage. Use her to get what you want."

"Hey, come on, man. All I want is a book."

"They say no deal, what do you do, shoot her?"

Chili smiled.

Michael didn't.

He said, "Why is everybody giving me a hard time?"

IT WAS DARK AND CATLETT STILL HADN'T SPOKEN TO the Bear. Had been calling him since coming home and getting no answer, the Bear's machine turned off. Right now Catlett was standing out on his deck looking at the night, trying to get his head to settle.

Looking at the view he started thinking about his great-great-grandfather with the cavalry sword, because that original Bo Catlett had lived on a mountain and must've had a view of his own, but without any lit-up swimming pools and girls laughing or, tonight, the cool sound of Jobim coming from down there. The original Bo Catlett had his view, had his sword, had his squaw wife—but what did he *do*? This Catlett's grandmother said, that time before she died, "Oh, he had plenty to do," but never said what. So this Catlett started thinking of western movies, wondering what people outside of cowboys did back then. They lived in little towns that had one street, wore six-guns and were always crossing the street going someplace, the extras in the movies. The stuntmen were always getting shot off of horses or off of roofs or falling through the railings on upstairs porches and balconies. Fall against the railing shot and it would give way every time, like the carpenters of the Old West didn't know shit about putting up railings. Bump against a railing shot, man, you're going through it . . .

And here he was leaning against a railing himself, his head having come all the way around a hundred years back to now.

You could bump against this railing all you wanted. It was California redwood, bolted together, built solid. The drop was about the same as looking down from a hotel room on the twelfth floor he had stayed in one time. If you fell through like in a movie, you wouldn't come close to that swimming pool. You'd hit on the slope partway down and from there it would be like falling down stairs, only you'd land in the scrub and shit where the coyotes hid. . . . Seeing this and thinking, Invite Chili Palmer out here.

Thinking, I don't know why, Officer, but it just give way on him.

Catlett picked up the phone from a deck chair, punched a number for about the twentieth time today and got him. *Damn.* The Bear's voice came on and Catlett said, "How you doing this evening?" having decided hours ago to be cool with the Bear, save his emotions.

"The guy faked them out," the Bear said.

"This Chili Palmer you speaking of? I *know* that much."

"You see on the news the drug bust at LAX? They picked up a guy from Miami. Alleged member of organized crime."

"You watching the news?" Catlett said. "What else? Watch some sitcoms 'stead of calling me?"

"I had to take Farrah to Costa Mesa, to her mother's. She had the news on and that's when I saw it. Then I had to stay a while and visit, talk about how I'm always late with the check. I got back, I had to eat. I figured you'd have talked to Harry, found out what happened. But I didn't actually give a shit if you did or not. I don't work for you no more, or Ronnie. I quit."

Catlett said, "This the man use to jump offa high buildings talking?"

"Into air bags," the Bear said. "There's no cushion under what you're doing. I got responsibilities, I got Farrah to think about."

"You always had Farrah. Took her on buys with you."

"I'm out of it, Cat. Ronnie picked up two keys for Palm Desert. I'll drop off the rest tomorrow morning and I'm done."

"Been giving it serious thought, huh?"

"All the way down to Costa Mesa and back."

"How 'bout we talk about it tomorrow? Tonight, later on, I got one for you doesn't involve any heavy work. Chili Palmer's staying with that woman, Karen? I need you to get me in the house."

"I'm already an accessory on one count," the Bear said. "You want to get in, bust a window."

"I'm thinking she might have an alarm system."

"Good, so don't do it."

"Something happened to you, huh? Like that tumble down the stairs shook you up."

"Or straightened me out," the Bear said. "It's different. It isn't like a stunt gag, you're ready, you know what's gonna happen. This guy doesn't fool around, he comes right at you. You talked to him, yeah, but you don't know him."

Catlett said, "Uh-huh," and said, "Bear, I had an idea. Listen to this."

Making it sound as though he was starting over and they were still friends.

"You get your saw—no, get your wrench, and fix my deck railing to give way like they do in movies. You know what I'm saying? Like when the guy gets hit he falls against it and it gives way on him? All you do is loosen the bolts that hold the upright part of the rail to the deck. So then I invite Chili Palmer out here to look at my view. Get him to lean over the railing, see what's down there . . . Huh? What you think?"

"This isn't a movie, Cat. This guy's real."

"It could be done though. Sure, loosen some bolts. I can see it . . . Except how would I get him out here? So I better go in the woman's house and do him. You helping me."

There was a silence on the line before the Bear said, "I'm not gonna do it."

"You sure?"

"I told you, I quit."

"I hate being alone, Bear."

"That's too fucking bad."

"I hate it so much, man, if I go down I'll plea-deal you in. Give 'em this ace burglar now one of the West Coast dope kings, if they go easy on the Cat. You dig? Tell 'em where you live, where you keep the product, all that shit they love to hear."

There was that silence again. This time all the Bear said was "Why?" in a quiet tone of voice.

" 'Cause I'm a mean motherfucker," Catlett said. "Why you think?" and hung up the phone.

It was fun playing with the Bear, putting fear in a man his size. Now forget him. He hadn't needed the Bear to do Yayo or the gas station man in Bakersfield or the fools he did over business, the one in his car waiting at a light, the other one on his front steps. He didn't sit down and *plan* doing those people. He saw the need and did them. Do this one the same way and don't think so much, worrying if there was an alarm system in the house. Harry said Chili Palmer had come in the house at night. He didn't say nothing about any alarm system going off. Chili Palmer had come in the house and turned the TV on and Harry had to go downstairs being the man, but without a gun, 'cause there wasn't a gun in the house, was there?

IT TOOK HARRY ABOUT TWO MINUTES TO DECIDE ON the Norwegian salmon—anxious to talk, get things going—and another Scotch. Chili kept reading the menu while Michael told them about the curious negative influence his father became in motivating his career. Harry was willing to bet Chili, after all the time he spent on the menu, would order a steak; and he did, the filet rare, baked potato, house salad, the soup, a half-dozen bluepoints and, yeah, another Scotch. But Michael wasn't finished telling about his dad, this tyrant who manufactured hairpieces and wanted his sonny to follow him in the rug trade, the headwaiter standing by. Then Michael had to look at the menu for a while, Harry willing to bet anything he wouldn't order from it. It was an unwritten rule in Hollywood, actors never ordered straight from the menu; they'd think of something they had to have that wasn't on it, or they'd tell exactly how they wanted the entrée prepared, the way their mother back in Queens used to fix it. The seven-million-dollar actor in the jacket a bum wouldn't wear told the headwaiter he felt like an omelet, hesitant about it, almost apologetic. Could he have a cheese omelet with shallots, but with the shallots only slightly browned? The headwaiter said yes, of course. Then could he have some kind of light tomato sauce over it with just a hint of garlic but, please, no oregano? Of course. And fresh peas in the tomato sauce? Harry wanted to tell him, Michael, you can have any fucking thing you want. You want boiled goat? They'll send out for it if they don't have one. Jesus, what you had to go through with actors. The ideal situation would be if you could make movies without them.

"WHAT FASCINATES ME ABOUT THIS ONE," MICHAEL said, "is the chance to play an essentially cliché-type character in a way that's never been done before, against his accepted image."

Harry liked the sound of that. He wished he could light up, so he could enjoy it more. Chili, busy eating ice cream, might or might not be paying attention.

"It's not unlike the way I saw Bonaparte in *Elba,*" Michael said. "The script had him morose, dour, bound by his destiny to play the tragic figure. I thought, yeah, that's the portrait we've all seen, with the hand shoved inside his coat. But why were his troops so loyal? Why were they willing to follow this neurotic guy, with the original Napoleon complex, to hell and back time after time, until finally Waterloo?"

Harry thinking, *To Hell and Back,* Audie Murphy, about 1955.

As Michael said, "What I did was separate the man from the historic figure, visualize a dichotomy, imagine him offstage making love, getting drunk, generally kicking back . . ." Michael grinned. "No pun intended."

Harry didn't get it.

"And you know what? I saw him rather impish in his off moments. Maybe because he was a little guy and I had to play him that way. I saw him childlike with a love of life, a mischievous glow. I have him telling jokes, mimicking his generals, I do one like a French Howard Cosell. I drink wine, smoke hash and giggle, I moon Josephine a couple of times in the film . . . Anyway it's this human side that my grenadiers sense, the reason they love *me,* not the historic figure, and are willing to die for me."

"Sure," Harry said, "you bring out that human side you've got the audience empathizing with you."

Chili said, "Why'd he put his hand in his coat like that?"

"It was a fashionable way to pose," Michael said. "And that's what I'm talking about. There's the pose of the character, as most people see him, and there's the real person who laughs and cries and makes love. I think the romance angle in our story is critically important, that it isn't simply a jump in the sack for either of them. These two become deeply in love. There's even a certain reverence about it, the way they fuck. Do you know what I mean? And it's totally in contrast to the guy's accepted character."

"From the way he appears in the beginning," Harry said.

Michael didn't even glance over. He went on saying to Chili—no doubt because Chili had spoken to him about it that other time—"Once their lives are in danger and you have the mob guy coming after them, it not only heightens tension, it adds a wistful element to their love. Now, because they have more to live for, they also have more to lose."

Harry said, "The mob guy?"

Michael, the typical actor, onstage, ignored that one too. A simple, honest question, for Christ sake.

"I also have to consider, I mean as the character, this is another man's wife I'm sleeping with. I know the guy's a schmuck, he's a sneak . . . By the way, what does he do?"

"He's an agent," Chili said, "and his wife, he handles, is a rock-and-roll singer."

Michael nodded. "Like Nicki. I like that. I don't mean for the part, but a character like her."

Harry stared at Chili now, Chili eating his ice cream and refusing to look over this way, Chili telling Michael, "We're still working on the ending."

Michael said, "You are?" sounding surprised. "I thought you were bringing the script."

"You have the first draft," Harry said, wanting to start over, make some sense out of this. "The one you read I sent to your house?"

He saw Michael shaking his head with that surprised look and Chili saying right away, "Basically it's the ending has to be fixed, but there some other parts too." The hell was he talking about? Now Michael was looking at his watch.

"Elaine wants us to come by tomorrow, sometime in the afternoon. How does that sound?"

Harry saw Chili nodding, so he nodded.

"I have to run," Michael said. "But what I hope to see, they begin to have misgivings about wanting the money. It becomes their moral dilemma and they try to rationalize keeping it, but in the end they can't." Looking at Chili the whole time. "Can they?"

"Which money," Harry said, "are we talking about?"

That got Michael's attention, finally, but with a kind of bewildered look on his face. "The three hundred large. What other money is there? I'm not being facetious, I'm asking, since I haven't read the script. I think their idea, ultimately, would be to let the husband keep it, knowing he'll get caught sooner or later. No, wait." Michael paused. "The mob guy gets to the husband first, the agent, and whacks him, knocks him off. But he doesn't have the money. Somehow the lovers have gotten hold of it. We see it piled on a bed. Make it a million—why not? The mob guy, who scares hell out of the audience, is closing in but the lovers don't know it. So now you've got the big scene coming up. But just before it happens . . . Well, it could be after, either way, but it's the shylock who makes the decision, they can't keep it."

Harry said, "The *shy*lock?"

Michael turned to him saying, "Look at me, Harry."

Harry was already looking at him.

Now Chili was saying, "That's not bad. I think you got it down."

Harry turned to Chili and back to Michael again.

"Jesus Christ, you mean all this time . . ."

But Michael wasn't listening. He was getting up from the table saying, "I should keep quiet, I know, till I've read the script, but I've got a feeling about this one. I'm that shylock. Really, it scares me how well I know him. I could do this one tomorrow, no further preparation."

"What am I thinking?" Chili said.

Michael grinned at him. "Well, I might need a week to get ready. But I'll see you tomorrow, right? At Tower." He started to go, paused and said, "Chil, work on that moral dilemma. Harry? Remember that time you turned me down for *Slime Creatures*? I'm glad you did. I might've gotten typecast."

Michael table-hopped and touched hands all the way out. Harry watched him before turning to Chili.

"All that time he's talking about your movie."

Chili nodded.

"That's what we came for?"

Chili nodded.

"You told Michael about your movie when you saw him that time? You never talked about *Lovejoy*?"

Chili finished his ice cream. He said, "Harry," getting his cigarettes out, "let's light up and have an after-dinner drink. What do you say?"

26

KAREN WAS WAITING FOR HIM. HE SAW HER COMING away from the front steps in a heavy-knit white sweater as he got out of the car. They walked around to the patio side of the house and over to the swimming pool that was like a pond with a clear bottom, leaves, dark shapes on the surface, Chili telling about the dinner with Michael, most of what happened, and finally asking her, "Guess who paid?"

Karen said that, first of all, high-priced actors never picked up the check. They had no idea what things cost. They seldom knew their zip code and quite often didn't know their own phone number. Especially guys who changed the number every time they dumped a girlfriend. Telling him this quietly in the dark. He felt they could be in a woods far away from any people or sounds or lights, unless you looked at the house and saw dim ones in some of the windows. They could have walked in the house when he got out of the car, but she was waiting for him with the idea of coming out here. It told him they were going to end up in bed before too long. He wasn't sure how he knew this, other than being alone in the dark seemed to set the mood, the idea of moonlight and a nice smell in the air, except the moon was pretty much clouded over. Her waiting for him outside was the tip-off. He didn't ask himself why she wanted to go to bed with him. It never entered his mind.

"So who paid, you or Harry?"

"I did."

"You felt sorry for him."

"Well, yeah, maybe. Twice in one day I have to explain something where he's already made up his mind I'm trying to stick him. Michael left, we sat there another hour and talked. You know what his omelet cost?"

"Twenty bucks?"

"Twenty-two-fifty."

"And he ate maybe half of it," Karen said.

"Not even that. The whole shot came to two and a quarter, with the tip, and we didn't have any wine."

"Harry went home?"

"Yeah, feeling sorry for himself. I said to him, 'This wasn't my idea, I didn't call it. If you wanted to ask him about *Lovejoy,* why didn't you?' Harry says, 'What, follow him out to the parking lot?' Harry had a point. Michael does all the talking and then he's gone, never mentioned the check. You know, at least offered. No—see you tomorrow at the meeting. Now I either have to make up something quick or forget the whole thing. Or let him do it. Michael knows more about it than I do anyway. All the time at dinner he's telling me how it should work: that the love part should be important and how he wants to play the shylock as a nice guy—like people don't mind paying him a hunnerd and fifty percent interest. You know what I'm saying?"

"That's what Michael does," Karen said. "He turns the story around to suit himself and then walks away. The shylock becomes a brain surgeon. The dry cleaner—who knows?"

"I'm thinking of making him an agent," Chili said, "and his wife, Fay, a rock-and-roll singer. It's a little different'n what I told you and Harry. She comes here with the shylock and they fall in love looking for Leo. Also there's a mob guy that's after them."

Karen stopped and turned to him. "His name Ray Bones?"

"Yeah, but I think I'll change it. I don't want to get sued. I've had enough of Ray Bones to last me the rest of my life."

They started walking again, strolling toward the house. Karen's shoulders hunched in the bulky sweater, hands shoved into the sleeves. She said, "What about Catlett?"

"He's not in it."

She said, "Are you sure? You have an idea for a movie based on something that actually happened, but now you're beginning to fictionalize. Which is okay, like bringing Fay into it more . . ."

Chili said, "After I saw that's what *Lovejoy* needed."

"That's fine—but what exactly are you keeping and what are you throwing away?"

"Well, if I have Bones as the bad guy, what do I need Catlett for? It's not about making a movie, it's about getting your hands on money without getting killed. Or it's about a moral dilemma, as Michael says. If they do get their hands on the money, can they keep it? Michael says no."

"So you resolve that," Karen said. "You have action, suspense, romance, good characters . . . You have that wonderful scene with Bones in the hotel room. He takes the locker key and you set him up." She paused and said, "It's cool the way it works, but you can't end the picture with it. What happens next, at the airport, is offstage. But if it did play as a scene you wouldn't be in it."

"You mean the shylock."

Karen said, "Yeah, right," thinking of something else. "What you might do is play the hotel room scene with Leo instead of Bones—it's too good to throw away. Leo finds the key, leaves to pick up the money and you call the DEA."

"I wouldn't do that."

"But you did."

"Yeah, to Bones. I wouldn't do it to Leo."

She said, "Well . . . I don't know. I like Catlett as a character, if you could use him somehow. Doesn't he fit into this at all?"

"He's Harry's problem."

"Isn't Harry in it?"

"I left that part out, the shylock looking for him."

He thought of Catlett again. He thought of the Bear, the Bear falling down the restaurant stairs, but didn't see how he could use that either.

Karen said, "I wouldn't throw anything away just yet," as they reached the patio and she turned to him. She looked cold, hugging herself with her hands in the sweater sleeves. "What're you going to call it, *Chili's Hollywood Adventure*?"

"That's a different story. I like it, though, so far."

She said, "What happens next?"

He said, "I'm ready if you are."

HE'D OPEN HIS EYES AND SHE'D BE WATCHING HIM, THE first time smiling, and he remembered her telling him Michael said funny things. Then she'd close her eyes and he'd close his, moving with her, all the time moving, and he'd open his eyes and she'd be looking at him again, face-to-face in the lamplight. She was feeling it, not just going through the motions, he could tell by her face, a certain look around her nose and mouth that was almost a snarl, but her eyes would still be looking: like she was riding a bike with no hands to look at something she was holding, doing two different things at once: her body turned on and having a good time, but her mind still working on its own, watching, until her eyes glazed over and it became more the way it usually was in those final moments of hanging on, no time to think or do anything but ride it out. She opened her eyes with kind of a dreamy look, thoughtful, and said it was like falling backwards . . . a time you could let go knowing you were safe. He wondered if she analyzed everything she did and had been watching, before, to see her effect on him. When Karen left the bed, went into the bathroom and came back a few minutes later, he got to see all of her at once—a picture he now had for life—before she turned the lamp off and got back in bed.

Chili had his arm ready in case Karen wanted to snuggle in, as they usually did after, but she stayed on her side and was quiet. They were alone in a different kind of dark now that they'd made love, a dark for sleeping. He thought, Okay, fine. Though had expected there would be a little more to it. It surprised him when she said, lying there in the dark, "I've been watching you."

"I noticed that."

"I think you could be an actor. I know you're acting sometimes, but you don't show it."

"You thought I was faking?"

"No, I don't mean *then.*"

"What was I doing? I was auditioning?"

"We made love," Karen said, "because we wanted to. That was the only reason."

"Yeah, but you were watching."

"For a minute."

"A *minute*—it was a lot longer'n that."

"Why're you getting mad? I say I think you could be an actor, you take it the wrong way."

"I don't like being watched."

"That could be a problem."

"Why would it?"

"If you want to act."

"I never said I did."

"You don't want to, then don't."

It was quiet for a minute or so.

"You don't mean become a movie star. More like a character actor."

"Let's talk about it in the morning. I'm beat."

"I ever made a movie, you know who'd go see it? My mother and my two aunts. Tommy, he'd go, for a laugh."

Karen didn't say anything, meaning that was the end of it.

He could see himself in different movies Robert De Niro had been in. He could maybe do an Al Pacino movie, play a hard-on . . . He couldn't see himself in ones, like say the one where the three guys get stuck with a baby. They don't know how to take care of it and you see these big grown-up assholes acting cute. Put on a surprised look and that was as far as they could take it. People liked that cute shit, they went to see it. But, man, that would be hard, try and act cute.

What else could he play? Himself? The shylock?

No, he'd start trying to act like himself and it wouldn't work, because acting wasn't as easy as it looked. He knew that much. No, what he needed . . .

He heard Karen's voice in the dark say, "I forgot to tell you. The Bear called."

Chili said, "Yeah?" even though for some reason he wasn't surprised. "He say what he wanted?"

"He left a number."

"I'll call him in the morning."

The Bear could wait. What he needed to think about was an ending. And maybe a title. *Get Michael.* Except that wasn't the movie, that was real life. He kept getting the two mixed up, *Chili's Hollywood Adventure* and whatever the other one was . . .

HE MUST HAVE HEARD THE SOUNDS COMING FROM downstairs, because something woke him up before he heard Karen say, "Not again." He turned over on his back and was looking at a faint square of light from the window reflected on the ceiling. Karen said, "It's Harry, downstairs." He could hear the sounds as faint voices now, a movie playing on the

TV in the study. "Harry pulling the same stunt on you," Karen said. "He was drinking, I'm sure of it, and got this wonderful idea." He saw Karen sitting up, her face and breasts in profile. Another picture to keep. The clock on her side of the bed—seeing it behind her—said 4:36.

"If he was drinking all night . . ." Chili let the words trail off before saying, "he'd be out of it, wouldn't he? How could he drive?"

"Ask him," Karen said, "he's waiting for you."

She turned to fix her pillows, puff them up, and sunk back in the bed.

"If I know Harry he'll act surprised to see you. 'Oh, did I wake you up? Gee, I'm sorry.' What happened at dinner, well, not forgotten, but put aside. This is Harry the survivor. Sometime during the past five hours or so he realized that if his project is dead, he'd better quick get a piece of yours. He'll offer to take over as producer . . ."

"I don't know," Chili said, wanting to listen for sounds, different ones than the TV.

But Karen kept talking.

"He'll get a writer, probably Murray, and handle all negotiations. He'll already have a plot idea and that's why he's here at four-thirty in the morning. He'll say he couldn't wait to tell you. But the real reason is he wants to be annoying. He still resents what he thinks you pulled on him, stealing Michael, and I know he doesn't like the idea of us being together . . ."

Telling him all that until he said, "I don't think it's Harry."

And that stopped Karen long enough for him to hear the TV again and what sounded like gunshots and that sharp whining sound of ricochets, bullets singing off rocks.

Karen said, "If it isn't Harry . . ."

"I don't know for sure," Chili said, "and I hope I'm wrong and you're right." It was a western. He heard John Wayne's voice now. John Wayne talking to the West's most unlikely cowboy, Dean Martin. Getting out of bed he said to Karen, "I think it's *Rio Bravo.*"

CATLETT SAT IN THE DARK WITH THE BIG-SCREEN TV ON loud the way Harry said Chili Palmer had done it; the difference was a movie instead of David Letterman and Ronnie's Hardballer .45 in his hand resting on the desk and pointed at the door part open. He believed the John Wayne movie was *El Dorado,* the big gunfight going on now with the sound turned up so high it was making him deaf, but he wanted Chili Palmer to hear it and come down thinking it was Harry paying him back. He'd checked to make sure Harry was home and not here and after so many rings he almost hung up, got Harry on the line slurring his words bad, the man almost all the way gone. He told Harry to go to bed before he fell down and hurt himself. All there was to do now was do it. Chili Palmer walks in the door—let him say something if he wanted, but don't say nothing back. Do him once, twice, whatever it took and leave the way he had come in, through the door on the patio he found unlocked.

He had waited this long so as not to be seen or run into by other cars on the street. Most went to bed early in this town, but some stayed out to party and drove home drunk when the bars closed or in a nod. Four A.M. was the quietest time. He had been here now since four-twenty. Shit. If Chili Palmer didn't come down in the next two minutes he'd have to go upstairs and find him.

CHILI PUT ON HIS PANTS AND SHOES, KAREN WATCHING him, and got out the Lakers T-shirt he'd bought at the airport to go with Karen's Lakers T-shirt if he got lucky. But when he did, when they came upstairs earlier and jumped in bed, he wasn't thinking of T-shirts. This one fit pretty well. Karen probably couldn't see what it was. He walked over to the bedroom door and stood listening. He was pretty sure the movie was *Rio Bravo.*

After about a minute Karen said, "Are you going down?"

He turned to look at her.

"I don't know."

She said, "Then I will," getting out of bed. "You're as bad as Harry."

He watched her pull on the bulky sweater and a pair of jeans. She looked about twenty. When she came over to the door he raised his hand and then laid it on her shoulder.

"What if it isn't Harry?"

"Someone else comes in and pulls exactly the same stunt?"

She was calm about it. He liked that.

"I think Harry might've told Catlett, and that's who it is."

She said, "Oh."

Maybe accepting it, he wasn't sure. "Or it could be somebody Catlett sent. You don't have a gun, do you? Any kind would be fine."

Karen shook her head. "I could call the police."

"Maybe you better. Or call Harry first, see if he's home."

She moved past him to the bed, sat on the edge as she picked up the phone from the night table, punched Harry's number and waited. And waited. Karen shook her head. "He's not home."

"He could be asleep, passed out."

"It's Harry," Karen said, coming away from the bed. "I'm sure. Paying you back."

Maybe, though it wasn't Chili's idea of a payback, the kind that kept you looking over your shoulder waiting to happen. He wanted to believe Karen was right. It was Harry trying to be funny. She knew Harry a lot better than he did. He wanted so much to believe her that he said, "Okay, I'll go. I'll sneak down the stairs." He looked through the doorway to the big open area that reached from the foyer below at a high domed ceiling above the curved staircase and the upstairs landing. "You stand over there by the railing, okay? You can see the door to the study. I don't want any surprises. You see anything at all, let me know."

"How?" Karen said.

"I don't know, but I'll be watching you."

TIME TO DO IT. CATLETT GOT UP FROM THE DESK WITH the big Hardballer ready to fire. He moved past the lit-up noisy screen where John Wayne and Dean Martin were shooting bad guys and ducking bullets singing off walls, the bad guys falling through those rickety porch railings. *El Dorado* was the name of it. Fine sound effects to go with what he was about to do. Loud, but not as loud as the Hardballer would be once he had it pointed at Chili Palmer. Catlett moved through the doorway into the front hall, heard his heels click on the tile and turned enough to face the stairway. He bent his head back to look at the upstairs railing that curved around the open part of the second floor and looked back at the stairway: did it quick to catch something dark there partway down, a shape against the light-colored wall. There was that moment he had to decide was it Chili Palmer or the woman and said Chili Palmer, though right then didn't care if he had to do them both, he was this far. Catlett raised the Hardballer to put it on the shape, got it almost aimed and a scream came at him out of the dark—a scream that filled the house and was all over him and he started firing before he was ready, firing as that scream kept screaming, firing at that shape dropping flat on the stairs, firing till that fucking scream turned him around without thinking and he ran down a hall to the back of the house and got out of there.

THE FIRST THING KAREN SAID WAS, "I HAVEN'T screamed in ten years," amazed that she could still belt one out. Chili told her it was a terrific scream, she ought to be in the movies. The second thing she said was, "We'd better call the police." And he said, not yet, okay? But didn't say why.

Now they were downstairs: Karen waiting in the kitchen, lights on, the television off, Chili looking around outside. She watched him come in shaking his head and noticed his purple and gold T-shirt for the first time.

"You said last night the Bear called?"

She nodded toward the counter saying, "The number's by the phone," and watched him walk over and look at the notepad next to it. "I have a T-shirt like that only it's white."

He said, "I know you do."

"Is that why you got one?"

She watched him with the phone in his hand now punching numbers. He waited and said, "Bear? Chili Palmer." She watched him listen for several moments before he said, "Yeah, well he tried. Tell me where he lives." He listened and said, "I'll find it." Then listened again, longer, for at least a minute, and said, "It's up to you," and hung up.

"You didn't answer my question," Karen said. "Is that why you bought it?"

He said, "I guess so," and turned to walk out.

"You're going to Catlett's house—why?"

"I'm not gonna spend another twelve years waiting for something to fall on me."

"What did the Bear want?"

"He's gonna meet me there."

27

CATLETT HAD PUT ON MARVIN GAYE TO PICK HIM UP, Marvin Gaye's voice filling the house now with "I'll Be Doggone." No sun yet: barely starting to get light out on the deck.

This tape he was playing had all of Catlett's favorites on it gathered from other tapes and records. It had "The Star-Spangled Banner" on it, Marvin Gaye doing our national anthem, and had "Ain't No Mountain High Enough" he did with Tammi Terrell, deceased. Both of them now. Marvin Gaye, the Prince of Motown, shot dead by his own father in the hot moment of an argument, a pitiful waste . . . Catlett thinking, And you can't shoot a man *needs* to be done?

If it was the man, Chili Palmer, on the stairs and not the woman. Trying to decide which was what had thrown him off at the time and then the scream coming to finish the job, a scream like he hadn't heard since *Slime Creatures,* Karen Flores doing her famous scream, which meant it must have been Chili Palmer on the stairs and maybe he did hit him and the job was done, 'cause Chili Palmer had gone down, shot . . . Or had dropped down to get out of the way. All that had been in his head coming home, thinking Karen Flores would call the cops when she quit screaming. That was the reason he wiped the gun clean and almost chucked it in some weeds going up Laurel Canyon; but didn't.

Came home, put his car in the garage part of the house, ran inside and changed from his black race-car-driver coveralls to his white silk dressing gown, barefoot. Mussed up the bed, mussed up his hair and then combed it again, Marvin Gaye doing his "Sexual Healing" now when he heard the car outside the front and thought of cops. He knew they couldn't have a court-signed search warrant this soon, so didn't worry about the gun; he went to the front window with a sleepy innocent expression ready. But it wasn't even a car. The headlights aimed at the house close went off and it was a van parked in the drive: the Bear getting out now, coming to the door with a suitcase.

Catlett let him in saying, "You know what time it is?" What anybody would say.

"I want to get rid of this," the Bear said, holding the Black Watch plaid suitcase Yayo had brought. "I came by last night after you called me, but you weren't home, so I came in to leave this stuff," the Bear said, talking all at once, "but then I thought no, I better deliver it in person and you check what's in here. Less what Ronnie took out for Palm Desert."

Catlett said, "Wait now. You came in my house last night?"

"I just told you I did," the Bear said.

This stove-up muscle-bound stuntman sounding arrogant. Catlett took it as strange. He said, "Bear, why you talking to me like that? I thought you and I got along pretty good, never argued too much. I always considered you my friend, Bear."

"I'm the one falls down the goddamn stairs," the Bear said. "But you take a fall, that other kind, and I go with you, huh? Well, I don't need a friend that bad."

"What?" Catlett frowned at him. "What I said on the phone to you? Man, I was putting you on is all. How'm I gonna scare you? I said, 'cause I was a mean motherfucker, right? When do I ever talk like that?"

"It's what you are, whether you say it or not," the Bear

said. "I'll tell you right now, I don't fucking trust you. I want you to look in this suitcase and see what's in it, so you don't say later on I took any."

Catlett watched the Bear lay the bag on the floor and get down on his knees to zip it open.

"Eight keys," the Bear said, "right?"

"Right. You want a receipt?"

He watched the Bear zip the bag closed and said to him on the floor, "Listen to Marvin Gaye doing 'Ain't That Peculiar,' Bear. Ain't it, though. You coming by this time of day, can't wait? How come you haven't asked me anything?"

Catlett watched the Bear get to his feet, the size of him rising up in that shirt full of flowers.

"You haven't asked did I get in the woman's house without you helping me. Did I do what I went in there for."

"You didn't," the Bear said, "or you'd have told me soon as I walked in. Then you'd give me some shit about keeping my mouth shut, saying I'm in it too."

Look at that, Catlett thought, surprised, but not taking it as strange anymore, seeing how the Bear's mind was working.

"I told you I quit and I meant it."

Telling him more than that.

"What's wrong with me?" Catlett said. "You talked to Chili Palmer, didn't you? Since you quit. When was it, last night? . . . This morning?"

The Bear didn't answer, or have to, Catlett seeing the dumbass half-a-grin on the Bear's face, trying to look wise, the Bear here because Chili Palmer was coming.

Catlett said, "Bear, I'm glad you stopped by," and left him, went in the bedroom and got the big .45 out of the bureau where he'd put it, slipped it in the pocket of his dressing gown and had to keep hold of it on account of the gun's weight and size. He heard two sounds then, as if timed to come one right after the other:

Heard a car drive up to the front.

And heard Marvin Gaye begin his "Star-Spangled Banner," recorded at the Forum before an NBA All-Star game: Marvin's soul version accompanied by a lone set of drums. Listen to it. A way to start this show by dawn's early light. Marvin's soul inspiring Catlett, setting his mood, telling him to be cool.

CHILI FOUND THE HOUSE LOOKING FOR A VAN PARKED in front, a little stucco Spanish ranch house, half two-car garage, it looked like, till he was inside and saw how the house was built out into space. Across the living room the doors to the deck were wide open. All he could see out there was sky starting to show light. He wanted to have a look and must have surprised Catlett and the Bear when he walked past them saying, "So this's one of those houses you see way up hanging over the cliff." Meaning from Laurel Canyon Drive. It didn't get any kind of comment.

He half turned in the doorway, light behind him now, to see the Hawaiian Bear standing by a suitcase on the floor, Mr. Catlett in his bathrobe, hands shoved in the pockets, soul music coming from somewhere in the white living room. Hardly any color showing at five-thirty in the morning. White carpeting, white sectional pieces forming a square, white artwork on the walls that might have spots of color. Green plants showed dark, the suitcase on the floor, dark, Catlett's face dark, his bare feet in the white carpeting dark. He would say he hadn't been out of the house. It didn't matter. Chili knew where to begin and was about to when he realized, Jesus Christ, it was the national anthem playing, some guy doing it as blues.

Chili got his mind back on Catlett and started over saying, "I've been shot at before—once by accident, twice on purpose. I'm still here and I'm gonna be here as long as I want.

That means you're gonna have to be somewhere else, not anywhere near me or Harry. If you understand what I'm saying I won't have to pick you up and throw you off that fuckin balcony."

"MY TURN," CATLETT SAID, FEELING MARVIN GAYE behind him and the big .45 in his right hand, inside the silky pocket.

He moved toward Chili Palmer saying, "You mean out there, *that* balcony? That's my sun deck, man. You gonna try your rough stuff I want to move us off my seventy-bucks-a-yard carpeting, so it don't get messed up."

The way Chili Palmer stood looking at him Catlett thought he'd have to show the gun; but the man moved, walked out on the deck looking across to where the canyon road cut through to climb over into the Valley. Catlett glanced aside, motioning to the Bear to go out there too.

"Say you been shot at before," Catlett said, following them out. "I can believe it. What I can't understand is you're not dead."

"I been lucky," Chili said, "but I'm not gonna press it. Okay, what can I do, go to the cops and complain? I read in the paper a guy was knocked off and dumped out'n the desert 'cause he was trying to ace this woman out of a movie deal and she had him killed. I was surprised—you know, it's only a movie. But it's high stakes, so I guess it can happen. I look at me and you in maybe the same kind of situation. I get shot at over it and I think, you bet your ass it can happen. But I'm in and you're out. You understand? That's the way it's gonna be."

"It cost forty million and some to make that movie," Catlett said, "the one the guy was killed over. But you know what? The movie bombed, man, and everybody lost money. It's high stakes and it's high risk too. What I'm saying, I'm not gonna let you be in my way."

He heard Marvin Gaye coming to "home of the brave," the end of the anthem, and felt a need to hurry, get this done. Time to bring out the Hardballer and he did, putting it on Chili Palmer standing in the middle of the deck.

"You broke in my house and I have a witness to it," Catlett said, glancing at the Bear. "Witness or accessory, I'll go either way." He said to Chili Palmer, standing there looking stupid in a purple Lakers T-shirt and suit pants, "Only no sound effects this time, huh? John Wayne and Dean Martin shooting bad guys in *El Dorado*."

"It was *Rio Bravo,*" Chili said.

"ROBERT MITCHUM WAS THE DRUNK IN *EL DORADO,* Dean Martin in *Rio Bravo,* practically the same part. John Wayne, he also did the same thing in both. He played John Wayne."

Chili couldn't tell if Catlett believed him or not, but it was true. He had won five bucks off Tommy Carlo one time betting which movie Dean Martin was in. He could mention it though he doubted it would interest Catlett much. So he got down to what this was all about and said to him, "Okay, you win. I go back to Miami and you become the mogul, how's that? I'm not gonna argue with anybody holding a gun on me." The biggest fuckin automatic he'd ever seen in his life. "I'll leave today. You want, you can see me get on the plane." Catlett kept pointing the gun, but with a fairly calm look on his face. Chili had a feeling the guy was going to say okay, go. And then maybe threaten that if he ever saw him again . . .

But it was the Bear, for Christ sake, who got into it then, the Bear saying, "I'm a witness, Cat. Go ahead, do it." And Chili saw the gun barrel come up an inch or so to point right at his chest.

"You don't have to," Chili said, "I'm telling you. It's not worth it, man."

That fuckin Bear, now what was he doing? Taking Catlett by the arm, telling him, "You got to set it up, have a story for when they ask you how it happened. If I'm in it, I won't do it any other way. It's like I used to choreograph fight scenes," the Bear said. "You're over there and he's coming at you. You don't want to shoot him and he knows it. So you keep backing away till the last second and you don't have any choice."

"Like I say, 'I warned him, Officer,' " Catlett said, getting into it, " 'but he kept coming at me . . .' Hey, but he should have a weapon, a knife or something."

"We'll get it later," the Bear said. "He's here . . ." The Bear took Chili's shoulders in both hands and moved him two steps back, toward the door, then motioned to Catlett. "You're around on that side. Yeah, right there. Okay, now you start backing away. Go ahead."

Catlett said, "You worked this in a movie, huh?"

"Now you go toward him," the Bear said to Chili.

Chili didn't move. He said, "You're out of your fuckin mind," and tried to turn, get out of there, but the Bear got behind him to grab hold of his shoulders again.

"This's okay where he is," the Bear said to Catlett. "You understand why we're doing this. You see it happen, you're able to remember each step when you tell it."

Chili watched Catlett, about five feet from the railing, the view of Laurel Canyon behind him, give the Bear a nod. "Don't worry, man."

"Okay, when I say go," the Bear said, "I duck out of the way. Give it two beats and move to the railing, quick, you're desperate now. Grab it with your hand, turn and press your back against it for support as you aim the piece with both hands. You ready?"

Catlett nodded, half turned, ready.

"Go!"

Chili wanted to turn, make a dive for the living room, but

the Bear was still behind him, his big arms going around him tight and he couldn't twist free, couldn't move because the Bear hadn't moved, the Bear not even trying to get out of the way.

That's why Chili was looking right at Catlett as Catlett looking back took two quick barefoot steps to the railing, got his left hand on it, the gun pointing out of his other hand, and kept going, screaming as the railing fell away behind him and Catlett, it seemed for a moment, hung there grabbing at space.

The guy who had sung the national anthem was doing "Ain't No Mountain High Enough." Which wasn't exactly true, Chili thought, standing at the edge of the deck looking down. He could see Catlett, the white silk robe, lying in weeds and scraggly bushes, more than a hundred feet from here, not moving. The Bear came up to stand next to him and Chili said, "Jesus, how'd that happen?"

The Bear started taking bolts and nuts, old used ones, out of his pants pockets. Wiping each one on his shirt before dropping it over the side, he said, "Beats the shit out of me."

LOOKING AT SKY, CATLETT KNEW EVERYTHING HE should have known while he was still up there looking at Chili Palmer instead of the Bear, the Bear too dumb to have the idea himself, shit, he had *given* the Bear the idea and the Bear had come in his house last night, even *told* him he did, but he kept seeing Chili Palmer instead of the Bear. Even knowing he was going to do them both he had listened to the Bear 'cause it sounded like movies and he said yeah, not taking even half a minute to look at it good . . . But, shit, even if he *had* taken the half a minute and said forget it and then did them both, he wouldn't know what the Bear had done to his deck, no, he'd walk out there some night hearing bossa nova or the nice sound of that girl laughing, look over the rail at the lit-up swimming pool down there in the dark, movie people having some fun, knowing how to live. He believed he was almost in their yard, but couldn't turn his head to look, couldn't move, couldn't feel nothing . . .

28

THE WAY CHILI TOLD IT WHEN HE GOT BACK TO KAREN'S and they were in the kitchen: "He fell off his sun deck and was killed."

She said, "He fell off his sun deck."

"The railing gave way on him for some reason. When he leaned on it."

She said, "The railing gave way . . ."

"Yeah, and he fell. I'd say about a hunnerd feet."

"You went down, looked at him?"

"The Bear did. I never would've made it, it's steep."

"It was an accident?" Karen said. "I mean you didn't hit him or push him and he happened to fall?"

"I'll take a polygraph neither one of us touched him."

"But you didn't call the police."

"Not with a suitcase full of cocaine in the house. Also he had that gun in his hand. He still wanted to shoot me."

Karen poured their coffee. She sat across from him at the kitchen table and watched him put two spoons of sugar in his and stir it slowly, carefully, smoking a cigarette. He looked up at her. She thought he was going to ask if she was still watching him, but he didn't. He smiled, stirring his coffee. He said after a moment, not smiling now, "You think I might've done it. I say I didn't, but you still think I might've. What can I tell you?"

Karen didn't say anything. He was a cool guy. Or seemed cool because she didn't know him and maybe never would. She thought, All right, the guy fell off his sun deck. She said to Chili, "Were you scared?"

"You bet I was scared."

"You don't act like it."

"I was scared then, not now. How long you want me to be scared?"

There was a silence. She heard him blow on his coffee and take a sip.

"The meeting's at two-thirty," Karen said. "Harry wants to pick us up."

THEY SAT AROUND THE COFFEE TABLE IN THE LIVING room part of Elaine's office at Tower waiting for Michael to get off the phone. Chili listened to Harry saying that as soon as this guy told him the story he knew they had a picture. Elaine saying that from what she'd heard so far it did sound off-trail, a shylock not your usual good guy. Harry saying that was the beauty of it, a hard-on type metamorphosized by his love of a woman. Elaine saying she hoped he didn't soften up too much, become limp. Chili thinking, Jesus Christ. Michael came over from Elaine's desk and took a seat next to Karen on the hard sofa. Chili, in his dark-blue suit, looked at Michael in his beat-up flight jacket thinking, What if it's that same fuckin jacket was at Vesuvio's?

They waited while Michael put his hand on Karen's leg, told her she looked great, then started explaining to everybody why he was leaving his agent who—they wouldn't believe this—could *not* acquire a property Michael wanted, could *not* make a deal with the writer, and if an agent couldn't make a deal with a writer, for Christ sake . . . Until Chili said, "You want to talk about that one or this one?" It got a surprised look from Michael and Harry, deadpan reactions from Karen and Elaine, and the meeting started.

ELAINE: "MR. PALMER?"

Chili: "Okay. Open at the dry-cleaning shop. You see the shylock talking to Fay, the wife."

Michael: "I thought the guy was an agent."

Chili: "I changed him back to a dry cleaner."

Michael: "You still don't have a script?"

Karen: "They're working on the moral dilemma."

Michael: "That writes itself. I want to know what happens."

Chili: "Yeah, that's what I'm telling you."

Michael: "Let's go to the third act and then come back if we want. You build to a climactic scene. What is it?"

Chili: "You're referring to the action, with Ray Carlo."

Michael: "Who's Ray Carlo?"

Chili: "He was Bones, I changed his name. Okay, Randy finally catches up with Leo . . ."

Michael: "Wait. Who the fuck is Randy?"

Chili: "Randy's the shylock. You need a nice-guy name. You don't want to call him Lefty, Cockeye, Joe Loop, one of those."

Elaine: "Sonny's nice."

Chili: "It's not bad. I know a Lucky, a Jojo, Momo, Jimmy Cap, Cowboy, Sucky, Chooch . . ."

Elaine: "Sucky?"

Michael: "Okay, I'm Randy, for the moment anyway. What happens?"

Chili: "They catch up with Leo the dry cleaner, Randy leans on him a little, not much, and Leo tells them, okay, the dough's out at the airport in a locker. So Randy and Fay have the key and are at the moral dilemma part when Ray Carlo shows up. Actually he's already there, searching the place when they get home from Leo's. Carlo, he's got a gun, takes the key offa Randy and Randy says okay, you win, the dough's out at the airport. Ray Carlo leaves to go get it and Randy calls the FBI."

Michael: "All he's doing is picking up money. What would they arrest him for?"

Chili: "They'd at least give him a hard time. Randy knows this and wants to see it, so he and Fay go out to the airport. They see the bust and look at each other with surprise, 'cause what's in that locker is not money but cocaine. You understand? Leo was setting *them* up, or anybody that got on to him."

Michael, frowning: "That's how it ends?"

Chili: "No, you still have Leo."

Michael: "I thought Carlo was the heavy."

Chili, noticing the way Karen was staring at him: "That's what you're suppose to think. No, that's the surprise. Leo's the bad guy, from the beginning."

Elaine: "Good. I like Leo."

Harry: "Leo has delusions of grandeur, wants to be famous, hobnob with movie stars, entertainers."

Elaine: "He could be fun to watch, while the other guy's just a heavy."

Michael: "Leo's a schmuck."

Elaine: "He's sort of schmucky, that's all right."

Karen: "He could have some funny lines, out of desperation."

Michael: "Wait a minute—"

Chili: "Yeah, he could be funny. I still think, though, he oughta fall off the balcony."

There was a silence.

Michael, quietly: "Okay . . . what balcony?"

Chili: "Leo's apartment, twenty floors up overlooking Sunset. He's with this starlet, they're drinking, doing coke, when Fay and Randy walk in. Basically what happens, here's Leo and here's the guy he's been paying for years and was always scared to death of. But right now Leo's flying on coke and booze and doesn't know enough to be scared of *any*thing, this little drycleaner. What he wants to do is put the shylock down—you know what I mean? Dishonor him, this guy he thinks of as a hard-on, a regular mob kind of guy." Chili paused. "Suddenly Leo jumps up on the cement railing of the balcony and says, 'Let's see if you got the nerve to do this, tough guy.' The starlet screams. Fay yells at him to get down. The shylock doesn't do nothing, he watches, 'cause he knows this guy basically is a loser. He watches Leo take three steps and that's it, off he goes, screaming all the way down twenty floors to the pavement."

There was a silence again.

Michael: "That's how it ends?"

Chili: "After that, they find the money in the closet. They have another moral dilemma talk, a short one, and take off for Mexico in a brand-new Mercedes."

Michael, to Elaine: "You know what I do in this picture? I stand around and watch."

Chili: "You want to shoot somebody? Or, hey, you want to play Leo? Take the dive?"

Elaine: "I don't know why, but Leo fascinates me. The little drycleaner with all that money. I'd like to see what he does with it."

Harry: "Sure, the guy must think he's died and gone to heaven."

Michael: "Elaine—"

Elaine: "He wouldn't have to take the dive, would he?"

Karen: "Not if he lives on the ground floor."

Michael: "Is it a comedy? At this point, who knows?" Grins. "I can see why you don't have a script. All you have is an idea, and you know what ideas are worth."

Chili: "Michael?"

Michael: "I'm going to London tomorrow. New York a few days and then grab the Concorde. But I'll put my writer on it first. By the time I get back next month we should have a treatment we can play with and then go right into a first draft."

Chili: "Michael, look at me."

Michael, grinning: "Right. That's what it's all about, right there, the look."

Chili: "You don't mind my saying, Michael, I don't see you as the shylock."

Michael: "Really . . . Why not?"

Chili: "You're too short."

HARRY WAITED TILL THEY WERE IN THE CAR, DRIVING along the street of sound stages toward the main gate.

"You have to be out of your mind, talk to a guaranteed box-office star like that. You blew any chance of getting him."

Chili, in the backseat, kept quiet. It was too hard to explain why during the meeting he started seeing Michael as Leo, thinking that if he wanted to play Leo, great; and after that couldn't see him as the shylock. It had nothing to do with the fact he didn't like the guy or trust him or would never loan him money, the guy was still a great actor.

Karen said, "Harry, we knew going in he'd back out sooner or later, it's what he does."

"Then what was the meeting for?"

"Elaine, she loves the whole idea, except the ending. You heard her, she thinks Pacino would be perfect."

Chili said, "He's kinda short too, isn't he?"

"They all are," Karen said. "You shoot up."

They drove through the gate and followed a side street to Hollywood Boulevard.

"What if," Chili said, "Leo hops on the railing and makes

a speech. Says how he sweated, worked his ass off all his life as a drycleaner, but he's had these few weeks of living like a movie star and now he can die happy. In other words he commits suicide. Steps off the balcony and the audience walks out in tears. What do you think?"

Karen said, "Uh-huh . . ." Harry said he wanted a drink and Karen said that wasn't a bad idea. Chili didn't say anything, giving it some more thought. Fuckin endings, man, they weren't as easy as they looked.

THE UNDISPUTED MASTER OF THE CRIME NOVEL

DJIBOUTI
A Novel

978-0-06-173521-9 (trade paperback)

Elmore Leonard brings his trademark wit and inimitable style to this twisting, gripping—and sometimes playful—tale of modern-day piracy.

ROAD DOGS
A Novel

978-0-06-198570-6 (trade paperback)

The further adventures of Jack Foley, out of prison but right back into trouble.

PRONTO

978-0-06-212033-5 (trade paperback)

A brilliant combination of suspense and black humor featuring Raylan Givens, the inspiration behind the FX series *Justified.*

RIDING THE RAP

978-0-06-212247-6 (trade paperback)

Raylan Givens returns to bust open a kidnapping ring in the sequel to *Pronto.*

COMFORT TO THE ENEMY AND OTHER CARL WEBSTER STORIES

978-0-06-173515-8 (trade paperback)

First time in print in the U.S.
A collection of 3 stories about the legendary lawman Carl Webster.

MAXIMUM BOB

978-0-06-200940-1 (trade paperback)

Florida Judge "Maximum" Bob Gibbs has thrown the book at so many felons, it's beginning to look as if one of them is throwing it back at him.

TISHOMINGO BLUES

978-0-06-200939-5 (trade paperback)

The Dixie Mafia is aiming to shoot high-diver Dennis Lenahan from the top of his 80-foot ladder.

RUM PUNCH

A Novel

978-0-06-211982-7 (trade paperback)

Cops try to use Jackie Burke to get at the gunrunner she's been bringing cash into the country for, but she hatches a plan to keep the money for herself.

FREAKY DEAKY

A Novel

978-0-06-212035-9 (trade paperback)

It's only after he transfers out of the bomb squad that Chris Mankowski begins playing with dynamite.

OUT OF SIGHT

A Novel

978-0-06-174031-2 (trade paperback)

Minutes after pulling into a prison parking lot, Deputy U.S. Marshal Karen Sisco meets legendary bank robber Jack Foley and the fun begins.

THE COMPLETE WESTERN STORIES OF ELMORE LEONARD

978-0-06-124292-2 (trade paperback)

This collection is a must-have for every fan of Elmore Leonard.

GET SHORTY

A Novel

978-0-06-212025-0 (trade paperback)

A Miami shylock, Chili Palmer, goes to Hollywood and becomes a movie producer. Why not?

LABRAVA

A Novel

978-0-06-176769-2 (trade paperback)

Ex-Secret Service agent Joe LaBrava gets mixed up in a scam involving a former movie actress and bad guys.

SWAG

A Novel

978-0-06-174136-4 (trade paperback)

Used car salesman Frank Ryan sells Ernest Stickley, Jr. on his "10 Rules for Success and Happiness in Armed Robbery".

BANDITS

978-0-06-212032-8 (trade paperback)

An unlikely trio targeting millions of dollars is sure to make out like bandits—if they survive.

BE COOL
A Novel

978-0-06-077706-7 (trade paperback)

Chili Palmer searches for his next big hit as murder blurs the line between reality and the big screen.

KILLSHOT
A Novel

978-0-06-212159-2 (trade paperback)

After witnessing a scam, Carmen and her husband must outrun the thugs bent on eliminating any living evidence.

FIRE IN THE HOLE
Stories

978-0-06-212034-2 (trade paperback)

Driven by terrific characters and superb writing, these short pieces are Elmore Leonard at his economical best.

MR. PARADISE
A Novel

978-0-06-211905-6 (trade paperback)

Elmore Leonard presents a whole new cast of characters—of the kind that only he can create—in this Detroit homicide book.

GLITZ
A Novel

978-0-06-212158-5 (trade paperback)

A classic Elmore Leonard novel, spinning from the lazy beaches of Puerto Rico to the mean streets of Miami to the jangle of Atlantic City's one-armed bandits.

SPLIT IMAGES
A Novel

978-0-06-212251-3 (trade paperback)

When homicide cop Bryan Hurd takes a vacation, he lands in Palm Beach and finds murder in the Sunshine State.

Visit www.AuthorTracker.com
for exclusive information on your favorite HarperCollins authors.

Available wherever books are sold, or call 1-800-331-3761 to order.